confetti
confidential

Holly McQueen has wanted to be a writer ever since
discovering that the nuns at her junior school would
let her off maths homework if she wrote a story
instead. After unexpected detours via law, magazine
journalism, and even musical theatre, she began
writing her first novel in 2006. Holly lives with
her husband in London. She still avoids maths.
Confetti Confidential is the third book in the Isabel
Bookbinder series.

Also by Holly McQueen

The Glamorous (Double) Life of Isabel Bookbinder
The Fabulously Fashionable Life of Isabel
Bookbinder

Holly McQueen

confetti confidential

arrow books

Published by Arrow Books in 2010

2 4 6 8 10 9 7 5 3 1

First published in Great Britain in 2010 by
Arrow Books
Random House, 20 Vauxhall Bridge Road,
London SW1V 2SA

www.rbooks.co.uk

Addresses for companies within The Random House Group Limited can
be found at: www.randomhouse.co.uk

The Random House Group Limited Reg. No. 954009

A CIP catalogue record for this book
is available from the British Library

ISBN 9780099545750

The Random House Group Limited supports The Forest Stewardship
Council (FSC), the leading international forest certification organisation.
All our titles that are printed on Greenpeace approved FSC certified paper
carry the FSC logo. Our paper procurement policy can be found at
www.rbooks.co.uk/environment

Mixed Sources
Product group from well-managed
forests and other controlled sources
www.fsc.org   Cert no. TT-COC-2139
© 1996 Forest Stewardship Council
FSC

Typeset by SX Composing DTP, Rayleigh, Essex
Printed and bound in Great Britain by
CPI Cox & Wyman, Reading, RG1 8EX

For Oscar Viry-Babel and Joshie Green,
with much love

Acknowledgements

Enormous thanks to the *real* Top Wedding Planner, Siobhan Craven-Robins, who took time out from working on her truly stunning weddings to give me invaluable advice and insight into how I might write about somewhat less successful ones. Thanks too for the snippets, for the wine, and very particular thanks, Siobhan, for taking me to the Designer Wedding Show, an inspiration if ever there was one. I hope I've done some justice to the real-life world of a wedding planner, but any errors I've made are mine alone.

Huge thanks, also, to the marvellous quartet of editors who saw this book through from beginning to end – Vanessa Neuling, Emma Rose, Gillian Holmes and Publishing Goddess Kate Elton. There might have been comings and goings but you never left me feeling anything but exceptionally well looked-after. Thanks too to Louise Campbell, Claire Round, and indeed to everyone at Arrow, with special thanks and appreciation to Louisa Gibbs, for the title.

And as ever, the most heartfelt of thanks to my agent Clare Alexander, for being Clare Alexander.

Chapter One

This is a big day for me and I really, really don't want to screw it up.

The moment my alarm clock went off this morning, I was up, out of bed, and into the shower. A swift, invigorating lather-up with a zingy grapefruit shower gel, followed by an equally invigorating scrub-down with one of those weird oily salt rubs that people keep giving me for Christmas, and I was fresh out of the bathroom less than ten minutes after waking up.

I do kind of wish I hadn't bothered with the weird oily salt rub, though. It left this slick, slightly pongy layer all over my skin, and I had to spend another ten minutes blotting myself with kitchen paper just so that I didn't look (and smell) a little bit like I'd spent the night sleeping in a giant chip-pan.

Once I'd blotted myself off, and thrown on my lovely cosy waffle dressing gown, I headed for the kitchen to make myself an energising cup of coffee. Well – I say 'headed' for the kitchen. My flat is so tiny that I'm actually *in* the kitchen the moment I step out of the bathroom. In fact, even calling it a flat is generous. It's what the estate agent I rented it from euphemistically called 'a studio' and what Mum and

1

Dad unappealingly call 'a bedsit'. I'm not wild about either term, to be honest, because the former makes me sound like I live here surrounded by half-painted canvases and empty bottles of absinthe, and the latter like I live here surrounded by half-written philosophy essays and empty cans of Strongbow. Neither of which is remotely close to the truth.

Anyway, while I was waiting for the kettle to boil, I started up my laptop and had a little nose through the online tabloids. This might just look like idle time-wasting, but in fact it's an extremely important part of my job. If I'm ever going to make it as a Top Wedding Planner, it's absolutely vital that I'm up to date on the tiniest developments in celebrity relationships. Even after just a couple of weeks in the job, I can already see that competition for the best clients is pretty brutal, so I'll need to be all geared up and ready at the slightest sign of any imminent engagement announcements. Think how impressive it would be if, only hours after you let the world know you'd decided to take the plunge, a wedding planner was calling you with a fully-developed plan for your big day. Perhaps a plan with lovely personal references to some of your favourite hobbies, and maybe incorporating elements from your recent romantic getaways in the Seychelles and Mauritius.

Though I'd have to be careful not to come across like a dangerous stalker at that point, obviously.

So. What relationship-related news is there in the ether today? Well, I see from the *Daily Mail* that the nice lady who presents that neighbours-from-hell programme on the BBC has been photographed coming out of the gym with a sneaky cigarette in her hand. And the *Mirror* is simply beside itself with excitement that somebody who almost made it through to the boot camp stage of *The X Factor* has admitted to recreational drug use and an addiction to lap dancers.

Well, you don't always strike gold. Besides, if everything goes well at my meeting today, I may not need to trawl about the tabloids trying to detect imminent celebrity engagements any more. I could find myself automatically catapulted to the very top echelons of the Wedding Planning circuit, the first port of call for any self-respecting star who's planning to get married.

Which would be completely brilliant, obviously.

While my cafetiere was steeping, I quickly made myself a piece of toast, and then went to eat it on my Power Plate machine. That isn't me having some bonkers, LA-style eating disorder, by the way, where you can only eat carbohydrates if you actually burn off the calories while you ingest them. It's simply because I have this great big Power Plate machine that I bought a few months ago, and there's literally nowhere else I can put it. With hindsight, it probably wasn't the smartest way to invest nine hundred quid, but I was working in the fashion industry at the time, and I was just getting a little bit tired of always being the only person in any given room with a muffin top creeping up over my jeans. Though obviously, giving up on actual muffins might have been a more sensible way to treat my neurosis.

Still, I will get around to using my Power Plate at some stage. And for the time being, seeing as I don't really have room for an actual table, it really is a jolly handy place to sit and eat my toast.

Anyway, now I've taken my nice steaming cup of coffee back up to my bedroom on the mezzanine level, so I can have a look in my wardrobe and decide what I'm going to wear today.

Actually, let me rephrase that – what I'm going to wear *with my black suit* today. Because black suits seem to be what all the Top Wedding Planners wear. My new boss, Pippa Everitt, who's right up there with the very best in the field, never comes to work in anything else. Obviously, seeing as I'm not yet a completely fully-fledged Planner myself, I'm not usually required to wear anything other than jeans and a freshly pressed T-shirt, but today I'm going to be conducting an important client meeting of my own. Correctly styling my brand-new Karen Millen suit might make all the difference between getting the gig, or not getting it at all.

Right. I think I'll team it with this nice, crisp white shirt, some minimal, elegant jewellery, and these sensible black peep-toe courts I bought *en route* to my boyfriend, Will's, office Christmas do, when I suddenly panicked that the skyscraper red heels I was wearing made me look less like a tax lawyer's girlfriend and more like a tax dodger's bit-on-the-side.

Then, because I'm worried this whole Look is just far too trainee accountant, I abandon the minimal jewellery, and sling on a huge pair of chandelier earrings and a bright turquoise bangle.

Which just makes me look like a trainee accountant on dress-down Friday.

So I replace the crisp white shirt with a slouchy grey V-neck T-shirt, ditch the boring black courts for my favourite spiky black stilettos, forget about jewellery altogether and just accessorise it all with the lucky Mikkel Borgessen clutch bag that has got me through big meetings before.

Yes. That's more like it. This is the Look that will catapult me out of the realms of assistant-hood and into the top echelons of celebrity wedding planning.

The thing is, when I took the job with Pippa Everitt, I knew it was going to sound like a bit of a backwards step. I've spent the last year working as Deputy Creative Director to a top fashion designer, no less, so stepping into the role of Pippa's assistant was always going to look retrograde. But you can't afford to be snooty about that kind of thing if it's going to help you get where you want. And being a Top Wedding Planner is what I really, passionately, want to do, more than I've ever wanted anything else before. And all right, as my friend Lara pointed out, that's pretty much exactly what I said about novel-writing when I really, passionately wanted to be a novelist, and it's certainly a lot like what I said about fashion designing when I really, passionately wanted to be a fashion designer.

But this is completely different. And I'll take any low-rung job if it gets me on the ladder.

Though if I could skip up a couple of rungs, that would be fantastic too. Which is why I need to spend just a few minutes tidying up some very important work right now, in time for my big client meeting.

I head down the stairs into my living 'area', reach for the leather conference file on the coffee table next to the sofa, and open it up to the notes I finally finished printing out at two o'clock this morning.

Though in some ways, I don't like to think of them as just plain *notes*. I like to think of them as more like an agenda. Or a strategy, perhaps. Or even – and I wouldn't admit this to just anyone – a kind of *manifesto*.

Because honestly, this is what got me all fired up about weddings in the first place. When my old boss, Nancy Tavistock, suddenly announced back in May that she was getting married, only a couple of months after her divorce was finalised, I immediately volunteered to help her out in any way that I could. And even though she hired Pippa Everitt to pull together a spectacular big day at spectacularly short notice, Nancy needed all kinds of extras that Pippa didn't and couldn't provide. Like, toing and froing with Nancy's lawyers to make sure all her legal affairs were tied up before she jumped into marriage with a penniless twenty-three-year-old male model. Like, tracking down a top personal trainer to make sure Nancy looked her absolute best in her own-label wedding gown (and, I suppose, before she jumped into bed with a twenty-three-year-old male model). Like, speaking repeatedly on the phone to Nancy's sisters in Chicago, and finally persuading them that even though they'd been jealous of her all their lives, they'd regret it for the rest of them if they didn't take up the invitation to fly first-class to London and watch their little sister walk down the aisle. And then, a couple of weeks later, as I watched a serene, newly toned, blissfully happy Nancy setting off to Syon House to get married, I realised that some of her serenity, and a little bit of her happiness, and pretty much all of the toning, was down to me.

So when Pippa took me aside between the dinner and the dancing to mention that she'd been impressed by my work, and would I consider coming and working as her new assistant, I jumped at the chance.

Because it's just so obvious that there's this huge gap in the market – not for plain old ordinary wedding planning, but for a *whole new kind* of wedding planning. You could call it 'holistic wedding planning', if that didn't bring to mind images of aromatherapy massages and Hopi ear-candling. You could call it 'ultimate wedding planning', if that didn't bring to mind shouty Territorial Army cadets doing shouty Territorial Army things in the Brecon Beacons.

But then I don't really think of it as Wedding Planning at all. I prefer to think of it as Bride Management.

I look down at the first page of my manifesto, and read my opening lines.

So just what is BRIDE MANAGEMENT ™?

It's the New Generation of Wedding Planning that'll guide you all the way from engagement to altar!

Hmm. Sounds a little bit stiff to me. A little bit formal.

. . . from opening the Tiffany's box to opening the door of the honeymoon suite!

Ugh, no. That one manages to sound both grasping and creepy in equal measure.

Wait. I've got it.

. . . from 'I Will' to 'I Do'.

Perfect.

Well, I think it's perfect. All I can hope for now is that Wendy Gordon sees it the same way.

The lobby of Gordon/Miskoff PR is painted a soft, flattering off-white, with pale wooden floorboards. There are low leather sofas, large black-framed mirrors, yucca plants in big pots, and lots of strategic up-lighting, presumably so Gordon/Miskoff's celebrity clientele don't accidentally catch a glimpse of themselves in one of the large mirrors and panic that they've suddenly started looking their age, and that Wendy Gordon had better get them a 'Fabulous New Look!' photo-shoot with *OK!* magazine double-quick. In short, apart from the up-lighting, it's pretty much the same as any other office, right down to the bored-looking girl on the reception desk, the bike messengers neglecting to remove their helmets as required by the sign on the swing doors, and the scowling man in the black suit surgically attached to his BlackBerry on the low leather sofa opposite me.

Over the last ten minutes, it has become clear to me that he's also a Top Wedding Planner, and therefore my competition for this job. Pretty tough competition, too, because he's been on the phone to all the top suppliers, the people that my boss, Pippa, also uses to source her flowers and her favours and her stationery.

'Yes, Caroline,' he's saying, now, to a woman on the other end of the phone who I assume is Caroline Quartermaine of Quartermaine Press, one of the top wedding stationers in London. 'I *did* say I wanted the seven-inch by four-point-five . . . well, I suggest you go back and check your records . . . no, my bride wants to look at a gold edge *and* a silver edge . . . well, Caroline, it would be an order for two hundred and fifty Save the Date cards, two hundred and fifty invitations, and a hundred and seventy-five Orders of Service, so I'd have thought you'd be extremely keen to make sure I don't start looking at other stationers . . .'

I shoot him a couple of sympathetic glances, which I think he takes to mean something else entirely, because quite suddenly, and rather rudely, he gets to his feet and goes to continue his conversation across the other side of the reception, near the potted yuccas.

Well. I was only trying to be friendly. I mean, I know we're competing for the same client, but that's no reason not to try and show a little bit of solidarity.

Besides, I know exactly how he feels. I've been a wedding planner for only a couple of weeks, but I seem to have spent approximately ten whole days of that on the phone to people like Caroline Quartermaine myself. Honestly, there's nothing I couldn't tell you about the intricacies of the stationery business. I can hold forth on all manner of trivia, from plate-sinking to blind embossing, from the ideal card thickness (600 gsm, in case you're interested), to the advantages of Palace Script over Copperplate. And don't even get me started on Half Post-Quarto sizing, or the best shade of tissue to line your envelopes.

I suppose it's no surprise, really, that the job isn't quite as much fun as I imagined it might be.

The thing is, I can't help feeling a tiny bit cheated by Pippa. Before I went to work with her, she made all these big claims about how I'd be accompanying her to client meetings, getting input on wedding design, and, most importantly of all, actually getting my very own brides to work with. But all she's done is get me to make phone calls and run errands, and, on more than one occasion, rustle up a pot of tea. Not to mention the fact that she's given up pretending any interest in my innovatory Bride-Management techniques, which I thought were the things she practically head-hunted me from my last job for anyway.

Head-hunting, incidentally, is certainly how I described my latest career move to my family. Dad has traditionally taken a pretty dim view of what he likes to call 'Isabel's job-hopping', so when I told him I was leaving Nancy Tavistock I knew I was going to have to make the move sound really, seriously worthwhile. As far as Dad's concerned, unless you're going forwards, you might as well be going backwards, which is why I wasn't going to tell them I'd gone from being Nancy's Deputy Creative Director to Pippa's mere Assistant. Hence the handy use of the word 'head-hunting', which is basically true.

And the equally handy use of the word 'Partner'. Which, basically, isn't.

Still, it's had the desired effect. Dad's been surprisingly silent on the whole issue, which for a Class-A shouter, blamer and disapprover like him, is pretty much an ideal result. And Mum, obviously, was always going to think the whole idea of a career in weddings was marvellous, as evidenced by the fact that she's phoned me almost every day since I started to ask if I've had the chance to take anyone dress-shopping yet, and if I'd be able to tell her if I ever ended up planning a wedding for someone really famous, like Jennifer Aniston, or Madonna.

Scowling Man has finished huddling by the yuccas, and has come to sit back down on the sofa opposite. He accidentally meets my eye, and clears his throat.

'Bloody stationers.'

'Tell me about it!' I roll my eyes, to show that I'm completely *au fait* with the stresses and strains in the life of the Wedding Planner.

'I mean, how hard can it be to get me a couple of samples?' He stabs a finger at his BlackBerry in exactly the same kind of end-of-his-tether, weight-of-the-world manner that Pippa also employs on a

11

regular basis. 'You'd think in this day and age, they'd be doing everything possible to improve their service. Virtually every bride I work with would be more than happy to send out an invitation on email.'

I nod. 'Or on a CD.'

'Sorry?'

'An invitation. On a CD.' I smile at him. 'You know, a nice, personalised message from the bride-and groom-to-be, giving all the details of the time and place of the wedding? Ideal when so many couples are choosing to get married abroad, or to have a three-day celebration in place of a more traditional event, and there's just so much more information to get through. We're finding it's ever so popular!' I add, which is a phrase I hear Pippa use when a client is proving reluctant to commit to something.

Scowling Man blinks at me. '*Really?*'

'Absolutely!' Well, it *would be* terribly popular if Pippa would actually give me the go-ahead to suggest it to any of her brides. 'I mean, we're in the twenty-first century now, aren't we? Just because weddings are big on tradition, there's no point in refusing to avail ourselves of the latest technology!'

He frowns. 'Well, surely if you wanted to avail yourself of the latest technology, you'd send out a mini MP3 player with the personalised message on it, not a crappy old CD?'

Oh.

Actually, he's got a point.

Though I don't think he had to be quite so deliberately rude about it.

I reach for my file, flip hurriedly to where I've written my 'Interesting and Innovative Invitation Ideas', cross out every reference I can find to CDs, and start scribbling in 'MP3 player' instead.

I really should have thought of this before. *Obviously* a personalised MP3 player is far more suitable for Summer Shelley's wedding invitation than a crappy old CD.

In fact, now I'm thinking it through, it's completely perfect. I mean, Summer Shelley sings, doesn't she? That group she was once in, Girlz 4 Ev-A, was meant to be the American answer to the Spice Girls. Though you'd probably have to assume that if they were the answer, then the question must have been something like 'Shall I shamelessly try to cash in on the Spice Girls' worldwide success by manufacturing a girl band with very little discernible talent for singing or dancing, but who look completely amazing in neon Lycra?' But maybe Summer just never really got to prove her natural singing talent, because Girlz 4 Ev-A were a terrible flop, and she's had to make her name ever since taking her clothes off for men's magazines, appearing on shows like *Celebrity Big Brother*, and, latterly, getting engaged to Tim Holland. Which has actually gained her far more notoriety than her semi-nude photo-shoots ever did, because he's the heir to a multimillion-pound retail fortune, and pretty notorious himself for his twin habits of a) relentless modelising and b) shovelling industrial amounts of cocaine up his nostrils. Though not any more, obviously. A stint in the Priory and hooking up with Summer Shelley have put paid to all that.

Anyway, maybe an MP3 of her singing a couple of nice, romantic ballads as her very own wedding invitation might give her stalled music career a whole new start! Summer could be back in the charts again, and all because of me and my Interesting and Innovative Invitation Ideas.

Well, all because of that and Scowling Man. I mean, credit where credit is due.

'Isabel Bookbinder?'

I glance up as my name is suddenly spoken. It's a tall, skinny girl in dark denim and horn-rimmed glasses, standing at the swing doors that must lead through to the main office.

'Hi,' she continues. 'I'm Natalie, Wendy's assistant. We're ready to see you now.'

'Great!' I get to my feet.

'And you're here from . . .' she glances at a clipboard, 'Pippa Everitt Weddings?'

'That's right!' I'm unable to resist a glance over my shoulder at Scowling Man, whose ears have pricked up at the mention of the eminent Pippa. 'She'd have loved to have been here today, but I'm afraid there was a dreadful emergency at the office.'

I cross my fingers behind my back as I say this. Because really, it's a little bit of a fib. Pippa not only wouldn't have loved to have been here today, but she doesn't, actually, know that *I'm* here in her stead.

The thing is, I was the one who answered the phone when Wendy Gordon called yesterday morning, and I just assumed Pippa would be thrilled about the possibility of planning a wedding for Summer Shelley. But as soon as I hung up and asked Pippa if she could squeeze in a preliminary meeting with Wendy some time this week, she gave me a long lecture on how I'm never supposed to agree to things without checking with her first, and an even longer lecture on how she hates working with celebrities, and how after the hell of planning her current celeb wedding, she'd only work with another one if somebody was holding a loaded gun to her head. And then she told me to call Wendy back and give her a flat-out, categorical No.

Which, obviously, I didn't do. I waited until Pippa had gone out for her client lunch, and then I called Wendy back and gave her a flat-out, categorical Yes.

Look, I do feel bad about going behind Pippa's back. But as soon as she realises that she won't have to do a thing, and that I'm the one who'll have all the hassle that comes with a celebrity wedding, I'm sure she'll understand. Besides, it'll be her wedding consultancy that will get all the amazing kudos, and the publicity from an exclusive magazine deal. Honestly, she'll be thanking me for it. I'm absolutely certain.

Natalie leads me through a corridor and into a large, bright office where a woman is sitting at a big glass desk. This is Wendy Gordon of Gordon/Miskoff PR.

Well, maybe Miskoff is the glamorous half of the partnership, responsible for the sleek offices and the trendy Marylebone location. Because honestly, for a well-known celebrity publicist, Wendy is a bit of a surprise. She's wearing a plain black trouser suit over a straining V-neck T-shirt, and I can see beneath the desk that her feet are shoved into a horrible pair of zebra-stripe driving shoes. Her round face is un-made-up apart from an unflattering slash of rose-pink lipstick, and her mousy-brown hair is cut in a short style that – and believe me, I should know about this – doesn't flatter its frizzy texture.

She doesn't get up. She doesn't even glance up.

'Is this one of them?' she asks, in a sharp voice.

'Yes, Wendy.' Natalie nods me towards the chair opposite the desk. 'This is Isabel Bookbinder, from Pippa Everitt Weddings. Pippa does send her apologies, apparently,' she adds, as she sensibly begins to retreat out of the office, 'but she's dealing with a huge emergency this morning.'

Wendy's head suddenly snaps upwards, and she fixes me with a beady stare. 'I *see*. Well, if Pippa isn't that interested in working on my client's wedding . . .'

'Oh, no! I mean, yes. I mean, of course she's interested!' I can feel myself getting warm in my Karen Millen jacket. 'And I'm sure, Wendy, that when you see the wonderful ideas she's put together, you'll realise just how truly committed she is.'

'All right. Let's see the wonderful ideas.'

I flip open my folder, and take out my manifesto. 'I

do apologise for the small alterations,' I say, handing a copy to her. 'Somebody failed to spot a typographical error, and so where you see the words "*MP3 player*"–'

'Yes, yes, there's no need to worry about things like that,' Wendy interrupts. 'We're only really interested in your suggestions for my client's wedding.'

'Absolutely!' I beam at her. 'Well, as you'll see from page one, which deals with the wedding design itself, we've really been inspired by the transatlantic nature of the couple's relationship.'

I have to say, I'm really pleased with myself about this bit. Summer Shelley being American and Tim Holland being British, I've come up with all these fabulous ways of incorporating both sides of their heritage.

'I'm suggesting a lovely traditional English garden party theme for the afternoon drinks reception – you know, dancing round the maypole, cream teas, big jugs of Pimm's or fresh lemonade – because obviously,' I lower my voice discreetly, 'I know that the groom might prefer a non-alcoholic option.'

Wendy says nothing.

'Er . . . and then that would be followed by a witty New York theme for the evening reception. I mean, what nicer way to welcome all their guests, from Britain and America alike!'

'Canada.'

'Sorry?'

'Canada. Summer Shelley is Canadian, not American. Her family will be flying in from Canada.'

Oh.

Well, this has put a bit of a spanner in the works of the witty New York theme.

'*Your guests will be able to wander between authentic New York street-food stalls,*' Wendy is reading aloud, '*where they can enjoy tasty treats from hot dog carts and delicious wares from pretzel stands – and not forgetting that glamorous old-time speak-easy serving Manhattans and Cosmopolitans (non-alcoholic also available).*'

'Which can all be perfectly easily adjusted to add some Canadian flavour!' I say, hastily. 'I mean, we could serve mini pancake stacks with maple syrup . . . er . . . maple-smoked bacon sandwiches . . . all served on horseback by Canadian mounties . . .'

Wendy's eyebrows pull down into an unimpressed V, and she scribbles a couple of notes on the pad on her desk. 'All right . . . so, I have a few questions about security. Obviously, there's going to be a certain amount of press interest in my client's wedding . . .'

I hold up a hand. 'Wendy. I can assure you that we would guarantee absolute paparazzi neutrality.'

'I'm sorry?'

'Paparazzi neutrality! If you just flip to page two . . .' I take her handout from her and turn over the page myself. 'You can see in detail our pledge to arrange top-quality security services. After all, nobody wants a repeat of those awful leaked photos of Catherine Zeta-Jones's wedding, do they? Or that sneaky photographer who almost got away with crashing Madonna's wedding up at Skibo?'

Wendy says nothing for a moment. But it's only because she's continuing to read page two. I mean, I know we got off to a bit of a shaky start, but I think she's starting to be just a little bit impressed by my manifesto. And just wait until she gets on to the appendix, with my Interesting and Innovative Invitation Ideas, and sees my suggestion about those MP3 players . . .

Quite suddenly, her head snaps up again.

'I'm sorry, but what the hell is Bride Management?'

I clear my throat. 'Well, traditional wedding-planning methods don't even begin to take into account the real strains and stresses faced by the average twenty-first-century bride, celebrity or otherwise. We're long past the days when a wedding planner was useful for nothing more than ordering the invitations and booking the string quartet. Nowadays there are many brides who want – no, who *need* – far more support than that.'

I'm so pleased all that came out right. I spent long enough practising it in front of the mirror last night.

But Wendy doesn't seem quite so impressed. In fact, she's started staring at me like I've just escaped from a nearby mental ward.

Maybe this isn't actually going quite as well as I'd begun to think.

'Perhaps it might make more sense if you have a little look at some of the fantastic special services we offer.' I take Wendy's handout again, and turn another page for her.

'It says here you can organise therapy.' She glances up at me. 'You mean massages and spa treatments?'

'No, I mean cognitive behavioural therapy.'

'You offer *psychiatric* services?'

'Oh Christ, no. Just Cognitive Behavioural Therapy. It's just this very *gentle* form of therapy, almost like reprogramming the way your thoughts work–'

'I know what it is!' she snaps. 'I'm just baffled as to why a wedding planner would arrange it.'

'Oh, well!' I flap a hand. 'The reasons are legion. It could be that the bride is having sleepless nights of worry, or that she's even suffering the occasional panic attack . . .'

'And personal training?' Wendy stabs the page with a stubby finger. 'Summer doesn't need her wedding planner to arrange a personal trainer! I'm pretty sure she already has one.'

'Ah, in that case, we could act as an all-important liaison between her trainer and Summer and her dress designer. You know, bring him along to fittings, so he'd be aware of everything he needed to do to get Summer looking her absolute best in her dress. Some serious triceps-toning, perhaps, if she's chosen a strapless style. Or if she's gone for something cut on the bias, then we'd be looking at squats, I imagine, and lots of lunges.'

Wendy takes a deep breath. 'Miss Bookbinder. Summer Shelley has appeared nearly naked in *Maxim*. She has promoted her lingerie range wearing only a thong and a pair of strategically placed Swarovski crystals. I don't think anyone needs to worry about getting her to do extra squats and lunges before her wedding day.'

'Oh God, of course. I only meant, you know, in case there are any nasty telephoto lenses lurking around, trying to snatch shots at unflattering angles.'

'Well, according to you,' Wendy gives a short, mirthless laugh, 'the paparazzi will have been sufficiently neutralised to eliminate that risk.'

Oh.

Well, I suppose I did kind of walk into that one.

'Look, Wendy . . .' I take a deep breath. 'I realise that some of what I'm suggesting here might sound a little bit unusual . . .'

'I think that would be putting it mildly.'

'. . . but it's just because we're trying to offer our brides a really special experience.' I put a hand on my chest, but then take it very swiftly off again when I feel my heart racing like the clappers beneath my ribcage. 'We're there for our brides twenty-four hours a day, seven days a week . . .'

'In that case, I really should be letting you get back to business.' Wendy rises from the chair – she looks even shorter, standing, than I thought she would – and extends a graceless hand. 'Thank you for your time.'

I get to my feet too. 'And thank you for your time. Will I . . . um . . . be hearing from you?'

Wendy sits back down, already reaching for her telephone receiver. 'Have a very nice day.'

Great.

I've blown it, haven't I?

My big chance, and I've blown it.

Well, there's no point in making a fuss. This is embarrassing enough as it is.

I head for the door. 'Oh, please pass on my warmest congratulations to Summer and Tim.'

Wendy nods. 'Bring the next one in, will you, Natalie?' she says into her phone as I pull open the door and head back out to reception.

Chapter Two

I can't help feeling a little bit self-conscious, as I jump on the bus that will take me towards Pippa's, in Fulham, that the other passengers are staring at me. Which is stupid, I know. I mean, none of them knows how badly that meeting just went. They're all far too concerned with their own lives, and getting to their own jobs on time. As my friend Lara always says, not everybody is thinking about you all of the time. And she's a top psychologist, so I tend to have a lot of faith in her on these matters.

In fact, I think I might just give her a quick call, for an emergency debrief. If there's anyone who can make me feel better about embarrassing myself in front of a hugely influential and important publicist, and wrecking my one chance to get my stalled career back up and running, it's Lara.

Damn. Her mobile is switched off. She must have started seeing her first patient of the day already.

I'm just leaving her a short, information-packed message when I hear the bleeping sound that means I have another call coming through.

No surprises. It's Mum.

Well, if there's anyone who can me feel better about

embarrassing myself in front of a hugely influential and important publicist, and wrecking my one chance to get my stalled career back up and running, it probably isn't my mother.

But I ought to speak to her anyway. She's been looking after my niece for a couple of days while my older brother Marley and his wife Daria attend a conference on Algebraic Topology in Applied Mathematics (no, *really*), and she'll probably be exhausted by now. So even if she can't make me feel better, maybe I can make her feel better. And at least that'll be one of us.

'Hi, Mum!'

'Oh, hello, Iz-Wiz! I was hoping I'd catch you!'

Actually, she sounds fine. 'Yes, I'm just on the bus on the way to work. How's it going with Hypatia?'

You know, I still can hardly believe the name Marley and Daria picked. I mean, obviously I had my concerns long before she was actually born, because Daria is Swiss, and I was worried she might try to name the baby Heidi or Muesli or something. So I put a lot of time and effort into researching and suggesting some really pretty Swiss names. Elodie, for one. Manon, for another. But in the event of it, they didn't go for a Swiss name at all. Being mathematicians, they elected to name their firstborn after someone called Hypatia of Alexandria, a Neo-Platonist philosopher who met a sticky end when, presumably having pissed off the wrong people (the Anti-Platonists?), she was stripped naked and flayed with oyster shells before being burned alive.

Yes. This is the woman my infant niece is named after.

'Oh, it's been lovely, Isabel! We've been to feed the ducks, and she's been out shopping with me and Barbara, and your father's been playing her bits of his Mozart records, because you know how good Mozart is at developing their little brains.'

Yes, and I know how keen Dad is to develop little brains. 'Has she asked about me at all?' I say, which is stupid, because she's barely six months old and hasn't so much as uttered a 'Mama' yet. But maybe all that Mozart might have worked already.

'Well, no, but I showed her your photo – you know, that nice one of you at Marley's wedding – and her face lit up, Isabel, it really did.'

The warm glow that spreads over me is actually cancelling out some of the horrible icky feelings about my disastrous meeting. 'That's brilliant!'

'Yes, and now she's having her little nap, so I thought I'd just give you a quick try. You know, see how work's going!'

'It's going fine, Mum. Busy.'

'Well, yes, I'm sure you must be.' Mum's voice has gone deliberately, and strangely, casual. 'I mean, being a partner in a firm organising a wedding for . . . oh, what's that girl's name again . . . Frank? Frankie?'

Oh. Now I know why Mum's calling.

This weekend is Pippa Everitt's big celebrity wedding, for Frankie Miller and Dean Davidson.

Obviously, he being an England footballer and she being an über-WAG, every newspaper in the country wants the details. Every newspaper including the *Central Somerset Gazette*, which is where Mum works two days a week, writing the 'Local News Round-up'. The wedding is at Lucknam Park, which is technically just over the border into Wiltshire. But then, not a lot happens in either Somerset or Wiltshire, so this is obviously going to be heavy fodder for Mum's weekly pages.

'Frankie Miller.'

'Oh, yes, that's right . . .' I can practically hear Mum sharpening her pencil. 'I bet it's going to be a really amazing affair! Lovely dress, I'm sure she'll be wearing . . .'

'Mum! Stop fishing! You know I can't tell you any of the details.'

'But it's not every day a celebrity gets married in this neck of the woods,' she's carrying on. 'And you know all the other local papers will be all over the story – the *Yeovil Express*, the *Bath Chronicle* . . . if we could just get the inside scoop –'

'Mum . . .'

'Honestly, darling, I'm a professional journalist! It would all be . . . whatsit . . . off the record.'

'*No*, Mum. Anyway, I don't even know all that much about it myself. I wasn't involved in any of the planning. And I'm not even going to be there on Saturday, because of Licky's wedding.'

This is true – and, I have to say, an enormous pity.

Just when I might have at least had the opportunity to go and be a dogsbody at a WAG wedding, instead of being a dogsbody at Pippa's office, I can't even go because I already have a wedding to go to. Licky – actually Alicia, but her childhood nickname has stuck – is an old friend of the family, who used to babysit for my younger brother, Matthew, and me, and who (I suspect) had a bit of a teenage fling with my older brother, Marley. I'm not really complaining – I've always liked Licky, and seeing as she's invited my entire family, I get the distinct impression she doesn't have that many people she can ask to her wedding – but it is a bit of a shame that I won't get to lurk about on the sidelines at Lucknam, observing all the bling and fabulosity of the footballers and their wives.

'Oh, yes, that reminds me – you do have something nice to wear to Licky's, don't you? I mean, you know how posh it'll be up at Broughton Hall.'

'Yes, I have something nice to wear.'

'A little suit?'

'No, Mum, not a little suit.'

'Oh.' She sounds disappointed. 'Well, something that matches, then, at least?'

I get up to change buses at South Kensington. 'Yes. Something that matches.'

'And a hat? Lara's wearing a hat.'

My bus lurches to a stop outside the tube station. 'How do you know Lara's wearing a hat?'

'Oh, she mentioned it on the phone.'

'You *phoned* Lara?'

'Well, she is Matthew's girlfriend! Obviously I phone her every now and then.'

You know, it's been a year now, but there are times when my brother and my best friend's relationship still fazes me. Like the times when I see this kind of ethereal glow around Lara that (I imagine) comes from finally getting together with the guy you were in love with for fifteen years. Or the times when I see Matthew watching her adoringly while she cooks in the kitchen, or reaching out to pat her on the bottom as she passes him by.

Or the times like this, when Mum tells me she phones Lara every now and then.

I mean, obviously, as Lara's friend, I'm thrilled that her boyfriend's mum is making so much effort with her. But that doesn't change the fact that . . . all right, this is probably going to sound a bit childish . . . well, she was *my* friend first.

OK. It sounds incredibly childish.

'I mean, I would never have done it with That Annie,' Mum is going on, probably crossing herself at the other end of the phone as she invokes the name of my brother's cheating ex-fiancée. 'But with Lara, it's different, isn't it? I mean, she's practically been family for the last twenty years anyway!'

'Yes, she has.'

'Oh, and there's still no chance Will is going to be able to make it to Licky's wedding?'

'No, Mum, still no chance. I've told you, he's got this

important seminar to give, at his firm's annual partners' meeting. There's just no way he can get out of it.'

She sighs. 'It's a shame. And it would be so nice to see how Will looks in a morning suit . . .'

Oh, Christ. Ever since I mentioned, the other week, that I was probably going to be moving back in with my boyfriend, Will, Mum's curiosity has reached close to fever pitch. Honestly, forget fishing for details about Frankie Miller – with Mum, it's a little bit like having my own personal *Daily Mail* on the other end of the line, angling to see if she's going to be writing 'Wedding Joy for Iz and Will' any time soon.

'Anyway, Iz-Wiz, I'd better go. I need to get Hypatia's things packed up before Daria gets here.'

'OK, Mum.'

'And you won't give me just the tiniest detail about Frankie Miller's wedding? Because I wouldn't quote you direct, you know, darling. I'd call you "an anonymous source".'

'No, Mum, I really can't tell you anything. Anonymous or otherwise. Look, I'll see you on Friday evening, OK?'

'Lovely, darling! Love to Will. Bye!'

Once I'm off my second bus, it's only a short walk to Pippa's house, a little way off Fulham Road. But I stop for a quick takeaway coffee at the Italian deli in Parsons Green, partly because I need a caffeine injection, but also because it'll delay me getting to Pippa's for another ten minutes more.

Look, don't get me wrong – I still think I did the right thing leaving my job with Nancy Tavistock. I had a brilliant time helping her set up the whole company from scratch, but by the end of it, I'd pretty much finished up as the office manager. I mean, at the start I had all this important input, and I was even taking all these fashion design courses so that I could really live up to the title of Deputy Creative Director. But then the label started to get really big, really fast, and Nancy had to hire lots more proper designers, and no amount of evening classes could make up for the fact that I didn't have a Master's from Central St Martins. Or that I was never going to be the world's greatest fashion designer.

It was a hell of a lot more *fun* working at Nancy's, though, I have to say.

The thing is, I wouldn't mind Pippa using me as a bit of a dogsbody if I really felt that I was learning something about how to design a wedding. But to be quite honest, I'm not even sure that's turning out to be true. Pippa is such a control freak that all her weddings seem to follow a fail-safe, if admittedly successful, formula. Her brides wear strapless, A-line Philippa Lepley (if they're a bit hippy/paunchy/saddlebaggy), or strapless, slinky Amanda Wakeley (if they're not). The floral arrangements are always beautiful, but never any more adventurous than daffs in spring, roses in summer, hydrangeas in autumn, and twiggy, Spartan affairs with holly and ivy in the winter. Throw in The String's The Thing!, a popular string quartet, for Frank Sinatra favourites during the drinks reception, and The Hot Trombone, a popular twelve-piece swing band, for yet more Frank Sinatra favourites during the dancing, and that's pretty much all you need to know about wedding design, Pippa-style.

Frankie Miller, though, is proving to be a tiny ray of resistance against the Everitt Orthodoxy. She's been badgering Pippa for all kinds of unapproved extras, from rose petals strewn down the aisle (Pippa thinks they're 'messy') to a group of clowns to entertain the children (Pippa thinks it's 'tacky'). Still, I'm crossing my fingers that one of Frankie's daring attempts at individuality is going to break through in the end, if only for the sake of Freedom.

Anyway, I'm here now. No point delaying any more. I fish my key out of my handbag, and open the front door.

That's just one of the other drawbacks about working for Pippa – the fact that her office is also her home. I mean, it feels slightly odd to be making cups of tea in your boss's family kitchen, welcoming your boss's children through the door when they come in at the end of the school day, and having your boss's husband yell 'Dar-*ling*?' down the stairs every five minutes when he's had to take the day off work with food poisoning. Admittedly this is about the most I've ever really noticed her husband, who does something incredibly time-consuming in the City and seems to have roughly the personality of an empty bookshelf.

But still – the close-knit quarters do feel somewhat off-putting.

I pick up two utilities bills, a Boden catalogue, and a postcard from someone signing herself 'Lucinda xxx' as I step over the doormat, and stop briefly to greet Jefferson, the ancient family Labrador, as I make my way down the hallway towards the office – in fact a slightly clammy, muggy conservatory that Pippa calls 'the garden room'. I can hear Pippa's plummy, head-girl voice even before I open the door.

'I mean, seriously, Sunetra, what the hell is she thinking?' Pippa is sitting at her desk on the far side of the garden room, black-suited as ever, and with the just-sucked-a-lemon expression on her face that I've learned is reserved for all discussions involving Frankie Miller. Sitting opposite her is Sunetra D'Souza, the features editor of *Sure!* magazine, who are the ones paying the big bucks for the exclusive rights to Frankie and Dean's wedding. 'We all agreed, didn't we, *no* fake tan?'

Sunetra is nodding. 'Well, now she's saying she feels a bit pasty and she'd just like "a little bit of colour".'

Wow. That was a viciously accurate imitation of Frankie's throaty Liverpudlian tones, and it reminds me why I don't like Sunetra. She's the kind of person who makes you dread what she might be saying about you behind your back.

I head for my own desk, tucked away next to the three tall filing cabinets where Pippa keeps meticulous records of all weddings past, present, and future.

'Morning, Pippa,' I say, as I slide into my chair. 'Hi, Sunetra.'

Pippa waves a rather regal hand in greeting; Sunetra doesn't.

'Is there some kind of a problem with Frankie Miller?' I ask.

'Oh, it's nothing, really,' says Pippa. 'Just a little bride management issue.'

Bride management? Pippa doesn't usually talk about bride management.

Christ, Wendy Gordon hasn't just called to complain about me, has she?

But the comment didn't seem to be directed at me, as such. And the snide eye-roll with which Pippa accompanied it implies she's using the phrase sarcastically, to highlight what a dreadful pain in the bum Frankie Miller is proving to be.

Oh, well, in that case, this could actually be a bit of an opening for me. I mean, if they want someone to speak to Frankie and persuade her that, actually, she'd look much better in the pages of *Sure!* without a radioactive tan, then I might be their woman! I've had enough fake tanning disasters myself to speak from bitter experience, for one thing, and I'm quite used to handling tricky celebrities, for another. And what a great opportunity to put my *actual* Bride Management concepts into action.

I clear my throat. 'Actually, Pippa, I have quite a lot of experience dealing with celebrities. I mean, they'd come into Nancy's all the time, wanting things changed on dresses they'd requested, and it can be ever so difficult to convince them that–'

'Well, you can take the girl out of the Wirral . . .' Pippa just cuts straight through me. It's so unbelievably brusque that for a moment I think she must be talking to me, but it's far ruder than that. She's just completely ignored the fact that I was even speaking, and started up another conversation with Sunetra. 'Seriously, Sunetra, I'm not having my wedding ruined by a Tango-tanned bride! And presumably she's planning to hose down the bloody bridesmaids with the stuff, too?'

'Over my dead body.' Sunetra runs her hands through her glossy, shaggy hair and stretches her arms up over her head. 'She's already quite orange enough as it is. Any more and my two million quid's worth of photographs are going to be a total laughing stock.'

Suddenly I'm less shocked by how rude Pippa has just been to me, and more appalled by the way they're talking about Frankie's wedding. *Frankie's* wedding, being the point. Pippa has just called it 'my wedding', and Sunetra has just referred to it as 'my two million quid's worth of photographs'.

Suddenly, the phone on my desk rings.

'Get that, will you, Isabel?' Pippa calls over, before I've even had the chance to pick up.

'It's probably Frankie,' Sunetra tells her. 'She wasn't happy when I talked to her about the fake tan this morning.'

'Oh God, well, if it is Frankie, will you tell her I'm

in a meeting, and I'll call her back before lunchtime?'

'OK, no problem.' I pick up the phone. 'Pippa Everitt Weddings, Isabel speaking.'

'Oh, hiya, Isabel.' It's the same husky Liverpudlian voice that Sunetra has just mimicked. 'This is Frankie Miller.'

'Hi, Frankie!' I can't help feeling a sudden rush of warmth towards her, despite the fact that she's actually been quite difficult whenever I've spoken to her these past few days, and she was nothing short of bratty when she came into the office last week to talk about the seating plan. 'Great to hear from you!'

'Is Pippa there?'

'She's actually in a meeting just now, Frankie. But I can take a message for the time being, and she can call you back in an hour or so?'

'Oh.' Frankie sounds a bit peeved. 'Well, can you tell her I just want to get her opinion on the spray tan thing? I've just had this chat with Sunetra, and she's really anti it, but I just wondered what Pippa thought.'

'Right.' I pretend to make a note on my message pad, even though Frankie can't actually see me. 'I'll let Pippa know.'

'I mean, if she's not keen, then I guess I'll forget about it. But I always feel that much better with a bit of colour, you know? More confident.'

'Yes, absolutely. But I'm sure you look just as great without it!'

'I look bloody awful without it! But Sunetra said it wouldn't fit in with the *ether* of the whole wedding.'

I'm going to assume she means ethos. 'Well, at the end of the day, it is *your* wedding, Frankie,' I say, lowering my voice. 'And the bride *is* the most person there on the day!'

'I s'pose . . . Oh, one other thing, Arabella. Can you tell Pippa me and Dean have changed our mind about the Bentley, and we want the Jag after all? I mean, Dean's already got a Bentley of his own, so it does seem a bit pointless getting one of them, doesn't it?'

Pippa's not going to be happy about this. The car-hire firm near Bath have been holding both cars for us while she and Frankie have been battling it out over which is the more appropriate. And Pippa has made it quite clear that, to her mind, the Bentley is the only way to go. 'Of course . . . um, it is a *vintage* Bentley, you know, Frankie. So it's probably quite different from Dean's one.'

'Yeah, but my little Harley, he saw the picture of the Jag, and he loves it 'cos it's red. He's saying, Mummy's going to get married to Daddy in a fire-engine car! So cute!'

'So cute,' I repeat.

'So will you let Pippa know I've changed my mind?'

'Yes, of course . . .'

'All right, then. Ta, Arabella!'

'No problem, Frankie.' I hang up the phone.

Pippa and Sunetra are deep in conversation about how to arrange the bridesmaids in the photographs so that the one they're calling The Fat One stands at the back. So I give it a couple of minutes before approaching the desk.

'Um, Pippa? That was Frankie. She wants to speak to you about the fake tan, and she's decided she'd prefer to use the Jaguar on Saturday rather than the Bentley.'

'No.' Pippa shakes her head, as though I'm her teenage daughter who's just announced she's getting a dubious piercing and going to Glastonbury for the weekend with her Goth boyfriend. 'You want the Bentley in the magazine spread, don't you, Sunetra?'

Sunetra shrugs in a way that isn't really a shrug at all, given that it indicates a firm opinion on something rather than any chance she's not that bothered. 'It's big, and it's white. It's what our readers want to see in a wedding issue.'

'But Frankie's little boy –'

'We had a dark green Aston Martin in the spread when we did Samantha Morrissey and Dylan Paterson's wedding,' Sunetra is going on, turning back to Pippa again as though I haven't even spoken. 'Honestly, it ruined a lot of the shots. I mean, Samantha might as well have been climbing out of a Vauxhall Astra.'

Pippa nods. 'Yes. Well, we'll stick with the Bentley. No question.'

I clear my throat. 'So, shall I call Frankie back and tell her, or will you mention it when you call later?'

'Oh, Christ, there's no need to tell her, Isabel. She'll

probably barely even notice on Saturday, anyway. Now, Sunetra, how does a cup of tea sound?'

'Love one, thanks, Pipps.'

'A pot of Earl Grey, if you don't mind, Isabel,' says Pippa, before returning immediately to the pressing topic of the unphotogenic bridesmaid.

Mind? Well, of course I mind! It isn't the making tea *per se*. Honestly, I'm happy enough to make tea, even for a condescending cow like Sunetra. But how am I ever supposed to develop my Bride Management strategy if people like Wendy Gordon just won't pay any attention, and if people like Pippa put bloody great obstacles in my way?

Not to mention the fact that Frankie Miller's little boy won't get to see his mum ride to the church in a car the colour of a fire engine.

I head for the kitchen, where I get the kettle boiling and start warming the pot the way Pippa likes, and then I nip back to my desk to get the car-hire firm's number from my contacts sheet. Then, once I'm back in the kitchen, behind a closed door and with the kettle making enough noise to cover me, I pick up the extension phone and dial the number for South-West Classic Cars.

Ted, the nice man who runs South-West, picks up after just a couple of rings.

'Ted? It's Isabel, from Pippa Everitt Weddings.'

'Isabel!' He sounds pleased to hear from me – unsurprising, given that up until a couple of weeks ago, his usual point of contact was Pippa herself. 'How are you this fine morning?'

'I'm really well, thanks. Listen, Ted, we've had a bit of a change of plan for the Lucknam Park wedding this Saturday.'

'The Smith/Jones wedding, you mean?'

Smith/Jones is the (somewhat unimaginative) codename Sunetra and Pippa have given to Frankie and Dean, to preserve anonymity as far as humanly possible.

'That's right. Now, I know we'd said we wanted the white Bentley, but have you kept the red Jag available?'

'Still available, Isabel! And I've fought off all comers to leave your Miss Smith the option, because it's our busiest weekend of the season.'

'I really appreciate it, Ted. So we can have the Jag on Saturday instead?'

'Fine by me. It's a nicer car for me to drive anyway. Handles a lot better on the bends.'

I listen to Ted expound on the virtues of the Jag for a few minutes, making polite noises about compression ratios and expressing as much interest as I possibly can in something called the torque, until the kettle has boiled. Then I put a couple of Cath Kidston mugs on a tray, pour the water into the teapot, and take Sunetra and Pippa their mid-morning refreshment.

Dear ~~Ms Ciccone~~ Madonna,

I would like to begin by saying what a huge fan I have always been of your work. ~~It may be many many years since~~ Ever since me and my friend Lara spent an entire summer working out the dance routine to 'La Isla Bonita', I have followed your career with great interest and admiration. On one memorable occasion, I even defended the publication of your Sex book to my (extremely small-minded and conservative) father, resulting not only in an ugly family row all the way up the M6 towards Edinburgh but also a ban on me watching Top of the Pops that lasted an entire school term.

However, it is not only your career that I have followed over the years, but your personal life, too. And this is the reason I am writing to you today: I wonder if I could ask if, the next time you get married, you might consider hiring me as your wedding planner. I am currently working for a Top Wedding Planner in London, but I very much hope, by the time you have found your ~~newest candidate~~ next husband-to-be, that I will be working on my own. What I lack in experience, I make up for in passion, enthusiasm, and Interesting and Innovative Ideas. I am sure that, being ~~a total control freak~~ a woman for whom attention to detail is paramount, you would appreciate the little touches that make my service so special. What better way to invite your *nearest and dearest to your Big Day than with a customised MP3 player featuring you singing a version of your mega-hit 'Holiday' with the words changed to 'Wedding Day'? And I am sure, ~~Madge~~ Madonna, that, having so nearly had your fingers burned with that interloper in the organ at Skibo Castle, you more than anyone would appreciate my guarantee of Total Paparazzi Neutrality. These, and many more, would be the perks that would await you if you were to avail yourself of my services.*

Perhaps the most sensible thing is for you to keep this letter on file, so that you have my details to hand as (and I am sure when!) you need them. ~~I cannot tell you how happy it would make my mother to know that I was planning~~ It goes without saying that your anonymity would be totally assured.

Yours in admiration

Isabel Bookbinder

PS Although I do not have a close working relationship with Stella McCartney, I would have absolutely no problem at all with her designing your wedding dress!

PPS I should also let you know that I am prepared to convert to Kabbalah if absolutely necessary.

IB x

Chapter Three

This evening I'm meant to be heading straight over to Will's, where my friend Barney is going to be trying out a menu for Simple Suppers, his brand-new at-home dinner-party catering service. But I've got to meet Lara to pick up the soda siphon I lent her when she threw that cocktail party for Matthew's birthday back in July. Because it was actually Barney's soda siphon, that he'd lent me when I *almost* threw a cocktail party for Will's birthday back in May. I had a bit of a panic when Barney called me to remind me to bring it over tonight, because if there's one thing he gets wound up about, it's people making merry with his kitchen equipment, and I couldn't remember for the life of me where the bloody thing had got to. Thank God, Lara had been keeping it safe, and now I'm meeting her near her office on Marylebone High Street to get it back.

She's waiting for me in Providores, looking terribly smart in grey pencil skirt and crisp blue shirt, her fluffy blonde hair smoothed out for work, and pinned up into a neat little pleat at the back of her head. There's a large glass of Sauvignon Blanc already waiting for me, and she's sipping from a smaller one herself.

I give her a quick hug before sliding into the seat opposite her and taking a long, desperate drink.

'Bad day?' she asks.

'Well, I've had better. Considering that pretty much all I've done all day is make pots of tea.'

'Oh, *Isabel*.' Her blue eyes flare wide with sympathy. 'Not tea.'

'Yes, Lara. Tea.'

'That was all she gave you to do all day?'

'Well, not *all*. I made several very important and interesting phone calls to suppliers.'

'Oh!' Lara sips her own wine. 'Well, that's not *too* bad, Iz-Wiz. I mean, I know it's not as much responsibility as working for Nancy, but you did say you were prepared to start again at the bottom for this job.'

'This isn't the bottom, Lars. This is way, way beneath the bottom.'

'So, why not say something? I mean, I know you don't like confrontation . . .'

'I'm perfectly happy with confrontation!'

'. . . and I know your schema tells you you're not supposed to challenge figures of authority . . .'

Schemas are this bit of cognitive behavioural terminology that Lara has a really big thing about. As far as I can tell, it's basically just a fancy way of talking about the way people interact with everyone else around them. So, I suppose you might be able to say that Pippa has a very *bossy* schema, or that Mum has a very *nosy* schema. I don't really understand the finer

43

points. Anyway, according to Lara (who ought to know) I have what's called an approval-seeking schema, which essentially means that I have this huge problem standing up for myself, especially when it comes to figures of authority.

'. . . but seriously, Isabel, if you're not even learning anything useful, then you need to call her on it. And sooner rather than later. I mean, you didn't leave a brilliant job with Nancy just to spend the next six months hoping Pippa throws you a bone!'

This is the bad side of having a best friend who's a psychologist. I mean, sometimes all you really want to do is have a bit of a moan, but Lara will be on at you to actually *do* stuff.

'No, absolutely. I will say something. I'll just wait until after Frankie's wedding this weekend. There's no point in trying to say anything to Pippa right now.'

'Well, as long as you do. Say something, I mean.'

'I will. Absolutely.' Time for a change of subject, I think. 'Oh, by the way, Lars, what time do you think you'll be able to leave for Mum and Dad's on Friday? Are you and Matthew still OK for mid-afternoon?'

'Actually, Iz, I was wondering if you mind if we changed the plan slightly. There are a couple of places the estate agent wants us to see, and it'd be a really good opportunity to have a look at them.'

Lara and Matthew have been talking for quite a while about moving out of her tiny flat to somewhere a bit bigger, and now they're actually going on viewings with estate agents, which is rather exciting.

Lara wants a proper guest-room for her small army of half-brothers and -sisters to come to stay, and Matthew wants space for . . . actually, I don't know what Matthew wants space for, but if I had to guess, I'd say it had something to do with rugby. With Matthew, almost everything has something to do with rugby.

'That's brilliant, Lars! Do you want me to come and have a look, too?'

'Actually, I was going to suggest that, Iz. I mean, seeing as it's kind of *en route* out to your parents, and everything.'

'What's *en route* out to my parents?'

'Twickenham.'

'Twickenham? What's in Twickenham?'

'Houses, Iz.'

Is it the large glass of Sauvignon, or is Lara not actually making very much sense?

'Houses that Matthew and I are looking at,' she explains. 'On Friday afternoon. With the estate agent.'

What?

'In . . . *Twickenham*?'

'What's wrong with Twickenham?'

'It's . . . *Twickenham*.'

Lara giggles. 'Come on, Iz. I mean, you should see what we could buy for the same price as a one-bedroom flat further in.' She leans down and roots around in her bag, bringing out a little bundle of estate agents' particulars. 'Look – we can get a three-bedroom house! With a small garden.'

'But you *want* to be further in! You don't *want* a three-bedroom house with a garden.'

'Actually, Iz, we do. Just look at some of these places!' She thrusts some particulars at me. 'OK, this one I like because we wouldn't have to do very much to it . . . whereas *this* one's in an awful state, but we'd be able to put a bit more of our own mark on it. This kitchen needs completely gutting, look . . . and we'd probably have to knock through this wall here to get proper natural light . . . But look what a blank slate the bathroom is! I mean, an ideal opportunity to put in a wet-room . . .'

I don't want to hear all about knocking through kitchens, or ideal opportunities for wet-rooms! I don't want to hear about home improvements at all! Not in *Twickenham.*

'But . . . how would I ever see you?'

Lara squints as though she's thinking hard. 'Hmm. You know, I'm not too sure about that, Iz-Wiz. I mean, they *say* people don't become invisible when they move to Twickenham, but obviously we couldn't be *completely* certain until we got there . . .'

I glare at her. 'You know what I mean.'

'I know what you mean, Iz.' Lara folds up the particulars. 'But it's not like it's Timbuktu or anything.'

'No, it's *Twickenham.*'

'Will you stop saying that?'

'Well, I'm just concerned for you, Lars! I mean, you seem to be the one making all the compromises in this relationship. Moving to Twickenham, when we all know Matthew's rugby obsession. *Compulsion*,' I add, because that sounds a lot more serious, and might scare Lara a little bit. 'And anyway, aren't you meant to be a feminist? Because it isn't terribly feminist to go around doing whatever your boyfriend wants you to do.'

'God, you sound just like my mother. It's nothing to do with feminism. And we're not moving there for the rugby.'

'It's just conveniently *close* for the rugby.'

'Conveniently close for Matthew to get to St Dominic's,' Lara says, giving me A Look. 'You know how much after-hours stuff he has to do with school, Iz. Besides, have you actually *been* to Twickenham? It's ever so nice.'

'Great. When I take the nine-hour round-trip to come and visit you, I'll look forward to the guided tour.'

'The fast train is thirty minutes into Waterloo,' Lara says in the careful, moderated tone of voice she usually reserves for use on her patients. 'Even South West Trains can't possibly make that take four and a half hours.'

I don't say anything. Because I know that anything I say will make me sound petty and pathetic. Mostly because everything I can think of *is* petty and pathetic.

'Come on, Iz-Wiz.' Lara sighs. 'You know I really want somewhere for me and Matt to settle down properly. A proper home.'

Instantly, I feel terrible.

Because of course I know that this is what Lara wants. And not just because she's always wanted to settle down with my annoying brother, but because she's yearned for a proper home most of her life. It's the kind of yearning people have when, like Lara, they've racked up too many step-parents to be counted on the fingers of one hand, and when they spent large chunks of their childhood decamping to an anonymous spare bedroom every other weekend and alternate Christmases.

'I'm sorry.' I reach across the table and give her hand a little squeeze. 'I'm being an idiot. And anyway, these places look amazing!' I look at the particulars, enthusiastically. 'You're absolutely right, that wall would need knocking through. And you could put a really nice kitchen in there . . . and . . . and maybe one of those big range cookers you've always wanted . . .'

'Exactly!' Lara beams at me. 'You and Will can come round for long Sunday lunches! And who knows, maybe you might even fancy moving nearby too! I mean, you can't stay in Will's flat for ever, can you?'

'Can't we?'

'Well, obviously not! I mean, it's a perfectly *nice* flat, Iz-Wiz, but it's not a family home for the next ten years, is it? You need somewhere with a proper big kitchen, and a bit of garden. Somewhere big enough for children, if and when they come along.'

I swallow. 'Children?'

'Oh God, I'm not suggesting you should do it

tomorrow, Iz.' Lara signals the waitress for the bill. 'But it isn't for ever away any more, is it?'

'I suppose not.'

'And talking of moving into Will's, how's the packing going? Do you need a hand taking anything round at any point? I'm sure Matthew would let you borrow his car.'

'No, no, all under control, thanks!'

'Great! OK, well, I probably won't see you before Friday. But shall we pick you up on our way through Fulham? Say, four-ish?' She leans down to give me a quick hug. 'Have a good time with Barney this evening.'

'Absolutely. We will.'

Chapter Four

Will's flat is in one of the tall red-brick Edwardian blocks overlooking Battersea Park, an inconvenient hike away from the nearest tube. Quite often I cheat for the last bit of the journey and waste five quid on a taxi over the river, or at the very least jump on a bus. But today I'm in the mood for pounding the pavement, so when I come out of Sloane Square station, I make a determined start up the King's Road in the direction of the Embankment.

I don't know exactly what it is, but I just feel unsettled.

Well, all right. I know what it is.

I mean, I thought I was meeting Lara to have a bit of a moan about Pippa, and to find out what she's wearing for Licky's wedding. Apart from the hat, of course.

I didn't realise we'd be discussing estate agents, and DIY. And, you know.

Babies.

Not that there's anything *wrong* with babies. Quite the opposite. Apart from the disastrous choice of name, which isn't exactly her fault, I'm as big a fan of Hypatia as I think it's possible for an auntie to be.

But then there's nothing wrong with wet-rooms, and I don't feel a burning need to get myself one of those any time soon either.

Besides, last time I checked, Lara was telling me to take everything one step at a time. I mean, this whole moving-in-with-Will thing, for example. She knows how long it's taken me to commit to that. Because I really wanted to be sure I was making the right decision, and that things are going to be different this time around.

Though, let's face it, they could hardly be *worse*. I lived there for a grand total of only twenty-five days last time, for eighteen of which Will was at work until midnight. And then there was this little misunderstanding when I thought he was having a torrid affair with his colleague Julia in the Cayman Islands, when actually he was just being nice because she was hugely pregnant and letting her use his air-conditioned room.

But I've been so excited about the move back in, and the last thing I want is to have the shine taken off just because some people – Lara, and Mum – are already shoving me in the direction of the next step. I mean, I just want to enjoy us living together for a while. Really enjoy it. Is that too much to ask? To live like one of those gorgeous, glamorous couples you always see in The White Company catalogue – all lazy Sunday lie-ins, and sexy pillow-fights, and wild, abandoned sex on top of crisp, cotton duvet covers . . .? Well, OK, you don't actually *see* the wild, abandoned sex in the White Company catalogue, obviously. But you do see a lot of bed-related activity. And that's what I want, just now, before one day I do really have to get down to the business of living like a proper grown-up for the first time in my life. Before I have to risk tarring the current perfection of my relationship with Will with scary talk of estate agents, and DIY, and moving to a better catchment area.

Honestly, it sends chills down the spine just thinking about it.

Oooh, and if this amazing aroma greeted me every time I put my key in the outside door at Will's flat – *our* flat! – then I'd be even happier about the move. God, it's making me starving already. I can detect onions, definitely, and woody, fragrant rosemary – or possibly thyme, I'm not brilliant at telling the difference – and something else sweet and buttery . . .

Whatever, it is, I'm sure it's going to be amazing. Barney's an incredible cook, and I really think Simple Suppers is a brilliant way to bounce back from the disaster that was his gourmet coffee-cart business, The Coffee Messiah. And I will call it a disaster. It finally went under at the end of July, costing poor Barney every penny of his savings and a huge chunk of his self-esteem.

I did try to warn him, by the way. Everyone did. The hottest May and June since records began, and Barney still refused to buy a blender and some ice-trays so that he could offer his customers cooling blended coffee drinks. Temperatures were hitting twenty-nine degrees before breakfast, and Barney was still sweltering away over his espresso machine, a one-man campaign against the swelling tide of coffee philistinism. It's just a shame that he had to hold back the Philistines at his own expense. Still, as Barney says, at least he never had to stoop so low as to actually serve anyone a Frappuccino.

Just as I'm about to head up the stairs, I see the door to Flat A opening. This is the flat beneath Will's, and it's inhabited by a very nice couple called Emma and Mark, who live there with their sickeningly adorable toddler, with another baby on the way. I've only ever exchanged the occasional cheery greeting and wave with Emma before, usually as I'm leaving the flat in the morning and she's on her way in some mad dash to work and nursery, but I suppose now that I'm going to be moving in, it would be nice to make more of an effort. A bit of community spirit, and all that. I mean, that would probably be a pretty grown-up thing to do.

'Oh, hi, Isabel!' She grins at me guiltily. 'You've caught me, I'm afraid.'

'Caught you?'

'Sticking my nose out into the corridor to inhale some of that gorgeous cooking smell.'

'Oh, that. Well, it's not a problem. Plenty of smell to go around!' Actually, that sounded stupid. And I don't want my nice new neighbour to think I'm stupid. 'I'd invite you up,' I carry on, 'but this is kind of an experimental dinner party, and I'm not sure I'd want to inflict it on you if anything's going wrong up there.'

'Experimental?'

'Yes, it's my friend who has his own dinner-party catering company. He's just trying out a few recipes on me and Will tonight.'

'Wow. That's an amazing idea.' Her eyes widen and she strokes her large baby bump thoughtfully. 'Especially for people like me who are far too lazy to do more than heat up a tin of beans.'

'Oh, well, I'll tell him you might be interested, shall I?'

'Definitely do that. And you and Will should come and have a bite with us one of these days too. He mentioned you were moving in pretty soon?'

'This weekend!' I say, in a voice that comes out unnaturally cheerful.

'Well, that's brilliant. And about time too! You two have been together for ages!'

I make an affirmative noise, and we agree that I'll get Barney to pop down later this evening and give her one of his cards, and then I head up the stairs with a little bit more of a spring in my step. Yes – that definitely felt grown up, chatting with the neighbours like that, and even doing a little bit of networking on Barney's behalf. And not at all scary, or Twickenham-y, or anything like that . . .

'Iz!' Barney turns round from the stove as I come into the kitchen. He's sweating, and his round face is alarmingly flushed, but he looks happier than I've seen him in months; almost back to his usual cheery self. 'Thank God, you've brought the soda siphon!'

'Yup. And I was just doing a bit of hustling for you, Barn, talking you up to the people downstairs!'

'Hey, thanks, Iz!'

'Not a problem. She was very impressed with all these amazing smells you're creating! You should pop down later on and give them one of your business cards.' I slip off my jacket and shoes. 'So, where's Will? Getting changed?'

'No, I've just sent him out to find Maldon sea salt. Can you *believe* he didn't have Maldon sea salt?' Barney shakes his head, genuinely overcome with sorrow for Will's soul. 'Didn't his mother teach him *anything* in the kitchen?'

'I'm not sure. She's Danish.' I mean, Danes mostly just eat a lot of bacon, don't they? In which case, there'd scarcely be any need to add Maldon sea salt to anything.

'Well, that doesn't explain a thing. The Danes eat excellently seasoned food.' Barney tuts. 'You're really going to have to shake things up a bit here when you move in, Iz. You're never going to manage with a Basic Storecupboard like that!'

I don't think it's the time to tell Barney that the Basic Storecupboard he installed for me when I first moved into my flat only stays as well-stocked as it appears every time he cooks for me because it hasn't actually been touched since . . . well, since the previous time he cooked for me.

'But you see, this is why it's so great that I'm practising on you guys today!' Barney beams at me. 'I've learned that I'm going to have to be extremely clear with my clients. You know, making *absolutely sure* they have the basics I need before I arrive.'

'Yes . . .' Oh, God, I do hope Barney isn't going to be quite so tyrannical about Simple Suppers as he was about The Coffee Messiah. 'Anyway, what are we eating? It all smells amazing!'

'Well, we're starting with a fresh mackerel tartare, with lemon and chives and a horseradish spuma . . .'

'Horseradish what?'

He brandishes the soda siphon at me. 'Foam.'

'Um . . . do you not think maybe you should *call* it a foam, Barn? I mean, I'm not being funny, but "spuma" sounds a bit off-putting.'

'I think the kind of people I'm going to be catering for, Iz, will be the kind of people who know what a spuma is. And if they're not, then my food will be a much-needed education!'

Oh God. It *is* going to be The Coffee Messiah all over again.

'Then for your main course,' Barney carries on, turning to stir a Le Creuset pan I never knew Will owned, 'you're really in for a treat. I'm trying out my version of the classic *lièvre à la royale*! Oh, I forgot to check, Iz – you do eat it, don't you?'

'That might depend on what *it* is.'

His eyes light up. 'It's a whole hare, completely boned, stuffed with foie gras, and marinated in a sauce of red wine and its own blood for twenty-four hours.'

I actually feel my stomach turn over, and I thank

God I didn't invite Emma-from-downstairs up for an impromptu bite. 'You're cooking a hare in its own blood?'

'*No*, Iz! You don't *cook* it in its own blood. Like I said, you *marinate* it in the blood, and then you roast it in some goose fat before braising it for four hours with a splash of *vino*!'

I stare at him. 'Barney, I thought you were calling yourself *Simple* Suppers.'

'Don't worry, Iz. Pud's ever so simple, to offset the main. I'm just doing home-made ice cream.'

'Oh, well, that'll be nice.' And *edible*, which is more than can be said for the main course of satanically slaughtered hare. 'What flavour?'

'There's lemon-and-thyme, raspberry-and-rosewater, dark chocolate-and-tobacco, and whisky-and-raisin. All served with salted caramel brandy snaps. Or they will be, if Will ever gets back here with the Maldon sea salt.' Barney turns round to look at me. 'Anyway, how was your day, Iz? Ooooh, you had your meeting with that publicity woman, didn't you?'

Barney is one of the very few people I keep filled in on some of my more unorthodox methods, mostly because he's just about the only one who can be counted on to be unflinchingly positive and non-judgemental. Besides, it's easy to be unorthodox with Barney, because he's pretty unorthodox himself. Just check out Exhibit A: the fact that he's seriously planning on serving his future clients bloody bunny and an ice-cream with tobacco in it.

I mean, you have to admire that kind of thinking. Even if you don't particularly want to eat it.

'Yes, that was today.'

'And? How did it go?'

'Oh, not especially well. I'm not sure the chemistry was right. I think maybe they're looking for someone a bit more . . .'

'Normal?'

I glare at him. 'I was about to say *experienced*.'

'Oh, Iz, you know what I mean!' Barney is opening the freezer door to give one of his ice-cream bowls a prod. 'I just mean . . . well, you're not exactly offering the run-of-the-mill approach, are you? It could take people a while to accept some of your ideas.'

'Yes!' He's exactly right. 'Yes, I think it will take a little bit of time.'

'Anyway, maybe you just didn't give the meeting your best shot today because you've got all kinds of distractions going on at the moment. I mean, finding another tenant for your flat, and packing, and all that. I'm sure as soon as you're settled here, you'll be able to sit down and have a think about how to proceed.'

Oh, that reminds me. 'Barney, talking of settling down, have you spoken to Lara at all recently? About her house-hunting in Twickenham?'

'*Twickenham?*'

I shrug. 'Apparently, it's very "nice".'

'That's precisely my point!' Barney's mouth has fallen open. '*God*, Iz, what's she thinking?'

I'm just about to explain all about the three

bedrooms, and the wet-room, and see what Barney makes of it all when there's the noise of a key in the front door. Will is home.

'The Maldon sea salt!' Barney gasps, practically bowling me aside as he rushes to get his hands on his all-important final ingredient.

'I'm so sorry,' I can hear Will saying, out in the hallway, 'but the poshest salt Sainsbury's seemed to have was this French one . . .'

'Sel de Guérande? Oh, well, that'll have to do, I suppose.'

'Are you sure?' Will is following Barney back to the kitchen, a tiny hint of desperation in his voice. 'Because honestly, it wouldn't be a problem for me to get in the car and head to somewhere different? You know, leave you to finish up all the cooking and then – Iz!' As he sees me, his face lights up with pleasure and what looks a little bit like relief. He's still in his suit from work, and Barney obviously didn't even give him time to take off his tie before sending him out on the salt-run, because it's pulled loosely down from around his neck. What with that, his ruffled hair, and the day's growth of light stubble on his jaw, he looks a tiny bit like an Armani model.

God, I love him when he comes home from work like this. I knew there was another excellent reason why I've been getting excited about moving in with him.

He heads across the kitchen to give me a kiss and, unusually, an extremely tight hug, inhaling the scent of my hair. 'You're here now! What I mean is,' he corrects himself, hastily, 'now that you're here, we can have a drink.'

'Yes, yes, the two of you must go and sit down with a nice glass of wine.' Barney shoos us towards the living room. 'The whole point of having Simple Suppers come and cook for you is for you two to relax! Oh, no, no, Will,' he adds, as Will reaches for a couple of glasses and the open bottle of red beside the fridge, 'I wouldn't go for a Rioja, not with a starter as delicate as the mackerel. Have you not got a nice crisp Vermentino, or maybe even a light Chablis?'

It's several minutes before we succeed in finding a wine that Barney deems appropriate and we can scurry to the safety of the living room to leave him creating his culinary masterpieces in peace.

'Iz, quick!' Will hisses at me, reaching deep down into his pockets and producing a family-size pack of peanut M&M's from one, and a couple of bars of Whole Nut from the other. 'Get some of this lot down you!'

I can't help succumbing to giggles as he tears the M&M's open with his teeth and pours a handful for each of us. 'Will! It's not going to be that bad! You know what a great cook Barney is.'

'I know what a great cook he *was*. Before he started worrying about gourmet dinner-parties and impressing his clients. Besides, it's already gone half-past eight,' he adds, popping the cork on the bottle of white that Barney has permitted us, and filling our glasses more-than-usually full. 'I skipped lunch today because I knew Barney would be cooking enough to feed a small army, and now I'm bloody starving!'

'Well, I'm sure it'll be nice when we do eventually get it.'

Will shoots me a look. 'He's cooking us some kind of hare marinated in its own juices, Iz. I mean, we're going to have to say something! I want Simple Suppers to work out for him just as much as you do.'

Maybe it's something to do with that non-confrontational schema Lara was talking about, but I'm not sure I can handle the fall-out from telling Barney that he might be better off just cooking a delicious roast and a nice apple crumble. 'Let's see,' I tell him, chinking my glass to Will's in the hope that he might get tipsy enough to forget the idea of *saying something*. 'Anyway, apart from being sent out to scour the shops for suitable salt, how was your day?'

'Unnnngh.' Will pulls a face, and pats his lap for me to prop my legs up on it. 'I'm swamped enough anyway without having to get this bloody seminar prepared for the partners' meeting . . . oh, but don't worry, Iz!' he adds suddenly. 'It's just a bit of a spike. Things will settle down right after this weekend. It's not going to be . . . well, like it was before. With you moving in, and everything, I mean.'

'I know.' I reach for the contraband M&M's and refill both our hands. 'It's going to be fantastic.'

'Exactly. Oh God, that reminds me, Iz, I've hired a van for Sunday morning, so we can move all your stuff over in just a couple of trips and avoid getting snarled up in terrible traffic all day.'

'That's brilliant, Will. Thank you!'

'And far be it from me to criticise, Iz, but it would be great if you – if *we* – could deal with the unpacking as soon as possible. I mean, we don't just want to dump everything in the spare room for the next three months! Sooner or later we're going to want to actually make use of that room.'

An M&M almost goes down the wrong way. '*What?*'

'Well, correct me if I'm wrong, Iz, but I do know the amount of paraphernalia you come with. I was assuming you might want to turn the spare room into some kind of storage space for your shoes, or for that bloody . . . that *extremely useful* Power Plate machine of yours. Or if you liked, we could make it into an office?'

'For me?'

'For both of us. But for you, mostly. I mean, you're not going to be working for Pippa Everitt for ever, are you? And when you do set up your own company, you're going to need a proper space to do it.'

I stare at him. 'Will . . . I'd love that.'

'Really? Then why are you looking a bit freaked out?' He suddenly looks a bit freaked out himself. 'Because we don't have to turn it into an office, Iz, we can just leave it as a spare room, for guests, if you'd prefer not to have the responsibility . . .'

'No, no, you've misunderstood.' I put my hand on

his leg. 'I'd love my own office here, Will! I was just worried for a moment, that you were suddenly thinking about turning it into a –' I'm about to say 'baby's room', but the last thing I want is for Will to think *I'm* trying to bring up the subject of babies. 'A wet-room.'

'A what-room?'

'A wet-room.'

He blinks at me. 'You mean one of those bloody stupid things where otherwise seemingly sane people turn a nice ordinary bathroom into a glorified communal shower?'

'Yes. Lara's thinking of having one, when she and Matthew move to their new place in Twickenham.'

'*Twickenham*? Why the hell are they moving to Twickenham?'

'Exactly!' God, I wish Lara could see the general reaction that her news is provoking. It does make me wonder if we shouldn't perhaps try some kind of intervention – lovingly sitting her and Matthew down and telling them our deep concerns. 'Something to do with having a garden, oh, and that wet-room . . . and bedrooms for the kids . . .'

'Wow. They're moving pretty fast all of a sudden, aren't they?'

'*Very* fast. *Too* fast.' I wave my arm expansively around the living room, with its view out on to the rustling tree-tops of Battersea Park. 'I mean, what's wrong with enjoying all this for a while, before anyone has to go dashing about making big life-altering decisions they can't take back if they suddenly change their minds.'

He frowns. 'Well, they could always just turn the wet-room *back into* a regular bathroom, couldn't they?'

'I meant the kids.'

'Ohhh. Well, yes. They would have a hard time exchanging children for a regular bathroom, I suppose. Probably the kind of thing the NSPCC frowns on.'

I can't help laughing, or suddenly scrunching down along the sofa to put my arms around him, and give him a long, lingering kiss on his lovely, soft lips.

'What was that for?' he asks, grinning at me.

'Oh, you know. Just a taster of how much fun we're going to have living together.'

'Fun?'

'*Fun,*' I say firmly.

'Well, in that case . . . He pulls me back towards him, and kisses me this time. 'Long may fun continue . . .'

'Iz! Will! Dinner!' It's Barney, calling from the kitchen, followed by an audible, 'Oh, shit!' A moment later he appears in the doorway, pulling his apron off and mopping his face with a tea towel. 'Sorry. Simple Suppers won't holler people in for dinner, obviously. Would you care to follow me?'

'Yes, Barney, we'd love to.' I panic, for a moment, about the M&M's, just as Will shoves them under the nearest cushion and gets to his feet.

'It smells great, Barn,' he says, holding out a hand to pull me to my feet, too. 'Though I should probably warn you, I do have one or two doubts about this hare you're serving . . .'

'Ah, well, that's what the feedback forms will be for,' says Barney, leading the way happily back to the kitchen. 'Now, they're entirely voluntary, of course, but I was thinking of asking people to score the food based on a few simple categories. You know – Depth of Flavour, Lightness of Touch, Texture, Presentation, and Seasoning . . .'

Will squeezes my hand tightly as we sit down in front of our plates of mackerel tartare and horse-radish spuma.

'This Much I Know'

Giving us the benefit of her wisdom this week is Isabel Bookbinder, glamorous Wedding Planner to the Stars.

- *I only became a wedding planner by accident, but as soon as I'd started, I found this was the one thing in my life I'd ever actually been any good at. Being there for people on one of the most important days of their life is a terrific high, and I found it pretty addictive right from the beginning.*
- *Brides get a bad rap, but they just need to be handled with the utmost care and attention. At the end of the day, this is* their *wedding: if they want to turn up with an orange fake tan, in a red car, or with an unphotogenic bridesmaid, then nobody* ~~especially not a stuck-up magazine editor~~ *should stop them. That's one of the most valuable lessons I've learned on the job.*
- *Grooms don't really get a look-in. But then women aren't allowed to go down coal mines, are they? Or should that be sweep for land mines? Either way, gender equality obviously has its limits.*
- *If there's one piece of advice I could give a young woman reaching an important crossroads in life, it would be just this: think twice before moving to Twickenham. That's all I've really got to say on the matter.*
- *My own relationship? It's excellent, thank you. Perhaps because I spend my days planning other people's weddings and helping them navigate through some of*

the choppiest emotional waters of their lives, I've never really seen the need to tie my own boyfriend down to anything more serious than living together. ~~Otherwise before you know it, you're living in Twickenham, with a range cooker, and a wet room, and oodles of children~~ *We adore each other, we're having fun. Isn't that all that really matters?*

Chapter Five

For crying out loud, who in their right mind is calling me at seven forty-five in the morning?

I pull the duvet up around my ears, tucking it nicely over the tips, then do my best to zone out my landline's horrible shrill ringing and doze off again.

Oh, thank God. It's stopped.

Only to start up again thirty seconds later.

OK, this had better be a really serious emergency we're talking about now. If I'm being hauled out of my lovely warm, cosy bed for anything, it had better be fire, or flood, or . . . what do they call it on the insurance forms? An Act of God? Yes. It had better be an Act of God, and a great big dramatic one at that . . . Shit. It's Mum.

'Mum?' I snatch up the phone from my bedside table. My heart is already starting to race, and I'm kicking myself for my stupidity in wishing for an Act of God. 'Mum, is everything OK? Are you all right?'

'It's not your mother, Isabel. It's your father.'

'*Dad*?'

Wait. Is that better, or worse, that he's the one calling me?

'It's not an emergency,' he carries on. 'There is

nothing wrong with anyone. I just wanted to try you before I left the house for school. And I did rather assume you'd already be up and about, I must say, Isabel. You're only a couple of weeks into a new job, after all. Don't you know how important it is to make a first-class first impression?'

I slide back under the duvet, wishing that a real-life Act of God would come and strike me down, sharpish.

'I am up,' I fib. 'I've been up since seven. I'm just a bit sleepy until I've had my coffee in the morning.'

'Ah. Well. I can certainly understand that. I would have phoned you yesterday evening, actually, Isabel, but it was rather late, and your mother mentioned that she thought you might be out for the evening.'

That'll be Mum's way of protecting me from Dad finding out that I might not have been sleeping in my own flat last night. His attitudes to pre-marital cohabitation, or even pre-marital sleepovers, are pretty much up there with the Victorians. Though fascinatingly, he seems to reserve the sharp end of his disapproval, as ever, for me. I mean, I don't see him causing any fuss about Matthew and Lara living together, in Twickenham or anywhere else on the planet, for that matter.

Anyway, as it happens, I *was* sleeping in my own flat last night. Even though Barney's dinner didn't finish until after midnight, and even though I'd have liked nothing better than to just fall into bed next to Will, I ended up getting a taxi back over here. Partly because

I was worried I was about to have a rather nasty reaction to the plate-and-a-half of *lièvre à la royale* I'd eaten, and I didn't want to put Will off living with me for the rest of his life. And partly because I've got quite a few bits and bobs to do before I'm ready to move out on Sunday, and what with the way Pippa's working me at the moment, every spare moment that I can spend here organising stuff is vital. I mean, I've got bills to pay, post to transfer . . . and OK, up until I got back last night, I hadn't *exactly* started my packing yet . . .

'So, Isabel, I had a telephone call from Susannah Britten-Jones yesterday evening,' Dad's continuing.

'Licky's mum? She called *you*?'

'Well, she called to speak to your mother, but I happened to answer the telephone and we had a very pleasant chat.'

This makes sense. Susannah Britten-Jones is one of those Women's Institute, parish council kind of women who Dad's always trying to butter up to come and chair fund-raising committees at the school. Despite the fact that he wouldn't usually give any of Mum's acquaintances so much as the time of day if they interrupted his evening with a phone call, I'm sure he was thrilled to be chewing the fat with Susannah.

'In fact, she was calling to ask about you, Isabel.'

'*Me*?'

'Yes. Apparently there are some last-minute problems with Alicia's wedding arrangements, and she was phoning to ask if you might be available to give a bit of a helping hand. It seems she'd heard you're working in the . . . er . . . in this field.'

Typical Dad, that he can't quite bring himself to voice the words that I'm working as a Wedding Planner. All right, he might not have actually shouted at me about it the other weekend, but it's still a very long way from any of the serious professions he really values.

'Anyhow, I told her you'd be delighted to help.'

I almost drop the phone in shock. Dad is prepared to unleash me on Susannah Britten-Jones? 'You did?'

'Of course I did.' His voice tightens. 'Isabel, you're not going to refuse to do a favour just because you do this for a living, are you?'

'What? No, no, not at all . . . I'd be really happy to help . . .'

'Good. Because I told Susannah you'd give Alicia a call this morning. Do you have a pen for the number?'

I scramble for the drawer of my bedside table, where, thankfully, I locate a Biro just in time to scribble down the number. Dad hates it when people don't have a pen at arm's reach; it's one of his many pet peeves.

'Please, don't forget to phone her, Isabel.'

'I won't!'

'And do try to accommodate whatever it is that Alicia needs you to do. Susannah has always been most helpful to me and the Governors, you know. And Jeremy was a very good friend of mine. I'd like to think our family can help his daughter now that he's not around to do it.'

I think calling Jeremy Britten-Jones, Licky's recently deceased father, a 'very good friend' is pushing it a bit. But I won't burst Dad's bubble. If he takes this kind of pleasure in associating with the great and good of the southern Mendips, then let him.

'Sure, Dad. No problem. I'll help Licky however I can.'

'Excellent. Well, I'd better be leaving for work now. I'm sure you should, too.'

'Yes. Absolutely.'

'Oh, and thank you, Isabel. We'll see you on Friday.'

And that's it. Just a click, as he hangs up the phone.

You know, when I do, finally, get to run my own Wedding Planning business, I'm going to be really, really careful about the way I treat my staff.

Though I suppose that when you're in the lowly, junior jobs, you never know how it'll really feel one day, when you're the one at the top of the pecking order. You might have all these big plans about how you're going to be this lovely, understanding boss, who mucks in with the tea rota, and knows the names of everyone's partners, children and pets, and takes everyone out to a nice lunch once a month just to say thank you for all their hard work and dedication. But then maybe when you do run your own company, perhaps you just automatically become the crabby, bossy control freak who takes all the fun jobs and leaves lists on people's desks headed with the words

ERRANDS – <u>ALL THIS MUST BE DONE **TODAY**,</u>
<u>ISABEL</u>.

Which is what greeted me next to my keyboard when I arrived at Pippa's this morning. And which is why, so far this morning, I have:

1) Jumped in a taxi to Sloane Square to collect the flower girls' silk orchid hairpieces from Basia Zarzycka, then dashed around Peter Jones to try to find silvery hairbands for them to wear instead, if Frankie decides she doesn't like the orchids;

2) Jumped on a bus to Harvey Nichols to pick up Frankie's gifts for members of her wedding party: to wit, four Marc Jacobs handbags for Bridesmaids (yes, really), one Yves Saint-Laurent handbag for Bride's Mother (yes, really), and one tube of Bliss Foot Patrol lotion and pair of matching Softening Socks for Bride's future Mother-in-law (Yes. Really);

3) Walked from Harvey Nichols to Harrods' toy department, selected two of their largest teddy bears, and arranged for Saturday morning delivery (complete with balloons) to Frankie's hotel so her three-year-old son Harley doesn't feel left out of all the excitement;

4) Jumped in another taxi to posh chocolatier on Piccadilly to collect eight thousand pounds' worth of specially commissioned 'Frankie and Dean'-embossed chocolates, served in boxes shaped like shoes (for the female guests) and footballs (for the men); and

5) Realised on my way out of the shop that chocolates in

fact say 'Francine and Dick', then stood around feeling awkward while posh chocolatier manager yelled on phone in mixture of French, English, and at one point what sounded a lot like Latin, before assuring me that teams of Parisian chocolate-makers were being mobilised even as we spoke, and that the re-embossed chocolates would be dispatched to London by first-class Eurostar by six o'clock on Friday morning.

All this, incidentally, while Pippa has swanned off to Lucknam Park for the day with Sunetra, charged with the arduous task of taste-testing the mini strawberry pavlovas and shot-glasses of Prosecco jelly that will form the guests' pre-dessert on Saturday.

I mean, couldn't Pippa at least have *warned* me that this is how I'd be spending my day? If I'd known, I wouldn't have come into work in my black suit and these bloody high heels. Nor would I have bothered putting on a layer of makeup or GHD-ing the frizz out of my hair. I'd have just rolled out of bed after Dad's seven forty-five alarm call, thrown on jeans and my only pair of Converse trainers, scraped my hair into a ponytail and been done with it.

And I would have looked better for it, too. Instead of looking like quite a cool, savvy girl-about-town, I look like an over-heated, frizzy, human ball of static who's just been pulled, repeatedly, through a hedge backwards.

And if that weren't bad enough, my mobile is

almost constantly ringing, with Pippa phoning me from the quiet luxury of Lucknam Park to demand that I run this errand, or call that supplier.

So I don't feel at all bad that I've made my way here, to the blissful peace of this little Italian trattoria just off Bond Street, for my midday meeting with Licky Britten-Jones.

When I got hold of her this morning, after Dad's call, she was already on her way up to town to pick up a bridesmaid's dress and to have lunch with her cousin – I assume the bridesmaid in question – who works somewhere near Hanover Square. Very sweetly, Licky suggested that I join them for lunch, which I'm seriously glad I accepted, if only so that I can just *sit*, for forty-five minutes, and take the pressure off the balls of my feet.

And sod it, I'm ordering us a bottle of champagne. It's not the kind of thing I imagine Licky would otherwise do, but she's getting married in forty-eight hours' time. We really ought to celebrate.

It's only as I take a sip from my glass that I notice that this guy at the table opposite is staring at me.

I mean, *really* staring.

Well, usually I'd be really flattered. Because, my God, he's good-looking. He's got all this thick, dark hair, and intensely black eyes, and I didn't even know cheekbones like that existed outside the confines of a Johnny Depp photo-shoot. But obviously, because he's quite so good-looking, and I'm doing my impression of a badly groomed, slightly sweaty girl who's just been pulled through a hedge backwards, he's not staring at me because he fancies me, or anything. In fact, the opposite is probably true – that he's staring because he can't believe I've actually come out like this. Men as good-looking as he tend to be the ones who only fancy supermodels.

But he's *still* staring.

It's starting to get a little bit off-putting, actually. And I can feel myself turning pink. I get my phone out of my bag and start fiddling with it, just so that I have something to do to distract myself. Oh, I know, I should text Barney, to thank him for last night's dinner.

Just wanted to say what a brilliant meal it was last night, especially loved the raspb+rosewater ice cream, thank you so much for doing all that cooking, I xx

A reply buzzes back twenty seconds later. *Didn't you like the choc+tobacco one?*

Of course!!! I text back. *All superb, as usual.* I busy myself perusing the menu for a couple of moments, until my phone buzzes again.

Not better than usual?

I sigh as I start tapping out my reply. *Barn. Of course better than usual. Ice creams sensational. Mackerel phenomenal. Hare*

I need to choose my words carefully here.

out of this world.

'Having trouble?'

It's the staring man. He's no longer just staring. He's speaking. At me.

'Sorry?'

'You just look a bit stressed about your text message. Actually, you look a bit stressed full stop, ever since you came in.'

'Oh!' I'm not quite sure what to say to this. Besides, my phone is buzzing again, with yet another message from Barney. *Did I leave soda siphon at W's? Any chance I could get it back by tomorrow night? Need to practise spuma. Spuma was awful, wasn't it?*

'Er . . .'

'Sorry. That sounds like I've been watching you.' He picks up the espresso cup that a waiter has just put in front of him and knocks back the contents in a single swallow. 'I haven't been watching you. Not in a creepy way, I mean.'

'No, no, I didn't think you were being creepy!'

He half-smiles, just for a moment. 'I was taking a professional interest, actually. I'm a photographer. You know, you have very interesting features.'

'Interesting' is clearly code for sweaty, shiny, and a bit funny-looking, with panda rings of mascara around the eyes'. 'Oh, right. I mean . . . glad to hear it.'

'Please, get back to your text messaging. I didn't mean to bother you . . .?' He pauses for my name.

'Isabel.'

'Nice name.' The half-smile returns. 'Your parents must be avid Jamesians.'

I must just be staring at him, because he carries on, in a slightly superior manner, 'Isabel Archer? *Portrait of a Lady*? By Henry James?'

'Oh, of course. One of my very favourite portraits . . .' I begin, just as there's a sudden flurry of activity from the entrance doors. It's Licky.

'Wizzie!' she squeals at me, as I jump up to greet her. 'Oh, my *God*, you haven't changed a *bit*!'

'Nor have you!' This is certainly true. She's just as sturdily built, with the same unruly cloud of frizzy, sandy hair, and that freckly skin that comes from being a pale English rose who spends most of their time teaching riding in the great outdoors, and it's entirely possible she was wearing those tapered jeans and that Puffa gilet the last time I saw her, almost a decade ago. 'It's really lovely to see you, Licks. It's been . . . what? Six years? Seven?'

'Yes, you came to my Donkey Sanctuary garden party at Broughton Hall! And do you remember, you were so sweet to me when I realised I'd been undercharging for entry? You said it wasn't so much about raising money as about raising *awareness*.'

I don't actually remember this. On the other hand, it does sound quite a lot like the kind of thing I would say.

'And Dan-Dan, too!' Licky turns to the staring photographer, who – hang on a minute – is getting up out of his seat and coming over to hug her, and plant a big, affectionate kiss on each cheek.

'*You're* the cousin?' It's my turn to stare now.

'Of course he is! Wizzie, this is Dan-Dan, my *favourite* cousin.'

'Well, that wouldn't be too hard,' says Dan-Dan,

wryly, as he extends a hand for me to shake. 'I'm Dan, by the way.'

'Isabel,' I say, shaking his hand – even though, of course, he already knows that.

'Look, Licks,' he says, 'I'm really sorry, but I'm not going to be able to stick around for lunch after all.'

'Oh, Dan-Dan!'

Dan is signalling a waiter for his bill. 'I know. It's a pain. But we've got a very important customer coming to look at a piece in the gallery, and I can't leave my assistant to handle him on her own. But I'm so glad Isabel's here,' he casts me a look, 'so that you haven't come all this way for nothing. And I'm still going to make sure I'm down at Broughton in plenty of time on Friday, if you need me to help out with anything.'

'That's sweet.' Licky gives him another huge hug. 'But aren't you coming down for the stag do anyway?'

Something flickers over Dan's face. 'I'm not sure, Licks. I'll do my best. But Marcus didn't actually invite me, you know.'

'Oh, I'm sure that was just an oversight! He's having *everyone*. I think even David might be going.'

'Yes. Well, like I say, I'll do my best.' He squeezes Licky's shoulder, then turns to me, fixing me with his inky eyes. 'It was lovely to meet you, Isabel, albeit briefly. I'm sure I'll be seeing you on Saturday, yes?'

'Of course you will! Wizzie's my brand-new wedding planner!'

Dan raises an eyebrow. 'Oh. Well, in that case, I'll

look forward to seeing the fruits of your labours on Saturday. As well as you.'

'Ooooh, *Wizzie*,' breathes Licky, as Dan heads out of the door, already pulling out his mobile phone. 'I think Dan-Dan liked you!'

'Don't be silly.' I flap a hand, and start helping Licky to a glass of champagne. 'I hardly think I'm his type!'

'No, no, you're exactly his type! All pretty and glamorous!'

I may have mentioned this before, but I really like Licky.

'Actually, you look a lot like his last girlfriend, Mia,' she carries on, wriggling her shoulders as she takes a sip of champagne. 'And she was gorgeous. He used to take all these beautiful photographs of her.'

'To sell in his gallery?'

'Oh, no, no, he doesn't really sell his photographs. They're more a hobby than anything else. And he's far too busy selling stuff by all these really trendy, expensive artists.'

'Paintings, you mean?'

'Paintings, sculptures . . . things he calls "installations" . . . honestly, Wiz, the last time I went to his gallery, the whole place was just filled with these six-foot-tall polystyrene coffee cups. It was meant to be a comment on disposability, apparently.' She pulls a face. 'Mummy said if someone was enough of an idiot to pay a hundred grand for a load of polystyrene, they ought to be disposed of themselves! Oooh, shall we order?' she suddenly asks, as a suave waiter brings us a bread basket and a little dish of olive oil. 'I'm starving. Do they have lasagne?'

We go ahead and order – spaghetti arrabbiata for me, lasagne and a side order of roast potatoes, unusually, for the bride-to-be – and then I top up Licky's glass as she dives for the bread basket.

'It's *so* nice of you to make the time to meet, Wizzie,' she says. 'Honestly, I was so chuffed when Mummy said she'd spoken to your dad, and that you wouldn't mind helping me.'

'I don't mind in the least! Anything I can do to help.'

'That's sweet!' There's suddenly a wobble in her voice. 'Because honestly, Wizzie, I don't think I've ever been so stressed. The workmen haven't got the marquee up properly yet, and my bridesmaid has food poisoning, so I'm having to draft in my cousin David's wife, and she's a whole two sizes smaller, and the Rolls we'd arranged to borrow from Mummy's friend isn't starting properly, so at this rate I'll be hitch-hiking to the church . . .' the wobble is getting more pronounced. '—And Mummy's buggered up a big patch of icing on the top layer of the cake and the little plastic bride and groom aren't big enough to cover it . . .'

'OK, OK, calm down.' I put my hand on top of hers. 'We can handle all this.'

'Really?'

'Really! I mean, it's all just logistics at the end of the

81

day, isn't it? All we need is a bit of a battle plan.' I take my leather file out of my bag, suddenly feeling pretty excited about the chance to put a bit of Bride Management into action. 'Now, tell me again . . . there's the marquee . . . the car . . . the vomiting bridesmaid . . .'

'The cake!'

'The cake,' I repeat. 'Well, for starters, that's incredibly easy to solve! My boss has all kinds of sample cake decorations lying around the office, so I'm sure one of them will be big enough to cover the icing disaster.'

Licky's eyes fly wide. 'Oh, that does sound good.'

'You see? Doesn't it feel better when you've made a start? Now, the car thing . . . oh, well, I think I can help with that.' Or rather, Ted from South-West Classic Cars can. 'How does a nice white vintage Bentley sound?'

'It'd be amazing, but I don't know how I could get one at such short notice.' Licky takes a miserable bite from her chunk of focaccia.

I wave a hand. 'Not a problem at all. Like I say, I happen to know of a lovely vintage Bentley that . . . well, that another bride won't be needing for her wedding.' I know it's only Licky, and I'd be extremely surprised if she had a hotline to the *News of the World* showbiz department, but it's still sensible to keep Frankie Miller's name well out of this. 'I'll just make a few calls and get it set up.'

'Oh, *Isabel*. You could do that?'

'Easy! Right, now then, this bridesmaid's dress business . . .'

'Well, that's where I was going after lunch, to see if I could find anything for David's wife at . . . hang on a second, she did give me the name . . . it's somewhere in Chelsea, I think . . .' Licky scrabbles in her tote bag. 'Oh, yes. The Wedding Shop.'

I stare at her. 'The Wedding Shop?'

'Yes. Is it not a nice shop, or something?'

'No, no, quite the opposite! It's a very nice shop. But Licky, their bridesmaids' dresses are by Vera Wang.'

Licky nods. 'Mm-hm. That's the name of the make that Sophie wanted.'

'But . . . are the other bridesmaids wearing Vera Wang?'

'Oh, no, but the other ones are just little flower girls! And Kitty – that's my friend who's down with food poisoning – she was just going to wear this nice full-length frock she got for last year's Young Farmers' ball.'

'Well, doesn't this Sophie have anything she wore to last year's Young Farmers' ball?' Rather than sending the bride-to-be trekking up to London two days before the wedding to pick her up a little something sassy from Vera Wang?

'Ooooh, no, Sophie really wanted something new. And I do want to give her what she'd like. She's being *so* kind, letting me use Broughton Hall for the wedding.'

I'm a bit confused. 'But wasn't that up to your uncle?'

'No, Uncle Tobes isn't at Broughton any more. David and Sophie moved in nearly a year ago, when David . . . well, they had a little bit of financial trouble, back in London.' Licky seems completely unembarrassed about airing her family's dirty linen, but then that's just the kind of guileless soul she is. 'David used to work in the City, but he had some problems – some of his deals went south, and the stress rather got to him – so it made sense for them to come home and take the Hall over. And Uncle Tobes is in an old people's home, not really with it any more, poor old thing. Sad, really. Daddy would be so devastated to see him, if he were still alive. He worshipped his older brother. At least he's been spared that, I suppose.'

I reach over the table and squeeze Licky's hand. 'I'm sorry, Licks. I know you would have liked to have your dad around on your wedding day.'

'Oh Lord, no!' Licky giggles, but her eyes are moist. 'I don't think Daddy would have been all that keen on poor Marcus. I mean, you know fathers and their daughters! It's rather a good thing they never actually managed to meet.'

'But I thought your dad died only six months ago.'

'Yes, yes. And Marcus and I have been together only since April. It has all been a bit of a whirlwind, Izzie-Wizzie! Which is partly why Sophie's been so great, pulling everything together at Broughton for the big day. She's actually turning the place into a proper venue, you know, all licensed for civil ceremonies and everything. She's going to start charging couples *thousands* to have their weddings there. But she's letting me use it for free. I mean, apart from a few basic admin costs, of course.'

Thank God, our plates of pasta are arriving, so I don't need to join in Licky's effusive praise of the woman who's charging her 'basic admin costs' to have her wedding at the family home. 'Well,' I say, as we dig in, 'I can stop by the Wedding Shop with you after lunch, if that would help at all?'

'Oh, Isabel, *would* you? I can't tell you how brilliant that would be! I'm a bit hopeless with clothes and things, but if you could help me pick something out for Sophie, I'm sure she'd be a lot happier with it!'

'Of course. It's practically on my way back to work anyway, so it's no problem.'

For a moment, Licky's eyes seem to fill with tears. 'You're a star, Isabel. I mean, I had no idea you'd be so good at all this! I just thought you'd volunteer to do a bit of flower-arranging on Saturday morning, or something . . . I mean, that's what Mummy said you'd probably do.'

Encouraged in this viewpoint by Dad, I have no doubt. 'Well, like I already said, I'm here for anything you need. It's just basic Bride Management.' I pick up the champagne, pour her a little bit more, and the raise my glass to chink against hers. 'Here's to the best day of your life, Licky! And to me doing everything I can to help you achieve it.'

Chapter Six

We're on our way to Chelsea in a taxi when I suddenly realise I haven't actually asked Licky the most important question about the coming weekend.

'So, are you starting to get excited now?' I beam at her. 'Just think – in barely forty-eight hours' time, you'll be married!'

'Yes!' Licky beams back. She's looking a little bit flushed from the lunchtime champagne. 'Isn't it amazing?'

'Amazing?'

'Well, I'm thirty-six next month, Wizzie.' She reaches into her bag and brings out a packet of fruit gums, which she offers to me. 'And I've never even had a proper boyfriend before. I was starting to think it was never going to happen for me!'

'Thirty-six isn't old!' I say, taking a green fruit gum and popping it in my mouth. 'And anyway, it doesn't matter if you're thirty-six, or forty-six. Or fifty-six, for that matter.' Though actually, never having a proper boyfriend until you were fifty-six probably *would* matter if it was happening to you.

'Maybe. Mummy says all that matters is that you find the right person eventually. And that when you know, you know.'

'Exactly! I mean, you and . . . God, I'm so sorry, Licky, I've completely forgotten your fiancé's name.'

'Marcus.'

'Marcus!' I repeat, with somewhat more enthusiasm than Licky has just managed to muster. 'You and Marcus are obviously the right people for each other. I mean, you'd hardly be getting married otherwise, would you? It's the most enormous step to take, even if you *do* know you're doing the right thing!'

'Mmm.'

'And even if you are a bit nervous now, Licks,' I add, patting her hand, 'just wait until you see him at the end of the aisle on Saturday. I bet *he* can't wait either.'

'Oh, yes, he's really excited! He's got loads of old friends coming, people he hasn't seen for yonks. So it's really just going to be like a big party for him. That's what he says.'

'Well, yes . . . but a very *special* party.'

'Oooh, no, the special party's going to be his stag do! Twenty-seven of them, converging on Bristol. Can you imagine?' Licky giggles, and pops a couple more fruit gums in her mouth. 'I was a bit worried at first, because his best man mentioned strip clubs and lap dancers and all that kind of thing, but Marcus told me not to be so silly. I mean, it's wrong to interfere, isn't it?'

I think maybe I'm starting to understand Dan's reaction earlier, when Licky brought up her fiancé and his stag do. I mean, just who *is* this Marcus guy, who calls his wedding day 'just a big party', and tells his wife-to-be not to be silly about his planned tour of Bristol's lap-dancing clubs eighteen hours before she walks down the aisle in a big white dress in front of all her friends and family?

'Right . . . though you *should* probably interfere a little bit, Licky, if it really bothers you.'

'Oh, no, no, it doesn't bother me! Besides, I want him to have his fun with his friends, before he has to come away on a boring old honeymoon with just me.'

I stare at her. 'Did he *say* that?'

'Well, no . . . it's just that I had to book the honeymoon, because he was ever so busy at work, and I thought it'd be really romantic for us to go to Rome, but I'd forgotten that Marcus much prefers beach trips . . . anyway, I'm sure he *won't* be bored, once we actually get there.'

I'm actually having to sit on my hands to stop myself leaning across the taxi, ripping Licky's (now I actually look at it, frankly hideous) engagement ring from her finger, flinging it out of the window into the path of the nearest bus and screaming at her to run for her life while she still has the chance. I just wish I'd got my hands on her a few months ago. She'd be an absolutely prime candidate for Bride Management, even if the end result was that she decided against actually getting married to this joker after all.

I can't help feeling a little shiver of excitement as our taxi pulls up outside the Wedding Shop, and we make our way inside.

This is exactly the kind of thing I hoped I'd be doing, when I started working for Pippa. I mean, who *wouldn't* want to spend their days in beautiful bridal shops, surrounded by these stunning creations in ivory satin and white lace, and advising an excited bride-to-be whether she looks better in . . . ooh, in something like that one hanging up there, with the fishtail skirt and halter neckline . . . or something more like this one on the dummy in the window – a strapless, layered creation with a contrasting dark ribbon around the bodice . . .

'Good afternoon, ladies!' A neat-looking brunette has appeared from the swing doors that lead to the back of the shop. 'Do you have an appointment?'

'No, I'm afraid not.' I smooth my frizzed-up hair with one hand, wishing I'd had the foresight to pop on a bit of lipgloss before we got here. 'But we have a little bit of a bridesmaid emergency, and I was wondering if you might be able to help. I'm from Pippa Everitt Weddings, by the way,' I add.

Thank God, the assistant picks up the shameless name-drop, because she nods. 'Well, we know Pippa, of course. I think several of her brides have used our wedding list service. In fact, we've probably spoken on the phone before now.' She extends a hand. 'I'm Kerry!'

'Ah, yes, Kerry!' I've actually never spoken to Kerry – or, indeed, to anyone who works here – but I'm not about to say that. Nor am I about to say that this particular emergency has nothing to do with Pippa.

'Well, it's lovely to put a face to the voice! Now, we have a bridesmaid down,' I go on, which is exactly the kind of paramilitary terminology that Pippa uses, 'and we're hoping to find something in Vera Wang for her last-minute replacement.'

'Oh dear. We only keep a very small selection of Vera Wang maids' dresses to purchase on the spot, and I'm afraid they all tend to be in . . .' she casts a discreet glance in Licky's direction, 'well, in *sample sizes*.'

'Actually, this is the bride,' I say. 'I think the bridesmaid we're talking about is probably a sample size, is that right, Licky?'

'She's a small size ten,' Licky announces, offering me – and Kerry, who declines – another fruit gum. 'She was quite clear I had to tell you that – a *small* size ten.'

Kerry considers this. 'Well, that might be possible . . . what are your colours?'

'Your colour scheme, for the wedding,' I translate, for a confused-looking Licky. 'The bouquet, and the table linen, and what the flower girls are wearing.'

'Oh, the little ones are wearing summer party frocks. And I don't really have a colour scheme. Mummy's just doing me a lovely mixed bouquet from the garden, and the flowers in the church are going to be mostly pink.'

'Well, we have some very beautiful bridesmaids' dresses in pink.'

'But Sophie specifically said, no pink.' Licky rifles

in her bag again and brings out her scrap of paper. 'She'd like midnight blue, or black . . . and preferably in a knee-length style so that she can wear it again. You know, to drinks parties, and that kind of thing.'

I'm glad to see that Kerry looks just as appalled by this Sophie's shameless attempt to wangle a free Vera Wang LBD as I am. She nods. 'I see. Well, we do have quite a few dark blues and blacks. Why don't you ladies wait here and I'll see if we can find something? I do have a bride doing a try-on session at the moment, so I may just have to leave you for a few moments if she needs anything from me. Actually, can I just ask – when you arrived, you didn't happen to see any photographers lurking around the corner, did you?'

'Er, no, I don't think so.'

'Right.' She sighs. 'I just have a feeling they're lying low until she comes back out.'

'Oh, really?' I say, ever so casually. Because it sounds like the bride doing the try-on is someone famous, and Kerry might tell me who it is if I come across as the blasé celeb wedding planner, who's seen and heard it all. 'They're such a pain, aren't they?'

'Tell me about it!' Kerry rolls her eyes. 'And bizarre, too,' she adds, lowering her voice to a whisper, 'to have three or four photographers chasing after Summer Shelley! I mean, it's not like she's Madonna or anything. Just shows you what the scent of a wedding will do, I suppose.'

I stare at her. '*Summer Shelley* is here?'

Kerry shoots me a funny look, which is hardly surprising given that I seem to have gone from blasé wedding planner to rubbernecking autograph hunter in the blink of an eye. 'Yes . . . anyway, I'll just go and check in our stockroom, see what I can find.'

'Fantastic! We'll just have a little look at some of these . . . tiaras! Were you thinking of a tiara at all, Licky?'

'I hadn't really considered it,' Licky says, as Kerry disappears into the back room. 'But some of them are lovely . . . Anyway, who is it she said was here?'

'Oh, just Summer Shelley.' I've got my composure back again – on the outside at least. Because this is completely brilliant! If there's any way I could actually get to *meet* Summer, I might be able to convince her to have a look at the manifesto I left with Wendy Gordon, and then who knows what could happen?

'Wow,' Licky breathes, 'a real live Spice Girl, here in the same shop.'

'Summer Shelley wasn't in the Spice Girls,' I hiss.

'No? Not the little blonde one?'

'No! She *is* blonde, but she was in a different group. Girlz 4 Ev-A.'

'Oh. Did they do that theme song for the *Charlie's Angels* film?'

'No, that was Destiny's Child.' I'm just about to add that Girlz 4 Ev-A were nowhere near as famous as that – not to mention that they were nowhere near as good as that – when Kerry suddenly comes back

92

through the doors with an armful of dark-coloured cocktail dresses.

'Easier than I thought!' she says brightly. 'Why don't you start with a little look through these?'

'Oh, I've got a good idea!' I take the dresses from her. 'Why don't I just nip back there and try them on? Then my friend can get a better idea of how they look off the hangers.'

Kerry's eyes flicker down to my waistline. 'Um . . . I *did* say they were a sample size, didn't I?'

'Yes, yes, but I don't actually have to be able to do them up or anything. Just pull them on so that we get a better idea of how they look with a body inside.'

'But my customer –'

'Oh, I won't disturb her. I'll only be a moment! Licky, why don't you ask Kerry to show you a couple of those tiaras you liked in the meantime?' I gesture in the direction of the tiara cabinet, then push the door open into the back room.

It's just as airy and light back here as it is out front. There are full-length mirrors on two walls, several tall bamboo screens to change behind, and more of those beautiful wedding dresses hanging from rails and hooks.

There's also a little gilt chair draped with a pile of very pink clothes, and a huge Louis Vuitton monogram bag that must belong to Summer Shelley.

I give a little cough. 'Hello?'

'Kerry? Is that you?' A breathy American – sorry, *Canadian* – voice comes out from behind one of the bamboo screens. 'I don't think I like this one as much as the other one. I mean, you know I said I wanted to feel like a movie star on my big day? Well, this one makes me feel more like a porn star . . .'

'No, actually, it's not Kerry. My name's Isabel.'

'Oh.' Summer Shelley's head appears around the side of the screen. 'Hi, Isabel.'

Her bright strawberry-blonde hair is pulled up into a high ponytail, and she's sporting the kind of Tango tan that would make Pippa and Sunetra throw up their hands in horror, but she's wearing only minimal makeup, which serves to make her look rather prettier and a lot younger than I expected. She's tiny, too – much tinier than she looks in photographs, and so obviously a sample size that I'd consider asking her if she minded hopping into a couple of these Vera Wang bridesmaid dresses to see what they look like on. But there's one thing that certainly isn't tiny or sample size about her – or rather two things, and they're currently bobbing up for air from within the corset of an ivory satin wedding gown. Wow. I mean, she was right about the porn star thing. I can hardly take my eyes off them for a moment, until I realise how rude it is just to stare at somebody's chest. My ex-boyfriend Ben had a colleague who did just that, and it's ever so off-putting. Summer Shelley is never going to choose a wedding planner who just stands around and *gawps*.

'Is Kerry available?' she asks, twisting this way and that to get a look at her back view in one of the full-length mirrors.

94

'Actually, she's just helping out another customer at the moment. But maybe I could give you an opinion? I mean, I *am* a wedding planner,' I say, casually, 'so it is kind of my area of expertise.'

'You're a wedding planner?'

'Mm-hmm. In fact, I had a meeting with Wendy Gordon about you only yesterday!'

Summer's blue eyes widen. 'You're not Henry Irwin, are you?'

Well. I know I'm not a sample-size boobalicious blonde, but are things really *that* bad?

'Um, no . . .'

'Oh, you know what I mean!' Summer giggles and catches my eye in the mirror. 'Are you *from* Henry Irwin? Because Wendy wants me to meet with him next week.'

Damn it. That must be Scowling Man.

God, he stole my MP3 player idea, didn't he? And used that to impress Wendy Gordon enough to get the job.

Right, well, I don't know if there's some kind of High Council of wedding planners that you can go to in cases of blatant breaches of ethics like this, but if there isn't, then it's something I'll be fighting for as soon as I'm in a position to do any good in this industry.

Not that I ever *will* be in that position if people like Henry Irwin keep nicking my best ideas.

'No. No, I'm not from Henry Irwin. I'm from Pippa Everitt.'

'Pippa who?' Summer frowns. 'Wendy didn't mention any Pippa anyone.'

'Pippa Everitt. She's a really top wedding planner. We're working on Frankie Miller's wedding this weekend, in fact.'

'*You're* doing Frankie Miller?' Summer's cheeks have flared pink beneath the layer of orange tan. 'Why didn't Wendy even mention you guys to me?'

'Perhaps she felt that Henry was more suitable,' I say, trying to sound gracious. 'I mean, I do hear excellent things of him. Although there may be one or two question marks over his scruples.'

'Oh?'

'Well, there are some wedding planners who are very happy to just recycle old ideas for new clients.'

Summer pulls a face. 'I don't want a *recycled* wedding.'

'Well, who would? I mean, you said it yourself, didn't you? You want to feel like a movie star on your big day.' Actually, this isn't a bad idea to run with. 'We could even give you a whole Hollywood theme, if you liked.'

'*Hollywood?*' Her eyes have lit up; clearly I've mentioned the magic word.

'Yes, if that's what you wanted. You could have a red carpet at the reception for all your guests to walk down . . . we could fit out your venue with big movie screens to show old movies during dinner . . . They could even show old home movies of you and Tim as kids, if you have any.'

I'm amazing even myself. I mean, this is a terrific idea! And Summer seems to think so too.

'Oooooh. I think the guests would *love* that.'

'And we could have all the menus and table plans printed out like old-fashioned gossip pages, and we'd get one of the top Frank Sinatra acts to perform . . . really it just depends how much fun you'd like to have with it. All the decisions would be entirely yours, of course.'

'Well, *duh*.' Summer is frowning, her mind back on Wendy's control freakery. 'I mean, it's *my* wedding. I should decide how the whole thing goes. And I should decide who's going to help me plan it.'

'Of course! In fact, that's a big difference you'd find with us. We really listen to our brides. Everything we do is truly bride-centric.'

Summer's eyes widen. 'Wow. Bride-centric!'

She looks impressed but I'm not completely sure she knows what it means. 'We'd be completely focused on you throughout the entire process,' I explain, 'doing anything wedding-related that you need. For example, I gather you were followed here today by three paparazzi photographers? Well, we'd make sure that didn't happen again.'

Summer gasps. 'You could get me followed by *more* than three?'

'Um, actually, I just meant that we could hire you some security people.'

'Oh.'

'But I'm sure we could get you *more* paparazzi!' I

say, hastily. 'I have all kinds of contacts within the media!'

'You do?'

'Absolutely. I'm an ex-journalist,' I tell her, which is basically true. I mean, all right, I only had this admin job on the *Saturday Mercury*, and I got kicked out because I accidentally exposed my boss's affair with the Home Secretary. But come to think of it, that little incident exposed me to my very own paparazzi for a while, so I'm sure I could track a few of them down! 'Plus,' I carry on, 'I also used to work in fashion, so I'd be able to give you really top advice on wedding dresses.'

'So you'd, like, come shopping with me?' Summer suddenly looks even younger, as a hopeful, eager expression crosses her pretty face.

'For wedding gowns, engagement party gowns, mother-of-the-bride gowns . . . whatever you want. Whatever you need. That's the beauty of our approach. I tell you what, Miss Shelley,' I carry on, reaching into my bag and pulling out my Smythson folder, 'why don't you have a little look at what I prepared for Wendy yesterday? If there's anything in there that takes your fancy, my number is right up there at the top. You can give me a call any time.'

'Excuse me?' Kerry suddenly pokes her head through the swing doors, looking rather annoyed. 'Is everything all right in here?'

'Oh, yes, perfectly OK, thank you.' I hurry towards her. 'But you were right – I don't think I can squeeze into any of these! This one's my favourite, though.' I hold up a midnight-blue dress, in matte satin and with a demure neckline that ought to scupper any of Sophie's attempts to upstage Licky on her wedding day. 'I'll come and see what the bride thinks! It was really nice to meet you, Miss Shelley,' I add, giving her my brightest, most professional-looking smile as I go out into the front of the shop to meet Licky.

After I've seen Licky off to Paddington, I finally head back to Pippa's for the rest of the afternoon. And actually, it's rather nice having the place to myself! I get the chance to rummage through Pippa's sample cake-toppers for a plastic bride and groom topper for Licky's wedding cake, and then I have a lovely chat on the phone with Ted at South-West Classic Cars, whose white Bentley is still, thank heavens, available on Saturday afternoon for Licky to hire. Anyway, once I've arranged all that, I sit at my desk with a nice cup of Pippa's Earl Grey, with some soothing background music filtering from the stereo, catching up on a few emails and then putting in a bit of extra work on my Manifesto. Plus I have a closer look at a copy of the standard Agreement that Pippa has all her clients sign, just so that I know the kind of thing I'll need to be putting in my own Agreement, if and when the time comes.

Well, just in case Summer Shelley *does* decide she wants to hire me, I really ought to . . . what's Will's favourite phrase? Make sure all the i's are crossed and the t's are dotted.

Oh, no, I mean the other way around. Obviously.

Anyway, it's all pretty useful stuff concerning schedules of payment and undertakings not to hire unauthorised suppliers, and I have to say, even if it doesn't make for a scintillating read, at least I've learned something. At about six thirty it becomes pretty obvious that Pippa isn't going to be back for a while, so I say good night to the nanny and the kids, who are also taking advantage of Pippa's absence to run riot in the kitchen, then I hop on the 295 to head over to Will's. I know he's working late tonight, in preparation for the partners' meeting, but I've got to locate Barney's soda siphon and drop it over to his flat. I mean, the last thing I want is to be held responsible for buggering up his spuma practice.

When I get to Will's, it's dark, and unnervingly quiet. So I switch on every light I can in the hallway, then head through to the kitchen to start trying to find where Will might have stored away the siphon when we were all clearing up together yesterday night.

Right. Well, the likeliest place is in one of the big cupboards to the right of the cooker. This is where Will keeps all his gadgety things that he uses once and never gets round to using again. Like that toasted sandwich maker he produced when, one chilly evening a few months back, I got this real craving for a cheese-and-tomato toastie. All of a sudden Will opened this cupboard door to reveal a whole arsenal of gadgets I'd never even known he had, including not only the toasted sandwich maker but also a working fondue set, a Japanese rice cooker, and a funny metal thing that looked like an uncomfortable hat but in which I think you're supposed to coddle eggs.

I open the cupboard and peer inside.

All right, well, it's not immediately visible . . . there's a bit of Magimix, without any other bits . . . the Japanese rice cooker . . . the weird hat-like egg coddler . . . Well, I'm going to have to move all of these out of the way to see if Will's gone and stuffed the siphon down the back, which it would be just like him to go and do.

But as I pick up the egg coddler, I can see that there's something nestling inside it.

Well, obviously it's not the soda siphon.

It's a little blue velvet ring box.

I recognise it right away. I mean, it's pretty weird to see it hiding here, in the egg coddler, when for the past twenty years or more it's sat on top of Mum's dressing table. She's always kept it there, despite Dad's carping on at her that she really ought to lock it away some- where safe. And despite the fact Mum usually gives in to Dad's carping, this is one thing she's stuck to her guns on, because the ring box contains her own mother's sapphire engagement ring, and she likes to be reminded of her. In fact, one Christmas when I was about fifteen and she'd had a little too much crème de menthe, she took me aside all weepy and said she would never let Nana's ring out of her sight, no matter what Dad said, until the day when her future son-in-law came to her and asked for it, in order to give it to me.

And now Will's got it. And he's hidden it here. Inside an egg coddler.

Which can only mean one of two things:

1) Will isn't really a tax lawyer at all, but in fact a daring international jewel thief, who has cosied up to me for eighteen months with the sole intention of getting his greedy hands on a vintage sapphire engagement ring; or
2) Will is going to ask me to marry him.

All right. Let's face it.
It's the second thing, isn't it?

Chapter Seven

Lara notices something is up the moment she and Matthew arrive to pick me up outside Pippa's house on Friday afternoon. She shoots me what's-going-*on* looks over her shoulder all the way to Twickenham, where Tania the estate agent is waiting for us – or rather, for them – outside an Edwardian semi on a quiet residential street.

Tania takes one look at Matthew clambering out of the car and, as is so often the way when women meet my brother, falls instantly and violently in lust with him. So she's clearly ecstatic when, after we've all trooped round the semi together a couple of times, marvelling at the opportunities for extension and improvement, Lara suggests that she, Tania, takes Matthew to look round the garden while we stay inside and try to visualise the dark, poky downstairs rooms all knocked into one huge kitchen/living room/diner.

'Right. What's going on?' she demands, the moment Tania has led Matthew out of the side door.

'Well, pretty much the usual, it looks like to me.' I nod out of the kitchen window, to where Tania is flipping her hair and giggling hysterically at, no doubt, Matthew's favourite gardening joke, which if I remember correctly is something to do with King Tut and chrysanthemummies. 'God, Lars, doesn't it annoy you, when girls are all over Matthew like that?'

'What? Oh, for heaven's sake, no. It's not like he ever responds, or anything.'

This is certainly true. And it's also pretty clear that Matthew has eyes only for Lara. On the short drive from Fulham to Twickenham, he told her he loved her twice, leaned over to give her a kiss four times, and solicitously bought her a chunky KitKat when he stopped for petrol near Mortlake.

'Anyway, I wasn't talking about Matthew's fan club. I was talking about you!' Lara's eyes are wide with concern. 'You look awful, Iz!'

This is probably because I had no more than two hours' sleep last night. Every time I closed my eyes, all these horrible disturbing thoughts kept popping into my head. Like, for example, the fact that Will must have gone to ask Mum if he could have the ring, which must mean that he's also gone and had 'The Conversation' with Dad. And for some reason, at three o'clock this morning, I just couldn't shake the vision of Will and Dad standing about in the study, both in full Edwardian dinner dress and muttonchop sideburns, for some reason, while Dad quizzed Will about his prospects and they both puffed away on foul-smelling pipes.

And all right, it probably didn't happen like that. Probably the way it happened was that, as soon as the

104

words, 'I'd like to marry your daughter' were out from Will's lips, Dad was sinking to his knees in astonishment that anyone would want to take me on, and kissing his putative son-in-law's hand in a pitiful display of gratitude.

And then there were all these other images that I just couldn't shake off. The vision of Mum phoning me five times a day, every day for a year, to discuss whether or not she should wear a hat or a fascinator, and her suggestions for a variety of matching items to go with the giant pouffy meringue she's guilt-tripped me into buying. The vision of Auntie Clem throwing a strop because I haven't invited every single one of her grandchildren, resulting in a spin-off strop from Dad because I've mortally offended his side of the family.

'It's not Pippa.' I swallow hard. 'It's Will.'

'What about Will? Oh, Iz-Wiz, you've not decided he's having an affair again?'

'No! The opposite.'

She frowns. 'What's *the opposite* of having an affair?'

'Oh, I don't know, Lars. How about asking someone to marry you?'

'Well, I suppose, but Will isn't going to ask –' She stops suddenly, her eyes widening. 'Oh my God.'

'Yes.'

'Oh, *Isabel*!' She opens her arms, all ready to throw them around me, but then lets them drop by her side again. 'Wait. It is *you* he's asked?'

'Well, thanks for finding me so unmarriageable!'

'No, it isn't that. It's just . . . well, it all just seems quite sudden, for someone like Will. And you've barely even moved back in with him yet.'

'That's the point!' I can feel my heart starting to race again, unpleasantly, the way it was doing when I was having all those visions about the muttonchop sideburns in the small hours this morning. 'I mean, has he gone *totally* insane?'

'OK, calm down, Iz. Just tell me how it all happened.' Despite herself, Lara's eyes are shining. 'Did he go down on one knee? Did he make a speech. Oooooh, the ring! Where's the ring?'

'No, none of that happened. He hasn't actually proposed yet.'

'Oh-kay . . .' Lara hastily applies her professional psychologist's expression, as though I'm one of her barmy patients who's just come in and told her I'm convinced the next-door neighbours are only putting up their side extension to spite me. 'Um, I think maybe you've been working too hard, Iz-Wiz . . .'

'I found the ring! Nana Hamilton's sapphire. He'd hidden it in an egg coddler.'

It's to Lara's credit that, instantly, she can make sense of this. 'Nana Hamilton's ring? Oh, Isabel. He really means it.'

'Precisely!' I think my racing heart might be about to develop into a full-blown panic attack. At least, that's what I'm hoping it is, because the alternative is a heart attack, which would just be *seriously* embarrassing.

*

'Look, Iz, you really do just need to keep calm.' Lara looks around for a chair to pull out for me, but nobody's lived in this house for what looks like decades, so she just pats the kitchen worktop and I lean against there instead. 'You're catastrophising.'

'You always think I'm catastrophising!'

'Because you always are! Now, what's the very worst that's going to happen here? Your gorgeous, kind, successful boyfriend, whom you adore, has decided to ask you to marry him. Discovering the ring has given you time to think about it. And you can say Yes. Or you can say No.'

'Lara, I can't say "No" to a free squirt of perfume in Selfridges.'

'Then say you need to think.' Lara shrugs, as if it's as easy as falling off a log. 'That's perfectly reasonable, Iz, when somebody springs a big surprise on you.'

I flap a hand. '"*I need to think*" is worse than "No". It's "No" for cowards. And I don't want Will to think I'm a coward as well as someone who doesn't want to marry him. He might never ask me again.'

Lara looks at me for a moment. 'But Iz, if you want him to ask you again, then you *do* want to marry him. One day at least.'

'Well, *obviously* I want to marry him one day at least. I think. But you have to be pretty sure about it, don't you? I mean, you hear about it all the time, people making the mistake of getting married when they weren't a hundred per cent sure. I read an article in *Glamour* all about it only the other week! Marriage Regret Syndrome, they call it.'

I pause, for Lara to nod sagely, and say yes, she knows that very syndrome, and has read a paper about it herself in *Psychology Review* only a couple of weeks back.

'Oh, *you* know,' I continue impatiently. 'People get all geed up about the idea of the romantic proposal and the big white dress, and then they go away on their big dream honeymoon to Phuket, and she spends their two weeks doing all kinds of adventurous things like snorkelling, and paragliding, and visiting all the amazing Buddhist temples, and her new husband just sits on a sun-lounger on the beach drinking beer and picking his toenails . . .'

Lara holds up her hands. 'OK, just slow down. For one thing, since when are you going to be the one snorkelling and paragliding? And I think we can safely say Will isn't a toenail-picker.'

'Can we?' I demand. 'Do we *know* that? For all I know, the moment I say I'll marry him and we've moved in to our new place in Twickenham together, and built the wet-room, he'll start showing his true colours. Maybe he's a secret belcher. Or . . . or a closet toilet-fouler . . .'

Lara actually suppresses a giggle. 'Honestly, Iz, I don't see it. I mean, far be it from me to sound like your parents, but Will is a lot of people's example of a dream husband.'

'Please.' I hold up a hand. '*Please*, Lars, don't bring Mum and Dad into this. Seriously, they're the last thing I need to think about right now.'

Lara doesn't say anything for a moment. Then she clears her throat. 'Are you sure? Because it sounds like they might be the first thing you're actually thinking about.'

'What do you mean?'

'Well, usually when you get into a state like this, it's something to do with your family. And given that weddings *are* about families, I wouldn't blame you for being a bit apprehensive.'

I don't say anything for a moment. Then something occurs to me, something that will shut her up on this front. 'Well, even if it is about my family a little bit, it's not *all* about them. I mean, I didn't even get round to starting packing for my move until the other night! Surely *that's* a sign I'm not really ready for any kind of serious commitment . . .'

'It's a sign you hate packing. And that you always leave it till the absolute last minute and then run round like a headless chicken shoving everything into black plastic bin-liners.'

'Actually, I've done extremely organised packing this time, I'll have you know. When I got back from Barney's dinner the other night, I boxed up loads of things, *and* I even used that label-maker you lent me!'

'Ha! So you *do* want the commitment of moving in with him!' Lara looks triumphant. 'Come on, Iz! Forget about all the big, scary wedding stuff. I mean, even if your wedding was a little bit about your family, your *marriage* wouldn't be.'

I let out a hollow laugh, which sounds all the more impressively sinister in the empty kitchen. 'Really? So if I *was* wrong about Will, and I realised I'd made a mistake marrying him, I wouldn't have to deal with Mum weeping and wailing and gnashing her teeth, and Dad thundering about the fact that I can never make a success of anything, and –' I break off as I see Matthew and Tania heading back up the garden path towards the kitchen. 'Look, I can't talk about it any more just now.'

'But, Iz –'

'Shush! Shush!' I flap at her. 'And don't say a word about this to Matthew! You know what he's like, he'll blab about it all through dinner, and I just don't want to have to discuss it with Mum yet.'

I mean, it's a complete bloody miracle she's kept quiet about it until now, frankly.

'I won't say a word, Iz.' Lara looks slightly hurt. 'You know I never do.'

'No. I know . . .' But I can't say any more, because the side door is opening, and Tania's hysterical giggles are resonating around the empty kitchen. And anyway, it's time to get going. Mum will be getting panicky that we'll be late for dinner.

The traffic heading south-west on a Friday is so abominable that even Matthew's bat-out-of-hell driving doesn't gain us much time. It's already gone half-past seven by the time we finally reach Shepton Mallet, and pull up on Mum and Dad's driveway.

Mum is already opening the front door as she hears the car doors shut, hurrying over to greet us all with kisses and hugs, and Lara and Matthew head inside with their bags to freshen up while I accompany Mum through to the kitchen.

'It smells great, Mum,' I say, sniffing the air appreciatively. 'What are we having?'

'Ooh, well, I read this article recently, Iz-Wiz, about someone having these incredibly famous shepherd's pie and champagne parties . . .'

'Jeffrey Archer.'

'Oh, was it?' Mum's face falls. 'Oh dear. Well, anyway, I was going to do a few big shepherd's pies, but then of course I remembered your dad doesn't like shepherd's pie, he only likes *cottage* pie, and then I thought if I was making the sauce for the cottage pie I might as well use it to make up some big lasagnes as well . . . and then I had a little bit left over, so I actually turned that into a rather nice chilli con carne.'

'So it's a cottage pie, lasagne, and chilli con carne and champagne party?'

'Well, sparkling wine, actually. You know what your dad's like about silly spending on wine. After all, as he said, it isn't worth spending good money on champagne when you're only eating plain old ordinary food.'

Typical Dad, putting the dampeners on Mum's shepherd's pie and champagne party. And anyway, the whole *point* of a shepherd's pie and champagne party is that you're drinking champagne with plain old ordinary food.

'Well, I'm sure it's going to be delicious, Mum. Can I help at all?'

'Oh, no, Iz, you go out and join the others in the garden! Besides, it's Hypatia's bedtime soon, and she'll want to see her auntie Iz before she goes up.'

God, I'd completely forgotten Hypatia was going to be here!

I wonder if Marley and Daria have dressed her in any of the little outfits I gave them last time I saw them. There was a sale on at Baby Gap, so I couldn't resist popping in and seeing if there was anything cool for her to wear. Because I do have this slight terror that Marley and Daria are going to dress her in . . . well, in mini versions of the clothes they wear themselves. Shapeless cardigans, tapered slacks, nondescript baggy T-shirts. Anyway, Baby Gap had all these adorable things – funky little hoodies, brilliant ra-ra skirts, cool jeans . . . Oh, and this amazing little T-shirt that I knew Marley and Daria would love, because it has the words 'Nice As' and then the symbol for pi stuck on it in little sparkly rhinestones! I mean, how great is that?

'Hello!' I sing out, opening the back door and heading on to the back patio.

Marley and Daria are sitting around the patio table, sipping glasses of sparkling wine. They both look pale and hollow-eyed, which under normal circumstances you'd obviously attribute to the pressures of having a six-month-old baby. But Marley and Daria tend to look pale and hollow-eyed pretty much all the time. In fact, I remember once seeing them only the day after they'd been away to Sicily for a ten-day holiday, and they still looked as though they'd spent the last week lying down in darkened rooms working on their algorithms.

Algorithms, by the way, are pretty much the only thing I know about what Marley and Daria do. They have very intense and high-level discussions about their work with Dad quite often, and the word algorithm features extremely heavily. Or rather, it's the only word that features heavily that I actually recognise, and am able to use in a sentence.

Anyway, I'm just about to ask where my favourite niece is when Dad appears from the French doors, holding her.

The first thing I notice is that she's not wearing any of the things I gave her. Unless . . . is that the 'Nice As Pi' T-shirt peeking out from beneath her dungarees?

No. It's a nondescript, baggy one.

Oh, well. Perhaps the rhinestone one didn't wash that well, or something. Or it's possible she's grown out of it already. Because she really has grown.

Plumped up all nice and pink, with the tiniest sprouting of fair hair in a wash over her little bald head, she looks not unlike Prunella Rebecca, my beloved Cabbage Patch doll from when I was five.

And the second thing I notice is that Dad's face is all lit up. I mean, he's radiating goodwill like Santa Claus. Which, if you knew my dad, you'd realise was about as likely as . . . well, as *seeing* Santa Claus.

'It's astonishing,' he's saying, to Marley and Daria. 'She seems to have the reasoning skills of an eighteen-month-old already! I mean, she quite clearly knows the difference between the square blocks and the triangles, and she's already starting to distinguish between the different sizes . . . you know, I think her colours aren't going to be too far off, either!'

Marley and Daria nod in their detached, contented way, as though Dad's talking about an especially interesting algorithm rather than their own child.

'Oh, well, that sounds really impressive!' I say. 'Well done, Hypatia!'

'Honestly, I think the sooner you can get her into some classes for gifted children, the better,' Dad continues, bouncing a stern-looking Hypatia on his hip and stroking her head in an unusually tender way. 'I must email you those studies I was reading, Marley, about accelerating development in the first twelve months . . . Oh, hello, Isabel,' he adds, suddenly noticing I'm here. 'I didn't know you'd arrived.'

114

'Just in time to see my beautiful niece!'

'Actually, Isabel, we'd rather you didn't use that word,' says Daria.

I blink at her. 'Niece?'

'Beautiful,' Marley corrects me. 'We feel very strongly that a little girl's worth shouldn't be judged on her appearance, so we're trying not to use those kind of subjective value judgements until she's old enough to be able to dissect their true meaning.'

Hang on a moment. So, it's OK to talk about classes for gifted children, and accelerated development, but calling her beautiful might . . . what? Actually make her believe she *is* beautiful?

But, as Lara's always pointing out about her half-brothers and -sisters, you must never, ever openly disagree with the way parents choose to bring their children up.

'Of course. I'm sorry. Well . . . er . . . is it OK to have a cuddle?'

'Oh, I'm sure she'd like that,' says Daria, earnestly. 'Physical closeness is very important in child development, especially when they're under a year old.'

'And it's nice for me too!' I say, then wish I hadn't when all three of them stare at me as though I've just said something hideously inappropriate. 'Well, it's very nice to see you, Hypatia!' I sing, heading over. 'Aren't you looking . . . er . . .'

Well, for God's sake, what do you say to a baby when you're not allowed to describe her as anything that might be a subjective value judgement?

'. . . bald.'

See? That's what you're left with.

And Hypatia doesn't look all that impressed, either. She blinks up at me from Dad's clasp with wide, blue eyes, not showing all that much willingness to be cuddled.

'Say hello to Auntie Iz!' I reach out to take her from Dad. 'Who's your favourite auntie?' Then I try out this silly face that I think she rather liked last time I saw her, where I kind of pull my lips back and cross my eyes and waggle my tongue.

Suddenly, Hypatia starts to howl.

'Oh, God, I'm sorry . . .' I shrink backwards as Daria hurries up to take her from me. 'Was I not meant to say "favourite"?'

'She's just a little over-tired,' says Daria, which I think is meant to be nice, but in her flat, Swiss tone comes out sounding suspiciously like a value judgement to me. 'I'll take her inside for her bottle. Marley, will you show me where your mother has put the formula?'

They vanish inside, with a wailing Hypatia.

So it's just me and Dad.

And he's not looking like Santa Claus any more.

'I'm sorry,' I repeat helplessly. 'I thought she might like it.'

'She's a very sensitive child,' Dad says irritably. 'And even if she weren't, pulling silly faces really isn't the kind of thing that adds very much to a child's development.'

I don't point out that I wasn't trying to add much to her development; that in fact there are a lot of people around her fully committed to adding to her development; and that all I was trying to add was a sense of light-hearted fun.

'No. I won't do it again.'

'I'm not sure you realise how very gifted Hypatia is,' Dad goes on. 'She's clearly an exceptional child. I was just watching her playing with some of her toys, and she can already distinguish basic shapes! I don't even remember Marley doing that when he was six months old.'

'And I'm sure *I* didn't!' I joke.

'Well, of course. I mean, those kinds of toys weren't your forte, Isabel. You liked . . . well, you liked things like drawing, didn't you?' Dad's brow wrinkles as he tries to remember. 'Plasticine?'

Nope. Hated them both. 'Yes. That kind of thing.'

We stand in silence for a couple of minutes, sipping our sparkling wine.

'So.' Dad sits in one of the patio chairs. 'Things going well? This . . . er . . . wedding stuff of yours?'

'Wedding consultancy. Yes, it's going very well.'

'Well. That sounds good, Isabel.'

'Yes. And I saw Licky yesterday, like you suggested.'

'Yes, Susannah Britten-Jones mentioned it to your mother. Good of you to offer your time.'

'Actually, it's not just my time, Dad. I've pulled all kinds of strings to get Licky a vintage car at the

117

last minute, and I've helped her with an emergency bridesmaid's dress. It's a little bit more than my time.'

'Oh, well, yes. I'm sure she really appreciates it.' Dad clears his throat. 'And William? Is he well?'

'Yes, he's well.'

'Not joining us this weekend?'

'He has a big partners' meeting tomorrow,' I say defensively. 'He couldn't possibly miss it.'

'Ah. Well, we'll see him soon, I'm sure.'

I shoot him a sideways look. Is he pulling the most amazing double bluff, or has Will not actually spoken to him about proposing after all?

'Why?'

'Sorry?'

'Why do you think you'll see him soon?' I throw back a good half of my wine. 'We don't have anything planned.'

Dad blinks at me. 'Well, I gather from your mother that you're planning to move in with him. So as your live-in boyfriend, I just assumed we'd be seeing him at some point, sooner rather than later.'

'Oh.' Maybe it isn't a double bluff after all. Maybe all those horrible visions of the muttonchop sideburns and the pipe-smoking aren't true. After all, it's perfectly possible that Will could have side-stepped Dad and just gone straight to Mum. Let's face it, it's what any reasonably sane person would do. 'Oh, OK.'

'And I must say, Isabel . . .' Dad turns his finest head-masterly gaze in my direction. 'I do wish you'd seen fit to discuss it with your mother and me first. You know I disapprove of cohabitation before marriage.'

I can't believe I'm hearing this. 'But I'm supposed to come and "discuss" it with you anyway?'

He blinks. 'Why ever not?'

'Well, it wouldn't exactly be a discussion, would it?'

'It certainly would.' Dad's eyebrows have shot upwards. 'Simply because I might disapprove, Isabel, doesn't mean you shouldn't come to speak to me. You don't even know *why* I might disapprove of it.'

'Because the neighbours might talk?' I can feel my hackles rising. 'Because I might burn in hellfire for all eternity?'

'Oh, *Isabel*.' Dad gets up. 'It's impossible to get anywhere with you when you're being this ridiculous.'

'I'm not the one who's being ridiculous,' I mumble, under my breath, just as – thank God – Lara and Matthew appear from the French doors.

Dad gives Lara a solemn, rather formal kiss on the cheek, and he and Matthew pat each other's shoulders, and I dart inside to grab a fresh bottle of sparkling wine from the fridge. I would stick around to help Mum, but she's deep in conversation with Daria, and anyway the smell of reheating mince is getting a bit overpowering, so I head back outside to top up everyone's glasses and completely refill my own.

'. . . and I'd be extremely interested in your perspective on it,' Dad is saying, to Lara. He's leaning across the patio table, his fingers in the pyramid shape he makes whenever he's got on to one of his pet subjects. 'In your professional opinion, I mean.'

'Oh, well, I'm not at all expert in educational psychology,' Lara says, rubbing her temples in the way *she* does whenever she's got on to one of her pet subjects. 'But certainly I'd say that six months does sound very early for the kind of cognitive reasoning you're observing. In fact, I could point you in the direction of a couple of quite interesting papers, if you'd like to get some really cutting-edge perspectives . . .'

I hand the bottle to Matthew, he obligingly pops the cork, and I sling a large quantity of the contents into my glass.

I mean, this is *weird*. Lara chewing the fat with my dad, and . . . and swapping cutting-edge perspectives. When only a few months ago, he was still the scary, bad-tempered man who once gave her detention when she was late handing in her geography homework, and used to shout at her when she and I got tipsy on left-over glasses of Pimm's at the Bookbinder Family Barbecues of the early 1990s.

'That would be terrific, Lara.' Dad sits back, and beams at her. 'And how is your own research coming on? That paper on social phobia sounded very interesting, the last time you were talking about it.'

'Oh, it's going pretty well,' Lara says. 'My research partner is coming up with some really excellent findings on the anterior cingulated cortex and its role in . . . oh!' She suddenly stops, and smiles in the direction of the French windows. 'Look who's coming!'

It's Hypatia, being carried outside by Daria again.

'I hope she's all right now,' I say, risking a smile in Hypatia's direction.

I don't believe it. She's smiling back! This is amazing! And she's even holding out her arms in my direction.

'La-La!' she says, joyfully. 'La-La!'

I get to my feet, my heart thudding with excitement. 'Oh, well, La-La to you, too, Hypatia, darling!'

Matthew lets out a loud shout of laughter. 'I think she means *Lara*.'

'La-La,' confirms Hypatia, scrabbling to get past me and towards Lara, to my left. '*La-La*.'

'Good God.' Dad's eyes widen. 'Can you believe that? It must be two months since she last saw you, Lara! And she remembers your name!'

'Oh, well, I'm sure it's just a noise she's making . . .' Lara is turning rather pink, and shooting flustered glances in my direction, so I flap a hand at her to show her it's fine.

Because it is. Of course it's fine.

I mean, it's hardly a surprise that Hypatia loves Lara. Who *wouldn't* love Lara? Just look at her now, bouncing Hypatia gently up and down on her knees, and singing a verse of a nursery rhyme that seems to have won Dad's approval for educational value, because he's beaming around with that Santa Claus look on his face again.

But just because it's completely fine doesn't mean it's all that easy for me to stand around and watch.

I pick up the wine bottle and head back into the safety of the kitchen.

Chapter Eight

Even though everybody else stayed up talking until the wee small hours – well, half-past midnight, which is a real night on the tiles by Mum and Dad's standards – I slipped upstairs to go to bed at about ten thirty. The plan was to get an early night so I'd be all bright-eyed and bushy-tailed for the big day of wedding work ahead, but in the end I only managed about three hours' sleep. I tossed and turned in bed for ages, listening to the merriment downstairs, and then I tossed and turned trying *not* to listen to the merriment downstairs. Which is a lot harder than you'd think. I've lived away from home for so long now that I'd forgotten that the whole place might as well have been built of balsawood for all the soundproofing it offers, not to mention the fact that both Dad and Matthew have the kind of resonant (OK, *booming*) voices that teachers seem to specialise in. I suspect it may well be something they learn at teacher-training college.

And at psychologist-training college as well, come to think of it. Because Lara was pretty much matching them decibel for decibel at times, punctuating the booming bass with light, bright laughter. It's odd, because I've never really noticed that Lara has an especially noisy laugh before. But I'm sure it's just a one-off, and down to poor-quality early-1980s building materials. Either that, or Dad and Matthew really were being unusually funny.

Then even after the racket subsided and everyone toddled off to bed, it wasn't as if I just slipped away into the Land of Nod. Because I suddenly had this overwhelming desire to speak to Will. God knows what I expected him to do, miles away in a conference centre in Reading, about my miserable evening. I suppose I just thought the sound of his voice might cheer me up. But he was obviously still living it up with all the other tax lawyers at his gala dinner, because when he answered his mobile it was too noisy to hear him properly, and he just kept yelling that he'd call me later, above the noise of what sounded – honestly – like a mariachi band. And even though I texted him not to worry about it, he woke me up calling back just after two. I was so groggy I just grunted a couple of my own call-you-tomorrows at him, only to find that somehow, half an hour later, I was still having a hard time dropping back off again. Throw in a five a.m. yowl from Hypatia in Marley and Daria's room next door, and it's no wonder that now it really is time to get up, I'm not so much bright-eyed and bushy-tailed as racoon-eyed and bushy-haired. And the less said about the attractive outcrop of pimples that's decided to pop up in the middle of my chin, the better.

Still, after a hot blast under the shower I'm feeling fractionally more human. And after twenty minutes in front of my dressing-table mirror performing all those clever makeup tricks you read about in magazines – the ones that promise to make you look like you've spent the last twenty-four hours sipping mineral water and sleeping on silken sheets when in fact you've binged on fizzy wine and dozed fitfully with your head wedged under a waffle-pattern pillow – I look quite a lot more human as well. Once I've slipped into my suit and my brand-new Kurt Geiger (very) high-heeled pumps, twisted my hair up into a chic librarian bun, and spritzed on the leftovers from an old but perfectly serviceable bottle of Anaïs-Anaïs I found lurking in my dressing-table drawer, I even feel capable of answering the call coming through on my mobile. Even though I can see from the screen that it's Pippa.

'Pippa!' I say, picking up. 'Good morning!'

'Is it? *Is it?*'

I'm guessing from her tone of voice that it isn't.

'I just wonder, Isabel, if you might like to explain to me why Frankie thinks she's arriving at the church in a Jaguar. And not a Bentley. *As had been agreed.*'

Oh, *bloody* Frankie.

I mean, what was the point of me going to all the trouble of arranging the car she really wanted as a *fait accompli*, if she was going to blab to Pippa on the morning of the wedding and make it a *fait . . . non-accompli*?

'Pippa, look, I'm really sorry, but –'

'What the hell were you thinking, going off-piste like that? This is *my* wedding, Isabel, not yours!'

'Well, technically, it's Fr . . .' No, Isabel. Not the time. 'I do apologise, Pippa, but I thought –'

'Well, don't! Don't *think*!'

'Yes, of course. I won't. I'm sorry.'

'Can you imagine what Sunetra would say if I called her up now and told her that despite everything we agreed on, that bloody red Jag is going to be in her photo-spread?'

'No, I can't.'

'You can't?' she spits. 'Can't what?'

'I can't imagine, Pippa. What Sunetra would say.'

There's a bit of a pause, during which I think she's working herself up to yell at me for being cheeky or something, but when it's followed by a thud, a bit of scuffling and some raised voices, I assume she's just put her phone down so she can go and trouble-shoot some wedding-related problem at the venue. She comes back on the line a moment later.

'Look, Isabel, I have to go. There's an RSPCA man just arrived to make sure we're treating the doves properly. I mean, Christ only knows what he thinks I'm planning to do with them. Whip them into a frenzy to make them fly faster, or bake four-and-twenty of them into the bloody wedding cake . . . I'm *joking*,' she suddenly bellows, presumably in the direction of the RSPCA officer. 'Isabel? I just want this car fuck-up sorted out, all right? You call your hire firm and tell them we want that Bentley.'

'Right, of course.' I hope to God Licky doesn't decide to pull a Bridezilla moment and weep that I'd promised *her* the Bentley; admittedly, it's unlikely, but the stress of a wedding can do funny things to people. 'Though if the hire firm has promised it to somebody else . . .?'

'Then that's your problem, Isabel. All I'm telling you is that if that Bentley doesn't turn up at Frankie's hotel at one-thirty this afternoon, you needn't bother coming in to work on Monday morning.'

And that's it. She's hung up.

Right. Well, I did my best for Frankie and her red-car-loving kid. But she's thrown a spanner in the works, and it isn't something I'm prepared to lose my job over.

I flick through my contacts list and find the number for Ted at South-West Classic Cars. It rings a few times and then switches to voicemail.

'Hello, Ted?' I begin. 'It's Isabel here – Isabel Bookbinder, from Pippa Everitt's office.'

There's a sudden tap on the door, and Mum sticks her head around it. 'Iz-Wiz, I'm doing some nice boiled eggs for breakfast, if you –'

I flap a hand at her to indicate the phone, and carry on leaving my message. 'Anyway, Ted, I'm afraid I need to switch round the cars for today. The Jag has to pick up at Broughton Hall, and the Bentley has to pick up at Charlton House Hotel, OK? Can you call me on this number, please, whenever you've got a moment, and I'll explain it all. Thanks!' I put the phone down. 'Sorry, Mum, that was an important work call.'

'It sounded it!' Mum looks impressed. 'Very high-powered, Iz-Wiz! To do with that WAG wedding, I imagine?'

I'm just wondering if Mum is being extra nice because she realises what a miserable evening I had yesterday or because she's still fishing for details about Frankie Miller's ceremony when she suddenly seems to clock what I'm wearing and her smile fixes and freezes.

'You look very . . . smart, Iz-Wiz. So you're assuming you'll have time to come back here after you see Licky this morning and get changed into your outfit for the wedding?'

'This is my outfit for the wedding, Mum.'

'Oh, *Isabel*. Not *black*.'

'It's a suit! You said you wanted me to wear a suit!'

'Well, yes, but not a *black* one . . .'

'I'm working,' I say evenly. 'This is what wedding planners wear to work.'

'Well, those look like extremely high heels to work in, darling. Anyway, you're not *just* working, you're a guest too! And you know what Susannah Britten-Jones is like – so traditional. All her posh society friends will be there! *And* the mistress of Broughton Hall!' she adds, suddenly coming over all Catherine Cookson and practically bobbing a curtsy at her reflection in the dressing-table mirror.

'Mum, I don't think you call someone "the

128

mistress" of a house these days. Besides, Sophie Britten-Jones can't exactly pass judgement on what people choose to wear. Not all of us have managed to wangle ourselves a free Vera Wang cocktail dress recently.'

'Oooooh.' Mum's eyes are wide at the first sign of gossip. 'You know, I'd *heard* she was a bit of a gold-digger. Jackie – you know, Scottish Jackie, on the social pages at the *Gazette*? – she told me the woman's intent on turning that beautiful old hall into a one-in, one-out wedding venue and conference centre.'

'Well, then, I honestly don't think you need to get all worked up about what she thinks of my outfit. Anyway,' I add, 'I've got a pretty top on underneath, so when I take my jacket off it'll look a bit jazzier.'

Mum brightens, as I hoped she would, at the concept of impending jazziness. 'That might be OK then, Iz-Wiz. I just don't want people thinking you're deliberately turning up to weddings in black just because . . . well, just because you're not married or engaged or anything yourself yet.'

'Mum! Nobody does that!'

'Oh, but they do, Isabel. I read all about this poor girl in New York, some top fashion editor – named after a fruit, might have been a prune – and when she was dumped by her fiancé just before her own wedding, she dyed her dress black and wore it to her sister's wedding a few weeks later as a form of protest!'

'It was Plum Sykes,' I tell her, 'and apparently that story's made up. You know – apocryphal.'

Mum makes the harrumphing noise she favours when she doesn't actually have anything to say, but won't be put in the wrong anyway. 'Well, all I'm saying is, Iz-Wiz, you don't want anyone thinking you're being funny about other people's weddings. Not when . . . well, not when things are going to be the way they're going to be.'

Oh, God. She's started talking in riddles. So she does know about Will's upcoming proposal, doesn't she?

I clear my throat. 'What do you mean, when things are going to be the way they're going to be?'

'Nothing! I don't mean anything, Iz-Wiz!' Mum is turning a bit pink. 'For heaven's sake, do I always have to *mean* something? Can't what I'm saying just be absolutely meaningless for once? Now, do you want any of these boiled eggs I'm doing or not?'

'Thanks, Mum, but I'm not sure I have time. A driver is coming from Broughton to get me in . . .' I glance at my watch. '. . . actually, they should be here by now.'

'A *driver* from Broughton.' Mum wriggles her shoulders with pleasure. 'Oooh, Iz-Wiz, should I wrap him up a nice bit of bread and cheese, in a cloth napkin, to take away with him? Or I could do some of these eggs hardboiled, and let him have a couple of those to take for the journey?'

It's that touch of the Catherine Cooksons again.

'No, Mum, it's fine.' I pick up my bag, head for the door and down the stairs, just as I hear a car pulling up outside in the driveway. 'Thanks, anyway.'

'But it's no bother! I've already done some of them for Hypatia's lunch. Oh, Iz-Wiz, have you seen her yet this morning? She's wearing the *sweetest* little T-shirt that Matthew and Lara bought for her, with a picture of a big yellow crane . . . I'd have gone for something with some nice flowers, perhaps, or a cuddly bunny, but Daria's ever so keen that we don't gender-stereotype her. And she does look lovely in it.'

'I'm sure she does.' I pull open the front door. 'Give her a kiss from me.'

'Oh, just come in and say bye to her, Iz-Wiz! She'll miss you all morning.'

'Mum, I can't keep the driver waiting. Besides, Lara's here for her to play with. She won't even notice I'm gone.'

As I head out on to the driveway, towards the battered, mud-splattered old Land Rover that's come to collect me, I notice that Dad is also outside on the drive. He's doing a wholesale tidy of his already immaculate Volvo – hoovering out bits of organic rice cake from Hypatia's car seat, shining the windows, picking bits of lint off the seat belts – in preparation for all the North Somerset VIPs who might walk past it this afternoon in the church car park.

'Off already?' he asks.

'Yes. To Broughton. I'm due to help Licky get ready.'

'Ah. Stressful time, the morning of a wedding. For the planner as much as the bride, I'm sure.'

Wait a moment. Is he trying to chat to me about *work*? Dad never chats to me about work. Well, only if you consider asking all kinds of intrusive questions about when I'm getting promoted and what further qualifications I need to add to my CV to be *chatting*.

'You know – nervous brides . . . weepy mothers . . .' He's obviously racking his brains for anything else he can possibly think of that might signify pre-wedding stress. 'Antique lace veils that suddenly disintegrate . . . ill-fitting shoes . . .'

'Yes!' I practically bark, keen to stop him before he starts ruminating on, oh, I don't know, *diamanté tiaras that pinch behind the earlobes* or *bridesmaids with water retention whose dresses won't fasten at the back*. 'Yes, that's exactly the kind of thing that often happens.'

'Of course.' Dad nods sagely, the way he always used to nod during the morning reading at weekly school assembly – as though he's really *learning* something, even if he's heard it a half-bazillion times before. 'Well, I'm sure it will all run smoothly today. And looking forward to seeing you in action, Isabel. Counting on you to do a decent job.'

Well, that's no pressure then. No pressure at all.

It's not the most comfortable ride cross-country to Broughton Hall. The Land Rover doesn't have the best suspension in the world, and Maurice, my driver, almost certainly doesn't have the cleanest driving licence in the world, to judge from the hair-raising manner in which we take most of the (many) bends in the road. What with that and Eminem's 'Lose Yourself' blasting out of the stereo at top volume, I'm feeling pretty rattled by the time we finally turn off the bumpy B-road into the long, gravelled driveway of Broughton Hall.

But the moment we do, my shredded nerves settle in an instant.

Because I think I'd forgotten how truly gorgeous this place is. Set in the middle of open parkland, it's built from pale golden Cotswold stone that almost seems to glow in the morning sunlight. It's shaped like a giant 'L', with two wings jutting out from the central section, which means that it has a beautiful, shady open courtyard to the front. And which, more importantly, means that if you lived here you'd be able to waft about saying fabulous things like, 'Put the guests up in the East Wing, Murgatroyd,' or, 'I think I shall take tea in the West Wing today; the afternoon light there is just too, too divine for words!' I mean, this is the way people always talk in dramas set in these kinds of houses on television.

Actually, thinking about it, if Sophie Britten-Jones wants to make some cash out of the place when she's not hosting weddings and conferences, she should consider putting it up for use on television. It could be the stand-out star of a luscious Austen adaptation, or some kind of *Jeeves and Wooster* comedy where amusing goings-on occur late at night on creaky back staircases and in prize-winning rhododendron bushes.

Maurice roars on up the driveway and straight round to the back of the house, where much activity is taking place. There are several spiky-haired young men lugging chairs and rolling table-tops towards the small white marquee set up on the lawn, a couple of burly Antipodean-looking blokes are going back and forth between the marquee and a large white van, humping big cardboard boxes with 'ATTENTION – BREAKABLE' plastered over the side, and a brunette in tight jeans unloading plastic crates filled with flowers out of another, smaller van.

I unbuckle my seat belt and clamber down from the Land Rover – which sounds a lot easier than it really is, if you happen to be wearing a tight pencil skirt and five-inch heels – then head over to the sexy brunette as Maurice reverses and disappears off back towards the driveway in a spray of gravel.

'Hello! You're the florist, I assume?'

'Yes.' She shoots me a suspicious look. 'And you are . . .?'

'My name's Isabel, and I'm the wedding planner for the day. But don't worry!' I flap a hand at her van. 'I won't be interfering at all, or getting in your way. You must just carry on doing whatever you need to do!'

'Wedding planner? Nobody told me there was a wedding planner.'

'It's just for the day. It's really quite usual, nowadays, for the bride to decide she might like a bit of help on the day itself, without all the expense of hiring someone to organise the whole thing.' I beam at her. 'Now, if there's anything at all you need me for, anything at all, then you must just give me a shout.'

'Well, if you're offering.' She turns back to her van and picks up a crate. 'These need to go inside.'

Oh.

I mean, really, what I had in mind when I said 'give me a shout' was her calling me on my mobile, giving me the opportunity to use my swanky new headset, and asking me to come and approve her centrepieces. Not lugging around a heavy, dripping crate of pink roses and trailing bits of ivy like an over-dressed dogsbody.

But I can't say that now, can I? I don't want the staff to turn against me before the day's even begun. Ideally, not at all, in fact. Obviously I'd much rather be a popular wedding planner, marshalling the troops through respect and a jolly good laugh, like some kind of favourite aunt, and not like . . . well, not like Pippa.

'They need to go through to the Saloon,' she directs me as I take the crate. Visions of ten-gallon hats, spittoons, and sarsaparilla flit through my head before she continues, 'It's the big reception room that faces out front. I need to set up a few vases there in case it pours later and they decide to move the drinks indoors while they're putting the starters out in the marquee. Just go through here –' she indicates a small side door to the main house, which has been propped open with a brick – 'all the way along the hall and then it's the fourth door on the right. You can't miss it. Oh, and when you've dropped that one off, you could always come back here and start taking some of these vases into the marquee.'

I give her a big smile and a noncommittal thumbs-up, and then head for the door with my crate.

I have to say, for a stately home that's quite so impressive on the outside, inside the Hall looks slightly disappointing. This side door leads into nothing more impressive than a long, narrow passageway, running the whole length of the West Wing. As I reach the fourth door on the right, I shove it open with my bottom while trying to hoist the crate a bit higher with my left knee . . .

Oh.

Now, this is more like it.

I'm in a long, thin, almost gallery-like room, flooded with light from half a dozen elegant floor-to-ceiling windows, offering views over the rolling parkland. The floor is laid with those black-and-white marble squares that always remind me of the Cinderella pictures in my *Children's Treasury of Fairy-Tales*, and the walls are panelled with solid wood that's been painted, in alternating sections, a warm ivory and the palest eau-de-nil. Presumably in readiness for the possible drinks reception, most of its furniture has been cleared out, apart from a couple of leather armchairs, an eau-de-nil chaise longue, and a huge mahogany bureau, all pushed back against the far wall. There's a lot of no doubt very valuable, heirloomy art decorating the walls – you know the kind of thing: oil paintings featuring wan-looking children with hoops and sticks, and a forlorn Pekinese who'd look quite at home in an RSPCA fund-raising advert . . .

'Can I help you?' The voice startles me, and I turn round to see a man hovering in the doorway. He's tall and thin, and there's a wan look about him that makes me wonder if he could be directly descended from the oil-painting kids with their Victorian play-things. Even though it's still only ten in the morning he's already dressed for the wedding – well, half dressed – in stripy morning-suit trousers that make him look even taller and skinnier than he probably actually is, a pale grey waistcoat with toothpaste spattered down the front, and a pair of battered sheepskin moccasin slippers.

'Oh, I'm sorry, I probably shouldn't have just let myself in, but the florist told me she needed a hand with a bit of the fetching and carrying.' I walk towards him, extending a hand, with some difficulty, from around the side of my crate of roses. 'I'm Isabel. I'm helping Licky today.'

The man doesn't extend a hand back at me, mostly because he seems to have been transfixed by the crate. 'I do hope you're going to put a cloth under that so it won't leave a stain on the floor.'

'What? Oh, God, yes, of course . . .' I glance around

to see if there might be a cloth anywhere. Of course, there isn't. 'Um, well, I'm sure the florist will bring some up when she comes in a few minutes.'

He makes a tutting noise. 'I certainly hope so. Honestly, these people! I'm only glad my father's not actually here to see what's happening to his house.'

'Oh, you're David Britten-Jones?' I didn't mean to sound that astonished. But seriously – *this* guy is related, by blood, to the gorgeous, brooding photographer I met at the trattoria the other day?

'I am,' he says, 'yes. And you are . . .?'

Haven't I already told him who I am? 'Um, I'm Isabel? I'm Licky's wedding planner?'

'Oh, the *wedding*.' David gives an exasperated sigh as he heads into the Saloon. I think he's about to help me by taking the heavy crate out of my arms, but in fact he's just gone straight past me to inspect the mahogany bureau, with an air of someone who's expecting to find it damaged. He stares, bleakly, at its polished wooden surface. 'The first of many, no doubt,' he adds, gloomily.

'Well, I think it's terrific! That you're allowing your family home to be used by so many happy couples, I mean.'

'*How* many happy couples?' he asks, turning to me with an appalled stare, as though I'm about to usher in six hundred couples for a Moonie ceremony.

'No, no, just the one today, of course! I just mean that it must be very exciting for you, having Broughton set up and running as a wedding venue.'

138

'Very exciting for me? That my wife wants to open my house to all comers, without the slightest regard for my feelings on the matter, just to make a quick buck?'

'Um . . .' What am I supposed to say to this? 'Well, Licky's not *all comers*, at any rate!'

'No, that's true.' His face softens, but this only makes him look more washed-out than ever. 'Sweet girl. I'm giving her away, you know.'

'How nice.' The crate of roses is giving me some serious back-ache, so I make a move to the side of the room, just to prop myself up against the wall. But David gives a yelp.

'Not near Flossie and Freddie!'

I'm starting to wonder if David Britten-Jones mightn't be one of those traditional English lunatics, the kind who hang around their aristocratic family homes cataloguing rare butterflies and frightening the servants. 'Flossie and Freddie?'

'The painting!' he repeats, shoving past me to put himself between me and an especially dreary oil painting featuring a smug blonde girl (Flossie?) and her even smugger miniature spaniel (I presume Freddie). 'You see, *this* is precisely why Sophie shouldn't be allowing Broughton to be used this way! When I think of all the damage that could be caused . . .'

'David?' This time the voice that comes from the Saloon's doors is one that I recognise immediately. It's Dan Britten-Jones.

He's nowhere near dressed for the wedding yet,

unless his plan is to wear faded blue jeans and a T-shirt with a picture of (I think) David Bowie on it. Mind you, maybe it *should* be his plan, given how gorgeous he looks.

'Daniel! This dreadful girl is trying to spill filthy water all over Flossie and Freddie!'

'Come on, David, I'm sure she's doing nothing of the sort.' Dan heads over and take the crate of roses out of my aching arms. 'She's just come here to help Licks out for the big day, that's all. And I'm sure you weren't deliberately trying to deface one of our valuable family paintings, were you, Isabel?' he adds, with a quick grin in my direction.

'No, no, of course not, I swear . . .'

'Well, then tell her she should be more careful,' David glares at me, but he seems reassured by Dan's presence. 'In fact, we should tell everyone they should be more careful.'

'Absolutely, Dave, I'll do that.' Dan removes a hand from beneath the crate to pat his brother on the shoulder. Despite the fact the crate wobbles precariously, David doesn't seem that bothered by imminent potential damage any more, and I wonder if his concern for his family valuables is more to do with some desperate desire for his own security and safety. 'Hey, why don't you leave me to deal with Isabel, and you can just go and have a cuppa in the kitchen? I nipped out and got the papers earlier. You can do the crossword for a bit, try to relax?'

'Yes, I could do that . . .' David is already

140

wandering back towards the Saloon doors. 'Don't tell Soph that's where I've gone, though.'

'No problem. I'll come and join you in a bit, Dave, as soon as I've sorted a few things out for Licky.'

Chapter Nine

'I'm sorry about that.' Dan turns to look at me the moment David has left the room. 'David gets quite stressed out about little things these days.' A muscle in his jaw tenses slightly. 'He's . . . not been that well.'

'Oh, don't worry, I completely understand. I'm sure I'd be the same if I had all these lovely things in my house.'

'Mmm.' He puts the crate down on the floor, seemingly totally unconcerned about water marks himself. 'He doesn't need to fret as much as he does, though. It's only because he doesn't trust Sophie to take care of things properly.'

'So, can you take me to wherever Licky's getting ready?'

Quite suddenly, his expression darkens. 'Yes. Sort of. Come with me.'

'Sort of?' I follow him out of the Saloon, scurrying like a geisha in my already slightly uncomfortable heels as I hurry to keep up with his loping stride. 'What do you mean? Is she all right?'

'Look, you'd better just see for yourself.' We reach the end of the same passageway I walked along earlier and he takes a sharp right turn that leads to a slightly scruffy back staircase. We start up it.

'Has there been some kind of problem?' My mind is racing over the possibilities, the scrapes that Licky, very far from *au fait* with all this kind of thing, could have got herself into. 'Oh God, she hasn't tried to do her own fake tan, has she?' I'm already reaching for my phone. 'Well, it's OK. We can deal with that. I'll just call my friend Lara and get her to dash to Boots in Shepton Mallet and pick up every bottle of nail polish remover she can find. We can sling Licky in a bath full of that, and –'

'No, it's not that.' We've reached the top of the stairs and Dan opens a door on to a much smarter-looking corridor that runs the entire length of this wing, above the Saloon. 'But good to know you'd have that base covered, if necessary.'

Is he taking the piss out of me? 'Actually, if you were a bride who woke up the morning of the biggest day of her life looking like she'd just been dip-dyed in Sunny Delight, you might not think my job is so silly.'

'I never said I thought your job was silly.' He stops, his hand on the handle of one of the doors that lead off the corridor. 'I actually think Licky could really use you right now. I mean, the whole point is, you're on her side, aren't you?'

'Well, of course I am.' It's an odd question. 'But I didn't know there was a side.'

'Trust me. There's a side.'

He opens the door into an airy bedroom. It's big

enough for not only an actual four-poster bed but also a little sitting area beside the leaded windows, with a battered leather armchair and a small Chesterfield couch. The whole place is unusually neat and tidy for the bedroom of someone who's getting married today, with none of the paraphernalia you'd expect – simmering hair irons, exploding makeup bags, recently discarded tights with ladders in them. In fact, the only evidence that a bride has spent the night in here at all is the big pouffy white dress hanging on the back of the wardrobe.

Right next to the wardrobe is a door, presumably leading to an ensuite bathroom. A tall woman, dressed in navy shorts and a T-shirt, is crouched in front of it. Her hands are resting on rather bony knees, and her head is pressed right up against the door.

'OK, now I'm starting to get annoyed,' she's saying, through the keyhole. 'This is just a total waste of everyone's time.' Her head spins round as she hears us come in. 'Oh, for God's sake, Dan. This isn't the time to bring one of your women here.'

I hate myself for this, but there's a tiny part of me that's secretly thrilled that I might just be pretty enough to be mistaken for *one of Dan's women*.

And I hate myself even more for the tiny part of me that's a little bit green about the notion that Dan has *women*. Plural.

He ignores the jibe; either that or the notion that I could possibly be one of his women is just too ludicrous for him to even bother denying it. 'Actually,

Sophie, this is Isabel. She's planning the wedding.'

So this is the infamous Sophie. David's wife, Vera Wang fan and – as Mum would have it – Mistress of Broughton.

She's slightly older than I imagined, closer to forty than thirty, and though she isn't exactly what you'd call conventionally pretty – her nose is too pronounced and her lips too thin for that – she's rather handsome, in a horsy sort of way. In fact, she reminds me of those girls at my school who carried on Saturday morning riding lessons long after the rest of us had moved on to Saturday morning mooching about the shops. She's got the same long, loose limbs, rosy-red cheeks and slightly annoying bouncy brown ponytail.

'Nobody told *me* there was a wedding planner.' Her frown deepens. 'Though what would I know? I mean, I am *only* the owner of the venue.'

'I'm not planning it in an official capacity,' I explain. 'I mean, I *am* a professional wedding planner, as it happens. But I'm also an old friend of Licky's.'

'*Friend*? Of Licky's?' Sophie repeats, in a deliberate pigs-might-fly tone that makes it clear just how hard she finds this to believe. 'In that case, do you think you can persuade her to come out of that bathroom any time soon? Say, in time to put on her dress and slap on some makeup and get in a car to head to a church to meet her bloody fiancé?'

'Sophie . . .'

'Oh, I'm sorry, Daniel, am I upsetting anyone?' Her

voice has gone high and sarcastic. 'Please, don't mind me! I've only got a hundred and fifty guests arriving at *my* house, expecting to drink the champagne and eat the food *I've* arranged from scratch . . . I mean, do you think your beloved auntie Susannah is going to stump up the cash for it all if she doesn't even get to see her daughter safely married off?'

A contemptuous smile flashes across Dan's face. 'Ah, yes. Cash. Lest we forget what's really the most important aspect of the day.'

It seems like Sophie's about to say something for a moment, but then she just performs an elaborate hand-washing mime and heads for the bedroom door. 'Fine. I'll send Susannah up here the moment she arrives. You can be the one to deal with her.' She flings the door open. 'I need to speak to the caterers, anyway.'

'Up to you,' Dan calls after her. 'I still think that's being a little optimistic . . .'

I stare at him, not quite sure how he's managing to stay quite so laid-back. 'Am I right in thinking that Licky is behind that bathroom door?'

'Yup.'

'And that she's refusing to come out?'

'Well, she hasn't actually *refused*, as such. But then, according to Sophie, who found her in there an hour and . . .' he glances at the watch on his tanned forearm, – '. . . twenty-five minutes ago, she hasn't actually said very much at all. Christ, don't *panic*,' he adds, as I dart to the door and start banging on it.

'Licky? Licky, can you hear me? This is Isabel.'

'*Still alive*,' comes a ghostly, ghastly voice from behind the door.

'Oh, that's what I've been getting her to say, every five minutes.' Dan has come up close – very close – just a fraction *too* close – behind me. 'So we know she's still alive.'

'Yes, I get that, thank you,' I whisper furiously at Dan. 'But it's not exactly ideal, is it? I mean, it's great that she's not killing herself, obviously. But there's a wedding she has to get to in two hours' time!'

Dan shrugs. ' "Has to get to." It's a very bossy way of putting it, don't you think? I mean, obviously you have a vested interest, being the wedding planner and all that . . .'

'I have no vested interest. But as Sophie pointed out, there are a hundred and fifty guests headed for St Joseph's, and a groom who'll be left waiting at the altar, and an awful lot of embarrassment and upset caused that might never be undone, just because of a little fit of completely understandable nerves.'

Dan's onyx-coloured eyes are fixed on me. 'Close to your parents, are you?' he suddenly asks.

'What?'

'I mean, you'd be able to tell them if you didn't want to marry someone, would you, when they were desperate for you to get hitched? You'd have the luxury of an open and honest conversation with them about that?'

I can feel my face getting warm. 'I don't understand what that's got to do with anything.'

147

'Well, maybe this isn't just a fit of nerves. Maybe locking herself in the bathroom is Licky's only way of getting her mother to realise that she doesn't want to get married. At least, not to the odious little shit she's supposed to be marrying today.'

I don't say anything for a moment. I'm remembering the conversation I had with Licky in the back of the taxi on the way to the Wedding Shop. Specifically, her fiancé's lap-dancing stag party, and the honeymoon he'd told her sounded boring . . .

I knock on the bathroom door again, more gently this time. 'Licky? It's Isabel again.'

'*Still alive.*'

'I know, Licks.' Her voice sounds so small and dismal that it makes my heart hurt. I take a deep breath. 'Listen to me. You don't have to get married today.'

There's a weighty silence from behind the bathroom door for a moment. Then there's a sniff. '*Really?*'

'Really. We can fix this. I promise. Now, look, I'll speak to your mother –'

'. . . And I'll speak to Marcus,' Dan interrupts me, leaning towards the door, 'so you don't have to face him if you don't want to.'

'And we can start calling the guests,' I continue, 'and tell them there's been a slight hitch. And none of them is even going to give it a second thought, Licky, I swear to you.' Well, one white lie isn't going to hurt; not if it saves a fraction of her self-esteem. 'People cancel weddings at short notice all the time!'

There's another very loud sniff. '*Really?*'

'Absolutely! You'll be like . . . like Julia Roberts! Or Jennifer Lopez!'

'Oh. I quite like Julia Roberts.'

'Exactly. And she got away with it, didn't she? Nobody remembers, now, that she left Kiefer Sutherland practically at the altar.'

'I certainly didn't know that,' Dan says through the door, before adding, in a lower voice that's intended just for me, 'Nice one, Isabel. I knew you were more than just a pretty face.'

I ignore him, with all my will. 'Please, Licky, just come on out. It's terrible, being shut away in the bathroom all by yourself like that.'

'Well.' Sniff. 'It is a bit cold and damp in here.'

'Precisely. So if you just come on out, I'm sure we can find you a nice cup of tea and warm you up a bit.'

There's a click as the lock slides back, and then the door opens. Licky peers out. Her eyes are red and puffy and her hair has been somewhat disastrously layered since our lunch on Thursday. Add in the bath towel that she's wrapped over her pyjamas to keep warm, and she looks more like a bag lady than a bride-to-be. Honestly, you'd have to have the hardest heart in Christendom to make her get married now.

'Oh, Licky.' I put my arms around her. 'It's going to be OK.'

'And you'll really tell everyone?' she gulps. 'Mummy . . . and Marcus . . .?'

'Yes. We'll handle everything. Nobody's going make you do anything you don't want to do –'

Quite suddenly – and, let's face it, at about the most unsuitable moment possible – my mobile phone starts to trill its 'Here Comes the Bride' ringtone.

'Oh God, I'm really sorry . . . that's just my boss, checking up on me.' I dart for my bag, which I've dropped beside the bedroom door, to stop the ringing, just as someone opens the door from the outside. It smacks, hard, into my head. 'Ow! *Fucking* hell . . .'

'Isabel? Are you all right?' Dan darts forward and pulls me sideways before whoever it is outside shoves at the door again. This time, without my head blocking it, the door opens, and a woman, whom I instantly recognise as Susannah Britten-Jones, barges in, in a pale pink silk suit.

'Oh, for heaven's sake,' she snaps, noticing me bending double and holding my hand to my head. 'What on earth were you doing in the way?'

'Auntie Susannah . . .'

'Not in the mood, Daniel.' She brushes past him and heads straight for Licky. 'Sophie just called and told me some nonsense about you hiding in the bathroom.'

Licky gazes bleakly down at her mother, who's a good head shorter than she, but no less terrifying for it. In fact, even in my compromised position – doubled over with half my head practically in Dan's crotch, and with one eye closed to stop it from hurting too much – I can see, straight away, why Dad is so keen to impress her. She must remind him, as she does me, of his mother, Granny Jean.

150

'Mummy –' Licky begins.

'And you're not even nearly ready!' Susannah puts her hands on her hips. 'What on earth have you been up to all this time?'

'Auntie Susannah.' Dan lets go of me. 'Look, you mustn't get all worked up, but we might need you to start ringing round and telling people not to come today.'

'I beg your pardon?'

I manage to straighten up, though I don't much fancy opening my left eye just yet. 'Mrs Britten-Jones, we've been talking to Licky, and it seems like the sensible thing to do is to . . .' There's something about the way she's looking at me that makes me hesitant to use to word 'cancel'. '. . . postpone the wedding for the time being.'

'I'm sorry.' Susannah holds up a hand. 'Who are you?'

'Oh, sorry, I'm Isabel. Isabel Bookbinder. John Bookbinder's daughter, do you remember? You asked if I'd come and help out with the wedding.'

'Oh! And this is what you call "helping out", is it? Postponing it for the time being?'

'I know you must be upset, Mrs Britten-Jones.' One of Lara's psychology tricks might be called for here – the one where, basically, you tell someone they're such a wonderful person that they can't possibly be thinking about doing something unreasonable. I don't know the technical name for it. 'But you've always been such a terrific mother to Licky, and I know the last thing

151

you'd ever want is for her to walk down that aisle thinking she's made the biggest mistake of her life.'

'Is that true, Licky?' Susannah – immune, it seems, to psychological tricks – turns to her daughter, who has edged back towards the bathroom, and is fiddling with the door handle as though she'd dearly love to dive back in and lock us all out again. 'You want to put a stop to this wedding? You want me to have to telephone all my friends, most of whom are probably already dressed up in their nice hats and new suits, and tell them I'm terribly sorry they've wasted their time and money buying those nice hats and new suits, and generously looking for nice presents to buy you?'

'No, Mummy, of course I don't want that . . .'

'Well, then!' Susannah heads for the wedding dress on the back of the wardrobe as if everything's forgotten, and starts to brush it down rather violently with the flat of her hand. 'Now, jump in the bath, Licky, and perhaps Sophie can come up and help you sort out your hair.'

'But Auntie Suze, Licks *really* doesn't want to do this!'

'Has she said that?' Susannah glares at Dan. 'Or have you and your new piece of totty put ideas into her head?'

People really do seem keen to pair me off with Dan today, I must say. 'Mrs Britten-Jones, if you just ask her –'

'I have asked her! And she's said she doesn't want to cancel! Now for Christ's sake, the pair of you, make yourselves useful, will you? Somebody needs to get over to St Joseph's and make sure the flowers have been done, and the Orders of Service put out.'

'Auntie Susannah –'

'*No*. Now, this wedding is happening. *Today*. Right, Alicia?'

Licky nods, misery flooding her face. 'Yes.'

'There we go, then. Not another word about it.' She snaps her fingers together. 'St Joseph's! Flowers! Come on, come on, come on!'

Well, I suppose that's it, then. Licky trundles mutely behind her mother into the bathroom, and Dan looks across at me and shrugs.

'Game over. Come on, then. Let's just do as we're told.'

Despite the Anadin that Dan digs out for me, my head is still pounding as, twenty minutes later, we head out of the Hall and on to the driveway. I'm expecting him to lead me towards the shiny silver BMW that's parked beside the outside windows of the Saloon, but instead we head for the ancient tomato-red Fiat Panda next to it.

'Sorry,' he says, obviously catching me glancing at the BMW in surprise. He's (half) changed into his suit for the wedding now, the pale grey waistcoat flapping undone around his shirt, and the charcoal morning coat slung over his arm to be shrugged on later. Naturally – annoyingly – it makes him look more broodingly gorgeous and gorgeously brooding than ever. 'That's Sophie's. We struggling younger sons can't afford the same perks as the chatelaines.'

'Oh, no, I wasn't thinking –'

'Yes, you were,' he says bluntly, but not rudely, holding the passenger door of the Fiat open for me to squeeze myself in. 'Don't worry. I'm quite used to it.'

'Quite used to what, exactly?' I give him a look as, by some phenomenon of spatial physics that Marley and Daria would no doubt understand, he crams his own long-limbed frame into the other side, behind the steering wheel. 'Women checking you out because they think you must have money?'

He can't hide a momentary grin. 'If the cap fits.'

'No, the cap doesn't fit.' God, how can someone be so nice one minute and so deeply smug and self-satisfied the next? 'Because I'm not checking you out. I have a very lovely boyfriend, as it happens.'

'Oooh. Good for you,' he says, as he starts the engine and crunches the car into gear. He's reversed and then started turning the car out towards the long driveway when he says, suddenly, 'Sorry. It's just been a difficult morning. I shouldn't take it out on you. You did a terrific job with Licky.'

'Not that terrific a job. She's still getting married this afternoon, isn't she?'

Dan doesn't have an answer for that. In fact, as we set off along the track across the parkland, we both descend into a gloomy silence, which is broken only when my mobile starts up its bloody 'Here Comes the Bride' ring again.

'Sorry . . .' I scrabble in my bag. 'I should get this . . . Hello?' I say, into the phone. 'Isabel Bookbinder speaking.'

'Isabel? It's Ted, South-West Classic Cars.'

'Oh, Ted! Thanks for calling back. Did you get my message? Can you reorganise the cars?'

'Yes, I did, Isabel. I'm just calling to let you know that it's no problem.'

'Oh, that's brilliant, Ted, thank you –' I stop suddenly, as Dan slams on the Fiat's brakes to prevent us from ploughing into the car that's just appeared around the corner of the track road.

Oh my God.

It's Will's car.

With Will in it.

'Fucking hell!' Dan snaps.

'Isabel?' An alarmed voice is coming out of my phone. 'Isabel, are you all right?'

'I'm fine, Ted, thank you . . . look, I'll call you back.' I cut the call, unable to stop my hands from shaking.

Because I think I know why Will's come here.

He's about to propose, isn't he?

I mean, what the hell else is he doing out here in the wilds of Somerset, when he's meant to be giving a seminar at a partners' meeting ninety miles up the M4 in Reading?

He's obviously realised who's in the car he nearly drove into, because he's getting out of his Golf and walking towards us.

'Oh God,' I hear myself murmur. 'He's going to do it. He's actually going to do it.'

'Do what?' Dan is staring at me. 'Do you *know* this guy?'

'He's my boyfriend.'

'Are you on the run from him or something? I mean, you seem terrified!'

'No . . . he's here to propose . . .'

Dan's eyebrows shoot up. 'Propose? Like, marriage?'

I'm so frozen that I can't even reply, or wind my window down as Will taps on it. Dan hesitates for just a moment and then leans across and opens it for me.

'Hi, mate,' he says evenly. 'Going a bit fast there, weren't you?'

'Sorry.' Will stares across at Dan, and then at me. He looks tired. Actually, scratch that, he looks exhausted. 'My sat-nav doesn't have this listed as an actual road, so I just assumed there was no real likelihood of anyone else roaring down towards me.'

'I wasn't exactly roaring,' begins Dan, just a fraction less evenly.

'Will, I don't understand.' Marginally unfrozen now, I reach for the catch on the car door and stumble out. 'What are you doing all the way down here? Aren't you meant to be in Reading?'

'Yes. But all I'm missing at the moment is Jonathan O'Hara's Taxation of Intangible Assets seminar.' Will gives a slightly nervous laugh. 'Let's face it, it's not as if there's anything tangible I'll be losing out on!'

Oh, Christ, a solicitor joke. I need to save him from himself as soon as possible.

'Dan, would you just give us one moment, please?' I ask.

Dan gives a half-shrug, half-nod, and turns on his car radio in an ostentatious don't-mind-me-I've-got-better-things-to-do manner.

'Who *is* this guy?' Will asks, rather tetchily, as we head towards his Golf for a bit of privacy. 'The groom?'

'The bride's cousin. Look, Will . . .' I slump against the side of the car. 'I just don't understand. Why did you have to come all the way down here like this, on a day when I'm working, *and* at somebody else's wedding? I mean, how did you even know I was at Broughton Hall?'

'Your mum told me, when I got to the house.'

'You've already been to the house?' My heart has started to race most unpleasantly. 'So they . . . they know you're here?'

'Well, yes. I mean, I think they were a bit surprised to see me. But I didn't tell them anything, Iz, don't worry . . .' He stops, suddenly. 'Hey, is your eye OK? It looks really bloodshot.'

'It's fine. The bride's mother hit me with a door handle.'

'She *what*?'

'It's nothing to worry about. Look, Will –'

'Well, of course it's something to worry about! I'm allowed to worry.' He reaches for my hand. 'I'm *supposed* to worry. God, Iz, as soon as I got your texts this morning, I knew I had to come.'

'My texts?'

'Yes. Telling me all about what happened last night, with Hypatia and everything. Look, I know what your family can be like, Iz. And I thought it might cheer you up to see a friendly face, even just for a few minutes.'

This isn't making very much sense. 'Wait a moment. You're here because you thought I needed a friendly face?'

'Oh, well, not just a friendly face. This too.' He pulls me towards him and wraps his arms very tightly around me. 'Any better yet?' he whispers gently in my ear. 'Because I'm not going to let you go until you're at least sixty per cent happier.'

Wait a moment.

He's *not* here to enact some embarrassing public proposal? He's here because he's dropped everything and raced ninety miles to make me feel better about my miserable evening with my family?

And *this* is the man whose proposal I was gearing myself up to reject? Just because I'm worried about . . . God, I'm not sure I can even remember what it was I was worried about. Wet-rooms, I dimly remember. And . . . and Twickenham. And Mum fussing over what hat to wear.

For *that*, I'd turn down the chance to spend the rest of my life with a man like Will Madison?

'Oh God, Will,' I mumble into his shoulder. 'I love you so much.'

'Well, I love you, too . . .'

'I can't believe . . . I mean, you came all this way . . .'

'It wasn't *that* far, Iz. I mean, it took me only an hour and a half, and really, once you get past that contraflow at junction fifteen, it's pretty plain sailing.'

I laugh. I can't help it. Even his fascination with motorway junctions is adorable at this very moment.

'But you know, Iz, I shouldn't be too long before I head back. I've got to get through that same contraflow again, and I do probably need to make sure I'm there for my own seminar!'

'Yes, yes, you should go.'

'Won't you have to let go of me first?' He grins down at me.

'Yes, sorry. But I'm just so happy that you came, Will.'

He plants a soft kiss on my lips before opening his car door. 'It's nothing, Isabel. You'd do the same for me.'

'Do you know, I think I would?' I croak. 'I actually really would.'

'I know you would. Now, could you get Fancy Dan or whatever his name is to back up to that passing place up there so I can get by and turn round?'

I shut his door for him and hurry back towards the Fiat, where Dan is waiting, a puzzled look on his face.

'That was a weird-looking proposal,' he says, as I clamber back in. 'No bended knee, no ring . . . For a conventional-looking bloke, he didn't exactly do it the right way, did he?'

'It wasn't a proposal, actually,' I say, with dignity. 'My mistake. Now, would you mind going back a bit so Will can turn round?'

Dan doesn't say anything for a moment. Then, quite sharply, he shoves the gear into reverse. 'Your wish is my command,' he says, mockingly, and puts his arm around the back of my seat so he can start the tricky process of reversing the Fiat.

Chapter Ten

St Joseph's really is an idyllic setting for a wedding, even one that's doomed to failure and misery before the bride has even walked up the aisle. It's in the ludicrously picturesque hamlet of Gifford Magna, about ten miles across country from Broughton Hall, where you drive down this narrow lane flanked by weeping willow trees before arriving at the churchyard itself. There's an artfully crumbling stone wall separating the churchyard from the lane on one side and the open meadows on the three others, where wedding guests are already starting to park their cars and meander in the fresh air before wending their way to the church.

Dan pulls the Fiat into one of the fields, as close to the church as possible, and starts to put on his morning coat as we get out of the car. He's barely said a word for most of the drive – apart from the apparently unconnected observations that Will seems a nice bloke and that the farm vehicle that was in front of us for a couple of miles was going far too bloody slowly – so I'm quite surprised when he says, 'All right, then. I'll go and track down these Orders of Service. You go and check out Auntie Susannah's flowers. Happy?'

'OK.' I reach into my bag for my headset. 'Now, it's probably best if I give you my phone number, so you can call me if there are any problems.'

'God, I don't know, Isabel, I'm not sure my phone is set up for long-distance calls.'

I glare at him. It's funny, but having seen him and Will practically side by side in the last half-hour or so, I'm suddenly failing to get whatever it was that made him so devastatingly attractive before. 'Fine. If you want to schlep all over the place every time you want to ask my help with something, be my guest.'

He's just about to say something in reply when his name is bellowed from a carload of guests pulling up into the space next to us, and a small army of women in pastel suits clamber out and start mobbing him. I leave him to his fan club – presumably a load of Susannah's chums with a taste for younger men – and head across the field on tiptoe in my (OK, OK, I admit it, extremely ill-advised) black pumps towards the church, and go inside.

The interior of the church is just as charming as the outside. There are oak pews, a flagstone floor, traditional stained-glass in the windows, and a charming, slightly decrepit organ just to the left of the christening font. Susannah Britten-Jones's flowers are pretty enough too – lots of pink roses spilling out of pedestal vases – though obviously with my wedding planner's hat on, I think there's a lot more that could be done, flower-wise . . .

Actually, with my bride's hat on, too.

Or should that be *veil*?

Because honestly, now that I'm standing here in the cool calm of St Joseph's, I'm actually starting to envisage what my own wedding day will be like if – wait a moment, *when* – it comes around. The first tiny frisson of excitement has started to run through me, and I have to say, it's an awful lot nicer than the total panic I was feeling only this time yesterday. I mean, Lara is completely right. My wedding isn't going to be about family strops. It's going to be about standing next to the man I adore more than anything in the world, and telling him that we'll be together until death us do part.

OK, I absolutely have to get in touch with the vicar and find out what we need to do to get married here. I can just *see* it – me gliding up this very aisle in ivory lace, carrying a lily-of-the-valley posy, just like Mum's got in her wedding photographs, and with my hair half up, half down, the way Will really likes it. And Will himself will be waiting for me at the altar, looking ridiculously handsome in traditional morning dress, with just the right shade of tie to bring out the chocolatey colour of his eyes, which will light up when he sees me . . .

My mobile has suddenly started ringing again, 'Here Comes the Bride' echoing tinnily around the empty church.

It's Pippa.

Oh, God. Please, *please* let everything be all right with the Bentley.

I cross my fingers – it's OK to do that in church, isn't it? Probably something I should check out before I contact the vicar – and answer.

'Pippa, hi! Is everything OK?'

'No, everything is not OK.'

'Oh, no, Pippa . . .'

'Mother-of-the-bride got herself into such hysterics when Bride put her dress on that she simply *had* to be given two double vodka and tonics to calm down,' she spits. 'Bridesmaids one through four have come to actual, physical blows over which one gets the best bouquet, as if *that's* going to make them look any less like Tango-tanned, pram-faced heifers. Oh, and I'm currently in the taxi with Flowergirl number three who's threatening to be sick all over her ballet slippers. I think she might have a migraine. Can six-year-olds get migraines? Anyway, who cares? It's just a complete fucking nightmare.'

'Yes, yes, terrible . . . but the Bentley turned up OK?'

'Yes, fine. It arrived at Bride's hotel just before I left.'

'Oh, thank God. I mean, I'm glad to hear it, Pippa.'

'So anyway, I need you to keep your mobile on at all times, Isabel. I might need you to head over here sharp-ish if things get any more out of hand.'

'Um . . . well, I am at a wedding myself.' The icy silence down the phone tells me this was the wrong answer. 'But absolutely, Pippa, I will make sure I have full access to my phone. Do please call me if you need anything at all.'

She doesn't bother to say anything else; she simply hangs up.

'Scuse me?' There's a voice behind me, and I turn round to see two men in morning suits loping up the aisle towards the altar. They're both in their late thirties, with matching receding hairlines and entirely unjustified expressions of self-satisfaction, and I know without even asking that one of these must be Marcus, Licky's fiancé.

The taller of the two nods at my black suit. 'The funeral's down the road,' he says, in a tone of voice that's probably meant to be bantering but just comes across as a bit aggressive.

I smile pleasantly. 'Actually, I'm here to help with the wedding.'

'That would be *my* wedding,' says the shorter one, stepping forward. He takes my hand in such a smarmy, exaggerated way that for a moment I think he's about to kiss it. But he just shakes it, holding rather too tight. 'Marcus McBride. It's very nice to meet you.'

'Good to meet you,' I fib. 'I'm Isabel. Is there anything you'd like me to do for you?'

'Nice of you to ask, darling. I can certainly think of one or two things you could do for me.'

Oh, *God*. Really? Half an hour before he marries Licky, he's hitting on the wedding planner? Dan was right: he really is an odious little shit.

'Well, if you don't need my help, then perhaps you could get on with a few things yourselves: starting to usher in some of the guests, getting the candles lit . . . just the things that will make the day run smoothly, you know. Minimise the stress for the bride.'

'Here comes the bride,' trills the best man, suddenly, in a singsong falsetto. 'All fat and wide!'

I glare at him. 'Fine. Whatever. Don't help. Stand around like a couple of silly schoolboys. It's not as if this wedding is exactly a match made in heaven anyway.' I take a step towards the doors, but Marcus blocks my way. The lascivious smile he was wearing just a few moments ago has vanished; he's quite obviously the kind of man who hates to be slighted.

'Hold up there, Girl Friday! You haven't even explained to me what it is you're doing at my wedding. I mean, *I* certainly don't know you. And you don't *look* like a friend of Licky's.'

'That's not true, Marcus,' the best man interjects. 'Doesn't Licky know some pretty fit birds from her riding events?'

'Well?' Marcus stares down at me. 'Is that how you know my fiancée? Through your interest in . . . riding?'

I take a very deep breath. 'Mr McBride . . .'

'Marcus. Please.'

'Mr McBride, there are a hundred and fifty of your wedding guests milling about outside and I actually really would appreciate it if you'd let me do my job.'

Over Marcus's shoulder, I can see Dan Britten-Jones coming through the church doors – obviously escaped, at last, from the pastel-clad harem. He's holding a large pile of Orders of Service in one hand, and a small box of white carnations in the other, and now he's seen us, he's heading our way.

'Isabel?' He strides all the way up the aisle, steps around Marcus as if he's a bit of litter that's accidentally been dropped, and looks at me. 'Everything OK?'

'Isabel and I were just getting to know each other a little better.' Marcus is regarding Dan with a smile that doesn't come anywhere near his eyes. 'I've not had the considerable pleasure of meeting her before.'

'I wasn't talking to you,' Dan says, 'actually.'

'*Ack-tually*.' Marcus mimics Dan's accent, which is obviously the closest thing to an insult he can come up with right now.

'Fuck you, McBride.'

'No, fuck *you*!' It sounds a lot less impressive when Marcus says it. 'I know you've already done everything you can to stop me marrying your cousin. But are you really going to stop me from just *talking* to pretty girls now?'

'If you're bothering them,' Dan says dangerously, 'then yes.'

'Oh, I'm so sorry,' says Marcus, laying the sarcasm on thickly. 'I totally forgot – *you're* the only one around here who's allowed to have a way with the ladies, isn't that right?'

'That's about the size of it.'

The best man gives another of his sniggers. 'Shouldn't we be asking *Isabel* about the size of it?'

Dan's eyes flash. He takes a very deliberate step closer to the best man. 'I'm sorry,' he says, 'would you mind repeating that?'

OK, things are getting a bit out of control here. It's all very nice that Dan feels the need to defend my honour, but the last thing this wedding needs right now is a fist fight. Quite apart from anything else, if Susannah Britten-Jones got wind of it, there's a very real possibility she'd actually self-combust, which wouldn't exactly improve Licky's day.

Well, not much.

'Righty-ho!' I say heartily, pulling Dan away from the best man by the sleeve of his morning coat. 'I think it's about time we started getting people in, don't you? They have all come here to see a wedding, after all!'

'Yeah.' Marcus is scowling at Dan's back. '*My* bloody wedding. Come on, Mike,' he adds, giving the best man the opportunity to step away from Dan without looking as though he's backed down about anything. 'I need a cigarette outside before the madness starts.'

'Try not to accidentally light yourselves, or anything,' Dan says, slightly too loudly, as they head for the doors.

'Dan!'

'Oh, I'm sorry, were you two getting on?' He pushes the Orders of Service in my direction. 'Because from where I was standing, it seemed like he was smarming all over you and refusing to let you out of the church.'

168

'Yes. They're idiots. But nothing I couldn't handle. And I don't think your auntie Susannah would thank you for almost starting a fight on her big day.'

'Then I beg your pardon,' he says, giving a mocking bow. 'I won't jump to your defence in the future. Obviously someone who's *very nearly* received a proposal of her own today knows precisely what she's doing.'

I feel my cheeks flame. 'There was a *reason* I thought he was going to propose,' I mumble. 'It wasn't just because I'm a bit stupid.'

'I never said you were stupid. Sorry.' Sarcasm is overcome by instant remorse again, and rather awkwardly, Dan shoves the Orders of Service in my direction. 'You handle these, can you, Isabel?'

'Yes, of course . . . I do know what I'm doing here, you know.'

'I know. I'll go and start ushering people in then, shall I? Roll up, roll up,' he adds, striding back out of the church. 'And just remember, folks – many a good hanging prevents a bad marriage!'

I hurry down the aisle after him. Just because it sounds like he's got a few more ideas up his sleeve about how to deal with Marcus.

Fifteen minutes later and the church is filling up nicely.

Oh, and this is no thanks to Dan, I hasten to add, who has spent the last ten of those chatting away to a blonde in a Jackie O pillbox and a dress that's just a

169

couple of inches more plunging than is truly appropriate, either for a church wedding or for her age.

Meanwhile I've been doing sterling work, including:

1) tracking down Reverend Harrison and Mrs Macmillan the organist, who were having tea, orange Club biscuits and a good old flirt over today's Sudoku in the vestry;
2) going pashmina-begging on behalf of an elderly great-auntie who's 'feeling the cold', despite her own admission that she's already wearing thermals underneath her pastel tweed suit;
3) project-managing the photographer who's just arrived (late) and who seems to be under the illusion that he's David Bailey on a fashion shoot with Kate Moss in the Bahamas;
4) assuring the chilly great-auntie that said photographer was shouting, 'Grit your teeth, love,' when he took her picture, and not 'Tits and teeth, love,' which is what he's been shouting at all his subjects for the last five minutes; and
5) actually gritting my teeth for long enough to speak to the best man and get him to get the groom into position so that when Susannah arrives, as she will do any minute now, the place might actually look like a wedding's about to occur.

All this, and I've been trying to put the occasional call in to Licky to make sure she's coping. Which she assures me she is. Though it's difficult to be absolutely sure that's what she's saying through all the sobbing.

Anyway, it's too late for me to try her again now, because the last time I called she hiccuped at me that Susannah was taking her phone away, presumably to limit the possibility of Licky making a break for freedom the moment she's alone in the back of the Jag. And even if I could call, I'm going to have to spend the next couple of minutes dealing with my own family, who are now heading across the churchyard, en masse, towards me.

Lara and Matthew are leading the way, followed by Dad, and Mum, resplendent in a brand-new peacock-green suit and a matching fascinator that looks as if it could have once been an actual peacock. Bringing up the rear are Marley and Daria, and, queen-like in her pushchair, Hypatia.

'Isabel!' Lara is putting on her incredibly sunny and positive voice. 'You look great! Doesn't she look great?' she adds, jabbing Matthew in the ribs.

He just grins at me. 'Like the headset, Wizbit. Oh, and if you're bringing in a plane to land, can you at least wait until after we've had the chance for a good old singsong of "Jerusalem"?'

I ignore him, distracted by the fact that Mum is looking flustered and close to tears. I think this might be the explanation for Lara's incredibly sunny and positive voice. 'Everything OK?'

'We had a little bit of a . . . an incident.' Mum sniffs,

tweaking some of her plumage to try to hide her eyes. 'We were worried we were going to be late. Susannah hasn't arrived yet, has she?'

Dad's face is white with fury. 'It's *terribly* bad form to arrive after the bride's mother!'

'Well, you can all relax,' I say. 'She's not here yet.'

'Oh, thank God.' Mum looks weak with relief. 'See, John? I told you it was going to be all right.'

'All right? You practically poisoned your only granddaughter!'

'What?' I stare at Hypatia. She's all kitted out in a little pair of pale grey dungarees and a blue blouse with a Peter Pan collar – oh, for the love of God, would it kill Daria to put her in a frilly pink dress, just for this one occasion? – and she looks rather smiley and cheery, and not at all like she's just been dosed with rat-poison by her favourite granny.

'I didn't realise she'd have such a terrible reaction!' Mum turns to Daria, imploring. 'It was only a couple of chocolate buttons, Daria, I swear! Just to keep her happy while she waited for us all to get ready. If I'd known it would make her sick . . .'

'But we have said many times, Moira, that we don't want her eating processed sugar.'

'Precisely!' Dad interrupts Daria. 'It practically rots the brain! What the hell were you doing, Moira, giving all that sugar to a sensitive child like Hypatia?'

'Well, if she's as gifted as you think she is, Dad, it's not as if it's exactly going to hurt. Rotting a few brain cells, I mean.'

'I *beg* your pardon, Isabel?' Dad's eyebrows have shot up.

'Look, all I mean is –'

'I think that all Isabel meant was that a little bit of sugar really isn't going to do Hypatia any long-term damage,' Lara interrupts. 'Honestly, Daria, there really is no evidence that I've ever heard of that suggests that developmental impairment can be caused by the occasional chocolate button. The studies I know you're thinking of, John, are generally much more concerned with children who consume a massive amount of E numbers, or MSG. And Hypatia's general diet is so wonderfully healthy that she really won't be harmed by a little bit of chocolate from her grandmother – who, after all, does love her very much.'

God. How *does* Lara do it? With one of her most brilliant psychology tricks to date, she's just managed to praise Marley and Daria for giving Hypatia a terrific diet, imply that Dad is a learned reader of the most up-to-date medical research available, and casually reiterate that Mum adores her grandchild and would never do a thing to hurt her. Honestly, the only person she hasn't bigged up in the last fifteen seconds is Matthew, and he's standing there staring at her anyway with a huge, soppy grin on his face that implies he knows he's won the lottery by going out with her.

Oh, and me, of course. She hasn't bigged up me. But then she has just been trying to help me out.

'Yes,' I say. 'That's exactly what I meant, Lara. Thank you.'

'Well.' Dad nods around at everyone, to show that, as decreed by him, the incident is over. 'Lara's right, I'm sure. And Hypatia does seem fine again now.'

'She does, doesn't she?' Mum looks like she might start crying with relief.

'Yes, though I think we should take her inside,' Marley says, 'so that she doesn't get sunburn.'

Given that the clouds have gathered thickly over the last hour or so, I think this is unlikely. But I'm not about to stop them going into the church and leaving me to get on with my job, so I hand them each an Order of Service and wave them through. But Lara hangs back for a moment and grabs my left hand.

'Well?' she hisses at me. 'Did Will find you? He came to the house, you know . . .'

'Yes, he found me. And no, he wasn't here to propose,' I say, anticipating her next question.

'Then what was he doing here? I mean, he came all the way from his meeting! I just assumed, when I saw him . . .'

'He just came to see me. He knew I was having –' I stop myself. 'He knew I was worried about the wedding today and he just came to give me a bit of moral support.'

'Oh! Well, that's amazing!' She gives me a quizzical look. 'And this is still a man whose proposal you *would* turn down, if he made it?'

'Well, things might have changed on that front,' I say, just as I see Maurice's Land Rover pull up and Susannah and Sophie start to clamber out. 'Look, I'll tell you about it later, OK, Lars? I should be getting on with my job now.'

Lara squeezes my hand. 'OK. Though it looks like you're doing a great job so far!'

Susannah is still in the pink silk from earlier, though she has added a gigantic pink hat and a slash of lipstick. Sophie is all gussied up in her navy Vera Wang, of course, and even I have to admit that she does look pretty splendid in it – tall and slim, with acres of her long legs on display. It helps that she's wearing her hair loose, which makes her look a little less horsy than before, and she's wearing some extremely expensive-looking heirloom-type jewellery in the form of a gold and emerald pendant and matching earrings.

I hurry across the churchyard towards them, keen to do a professional job.

'Mrs Britten-Jones! Everything all right back at Broughton?'

'Yes, it is, in fact,' she says, in a tone of voice that means she might just as well add 'and no thanks to you'. 'Licky's car arrived just before we left, so I assume she and David are on their way.'

'Ah, yes, the Jaguar I arranged.' I want to remind Susannah that I have, actually, done my very best to make sure things go well with this wedding. 'I hope it was all right?'

Susannah sniffs. 'It was fine. A convertible, though,

so God knows what it'll do to her hair on the ride over here.'

Honestly, there really is no pleasing some people.

'Well, I'm sure you'll want to go inside and greet people,' I say, brightly, handing her an Order of Service, unable to shake off my sense of relief when she takes it from me and marches through the church doors. 'And Sophie, I presume you'll want to stay out here so you can walk in behind Licky and David when they get here.'

'In front.'

'Sorry?'

'I agreed it with Licky. I'm walking in front.' She tosses her hair over one shoulder. 'Like they do in America.'

'But we're in Britain!' I say lightly. 'And it is supposed to be the bride's big entrance!'

Sophie shrugs. 'I'd prefer to do it my way. Hey, Dan,' she suddenly calls over my shoulder, to where Dan has just emerged from his lengthy chat with the inappropriate blonde, and come out of the church to wait with us. 'You were at dinner last night. Licky said it was perfectly OK for me to walk in ahead of her, didn't she?'

'She did, Sophie, yes. Under absolutely no duress whatsoever.'

'Oh, fuck off, Dan.' Sophie pulls a little gold compact from her shoulder bag and starts examining her lipstick. 'If she'd wanted it any different, she could have said so.'

'Mmm. Just like she could have told her mother

earlier that she didn't want to go through with it, maybe, if she'd been able to speak to her on the phone rather than having to confront her in person.'

'Well, if you don't realise why I *had* to call Susannah . . .'

Thank God, my mobile has started to ring, so I can step away from Row Number Seven Thousand of the Day and take the call.

'Excuse me, I really have to take this . . .' I press the button on my headset. 'Isabel speaking.'

The sound that comes out of the phone is almost . . . inhuman. In fact, I don't even realise it's an actual voice for a couple of seconds, until I glance into my bag at my mobile and realise that it's Pippa.

'Pippa? Is everything all right?'

'*Isabel* . . .'

Well, it was a recognisable word, at least.

'*What the hell have you done?*'

OK. Six more recognisable words. Not ones I'm particularly pleased to hear, though, it must be said.

And they beg the immediate question – what *have* I done? Has there been a terrible problem with the flowergirls' hairbands? Was it my choice of the plastic ones that, pinching behind the ears, has caused one of them to suffer migraine-related sickness? Have the eight thousand pounds' worth of chocolate wedding favours turned up all melted inside the boxes?

'Pippa, perhaps if you could just explain what the problem is . . .'

Over the churchyard wall, I can see that a wedding

car has just turned into the lane and that it's moving at a stately pace towards us.

Wait a moment.

This can't be right.

It's not a red Jaguar. It's a white Bentley.

Oh, *shit*! This is the problem! This is why Pippa's going mental on the other end of the phone. I don't know how Frankie did it, but somehow she's managed to get hold of the Jaguar after all, and she must have just showed up at church in the banned red Jag, wrecking Sunetra's photo-shoot and undermining Pippa into the bargain.

'Pippa, I swear, this isn't my fault. I called South-West Cars like you asked, and told them to send the Bentley to Frankie! She must have called them back herself and rearranged the red Jag again.'

'The red Jag?' Pippa is actually snarling. 'You think the *red Jag* is my biggest concern right now?'

I don't understand. And I'm just about to tell Pippa that I don't understand when the Bentley pulls to a halt, a little further back along the lane than it should, one of the back doors is thrown open, and a bride clambers out.

She throws back her veil, stares up at St Joseph's in all its late summer glory, and lets forth a scream that might wake the dead in the churchyard all around us.

'Where the *fuck*,' she yells, in the broadest of Merseyside accents, 'am I?'

This bride is not Licky Britten-Jones.

It's Frankie Miller.

Dear Frankie

First, I would like to apologise from the very bottom of my heart for ~~ruining~~ making a bit of a mess of your wedding day. In my defence, I would just like to point out that at least, in the end, you did in fact make it to the right church, and only approximately one hour after your scheduled arrival time, and that at the time of writing you are, finally, happily married to your ~~millionaire~~ charming and good-looking Premiership footballer husband. So, well done on that!

That said, I would very much like to deal with the several points that you, and other members of your ~~terrifying~~ large and obviously close family have made to me both on the phone and in person over the last few hours.

1) I am painfully aware, Frankie, that (as you may recall, you screamed at me repeatedly outside St Joseph's church earlier this afternoon) your big entrance into your own wedding venue was, unfortunately, ~~completely fucked~~ not as you had wished it to be. I do understand that having another bride walk down the aisle towards _your_ fiancé, watched by 200 of _your_ family and friends may have put the dampeners on your own, no doubt spectacular, arrival an hour or so later. However, I think we should focus on the positives

here. *As I have already said, you did* ~~eventually~~ *make it down that aisle yourself! And how deeply must your fiancé and your guests have relished that moment when it eventually came, having waited that much longer for it themselves?*

2) *Regarding a point* ~~repeatedly~~ *made to me by one of your extremely spirited bridesmaids on the phone just a short time ago (how _did_ they get my number, do you know? Not that it's a problem! Always a pleasure to speak to any of your friends!), unfortunately I have no good explanation for why the Other Bride, Alicia Britten-Jones, managed to get halfway along the aisle before realising that this was not the church at which she was due. I can only guess that, due to a recent change of heart about actually getting married today at all, Miss Britten-Jones was in an unusually fragile state of mind and not sufficiently aware of her surroundings.* ~~Besides, did you see the veil she was wearing? She should have been given night vision goggles just to see out from under that thing!~~

3) *Re: your doves. Again, I can only apologise. I do know how disappointed you must have been that, due to the seemingly draconian laws regarding the welfare of working animals in this country, the dove handler was unable to stay any later than 3.15 p.m., thereby rendering the dove release on your arrival an impossibility. If it would make you feel better, I am perfectly prepared to take up the matter with the RSPCA, possibly even going so far as to lobby Parliament for changes to this unacceptable system.*

Alternatively, as has already been suggested to me on the phone by your delightful mother, I am fully prepared to reimburse you for the cost of the doves, if you would be prepared to accept this in monthly instalments. However, I am afraid to say that I am not prepared to undertake any of the other suggestions made by your mother, regarding the doves and what she would like me to do with them. I really do think the RSPCA would be justified in having a thing or two to say about that.

4) *Finally, regarding a series of text messages I have just received from several of your brothers, although I am fully prepared to accept total responsibility for my part in this ~~fiasco~~ ~~debacle~~ muddle, I honestly do not think it is fair to ask me to take the blame for the fact that, due to your late start, your outdoor drinks reception was compromised. While it is a terrible shame that the previously glorious weather turned to heavy showers at approximately five forty-five p.m., just as your guests arrived at the reception venue, I am sure that you can understand that this is, to an extent, the luck of the draw. Contrary to the ~~violent~~ vigorous claims asserted by your brothers, I obviously have no means of controlling the weather. Though please be assured, Frankie, that if I did, I would have wished for only sunshine for you!*

Given that, at the end of the day, no terrible harm has really been done to anyone here, I wonder if you might find it in your heart to ~~call off your attack dogs~~ have a quiet word with the more eloquent members of your ~~vast~~ extended family, and remind them that still and all, you are now the happily married Mrs Dean Davidson, and that no good can come from threats of violence. ~~And maybe one day this will all make an amusing story to tell your grandchi~~ I wish you very many years of happiness together.

   With very best wishes,

   Isabel Bookbinder

PS As I say, I am more than happy to stump up for the cost of the doves, but I hope you will understand if I do not give you my home address to send the bill to. Do please text me the amount required.

PPS Not that I am implying by this that your brothers are the sorts to act on their threats! I am sure that, like you, they are a credit to your extremely lovely mother. In fact, why not tell her I said that?

   IB xx

Dear ~~Susannah~~ Mrs Britten-Jones,

~~Hopefully by the time you receive this, you'll have managed a couple of decent nights' sleep and things won't seem~~
~~I can only hope that you suffered no adverse reaction to that Valium that~~

I cannot express how truly sorry I am for my role in today's unfortunate events. Quite obviously, and contrary to the ~~abuse you hurled at me~~ opinions you expressed earlier, I had no intention of putting such a spanner in the works of ~~Licky's your~~ Licky's Big Day. Despite the reservations I may have had this morning about ~~forcing~~ persuading Licky to go through with the marriage, I absolutely did not, as you put it, 'cook this whole thing up just to make it easier for Licky to pull out after all.' ~~Quite apart from anything else, if I had really been scheming to put a stop to the wedding, don't you think I would have arranged something that didn't make me a laughing stock in front of an entire congregation, and didn't result in the instant loss of my job with Pippa Ev~~ The other bride at the centre of this mix-up, Frankie Davidson (née Miller), did in fact go through with her wedding this afternoon, albeit an hour and a half later than planned, so I hope that you can recognise that it would have been perfectly possible for Licky to turn up at St Joseph's if she had really wanted to. Surely the fact that she took this as a ~~sign~~ golden opportunity to do a runner should indicate to you that there were deeper reasons for her no-show than the regrettable mix-up of the wedding cars? I am sure that, *when you have had the time to reflect on this, you will see that not all the blame can be laid at my doorstep. Shall we agree that I will shoulder ~~60%~~ ~~40%~~ 50% of the responsibility, and that the rest can be put down to events beyond my control?*

For this reason, I would appreciate it enormously if you would have a quiet word with my father, Mr John Bookbinder, and try to convince him that you have backed off from the view that, to sum up your earlier ~~accusations~~ views, I am 'a scheming little bitch' who has ruined your chances of 'getting so much as one lousy grandchild'. As I am sure you will understand ~~if you have ever spent more than five minutes talking to him~~, my father can be a critical man at the best of times. You were probably too ~~hysterical~~ upset to notice the look on his face this afternoon, but I can assure you that, without your intervention in this matter, his already low opinion of ~~my abilities~~ ~~my talents~~ me will very likely plumb new depths. ~~In all the years I have known and irritated him, I have honestly never seen him quite so~~

~~I'm not kidding when I say that he looked at me as though I'd just~~

~~It's hard to describe but~~

~~I don't know if he's ever going to forgive me for~~

~~I just wish he wouldn't~~

~~Why can't~~

Chapter Eleven

There's a book Dad forced me to read when I was younger – I think it was *Great Expectations* – where this miserable old lady called Miss Havisham never leaves her house, instead spending all her time wafting about in her wedding dress, picking at mouldering cake, with all the clocks stopped at the exact time, on her wedding morning, that she got a letter from her fiancé announcing that he wasn't going to marry her and that he'd pinched all her money.

I'm just wondering if I could get away with something similar.

I mean, not that I'd need to wear a wedding dress, of course. It's not *my* wedding day that's been shot to hell. Far more appropriate that I wear this exact same black suit and these same black pointy pumps, given that this was what I was wearing at the moment – five past three, stop all the clocks – when my career took a deathly nosedive into oblivion.

I'm not sure quite how rigid you have to be on the shoe front, though. Because after almost twelve hours wearing these bloody (literally – my heels are now finely grated all over the insides) high-heeled pumps, I think even mad old Miss Havisham would slip on a nice pair of comfy Ugg boots. Even if they didn't go with the rest of her outfit. Which is what I'm doing now, as finally – *finally* – I get back to my flat after my day of Wedding Armageddon.

Well, OK. Maybe Armageddon is a teensy bit of an exaggeration. I mean, I've been thinking about it all the way to London in the back of Matthew's car, not to mention discussing it with Lara, who tried to remain as relentlessly positive as ever. And we both agreed that there is at least one major bright spot to this whole fiasco, which is that, albeit inadvertently, I've prevented Licky from marrying Vile Marcus. The last we heard from her was at about five-thirty this afternoon, long after the wedding guests had dispersed from St Joseph's, when Dan managed to sneak away from attending to Susannah's hysterics for long enough to let me know he'd just had a call from Licky at the Gatwick Travelodge. I gather she's jetting off on honeymoon, solo, tomorrow morning. Honestly, the sheer triumph of this is almost enough to outweigh the sheer hideousness and misery of everything else that's happened since five past three this afternoon.

I said *almost*.

As I shove my battered, aching feet into my Uggs, the phone next to my bed starts to ring, making me jump. It's unsurprising, as the ringing of phones has precipitated most of the horrors that this day has had to offer. In fact, the only call I've had all afternoon that hasn't contained recriminations, threats, or firings was the one from Ted at South-West Classic

Cars, explaining to me kindly and patiently, as though *I'm* the idiot here, that I really should have made it clear to him that changing the brides' pick-up locations *also* meant that the corresponding drop-off locations had to be changed too.

But neither Pippa nor Frankie, nor any of Frankie's entourage, can possibly have got hold of my unlisted landline number, so I think it should just about be safe to answer this one.

I pick up. 'Hello?'

'Isabel?'

'Mum.'

'Oh, *Isabel*.'

'Yes, OK, Mum. I know.'

'Well, it wasn't totally your fault, darling.' She's whispering, which means she's probably shut herself in the bedroom, where she always goes to make phone calls that she doesn't want Dad to know she's making. 'I mean, from what it sounded like, it's that man from the car-hire place who really ought to be apologising to people! He's the one who sent the drivers off to the wrong churches!'

I can feel a lump growing in my throat, which is what I knew would happen the moment anyone tried to be nice to me about all this.

'And those two silly girls . . . I mean, I know the Waggy one isn't from the area, so she wasn't to know her car was taking her the wrong way. But Licky! Poor thing, I know she's not the smartest penny in the toolbox, but –'

187

'It wasn't her fault, Mum. She was a bit out of it. If anyone should have noticed, it was David Britten-Jones.'

'Well, yes . . .' She's not keen to criticise the Master of Broughton. 'But he's a bit eccentric, isn't he? You know, I was just on the phone to Barbara – she sends her love, by the way, and says you mustn't worry, everyone makes mistakes – and she was telling me she's sold a nightie to one of the ladies who cleans at Broughton and she said he's forever shutting himself away with his antiques and his paintings.'

'Mmm.' I'm not in the mood to discuss David, or indeed any of the other Britten-Joneses, right now. 'Look, Mum, I've just got in and I'm exhausted . . .'

'Oh, yes, you go, darling. I just wanted to say that I thought you were doing a marvellous job up until . . . well, you know. Do you think your boss – what's her name, Pippa? – will calm down in a couple of days' time? Maybe let you come back to work for her?'

'Maybe.' It's a total lie. Pippa is no more going to let me come back and work for her than she'd let the Child Catcher from *Chitty Chitty Bang Bang* babysit her kids. 'We'll see.'

'Oh, well, I thought she might! I mean, you're her partner, aren't you, Iz? It's not really right of her to go around firing her partner.'

'Mmmm. Well, maybe it's a case of me not being that comfortable working for her any more.'

'Yes, I see. But you never know, Iz. I mean, people

188

all calm down eventually, you know. Even your father . . .' She takes a deep, rather sharp breath. 'Well, he'll calm down, too. Sooner or later.'

Yes. Well.

Based on the twisted expression on his face as he stamped back to the car earlier this afternoon, not to mention the fact that he seemed so deeply wearied by the whole sorry affair that he couldn't summon himself to address so much as one word to me, even in anger, I'd say it's a lot more likely to be later rather than sooner.

'It was just a bit of a blow for him, this all happening with Susannah Britten-Jones. Especially after he actually recommended you to her.'

'I realise that, Mum, thanks.'

'He's got an awful lot on his plate right now, Iz-Wiz, and you know how tired he gets at the start of a new term . . .'

'Mum, I really do need to go now. But I'll speak to you on Monday, OK?'

'Oooh, yes, I forgot, you'll be busy all day tomorrow doing your move, won't you, Iz-Wiz? Well, that'll be something nice for you to focus on! Take your mind off work for a bit!'

'Yes. Thanks for calling, Mum. I really do appreciate it.'

After I've hung up, I sit on the edge of the bed for a few minutes. I'm too exhausted to get up, and anyway, I'm thinking about what Mum's just said about my big moving day tomorrow.

I mean, if there's one good thing that's come out of today apart from Licky's daylight flit, it's the fact that every last one of my reservations about moving on to the next stage with Will have well and truly melted away. In fact, maybe today's career implosion is actually a bit of A Sign. Is someone up there trying to tell me I'm far more cut out to be a full-time wife and mother than anything else? Let's face it, I could hardly be any more of a failure in those departments than I have been as a wedding planner.

Yes. It's definitely A Sign.

So what I think it's best to do now is devote the next twelve months to arranging our own, spectacular wedding. Obviously St Joseph's might be out of the question – to be honest, the further away from Susannah Britten-Jones, the better – but there are still plenty of other lovely locations I could think about. Venice, perhaps – not only thousands of miles from Somerset, but the one place on earth where I can guarantee there won't be a problem with the car hire. I mean, unless Ted is thinking of opening up a South-West Classic Gondolas any time soon, I should be safe.

I head down the stairs into the kitchen/living-room, locate the only thing I can face making for a late supper, which is a pot of raspberry yoghurt and a box of Alpen, then head for the sofa and pull out a sheet or two of scrap paper from underneath one of my moving boxes. I'm sure Lara would heartily approve of the idea of starting up a cheery, positive To-Do List under the circumstances.

Right. Item number one is nice and straightforward – *Plan huge (Italian?) wedding a.s.a.p.*

Now, what to focus on for the next stage of my brand-new life plan? Well, obviously as soon as we're married, we'll need to take Lara's lead and move out to some rambling house on the outskirts of London, which I can then do up from top to bottom. Because that's practically a full-time job anyway, if you think about it – all that traipsing about to Fired Earth and Habitat to find the perfect finish for our brand-new wet-room (yay!). Not to mention the fact that we'll need a suitable family bathroom, too, in preparation for Phase Three of the plan: kids. We'll have two. No, three. Two boys and a girl. No, two girls and a boy. Aisha, Aurora and Zack. No, Aisha, *Jemima* and Zack. Except what if the girls are twins? Then I think we'd be better off with *Jessica*, Jemima and Zack. Unless Jessica isn't a twin, and the other two are the twins. So then really it should be Jessica, *Zoe* and Zack. Or I could stick with the name Jemima and then call her twin *Jack*. Hang on, maybe I'd be best off with the twins being boys, and then they could be Jack and Zack, and their older sister could be Aisha . . .

As I hear a key in my front door, I shove my by-now scribbled and chaotic to-do list into my handbag, and leap to my feet. Because the only person who has a key to my flat is Will, and the last thing I want is to ruin his big surprise proposal by letting on that I've already picked out our kids' names. Well, *nearly* picked out our kids' names.

'Will!' I hurry towards him as he comes through the door, weary-looking but gorgeous in his dressed-down khakis and white shirt, and fling my arms around him. 'God, I'm so glad to see you!'

'I didn't even know you'd be here yet!' He sounds astonished. 'I assumed I'd be waiting up for you until two or three! Did the wedding finish early?'

I just inhale the warm, slightly citrussy scent of his neck for a moment before I can bring myself to answer. 'Yes. No. Sort of. I mean, it kind of didn't happen at all.'

And then it all pours out. Will is completely brilliant, of course, and just stands next to me while I perch on one of the packing boxes, holding my hand, and listens while I tell him everything. He agrees in all the right places, too – that it's as much Ted's fault as mine; that David Britten-Jones really should have noticed the car wasn't heading towards the church where half his family have been married or are buried; that it might be a good idea to send somebody else round to Pippa's office to pick up my things. And he adds his own twopence worth, too – that Susannah Britten-Jones will get over it; that Frankie Davidson née Miller will forget about the whole thing just as soon as she's sipping piña coladas out of a coconut on her honeymoon; and that Dad might have reacted badly but that's just because he doesn't know any other way to express himself when he feels awkward or embarrassed.

Which really is an extra twopence worth, because I

don't know exactly where Will got the idea I was bothered by Dad's reaction. It's not like I even mentioned it, or anything.

Anyway, once we've been through all the basics, he leans down so he can take my face in his hands and says, 'Look, Iz. It sounds dreadful. But let's just try and put things into a bit of perspective. Nobody got hurt. Nobody died. There was no *actual catastrophe*. Frankie made it to her wedding perfectly OK in the end, didn't she? And from what you've told me about Licky's almost-husband, it sounds like she dodged a bullet.'

I nod. 'A big bullet. Actually, one of those horrible dum-dum bullets that get lodged right inside you and cause maximum damage to all your live tissue . . .' I catch Will looking at me with alarm. 'I saw a few minutes of this documentary about Special Forces the other day while I was waiting for *Mad Men*,' I explain. Which is basically true. And certainly sounds a lot better than admitting I was really waiting for *Keeping Up with the Kardashians*.

'Right.' Will grins. 'And you know, Iz, just because this particular wedding didn't go exactly to plan, doesn't mean you're never going to get to show your family – your dad – what you can really do. I mean, this was all just about impressing snooty Susannah Britten-Jones for him, wasn't it? Wait until he gets to see what you could do with a wedding you're *really* in charge of.'

I stare at him. 'What? I mean . . . what wedding are you talking about?'

'Oh, well, you know . . .' He shrugs, hyper-casual, and then brings himself up to his full height, staring around the room. 'This is going to be a job and a half tomorrow, isn't it? In fact, I wonder . . . yes. Maybe we should sit down and talk about this now.'

'Talk about?' My heart has started to pound. 'Talk about what, Will?'

'Well, I was planning to wait until tomorrow, but I wonder if this evening is more appropriate.' He takes a deep breath. 'Isabel . . .'

'Wait!' I suddenly yelp, jumping off my box. For fuck's sake, he can't do this now! Not while I'm in my slightly sweaty work suit and my Uggs, with makeup smudged around my eyes, and bits of muesli and raspberry seed stuck in my teeth! I mean, my God, I may not be a Top Wedding Planner any more, but I couldn't possibly live this down if people found out this was how I'd received my big proposal! 'I just need a quick shower,' I say, pushing past him and dashing for the stairs to the mezzanine. 'Can you give me five minutes?'

'Oh, OK . . .' He looks disappointed for a moment, but then he brightens. 'Maybe I should fix us a little something to eat. I'm starving. Do you have any eggs? We could have an omelette with a nice glass of wine?'

'Perfect!' Oooh, I can just hear myself, ten years from now, telling this story to Aisha, Zack and Jack. Or whatever their names are. *Omelettes always remind me of the night your father proposed*, I'll say to their shining little faces, while I make them omelettes in our beautiful Mark Wilkinson country kitchen. *In fact, my darlings, making an omelette is a good way to describe our happy life together. You take a little pinch of consideration, a good dollop of humour, whisk it all together with a whole lot of love and then pour it into a heavy-bottomed skillet . . .*

I mean, it needs work, obviously. But this isn't going to be until Aisha and the twins are ten and eight! There's plenty of time to get it right. What there isn't plenty of time to get right just now is *me*. What I wear, how I do my makeup . . . I mean, the omelette story is going to lose a lot of its charm if the picture the kids have to accompany it is a dodgy mobile-phone shot of me in jeans and a crumpled T-shirt with hastily applied blusher and a limp hair-do.

I grab my phone as I dive into the bathroom, lock the door behind me and switch the phone on. By the time I've tipped my head upside down to zhush up my hair and get the blood running to my cheeks, my mobile is ready to dial Lara's number.

It rings several times before switching to answerphone.

So I ring it again as I start shedding my clothes.

Just as I'm about to try our emergency code, she picks up.

'Isabel?'

'Lars? Oh, thank God! Listen, I need your advice.' I turn on the shower, so Will won't be able to hear me in the kitchen/living room below. 'OK, I think Will's about to do the big proposal, and I want to know what you think I should wear.'

I pause, for a moment, for her scream of excitement. When it doesn't come, I carry on.

'I was thinking of just going back downstairs in my kimono dressing-gown – you know, the one you bought me when you went to that conference in Hong Kong – but I don't know if that's going to look particularly good if we take a photo or anything . . .'

'Iz, stop. I . . . look, I'm actually really glad you called.'

'Are you all right?' I hop on one leg to get my tights off, managing not to howl out in agony as I pull a large chunk of my heel with them. 'You sound weird.'

'I'm fine. I mean, I'm better than fine. But . . . well, no. I'm worse than fine. In some ways.'

'You're not making any sense, Lara! And I really don't have time for you not to make any sense just now . . .'

'Oh God, Iz.' She takes a deep, shuddery breath. 'Matthew just proposed.'

I catch a sudden glimpse of myself in the mirror above the sink – wild-haired, red-cheeked and open-mouthed. 'He *what*? Oh my God, Lars, you too? This is incredible!'

'With Nana Hamilton's sapphire,' she interrupts. 'That's the ring he just gave me.'

Ohhhhhh.

My face, in the bathroom mirror, looks like I've just been hit with a dum-dum bullet.

'He said he asked Will to look after it for him this last couple of weeks, ever since he brought it back from your parents'.' Lara is going on. 'He didn't want me to find it lying around the flat, and he thought Will was a far safer bet than any of his stupid rugby mates . . .'

The bathroom's unflattering strip lighting seems to be glowing brighter and brighter and everything else seems to have gone a bit fuzzy. I open my mouth to speak, but no words come out.

'Iz, I'm so sorry! It was meant to be *your* ring. *Your* proposal.'

'Don't be silly.' Some kind of autopilot is kicking in, and I'm dimly aware of the fact that I don't want to ruin this huge moment for Lara. 'This . . . this is incredible news. I mean, you've said yes, haven't you?'

'Of course, but, Iz –'

'No buts.' I sit down on the side of the bath. 'I'm thrilled for you, Lars. Really and truly. How did it happen?'

'He surprised me while I was making cheese on toast!' There's a sob of happiness in Lara's voice that she can't disguise.

'Cheese on toast!' I swallow, hard. 'That's going to be an amazing story to tell your children!'

'It was only half an hour ago, Iz, and I was just about to call you, and then Matthew opened some champagne . . .'

'Oh, Lars, you must go. Go and drink your champagne. In fact, Will and I will drink a toast to you ourselves, right now!'

'Iz . . .'

'Honestly, Lara, I'm so happy for you. This is everything you've ever wanted. Give Matthew a big hug from me, won't you?'

'I will.'

'And we'll talk more tomorrow. Bye!'

I turn off the shower, smooth down my hair, pull on my waffle bathrobe and open the bathroom door.

The nutty aroma of frying butter is floating up the mezzanine stairs as I head down them to find Will at the stove, gently stirring a pan, a bottle of red wine in his hand. He turns round with a smile as he hears me.

'Hey! I could only find this pan. And I've no idea where you've packed your glasses, so we're going to have to be savages and drink from the bottle!'

'OK. No problem.' I grab the wine he offers me and take a big glug. 'So, Lara just called me. She and Matthew have just got engaged.'

Will spins round. 'He did it *tonight*? Oh shit, sorry.' He claps a hand over his mouth. 'You weren't meant to know that I knew.'

'That's OK. Lara told me you were hiding the ring.'

'I know I should probably have told you, Iz, but Matthew swore me to secrecy.' He turns back to his omelette pan. 'I can't tell you how stressed I was about it, worrying that you might find it and ruin the surprise for Lara!'

'Right.' I clear my throat. 'It's my grandmother's sapphire ring, as it happens. The one Mum always told me was meant for me one day. Apparently she told Matthew exactly the same thing.'

'God, Iz, your mother!' Will shoots me a sympathetic look as he shakes the finished omelette on to a plate he's found somewhere, then picks up two forks and hands one to me. 'Dig in!'

'Actually, I'm not all that hungry any more.'

'Really? Are you OK?'

'I'm fine.' I take another gulp of wine. 'Big news for Lara!'

'Huge news. And presumably she'll want your help planning everything!'

'Yes. Presumably.'

'Well, there you are, then.' He reaches out and strokes my cheek. 'That can be your first big wedding commission to impress your family with.'

'Oh. *That's* what you meant.'

'Sorry?'

'Nothing . . . but . . . look, you said we had something to talk about? Something you'd been planning to ask me tomorrow?'

'Oh God, yes. Nearly forgot!' He swallows a mouthful of omelette and takes the wine bottle from me. 'It's quite a big thing to think about, Isabel. And you can say no if you want to.'

'Say no to what?'

'Well, how would you feel about the two of us getting a joint mortgage?'

The final shred of hope I've been clinging to for the last three minutes has just been wrenched away. I sit down on one of the bar stools. 'A joint mortgage.'

'My five-year fixed rate is coming to an end, you

see, and there are some really worthwhile deals out there. Now, obviously I'm not suggesting you cover half of it, because I know that might be a bit of a stretch for you at the moment, but I thought we could have a chat about what you do feel happy with, even if it's just ten per cent. Anyway, it's not really about the money, it's more about you starting to get your credit rating on track . . .'

He carries on, about things like base rates and something called a tracker mortgage, and I just sit and nod along, realising that this really is my very own Miss Havisham moment, and wondering if I can stop the garish green digital clock on the oven at nine-seventeen, and if I'm doomed to eat mouldering omelette for evermore, and I don't even realise I'm crying until Will's expression changes to one of horror.

'Iz! Oh, my God, what's the matter? Do you need a tissue? Is there one in your handbag?'

'No!' I dive for my bag myself, before Will can get there and pull out my stupid To-Do List in lieu of a tissue. 'No, I'll get it . . .'

'I don't understand,' he says, after a moment, as I scavenge an ancient, already-used tissue from a side pocket and ineffectually blow my nose with it. 'I thought you'd be pleased about this, Iz. I mean, I know the thought of planning for the future scares you, but this actually isn't scary at all!' He comes over and puts both hands on my shoulders. 'It's just a bit of boring old financial nuts and bolts, sweetheart. It's not life-altering. Not like a wedding or anything, God forbid!'

'God forbid,' I echo.

'So there's really no need to be upset. And there's no need to make a decision about this tonight, either. I probably shouldn't have brought it up. You're tired. It's been a hellish day for you.' He draws me into a hug. 'We can talk about this another time, OK? Any time you want. Oh, sweetheart . . . you really are exhausted, aren't you? But there's no need to cry . . . no need at all . . .'

Chapter Twelve

OK. Let's face it. The whole reason old Miss Havisham had a seriously big problem was that she was a Victorian. Or an Edwardian? It's something I'd have to look up. But the point is, the only reason she went a bit loopy when she realised she wasn't going to get married after all was because in those days, not getting married was the *Absolute Worst Thing* you could possibly do. Beating starving orphans and sending poor people to their deaths in the workhouse were all fine and dandy by the standards of the day (again, it's something I'd have to check) but remaining unmarried was absolutely beyond the pale. A crime against nature.

But today, in the glorious twenty-first century, things are totally different. I don't *have* to get married! Barely forty-eight hours ago, I didn't even *want* to get married! The whole thing was giving me the heebie-jeebies, all that waltzing about in a big white frock and cutting a five-hundred-quid cake with a ceremonial sword. In fact, when you think about it, weddings really are completely ludicrous things. Will is quite right to focus on sane, sensible matters like his base rates and his five-year trackers, and all the other stuff I'm going to read up on just as soon as I've got the time. Just as soon as *we've* really had the time to have a bit of that footloose-and-fancy-free fun we were both talking about only last week. Because let's face it, there's no point in dashing straight into a joint mortgage if he can't even be bothered to ask me to marry him!

Not that I'm bothered, either one way or the other!

And anyway, even if I *did* want a bit of wedding-based excitement in my life – which I don't. I mean, God forbid and all that – I've got Lara's wedding to think about! I'm the best friend of the bride, the sister of the groom, and the professional(ish) wedding planner, so it's basically going to be a triple-whammy on the weddings front for the next few months.

In fact, I did a lot of thinking about Lara's wedding yesterday, while Will and I were moving all my stuff out of my flat and over to his. Well, to be fair, he did most of the moving all my stuff out of my flat and over to his, and I concentrated on all the very important unpacking at the other end. Anyway, I've realised that Lara and Matthew's engagement honestly couldn't have come at a better time. Pippa firing me may have seemed like a disaster on Saturday, but I was only ever working for her to get some experience before setting up on my own, doing things my own way. And this is going to be a terrific opportunity to do just that.

Plus, obviously, it's the chance to show my family that I'm not just a complete idiot who can't even get the right bride to the right ceremony.

'Morning.' Will has stuck his head round the

bedroom door. He's all ready for work, freshly shaved and handsome in his dark grey suit and crisp blue shirt. If we were in a movie right now, on our first proper morning of living together, I'd be grabbing him seductively by the tie and pulling him back into bed. But we're not in a movie, and anyway I'm in my rattiest old pyjamas and still covered in a layer of grime from yesterday's move. Plus I know Will likes to be at work on time on a Monday, no matter how tantalising the trade-off. 'Sleep well?'

It's a slightly formal question. 'Yes, very well, thank you,' I reply, in a slightly formal way.

'Good! I've made you a coffee and left it on the table. Maybe when I get back this evening I could show you how to work the coffee machine?'

'Oh, it's no problem. I quite like using my little individual filters anyway. Though you must never tell Barney that,' I add, in a slight panic. 'Not even if he tries to trap you into admitting it.'

Will grins. 'Well, I should be getting on. But you're OK knowing where to find everything? You know how to work the shower?'

'Will, I have stayed here one or two times before. Remember?'

'Yes. Of course. And you've got plans for the day?'

Has he suddenly turned into the concierge of his own home, or something?

'Well, I'm going to go round and see Lara. You know, get the ball rolling on some of the wedding plans.'

'That soon?'

'*Yes,* that soon! Time and tide wait for no man, Will, when it comes to weddings. *Bloody* weddings,' I add hastily, just in case he was under the impression I sounded too enthusiastic about the idea, or anything.

'Right . . . Look, are you sure you're OK, Iz? You were a bit quiet yesterday, and you seemed so down on Saturday night.'

'Down? Me?'

'You cried for an hour and a half.'

'It had been a *very long and difficult* day,' I tell him.

'I know, but . . . well, you are happy, Iz, about us moving in together?'

Oh, God, I should really have made a bit more of an effort on our first proper morning together, shouldn't I? Maybe he really is expecting me to grab him by the tie and pull him back into bed. Well, it's never too late, I suppose.

'Will, darling, I'm ecstatic,' I purr, already pushing back the duvet in a seductive manner. 'Couldn't be happier . . .'

'Well, I'm glad. Just wanted to be sure.' He glances at his watch. 'Shit, Iz, I really do have to dash. See you this evening, yeah?'

'Yeah.'

'Oh, and I've left some of those mortgage brochures on the kitchen table, for you to have a little look at whenever you've got a moment. No pressure, of course!'

'Oh, yes. About that . . .'

'And I thought I'd pick up something for dinner on my way back, yeah? We'll have a cosy evening in with a takeaway and a DVD? Good plan?'

'Excellent plan,' I say, which seems to reassure him before he heads out of the door. 'Looking forward to it.'

Unfortunately I don't have the time to make any headway with the unpacking this morning, because I have far too much that really has to be done before I head round to Lara's later on. First off, I headed straight over the river to the Smythson shop on Sloane Street, where I picked up a really useful engagement present for Lara in the form of a gorgeous little hot-pink notebook with 'Wedding Planner' stamped on the front, plus an identical one for me, so that I can start filling it with all the notes I'll need for her wedding. While I was there, I also took the plunge of placing an order for my very own personalised stationery, which is obviously a total necessity now I'm setting up on my own. It took quite a bit longer than I thought, as I hadn't actually finalised the wording before I started placing the order. But the sales assistant was ever so sweet about it, and even got in on the act herself, helping me decide on a name for my brand-new wedding consultancy. We both agreed that 'Isabel's Wedding Belles' was unpleasantly redolent of a bridal boutique in small-town Kentucky, and that 'Isabel's Holistic Weddings' sounds like I might only be interested in organising New Age weddings at Stonehenge, where the bride and groom do a naked fertility dance, and the guests plait their beards in coloured ribbons. So finally we agreed that, for the first hundred business cards, at least, I was probably best off with a simple 'Isabel Bookbinder: Individual Weddings'.

Though a couple of hours later, my order already winging its way to Smythson printing HQ, I'm wondering if I shouldn't have gone for something more like 'Bespoke Weddings', or 'Exceptional Weddings'. But the assistant suggested this really clever design where the *I* of Isabel was also the *I* of Individual, and she was so sweet and enthusiastic about the whole project, and promised to come straight to me whenever she's engaged herself, that I really couldn't have said no.

Anyway, after that I headed straight across town to the Wallace Collection in Manchester Square, to have a little look around and see if it might be a suitable location to hire for Lara and Matthew's reception. Lara dragged me there one damp Saturday a couple of years ago, and as we marvelled at all the paintings and antiquities (well, she was marvelling; I was in a bit of a mood because I thought the plan had been to go to Selfridges) she declared that this would be the perfect place for her wedding one day. And even way back then, while Matthew was still happily with his ex-girlfriend Annie, Lara was actually envisaging gliding up the carved staircase to be joined in holy matrimony *with Matthew*. So here's my chance to give her that dream day she was thinking of! I took a few photos with my mobile, and then I found somebody in charge and gave them my name and number so that they can call me to schedule a proper visit with Lara one day next week.

And then I went and sat in the very nice atrium café and had a big cappuccino and a huge slice of sticky lemon drizzle cake, which made me more convinced than ever that this would be a great location for me to work with.

After that, it's just been a quick pit stop at WH Smith for every up-to-date bridal magazine I can lay my hands on, and now I'm getting off the tube at Queensway to head to Lara and Matthew's flat.

I'm just thinking that I should probably call Lara to let her know I'm coming when my mobile starts to ring.

Surprise, surprise. Mum.

She tried me on and off a couple of times yesterday morning, but obviously I was busy with the move, so there was really no very good opportunity to speak.

Besides, I wasn't exactly sure what I was going to say.

But now that I've had time to think about it, and now that I'm completely OK with the fact that Lara's ended up with Nana Hamilton's sapphire, instead of me, I think it might actually be a good idea to speak to her. After all, she's bound to have approximately eight million ideas about the wedding, and it's going to be my duty to see that only the harmless ones get through the net.

'Iz-Wiz! It's only me! I tried you yesterday!'

'I know, I'm sorry, I was a bit busy . . .'

'But have you heard?' Mum sounds like she's about to bubble over. 'Have you heard about Matthew and Lara?'

'I have, Mum, yes. She called me on Saturday night. It's brilliant news.'

'*Saturday* night?' Mum sounds slightly put out. 'Oh! They called us on Sunday morning.'

'But Mum, surely you did already know about it? I mean, Matthew must have come and asked you for Nana Hamilton's sapphire.'

'Oh, yes . . . Actually, I did really want to speak to you about that, darling. Now, I know I once told you that ring would be yours one day . . .'

'Once?' I say. But lightly. Good-humouredly.

'. . . but I think I might have said that to Matthew, too. Well, not that it would be *his*, of course, but that he could give it to the girl he wanted to marry. He obviously never even *thought* about asking me for it when he asked That Annie to marry him – which I think is incredibly revealing, don't you, Iz-Wiz?'

'Yes.' I swap my phone to the other hand so that I can give my left arm a bit of a break from carrying roughly eight hundred pages of wedding magazine. 'Very revealing.'

'And you know, darling, I did do a bit of Googling, and it does seem that it's *far* more traditional for a family engagement ring to be passed down the males in the family. So I'm *sure* Will's mother has a stunning family engagement ring she'll be giving Will to pass on to you, whenever the time is right! Probably something far, far better than Nana's little old sapphire!'

'Mum . . .'

'I mean, the Danes have incredible taste in jewellery, don't they? I remember seeing a picture of that Australian commoner who married into the Danish royal family, and she was practically dripping in diamonds!'

I think it's time to stop Mum before she has me married off into the Danish royal family – Will's mother may be posh, but she's not *that* posh – and anyway, I'm almost at Lara's.

'Mum, honestly, don't worry about it.'

'And you know, I'm sure the day will come, very soon, Iz-Wiz.'

'What day?'

'When Will proposes to you! Because I don't want you getting all upset about the fact that your younger brother is getting married before you. I mean, you're not even thirty yet! There's still time before you have to start panicking.'

'I'm not panicking, Mum.'

'Well, good for you, Iz. You're being ever so brave.'

'Right. Look, Mum, I'm just getting to Lara's, so I should go . . .'

'Ooooh, are you going to start discussing the wedding with her?' Mum is starting to sound a bit like a whistling kettle, excitement building up inside her and then exploding up through the spout. 'So exciting, Iz-Wiz! Now, one thing you must do right from the start, if you would, is try and find out exactly how many of her ex-step-parents she's thinking of inviting to the wedding. Because the longer your father has to get used to something a little unorthodox like that, the better.'

'Fine,' I fib. 'I'll do that. But you know, Mum, Dad is just going to have to go along with whatever Lara and Matthew want. It is their wedding, after all.'

'Oh, *I* know that, of course, darling! But you know what your father's like. And though he's terribly fond of Lara, he's never exactly been a fan of that mother of hers . . .'

There's something about the way Mum says 'that mother of hers' that reminds me that she's never exactly been the biggest fan of Lara's mother either.

'OK, Mum. Look, why don't I give you a call tomorrow, and I can fill you in on a few of the things that Lara and I discussed?'

'Oh, that would be wonderful, Iz-Wiz!' Her tone of voice suddenly changes. 'Wait a moment, darling – are you saying you're actually going to be *planning* things for Lara?'

'Well, we're going to be making a start.'

'But . . . in an official capacity?'

'What's wrong with that?'

'But after what happened on Saturday . . .' She takes a deep breath. 'I mean, your father . . .'

'What about him?'

'It's just that he's already told Matthew he'd like to

contribute to some of the costs of the wedding. I don't know how happy he'll be about . . . well, about the chances of his money possibly going to waste. You know, if there's a repeat of what happened with Licky.'

'There isn't going to be a repeat. And obviously I have to help Lara with her wedding plans. I'm her best friend! Have been for the last twenty-odd years, in fact,' I add, pointedly.

'I suppose that is true.'

I give up. 'Look, I have to go now, Mum.' I ring the doorbell outside Lara's flat. 'I'll call you later, OK?'

'OK, darling, but do mention to Lara that you think it'd be really nice if she decided to have a little flower-girl . . . I mean, even if Hypatia's only eighteen months when they get married, she could probably toddle up the aisle in a pretty dress. And Daria wouldn't be able to say no to that, would she, if Lara was begging her . . .?'

'Will do, Mum. Bye!'

It's only a couple of moments before Lara opens the door.

'Iz?' She blinks at me. 'I had no idea you were coming!'

She's wearing her usual at-home outfit of yoga pants, vest and reading glasses, her hair hoicked into a topknot with an ancient scrunchie, but she looks . . . it's hard to describe . . . all kind of glowy, and radiant, and . . .

I gasp. 'Are you *pregnant*?'

'What?' She hauls me indoors, I think before her upstairs neighbours, an elderly Catholic couple who already disapprove of her cohabiting with Matthew before marriage, can hear anything. 'For crying out loud, Iz, one step at a time!'

'So you're *not*? Pregnant, I mean.'

'No. I'm not. What makes you think I am?' She grabs her stomach, suddenly self-conscious. 'Oh, God, am I *fat*?'

'No, you're not fat.'

'Matthew cooked me bacon and eggs for breakfast, that might have made me a bit bloated.'

'You're not bloated.' I close her front door behind us and follow her through to the kitchen. 'You just look extremely pretty, that's all. *Glowing*. But it must just be the engagement.'

'Oh, Iz.' Lara turns to me, her hands up to her face. She may be looking exceptionally pretty right now but she's so tiny and blonde that this particular expression can't help but make her resemble Macaulay Culkin in *Home Alone*. 'Oh, Iz, I don't know what to say.'

'About what?'

'*You* know . . . what we thought when you found the ring . . . and I know the ring was meant to be yours.' She sits down heavily at the kitchen table. 'I've told Matthew it might be better if he went and bought a different ring.'

'Lara! That's ridiculous!' I sit down opposite her and grab for her left hand. 'It looks amazing on you,' I say, staring down at the sapphire glittering on her

213

finger. 'Honestly, it suits you far better than it was ever going to suit me!'

This is true, by the way. Not only does the bright, intense blue of the single sapphire work brilliantly with her skin tone, but the ring's proportions are much better on Lara's delicate little hand than they would have been on my oversized one.

'Really?'

'Really. And come on, Lars, let's cheer up about all this a bit! I mean, you and me are going to be sisters-in-law, for God's sake! How brilliant is that? After all these years of me being the lone voice in my family's wilderness, now you're going to be there with me. We'll be like . . . like Princess Di and Fergie!'

Lara's eyes widen. 'Both divorced and one of us dying a tragic death in Paris?'

'No! They ganged up against the royal family, didn't they?'

'Oh . . . yes, I see.' She looks a bit uncertain. 'But you know, I can be on your side, Iz, without actually having to *gang up* against anyone.'

I wave a hand. 'That's not really important right now. The main thing is that you've been dreaming about marrying my stupid brother since you were fourteen . . .'

'And a half.'

'. . . and now all your dreams have come true! So you've got to chill out about Nana Hamilton's ring. I just made a silly mistake about it, that's all. Let's face it, it's not even as if I wanted Will to propose!'

'But I thought, outside St Joseph's, you said –'

'And there's so many more important and exciting things to discuss!' I get up and start to fill the kettle. 'Can I make some tea, and then we can start going over some of the basics?'

'Basics?'

'Yup.' I switch the kettle on and sit back down, reaching into my tote for the Smythson stuff I put there earlier. 'Now, this is your engagement present from me, as your best friend,' I explain, handing over one of the slim blue boxes, 'but it's also what I give my brand-new clients at our very first meeting.'

Lara blinks. 'What brand-new clients?'

'Well, you're the first, obviously. But I thought it might be a nice gesture, for me to hand each of my brides a Smythson notebook on the first day, no? I mean, you're pretty much my guinea pig on this one, Lars.' I lean forward. 'Open it! Have a look! Tell me what you think.'

'Oh . . . well, it's a really nice thing to do.' Lara, prompted by my stare, starts to open her box to reveal her pink notebook. 'It's lovely, Iz! And very useful, I'm sure.'

'Exactly!' I take my own notebook out of its box and turn to the first page. 'So. I think we need to start with a bit of a getting-to-know-you chat, don't you? So I can begin to work out the kind of things you like, that you don't like.'

'Getting to know me?' Lara actually giggles. 'Iz, you've known me since I was six.'

'Yes, as your friend. Not as your wedding planner. And over the next few months, Lars, there are going to be times when I need to be your wedding planner first and your friend second.'

She nods solemnly. 'I see. And will you let me know when those times are, so I can prepare myself? I mean, it could be awkward if I got it confused.'

I glare at her. 'You're not taking this seriously.'

'I'm sorry.' She gets up and starts to make the tea. 'I just didn't realise that you were thinking of coming on board as our wedding planner.'

I clear my throat. 'Don't you want me to?'

'Oh, it's not that! It's just . . . well, I don't know what we can afford at the moment, Iz, and I wouldn't feel comfortable having you do this without us paying you.'

'You don't need to pay me! Look, Lars, this is a terrific opportunity for me to start up on my own. Just think of all the experience I'll be gaining! Not to mention the fact that planning my best friend's wedding is worth far more to me than money.'

'You're so sweet. But are you sure we even *need* a wedding planner? I mean, we're only thinking of a very simple ceremony, and a low-key reception for close friends and family.'

I roll my eyes, knowingly. 'Lara. Simple, low-key weddings are neither simple nor low-key to organise.'

'Aren't they?' Lara looks alarmed.

'No. In fact, often they're by far the most complicated. I mean, you want your day to be special, don't you, even if you're trying to keep it fuss-free?'

'But it will be special, no matter what.' Lara's got that glowy thing going on again, as she sits down with the pot of tea. 'I'm marrying Matthew!'

Oh dear. I can see that we're going to have a few problems here. Time to start getting down to brass tacks. 'Look, let's just get a few of the details down, and then we can see where we are. So, you're Miss Lara Alliston . . .' I'm about to start writing this down in my notebook when I hesitate. 'Or would you prefer "*Ms*"?'

'Well, technically, it's "Dr".'

I just write 'Lara'. 'And you're marrying . . .?'

'Matthew Bookbinder. That's B-o-o-k –'

'Now, your preferred date,' I interrupt. 'Do you see yourself as a summer bride? A winter bride?'

'Oh, a summer bride, definitely.'

I glance up at her. 'Really? Because summer weddings really aren't all they're cracked up to be, you know. Either you get all geared up for a beautiful day and it buckets down, or it hits thirty degrees before lunch and everyone is either passing out, getting sunburn, or sweating unattractively in the wedding photos. Plus the really popular wedding venues can be booked in the summer months up to two years in advance.'

'Oh, well, I don't want sweaty wedding photos, obviously. But the venue shouldn't be a problem. I mean, Matthew and I were already thinking it might suit us best to have the reception at The Beeches, in the garden.'

217

'At your *mother's* house?'

'Yes, she offered when I called her to let her know we were engaged.' Lara rolls her eyes. '*You* know my mother, Iz. Offering us her house is her way of pretending she's got involved, without actually having to put in any time or effort. And I know it's a bit fraught in some ways, but Dad and Melinda won't have a problem going there, and I don't think Clarrie or Cassie will mind. And Stefan would come to my wedding even if I was planning to host it at the gates of hell, so the only person I think it'd be tricky for is The Brad, and I'm not even completely sure I'm going to be inviting him anyway.'

That little collection of names she's just reeled off, apart from Melinda, her dad's current wife, are The Ghosts of Step-parents Past. And not a Wicked one amongst them, unless you count The Brad, who wasn't so much Wicked as Texan, which wasn't really his fault, and Loud and Overbearing, which, I suppose, was. And Lara, bless her, has managed to negotiate such good relationships with all of them that she wants them all at her wedding.

I suppose this is where Mum's fears about Lara's complicated family situation may be just the tiniest bit justified.

'But . . . er . . . I thought your mum hated Stefan. Is she really going to welcome him into the house she spent most of their marriage trying to throw him out of?'

'Catherine can lump it.' Lara's face hardens, the

218

way it often does when she talks about her mother for too long. 'We all know the main reason she's got such a problem with Stefan is that he's the one who brought me up while she was flying around the world attending her medical shin-digs and picking up Texans.'

While this may be a tiny bit harsh with regard to Catherine, who I've always rather liked – I mean, it was only the *one* Texan she ever picked up, to my knowledge – Lara is certainly right about poor Stefan. He was the one who attended her parents' evenings, the one who waited with her patiently in the school car park on the day the A-level results came out, keeping her calm with a flask of camomile tea and his home-made kipferls, and the one there with a shoulder to cry on when her anticipated four A grades were actually three As and a B.

'Anyway, I think the least she can do is let us have The Beeches for the wedding,' Lara is continuing. 'I doubt she'll take very much interest in the rest of the wedding. Though she did say she'd like to arrange a dinner with your parents when I called her yesterday, can you believe it?'

'Oh, well, that's something I could sort out for you!' I offer, seeing a golden opportunity to get in at the early stages and silence Dad as to whether I'm capable of organising successful events. 'Barney could cater!'

Lara sips her tea dubiously. 'Don't you think Catherine and your parents under the same roof is going to be a stressful enough experience as it is?'

'Oh, he'll be fine. You know how terrific his food is.' When he's not drowning fluffy bunnies in their own blood, that is. 'Come on, Lars, let me arrange this for you. Look, Mum's going to insist on some kind of meeting with Catherine anyway, so we're much better off maintaining the control.'

She sighs. 'All right. But can you liaise with Catherine about this? I mean, if there's one favour you can do me, as my wedding planner, it's keeping my mother at arm's length.'

'No problem.' I make a note in my wedding book. 'Well, OK, then, if you're set on having the reception at The Beeches, we could probably manage a summer wedding. An English country garden theme, perhaps . . .' Well, I might as well give Lara one of the ideas I had for my own wedding. It's not as if I have any use of it. 'Flowers arranged in mismatching teacups and jam jars, an old-fashioned marquee, you in something bias-cut and beaded, maybe a vintage lace shawl . . . I'd better get us a couple of appointments at Tania Packham and Sassi Holford,' I add, making another note. 'You'll have to let me know how your diary's looking for the next couple of weeks.'

'For dress-shopping?' Lara has finished her tea and is glancing at her watch as though she'd really like to be getting back to typing up her clinical notes, or *Loose Women*, or whatever it is she actually does on her days working from home. 'Can't we just have a mooch around Chiltern Street one lunchtime?'

'Lara! We need to schedule in some proper appointments!' My phone has started ringing; it's a mobile number I don't recognise so I'm not about to touch it in case it's another of Frankie Miller's cohorts calling to leave me a death threat. 'Not to mention the fact that there's going to be a long waiting list at some of the best places.'

'Aren't you going to get that?'

I shake my head. 'You're my bride, Lara. I am one hundred per cent focused on you at all times.'

'I'll settle for ninety-five per cent. And I've got a lot to be getting on with myself, anyway.' Without warning, she picks up the phone herself, ignoring my flapping hands. 'Isabel Bookbinder's office, how may I help you? . . . Yes . . . yes . . . she's right here. Someone called Summer Shelley,' she mouths at me, handing the phone over.

'*Summer Shelley*?' Whoops. I didn't mean to say that actually into the phone itself. 'Hi, Summer! This is Isabel. How are you?'

'I'm good!' It's Summer's tinkly American – sorry, *Canadian* – voice, sweet as apple pie – sorry, maple syrup.

'How can I help you?'

'Well, I've had a bit of a . . . I guess you'd call it a setback. Regarding my wedding. Actually, regarding my planner.'

'Mm-hmm, mm-hmm.' I'm trying to sound super-casual. 'That sounds unfortunate.'

'Yeah. And I guess I'd really like to speak to you about some stuff. See if maybe you can take the reins.'

'Sure, Summer.' My voice may be casual but my heart, banging away in my ribcage, isn't getting the message. 'That sounds good. Would you like to schedule a meeting?'

'Oh, that'd be great, Izzie. Can you come over tomorrow morning?'

'Tomorrow morning?'

'Yeah, I know it's really short notice, but . . . well, that's the issue I'm dealing with.'

Oh, *I* get it.

Lara may not be pregnant, but it sounds a lot like Summer Shelley is.

'You can just bring over the presentation you took to Wendy's,' she's going on. 'I mean, that all sounded pretty great. Can you come to my house at around ten tomorrow?'

'Yes, that's absolutely fine.'

'Oh, and it can just be you, if that's easier. It doesn't have to be Peppa as well, not at this kind of notice.'

'Peppa?'

'Oh, I'm sorry, I'm crap with names. Your boss?'

'*Pippa*.'

Of course. Summer has no idea I don't work for Pippa Everitt any more.

Well, my new job status isn't something I'm going to start trying to explain over the phone. I'll tell Summer all about it tomorrow, face to face. I mean, not *all* about it, obviously. Probably not the best way to start things out with a new bride, filling her in on every detail of the last wedding I botched.

'Yeah, I knew it was something like that. So, I'll see you tomorrow, Izzie, yeah?' She gives me an address with a swanky SW3 postcode, before blowing a noisy kiss down the phone. 'Love ya loads!'

'Er, same here,' I say, as Summer hangs up.

Lara is grinning at me. 'Does this mean you'll only be giving me fifty per cent of your focus?'

I'm already getting to my feet, conscious that my presentation could do with a lot more work. 'Absolutely not! But I really need to get going now, Lars, if that's OK with you? I mean, I think we've made some good progress already, and I'm going to leave these magazines here for you to have a good look at.'

'It's fine. Honestly, Iz. I want you to focus on your other clients more than me, OK? I mean, you've been so great, so understanding . . .'

I give her a quick hug and head for the door. 'Don't you worry about a thing, Lara. It's all completely under my control!'

Chapter Thirteen

The swanky-sounding SW3 address Summer gave me is tucked away down a particularly quiet side street a stone's throw from the King's Road. It's a pretty pink-painted terraced house of the kind that I think are called artisans' cottages, even though the average artisan would have to sell his entire family into slavery to afford just one mortgage payment on the thing.

I'm fifteen minutes early, so I lurk around for a bit until one of the neighbours opens her door and very pointedly stares out in my direction while talking on her phone, presumably to Chelsea Neighbourhood Watch to tell them an interloper is hanging about outside with a big bag containing all kinds of breaking-and-entering equipment. So before I'm hauled off in an unmarked Range Rover, blindfolded with a pastel pashmina and beaten about the head with Mulberry handbags, I decide it's probably best if I just ring the bell and ask Summer if I can come in.

Anyway, if Nosy Neighbour actually challenged me about what was in my huge bag, I'd have been quite happy to show her. It's just filled with all the bits and bobs I sorted out yesterday afternoon and evening, so that I'd have something really good to bring Summer

224

Shelley for our first official meeting. I've brought her a Smythson wedding notebook, of course, and I picked up another round of those bridal magazines, despite the fact that I can barely afford either them, or the osteopath's appointments I'm going to need after lugging them about all morning. I've also brought along my whole presentation, with the tweaks and adjustments I made to it last night.

I have to say, I can only hope Summer appreciates the hard work I've gone to, because it managed to make me distinctly unpopular with Will. He came back home bearing wine, flowers and yummy treats for dinner from my favourite Lebanese deli only to find me chained to my desk the whole night. Metaphorically chained, that is. Not literally. Not in a sexy we've-just-moved-in-together-and-this-is-my-housewarming-gift-to-you kind of way.

'Go away!' Summer's voice suddenly comes out of the intercom next to the buzzer. 'I'm not coming outside!'

'Er, Summer?'

'Yeah?'

'It's me. Isabel.'

'Oh, *Isabel*! I'm so sorry.' There's a buzz and a click as the front door opens. 'Come on in!'

I avoid the temptation to turn round and give Nosy Neighbour a cheery wave, and go on through.

Looking around, I can tell straight away that this place must belong to Sir Peter and Lady Holland, Tim's parents. I'm in a rather dingy hallway, done up in a heavily dated fashion, all William Morris wallpaper, fitted carpet, and that kind of expensive furniture – a console table, a large chest, a hat-stand – that seems to be carved from solid oak. There are touches of Summer around, though, in the python-skin Zagliani handbag strewn across the console and the pink baker-boy hat hooked on to the hat-stand . . .

Oh, and the fact that she's bouncing down the stairs to greet me.

'Hey!' She flings herself at me for a hug, squashing her ample chest into mine. 'Sorry about that, yelling at you over the intercom. I just thought you were paparazzi, you see.'

'That's OK.'

She pulls a face, rolling her heavily mascara'd eyes. 'How many of them did you see out there? Three? Four?'

I haven't the heart to tell her the truth. 'Oh, er, yes. Three. At least. I think they were headed round the corner, though,' I yelp, as she makes as if to open the door and peer outside. 'Probably got bored with waiting.'

She looks slightly downcast for a moment, then perks up again. 'Anyway, it's great that you're here, Izzie! Won't you come through so I can fix you something to drink?' She leads the way through the hall into a sitting room, complete with Liberty-print curtains and a velvet Chesterfield, and finally to a big kitchen at the back. This is done out in that slightly peculiar way rich people often have their kitchens, with all kinds of mismatching units and a huge range cooker – the only slightly jarring note being the big treadmill positioned next to the fridge.

'Oh, just like me! I keep my Power Plate in my kitchen,' I explain. 'Well, in my old kitchen. I live with my boyfriend now and he's made me put it in to the spare bedroom.'

'Oh, I only just moved it in here. And right next to the refrigerator, so if I'm tempted to snack on anything, I make myself do twenty minutes on the treadmill first.' She pats it. 'Aren't you pleased?'

'Um, pleased?'

'So I'm in great shape for the wedding!' She looks rather hurt as she passes me a mini bottle of mineral water from the fridge and opens one herself. 'I thought you were meant to be taking a close personal interest in that kind of stuff.'

'Of course, I'm sorry. But you're already in great shape, Summer!' This is true. And even in her skintight leggings and hot-pink vest, there's not yet the slightest sign of her baby bump. 'You really mustn't worry too much about that kind of thing. Especially not now!'

'*Especially* now!' Summer corrects me, hopping up on to the treadmill. 'Hey, would you mind if we did this meeting while I do a little bit of a workout? It's just that I've got this really hectic morning, with you, and with this guy from the TV company, and I won't get a chance to burn off my breakfast otherwise.'

'No, that's fine . . . but what was that about a TV company?'

'Oh, yeah, that's right. I should tell you about that.' She pushes a couple of buttons on the treadmill and sets about a fast walk, pumping her arms behind and in front. 'Wendy's got me my own reality show, can you believe it?'

'A reality show?' I stare at her. 'All about you?'

'Yeah! It's gonna be on Living TV!' She beams at me, unable to suppress her excitement. 'A six-part series, all about my preparations for the wedding. I'm telling them I think we should call it *A Summer Wedding*,' she continues, 'because then if I get another series it could be all about, like, me going on holiday, and we could call that one *A Summer Holiday* –'

'Or the next one could be about your pregnancy,' I interrupt, getting a bit carried away with the excitement of all this. I mean, does this mean *I'm* going to be on this TV show? Because that would be the most incredible publicity for Isabel Bookbinder: Individual Weddings! 'And then obviously you'd call it *A Summer Baby*!'

'*Ewwww*.' Summer wrinkles her nose, disgusted. 'I don't want to get pregnant, Izzie! Not even for a cool TV show title!'

'So . . . you're not pregnant now?'

Now her eyes widen in abject horror. 'Are you saying I look *fat*?'

'No! Christ, no!' I really need to find a better way of asking that question. 'Look, I just assumed that it might be the reason you wanted to move the wedding forward.'

'Because I'm *pregnant*? Before I'm even *married*? Lord, Izzie, what on earth do you think of me?'

'I'm sorry. I didn't mean to offend you. I was just wondering what your reasons might be. None of my business, really.'

'Oh, well, it's this whole sex tape business, of course.'

I stare at her. Her fast walk becomes a slow jog. I clear my throat. 'And this would be . . . *your* sex tape?'

She nods. 'Uh-huh. Wendy got this call a couple nights ago from some guy trying to sell her a tape of me, you know, doing it with him. Well, I'm gonna tell Tim it's just *some guy* but actually it's this guy I used to go out with,' she adds, as though her fiancé might prefer the idea that his wife-to-be filmed herself shagging a random stranger rather than somebody she was actually in a relationship with. 'Two hundred grand he's looking for! Can you believe it?'

I'm not sure there's any good way to answer that question. 'Well, I suppose that when people know you're marrying into money, they all come crawling out of the woodwork.'

'Crawling out of the woodwork is right. Anyway, Wendy thinks this guy's a real slimeball . . .'

'Understandably.'

'. . . and that even if we offer him what he's asking, he might just go ahead and post the tape on the internet anyway. Which is why the quicker I'm safely married, the better.'

'You don't think Tim will marry you if he knows about the tape?'

'Oh, no, it's not that. Tim's cool with it. The problem is his mother.'

She says the words 'his mother' like some people might say the words 'rat infestation'.

'I mean, you can see the kind of woman she is.' Summer waves a hand. 'Just look at this place! When I first saw it, I was so excited to be living in this cute little pink English cottage, and I thought I'd have such fun doing it all up *my* way. You know, really put my stamp on the place?'

'Yes, of course. Like, putting in a wet-room. That kind of thing.'

'Exactly! I mean, it's meant to be my home too, now. But she won't have it. I'm not allowed to touch so much as a scrap of this lousy wallpaper. Until I'm the new Mrs Holland, apparently, I don't get to do what I want. And it's not just that, Izzie . . .' She's warming to her theme, and I wonder again if she's got any actual girlfriends over here to share this kind of stuff with. 'We have to go for lunch with the whole family *every* *Sunday* – it's like an *order* or something . . . and I just have to sit there while she totally ignores me, and his snooty sisters make little comments to her about what I'm wearing – like hotpants are *totally* inappropriate for a family lunch, or something. I mean, for Chrissakes, it's not like I've turned up naked!'

'Mmm.' I make my very best sympathetic agreement noise. 'Well, they do sound like the kind of people to object to a sex tape.'

'Exactly! She doesn't want me marrying Tim anyway, so she'll latch on to anything to stop it going ahead. I mean, she's told Tim they're only prepared to fork out a million pounds to pay for this wedding! People with their kind of money! Isn't that ridiculous?'

'Ridiculous,' I echo, feeling my way to a seat at the (solid oak) table, and sitting down very suddenly in it.

This wedding has a budget of *a million quid*? I mean, I suppose if I'd stopped to think about it, I'd have assumed it was hardly going to be strung together on a wing and a prayer – after all, this is Tim Holland, scion of multimillionaires, that we're talking about.

But if the standard fee for a wedding planner is ten per cent of the total budget . . .

I'll be getting a *hundred grand* for my first ever paying wedding job?

I haven't earned a hundred grand, total, in my entire working life so far.

'Oh, no, are *you* worrying about our budget, too?' Summer is staring at me, the corners of her lipglossed mouth downturned as she continues her jog. 'That was one of the other planner's big issues.'

'Henry Irwin, you mean?'

'Uh-huh. When Wendy told him we'd need to move the wedding forward, he said we couldn't possibly do the wedding we want as quickly as we need it without sticking a sweetener on for all the suppliers. You know, offering to pay them fifty per cent more to get them to fit us in at short notice?'

'Yes . . . but honestly, Summer, I really think that even if that's the case, we should be able to arrange everything you want within that budget.'

Summer gives a slightly breathless whoop. 'I *knew* you'd say that! I think he was just trying to hustle us, you know? I mean, he was trying to demand twenty per cent of the budget for his fee, can you believe it?'

'No, I mean, ten per cent is more than reasonable . . .'

'Really? 'Cos we were already going to pay him fifteen per cent, so I kind of assumed you'd be wanting the same?' Summer flaps a hand. 'Oh, well, you sort all that out with Wendy. I'm not that bothered, Izzie, as long as you get me the day of my dreams.'

'Of course,' I bleat, feeling slightly wobbly at the prospect of even more cash being chucked at me. I reach down by my feet for my bag, to get the Agreement and the notebooks out. 'So, we should probably start talking about a few of the specifics, try to lock down a decent venue for . . . well, what date were you looking at?'

'October the seventeenth.'

I drop my bag to the floor. '*October* the seventeenth? But Summer, that's . . .' I do a rapid calculation in my head, '. . . three and a half weeks away!'

232

'Wow. I guess it is. That's really soon, huh?'

'It's really, *really* soon. I don't even think I could find you a venue that would have availability in that time.'

'Oh, yeah, that was Henry's big problem. He had us all booked in at this place called Cliff's Den.'

'Cliveden,' I translate.

'Oh, yeah. But that was when we were thinking of late August next year. Henry said he didn't know where in the hell he was going to be able to fit us in this October.'

I stare at her, wondering why she's sounding quite so complacent about this fact. And then it dawns on me. She doesn't intend to get worried about it. I'm the wedding planner. She's paying me to get worried about it.

'OK . . .' I take a deep, calming breath. 'Well, maybe the best place for me to start is to call around some of the nicer venues. There's just a chance there might have been a last-minute cancellation –'

'I don't want some other girl's sloppy seconds!' Summer's pretty face has formed into a dangerous-looking pout. 'Look, can't you just get Peppa to pull in a few favours?'

'Peppa?'

'Your boss! Peppa!'

Oh, shit. The Pippa issue.

'I mean, Henry Irwin said she was the only person he could think of who'd be able to do a decent job in the time available. And you know, Izzie, I would have called Peppa herself, but I thought you and me had a bit of a connection.' Her voice has hardened slightly, to match the pout. 'But if you don't think you're the right person to take the lead on this, then I can just call Peppa and get her to take over.'

'No! I mean, no, don't call Peppa. Pippa.' I'm not about to blow my huge chance – the TV exposure, the pay cheque, the proper *client*, for Christ's sake – by letting Summer call Pippa and find out that I'm kind of a renegade. 'Look, Summer, I'm quite sure that I can arrange things just the way you want them, OK?'

'You can get me my Hollywood wedding?'

'Yes.' Well, it's going to be as manageable as anything else is in less than one month.

'And you can still arrange all that other stuff you were talking about? The personal training, and the therapy sessions?'

Oh God. Bride Management. 'I'm sure we can work something out.'

Summer punches the air and gives a little whoop as she speeds up to a faster run. 'That's great,' she puffs. 'OK, so I'll have Wendy link you up with my schedule. Then you just start filling it up with whatever you think we need. You say I need Botox, I get Botox. You say I need colonic irrigation, I get colonic irrigation.'

'Well, I suppose I was thinking more of some regular pedicures and a weekly deep hair treatment,' I mumble.

'Yeah, yeah, that too. But I want the works, yeah? The whole package. I'm completely in your hands, Izzie.'

I'm wondering if the most sensible thing I can put into Summer's schedule the minute I'm out of here is a week at a Bikini Boot Camp in Arizona, or daily sessions with a life coach. Because I have this concern – OK, OK, this full-blown panic – that Summer is not, perhaps, quite the easy-going bride I'd imagined her to be.

There's a sudden, sharp buzz from out in the hallway that makes me jump, and Summer gasp with excitement.

'Ooh, that'll be Wendy with my TV producer! Would you go and let them in, Izzie? I really need to get another ten minutes in on this thing, wouldn't you agree?'

'Oh, yes, ten more minutes. Keep it up! Er – you go, girl!' I say, trying to disguise the fact that right now, I couldn't actually care less whether she uses the next ten minutes to run on her treadmill or to stuff her face with Ben and Jerry's Phish Food. It seems to work, because she gives me another of her little whoops as I head to open the front door.

Standing there is a skinny young man with a rather straggly beard, wearing an earnest expression that looks like he's right at this moment attempting to work out whether his doctoral dissertation should be on eighteenth-century French literature or child poverty during the Industrial Revolution. And next to him is Wendy Gordon, wearing an expression that looks like she's right at this moment attempting to swallow an entire wasp.

'Oh God, I should have remembered you were going to be here.' Wendy pushes past. 'This is the

235

producer from Zenith TV,' she adds, jerking her head in Weirdy-Beardy's direction.

'Zenith?'

He winces visibly. 'I'm not *from* Zenith TV, I'm a freelancer. I've done work for the BBC,' he adds, as he comes through the door in Wendy's wake, 'and several other extremely highly regarded independent production companies . . . but you know, it's tough out there . . .'

'Hey, it's fine,' I assure him, before he can produce an actual copy of his CV to prove that he doesn't spend all his time making tat for obscure production companies. 'I just thought Summer said the show was going to be on the Living channel.'

'Well, that all depends on who we can get to buy the show from us.' Weirdy-Beardy prickles defensively, behind his facial hair. 'I mean, Zenith *does* sell things to Living sometimes. I'm sure once we've finished the show . . .'

'It's OK,' I tell him. 'You don't have to butter me up. I'm just the wedding planner.'

'Oh, right. I assumed you were a friend, or something.' He looks relieved for a moment, an expression that is quickly replaced by astonishment as we head into the kitchen, to see Summer on her treadmill, by now striding up a sharp incline towards the fridge.

'Hey!' Summer gives him a flirty little wave, as though she's passing by on a brisk cliff-top stroll. 'Sven, right? Good to see you again.'

'It's . . . great to see you.' Weirdy-Beardy's – sorry, *Sven's* – mouth is half-open, though whether it's surprise at Summer's incongruous treadmill session, or lust at her bobbling, bouncing breasts beneath the pink vest, it's impossible to tell. I'll give him the benefit of the doubt and assume it's surprise, mostly because he looks like his usual type of woman is a vegan Goth reading Moral Philosophy at Brighton University.

'You've met my wedding planner, Isabel?' Summer goes on. 'I guess you'll want to be talking to her a lot throughout this whole filming process. And, Izzie, you should make sure you're keeping Sven in the loop with all your plans. I want my film crew to have completely unrestricted access, OK? And if that means I'm the first person to have colonic irrigation on national television, then so be it.'

'Actually, I think a couple of people may have already beaten you to that,' I say.

'Oh.' Summer glances at Wendy. 'Well, can *you* think of anything I can get done for this wedding that'll be a first on national television?'

'We'll come up with something, darling, don't you worry about that.' Wendy is taking a packet of cigarettes out of her handbag. 'Isabel, will you come and join me outside for a quick smoke break while Sven and Summer have a bit of a chat?'

'Actually, I don't smoke . . .'

'You don't have to. I just like the company.' She's holding the back door open for me. 'Makes me feel like less of a social outcast for my nicotine habit.'

I can tell I'm not going to get out of this one.

I follow her outside on to the patio, counting the seconds before she says something aggressive. One . . . two . . .

'So. I see you got what you wanted, then.'

Three. Just as I suspected.

'Sorry?'

'Summer. It worked. Ambushing her in the Wedding Shop.'

'I didn't ambush anyone.' I take a deep breath, which is a mistake, because Wendy has just lit her cigarette. Once I've stopped coughing, I continue. 'Anyway, how could I possibly have known Henry Irwin was going to back out when Summer changed her time-scale?' I'm tempted to add that with less than four weeks' notice, Wendy should be grateful they're getting a wedding planner at all, but I don't want to anger the beast.

Still, she almost seems to know what I'm thinking, because she suddenly says, 'I had meetings fixed up with two other planners for today, you know? Jenny Jones said she'd be happy to work with us. And Maureen Brady was going to bump a couple of her weddings on to one of her assistants so that she could give us her full care and attention for the next four weeks, if we wanted it.'

Shit, those are two extremely well-known wedding planners she's just mentioned. And it sounds like Wendy would be only too happy to send Summer's wedding their way instead of mine.

'That's nice,' I say evenly, 'but there aren't any

substitutes for the terrific feeling a bride gets when she really *likes* her wedding planner. And Summer and I are getting on so well already, it would probably be a mistake to try your luck with a planner who's not even met her yet. Personality clashes can be dreadful things.'

'Hmmm. Well, Summer does seem to like you,' she says, her tone making it quite clear that this is nothing but a source of irritation to her. 'And I've heard good things about Pippa Everitt Weddings, so I suppose we can rely on you to produce the kind of wedding we need. Even if you do still insist on fannying about with all that Bride Management crap.'

'It really isn't crap, Wendy. In fact, I think you'll find –'

'Yeah, yeah. So, I guess Summer has told you she's prepared to pay ten per cent of the total budget?'

'Actually, she had mentioned . . . yes. Ten per cent,' I say, hastily, as Wendy puts her wasp-chewing face back on again. I'm not going to risk angering Dragon Lady any more than I already have by pushing for the extra dosh. 'That all sounds fine.'

'OK, then.' She blows out a cloud of smoke. 'So, let's have a look at Pippa's contract, then.'

'What?'

'Her contract,' Wendy repeats, her eyes narrowing. 'I assume she usually likes her clients to sign one? And I assume she's not dozy enough to send you out to an important meeting without bringing one with you?'

Shit.

'Er . . . it might be easier for me – for her – to just send you one in the post –,' I begin, but Wendy interrupts.

'Bloody hell, Isabel, do you really think we have all the time in the world to get this locked down?' She starts rifling in her bag for her mobile. 'I'll get one of my couriers to head over to her office and pick one up later this afternoon . . .'

'No! I mean, there's no need for that!' I'm scrabbling in my own bag now, hoping against hope that I might still have one of those copies of Pippa's Agreement I took away to study while I was still working for her. Oh, thank God – they're still here. Slightly scrunched and battered, but still here. 'Silly me – I did bring one with me after all!' I say, handing it over and feeling a flood of relief as some of the suspicion ebbs away from Wendy's face. 'I'm sure you'll find it's all totally standard!'

Wendy studies it for a moment. 'You want fifty per cent of your commission paid upfront?'

'Well, that is normal practice within the industry . . .'

'Fine.' She folds the Agreement in two. 'I'll get Summer to sign it before you leave. And I'm sure Tim can pay the money later today.'

'He can access fifty grand just like that?' I can't help blurting.

Wendy shoots me a look of scorn. 'Fuck's sake, Isabel, this is Tim *Holland* we're talking about. He carries three grand cash everywhere he goes in case he fancies calling up his dealer. Do *not* tell anyone I said that,' she adds, fiercely, as though I'm about to send a text message to the *News of the World* revealing that Tim Holland might not have kicked the drugs after all. 'Now, would Pippa prefer a cheque for her fee, or is a bank transfer more convenient? And I assume she has some kind of client account for the rest of the actual wedding budget to go into, so she can pay suppliers out of that herself?'

Oh bloody hell. I hadn't thought about any of this. But she's right. I am going to need to pay a shedload of people if this wedding is ever going to get off the ground, and it's not like I have the best part of a million quid sitting around in petty cash to get the ball rolling.

'Not a cheque,' I say hastily. 'Definitely not a cheque.' The last thing I need is a useless cheque written out to Pippa Everitt that I won't be able to pay in anywhere. On the other hand, if I give her the details of my own current or savings account, it's going to be pretty obvious that the money isn't being paid to Pippa Everitt either. 'Actually, the way we usually do things is that each of Pippa's staff operates out of their own separate work account.' I can feel sweat condensing in my armpits. 'So why don't I give you those details to pass on to Tim?'

Wendy is eyeing me the way I imagine a stalking lioness regards her still-living lunch. 'That sounds odd.'

'Oh God, no, not at all! It's quite usual, in fact.

241

Many wedding planners, Pippa amongst them, feel it's the best way to give their staff total freedom and creativity . . . a sense of responsibility . . . project management . . . stakeholders . . .' I tail off as I run out of jargon.

Wendy carries on eyeing me for a long moment, then she stubs her cigarette out on the nearby wall. 'All right, then. Anything to get this bloody juggernaut moving. But I'll want to see detailed invoices and records of all the payments you make. Understood?'

'Totally! Completely reasonable!' My hand is shaking, slightly, as I type the details of my savings account into the BlackBerry she shoves at me. I'm trying not to think about the reaction at the computer terminals of the Abbey when my ancient account, that has been on famine rations of no more than four hundred quid since Dad made me open it the day after I turned eighteen, is suddenly engorged with hundreds of thousands of Holland family dosh. 'And I want you to know, Wendy, that I – that *we* – will get moving on this right away.'

'You'd better. Summer will want to have her invitations printed and sent out as soon as possible.'

'Or recorded, of course! If she'd like to try the MP3 option,' I add, when she looks at me blankly.

'Christ, Isabel, you're not still banging on about that, are you? When we've only got a few weeks to get this whole bloody thing together?'

'No, of course. Traditional invitations are probably the better option.'

'Too right they're the better option. Now, are we going to have the venue booked before this weekend?'

'Well, I'll certainly do my best!' I can feel sweat beads forming on my upper lip. 'I mean, Pippa and I will do *our collective* best.'

'I suppose I'd better put you into my speed dial,' she adds. 'Oh, and Pippa Everitt's number, too, in case I can't get hold of you in an emergency.'

'Of course!' I give her my mobile number and then just shove a load of plausible-sounding sevens and nines together to construct a fake mobile number for Pippa. 'Though I'd really rather you did everything through me,' I go on, as casually as possible. 'Pippa . . . well, I hate to say it, especially when she's such a terrifically good planner, but she can be a teeny bit of a snob when it comes to these celeb-type weddings. The last thing either of us needs is her upsetting the bride with an ill-judged remark in the run-up to the big day, right?'

'Right.' Wendy is looking at me in a way that, if I were being paranoid, I'd call extremely suspicious. 'That's the last thing we need.'

I leave Wendy smoking, take my leave of Weirdy-Beardy and Summer – something Summer's prepared to let me do only if I swear I'll call her *first thing* tomorrow morning to discuss her schedule – and make my way back out on to the street and up towards the King's Road.

It's only when I'm collapsing with an emergency Frappuccino at Starbucks that I notice the sharp pain on the left side of my neck, and realise that I'm still lugging around the bridal magazines and the Smythson notebook that I was supposed to be giving Summer.

I really hope I'm not going to end up with more reason for a pain in the neck than that.

GMTV, with Kate Garraway and ~~hot~~ Ben Shephard, 14 July

KATE GARRAWAY Now, we come to the next stage of this year's GMTV Interactive Wedding competition! We've whittled our three possible brides-to-be down from over seven thousand entries, and today we're asking you, the viewers, to vote on your favourite couple who will then win the wedding of their dreams!

BEN SHEPHARD But one thing you don't have to vote on is the ~~lady girl~~ woman who'll be making this dream wedding possible – and that's Top Wedding Planner Isabel Bookbinder, who joins us in the studio now.

KATE Yes, good morning, Isabel!

ISABEL BOOKBINDER Good morning, Kate. And a very good morning, Ben.

KATE Well, we're extremely excited to have a wedding planner of your ~~fame notoriety~~ calibre organising this year's Interactive Wedding.

ISABEL Thanks, Kate! I can hardly believe I'm here. It all started only a few months ago, when I was asked to plan a wedding for a Canadian ex-pop starlet and an heir to a colossal retail fortune . . .

BEN You mean Summer Shelley and Tim Holland?

ISABEL [fluttering her eyelashes in the direction of square-jawed, broad-shouldered Ben] Oh, Ben, stop it! You know I can't breach my clients' privacy.

BEN [moving just a fraction closer to Isabel on the sofa] And of course, that was just the beginning for you, wasn't it? Ever since then you've been using your incredible talent to plan cutting-edge weddings for a whole host of top celebrities.

ISABEL *[laughing] You're too kind, Ben! All I will say is that I'm currently working with a top American sportsman who's marrying an extremely famous Irish pop star, and planing a fourth wedding for a ~~craggy old~~ veteran rock star who's recently become engaged to a very young supermodel from Slovakia. Or Slovenia. I always have a problem remembering which.*

KATE *Lovely, yes, but obviously today you're here to help the viewers vote on some non-celebrity clients, our three GMTV couples, all hoping to win the wedding of their dreams. Now, in your experience, Isabel, what do you think our viewers should take into account when they vote for one of our couples? Should they be looking for the most amazing meeting, the most romantic first date, the best proposal . . .?*

ISABEL *Well, obviously proposals are extremely important. But at the end of the day, the most important thing is that all three ladies did get a proposal! ~~They didn't have to sit and watch their best friend get the sapphire engagement ring that was~~ So it shouldn't really matter if he pops the question at the top of the Empire State Building, or just asks you over a takeaway pizza in front of The X Factor. The important thing is that your boyfriend asks you to spend the rest of your life with him.*

BEN *[sympathetically, with a hand on Isabel's knee] You sound as though you're speaking from personal experience, Isabel. ~~Perhaps after the show we could grab a coffee and I could offer you a broad shoulder to cry on.~~*

ISABEL *Oh, no, not at all, Ben. I'm far too busy with my*

fabulous wedding planning career to think about my own engagement or wedding at all!

KATE Spoken like a true professional. Well, Isabel, it was great to have you on the show this morning.

ISABEL Thanks so much, Kate.

BEN No, thank you, Isabel. It's been an absolute ~~joy~~ pleasure to have you.

ISABEL And it would be an absolute pleasure to have you.

Ad break

Chapter Fourteen

I'm never one to admit defeat, but I think I may have bitten off just a little bit more than I can chew here.

The three and a half weeks I have to arrange Summer Shelley's wedding have slipped, before my very eyes, into exactly three weeks, and I'm not sure what I've got to show for it.

Actually, scratch that. I know exactly what I've got to show for it. Nothing. Zero. Zilch. Zip. Nada. And whatever other words people use when they mean that three whole days have gone by without making anything that could be considered the smallest amount of progress. Apart from the terrifyingly large amount of money that's now sitting in my savings account, you might not even know I was planning a wedding at all.

Almost two days were taken up on Wednesday and Thursday phoning round practically every suitable venue I could possibly think of – and quite a lot of distinctly unsuitable ones – to see if any of them could squeeze in a wedding for a hundred and fifty guests with twenty-four days' notice. Followed by an entire day yesterday spent trekking to a ruined castle on the Welsh borders whose manager had assured me on the phone that yes, October the seventeenth was free. And I got all excited when I got there too, because the castle was extremely dramatic-looking, with romantic turrety bits, and a moat, and those little slit windows that you can pour boiling oil through, which could come in handier for a wedding than you'd think. So imagine my disappointment when it turned out the manager had misunderstood my request and only had October dates available *two years from now*.

Progress has been equally limited on pretty much every other front, too. Most of the high-end florists wouldn't even take my call until I took the risky option of dropping Pippa's name to one of them, who has agreed to let me have one of her junior florists for the day, as long as the venue is no more than a three-hour drive from central London. It's an even worse story at the top cake-makers, no fewer than three of whom have suggested that I consider buying plain iced fruit cakes from M&S and decorating them with fresh flowers, an idea that will have my credibility with Summer even more ruined than that Welsh border castle. And at the rate I'm going with my trawls through *Spotlight*, the hundred grand or so that Summer has earmarked for a fabulous band is probably better spent on a karaoke machine, a hundred bottles of vodka, and gold-plated earplugs for any guest who doesn't get pissed enough to want to sing.

In fact, *Spotlight* is where I am now, hunched over my laptop on the desk in the spare room, wondering whether or not I should bother contacting this slightly creepy-looking Frank Sinatra tribute act, and avoiding my mobile, which has been ringing on and off for the last five minutes.

I don't want to answer, because I know it's going to be Summer. And the reason I know this is because she's already called me four times this morning, to ask:

1) what she should wear for her first appointment with Kieron, one of the personal trainers at my gym, who's agreed to train Summer at home (about the only concrete thing I've managed to accomplish this week), and whether she'd be better to put her hair up in a ponytail or some really cute bunches;

2) if she should eat a melon medley or a tropical fruit salad for breakfast before she goes;

3) if she should eat *only the watermelon* in the melon medley because she's heard that's meant to be good for banishing water retention and that regular melon is hard to digest; and

4) why I didn't return her call when she left the message about the watermelon in the melon medley, because if I want to preside over a wedding with a bloated bride walking down the aisle, then that's the right way to go about it.

Though she may not have actually used the word 'preside'; it doesn't sound much like Summer, to be fair.

The phone stops ringing and I hear Will speaking into it. Which surprises me until I remember that he knows about only one of Summer's calls this morning: the first one, at eight-fifteen. The one that made him decide to haul himself off for a jog in the park seeing as our Saturday morning lie-in had already been disturbed. He's got no way of knowing that she's called every half-hour since, and that, like a stray dog, it might be best to pretend we haven't noticed her.

And I have to say, if there's one thing that's annoyed me most about Summer this morning, it isn't the inane queries about hairstyling or tropical fruits. It's the fact that she disturbed that Saturday morning lie-in. The first Saturday morning lie-in Will and I would have had since I moved in. I mean, if you believe The White Company catalogue – and really, is there any reason not to? – this was meant to be prime time for that sexy, flirty pillow-fight while wearing crisp pyjama bottoms (him) and matching top (me). And believe me, after the week we've had, a sexy, flirty pillow-fight would have been especially welcome.

It's not that there's anything fundamentally *wrong*, by the way. It's just that I've felt so guilty about being busy this week, and Will's been so eager to encourage me and let me get on with it that we've both ended up being ludicrously polite and considerate towards each other. We're so busy with *I'm-so-sorry-but-would-you-minds* and *don't-worry-not-at-alls* that I don't think we've had a proper conversation all week.

There's a knock on the door, now, and Will pops his head round it. 'Oh, sorry, Iz. I wasn't sure if I was meant to disturb.'

'No, no, don't worry about it! Not a problem.'

He waggles my phone at me. 'That was your number-one client. Sunshine? Sunny?'

'Summer.' I catch the phone as he throws it to me, and put it down on the Power Plate, to the left of the desk. 'What did she want this time?'

'She seemed to be wanting your expertise about the number of calories in something called a melon medley. If that makes sense?'

'Oh, it makes sense.'

'And all I really gathered was that she needs you to call her back to assure her that a calorie is exactly the same thing here as it is in Canada. I mean, I did my best, obviously,' he goes on, 'but she didn't seem to want to hear it from me.'

'Well, thanks for trying. I'll give her a call before I head out.'

'Oh, that's right. You're dress-shopping with Lara today, is that it?'

I nod. 'I'm sorry, I know it's a Saturday, but Lara's busy both of the next two weekends and we do need to make some headway on the gown front.'

'That's OK, Iz. I understand how important this is to you.'

'Well, yes, but I just wanted to say how sorry I am . . .'

'Please. There's no need. It's not like I haven't got

252

about a million emails I need to catch up with. Plus my trainee has made a mess of some drafting, and you know how much I enjoy a good day wrestling with a contract. Oh God, that reminds me, Iz . . . I was wondering if you'd like me to draw up any kind of contract for you? You know, to give to this Summer person of yours – and to any of your future clients, for that matter.'

Probably better not to tell him that actually, I gave Summer Pippa's standard contract. 'Well, yes, we probably should get round to something like that sooner or later . . .'

'Sooner rather than later, Iz!'

'Yes, yes, but there's no real rush. Honestly, Will, most things in the wedding planning business are done by . . . er . . . gentleman's agreement.'

'Gentleman's agreement?' he echoes.

'Or ladies' agreement. I mean, it is a wedding, obviously. And there's no reason to be sexist.'

'Isabel, you can't be serious. How can you guarantee that this Summer girl is going to pay you? How can you be sure she isn't going to take all the ideas you've given her and go off to a rival wedding planner? And come to think of it, now that you're operating your own business, we really should have thought about getting you properly insured.' Will is looking fretful. 'Some kind of public liability insurance, at the very least.'

'I'm not a public liability!'

'No, that's not what I mean . . . Look, I'll do a bit

of research later today, and compare a few rates. Oh God, Iz, I completely forgot to ask – did you get a chance to look over those mortgage deals I left out for you the other day?'

'Yes, I had a quick look.' Which is only *partly* a fib. I mean, I *did* have a quick look, but honestly, I think you'd be amazed at just how truly tedious a mortgage application booklet can be. Low though my expectations were – I mean, it was hardly going to be like flicking through *Grazia*, was it? – I practically gave up the will to live. 'Some very interesting points, I felt . . .' I clear my throat. 'But there's no hurry, is there?'

'Sorry?'

'Well, we had said we were just going to have loads and loads and loads of fun together, when I first moved in. Not that picking out a mortgage *isn't* fun, in its own way! It's just that –'

'Oh God, of course. I'm sorry. Let's forget I even mentioned it.' Will is turning slightly pink.

'Oh, but I don't want to *forget* it. I just thought we could hold off for a little while longer, that's all. It's a big decision.'

'You're right. Like I said. Let's forget I mentioned it.' He takes a deep breath and plasters a slightly strained smile over his face. 'So! Shopping with Lara, hey? That should be entertaining.'

'Yes . . .' I get to my feet. 'In fact, I really ought to be heading off. I need to get to lunch before Lara's mum turns up.'

Will's eyes widen. 'Her *mum* is joining you?'

This is the only potentially dark cloud over the afternoon I've planned in London's finest bridal boutiques with Lara. It's not so much the fact that, somewhat out of the blue, Catherine wants to join us. It's more the fact that I haven't, yet, had the courage to tell Lara about it.

'Isn't Lara going to be a bit pissed off about that?' Will carries on. 'I mean, I've always thought she finds her mother a bit difficult.'

'Yes, OK, she probably is going to be a bit pissed off!' I get up and head for the door. 'But what was I supposed to do? Catherine completely blind-sided me when I called her about the engagement dinner the other day. The only reason I even mentioned dress-shopping to her was because I never thought she'd want to come!'

'Ah. Well, I'm sure it'll all be all right. Nothing a couple of pre-shopping drinks can't cure.'

Yes. He's right. And anyway, Catherine can be a real hoot. Probably it'll be even more fun with her there. Lara's bound to realise that. 'Exactly! We'll have a great time. I mean, it's wedding-dress shopping. How bad can it be?'

'Well, horrific, I'd have thought. But then I'm not you. And for the love of God, Iz, don't come home with a white frock costing three grand and a matching pair of Manolo Choos!'

I blink at him. 'Sorry?'

'Oh, whatever they're called.' He leans down to give me a swift kiss before heading for the shower.

'You know all this wedding malarkey just goes in one ear and out the other, with me!'

By the time I arrive at The Wolseley, where we're meeting for our pre-shopping lunch, I've mulled over Will's parting comment in my mind so many times, I'm starting to wonder if I just imagined it after all.

And even if he *did* say what I think he said, then it's not exactly a big deal. I mean, all he was really saying was that he'd rather I didn't go out and spend three thousand pounds on a big white dress. Well, what man in their right mind would *want* their girlfriend to go out and spend three thousand pounds on a big white dress? That would obviously be a completely crazy thing to do, if you weren't going to be getting married any time soon.

Still. Does he have to make it *quite* so obvious we're not going to be getting married any time soon? What's next – a Valentine's card signed 'Much love, a Confirmed Bachelor'? Loud retching noises every time we walk past a church with a wedding going on? Loud retching noises every time we walk past a couple holding hands, like my first-ever boyfriend Michael used to make?

Or is he just getting his own back on me because I put paid to the idea of the joint mortgage for the time being?

The nice lady on the Wolseley's front desk shows me to our table, where I sit for just a couple of moments trying to spot celebrities – disappointingly thin on the ground this lunchtime, I must say – before I see Lara's mother heading across the room towards me.

Catherine Greene – *Professor* Catherine Greene, to give her the correct title – looks just as fabulous as she did when I last saw her three years ago. Her hair is expertly styled in a chic crop, she's dressed in a beautifully cut navy trouser suit with stylish mannish brogues and an Anya Hindmarch handbag, and the only resemblance to Lara is in her petite frame and in the blue-grey shade – though not the expression – of her eyes. Seeing her sweeping imperiously across the restaurant takes me immediately back fifteen years, to sleepovers at Lara's, when we'd wait up until the small hours for Catherine to come back from her date with whatever man she was seeing at the time. Then she'd sit on the end of our beds, smelling exotically of wine, cigarette smoke, and Mitsouko, and tell us what with hindsight must have been a rather censored version of her evening. I used to absolutely love it. I mean, Mum and Dad's once-yearly anniversary dinner dates, with Mum in a panic that the babysitter would be late, and Dad getting into an argument with the taxi driver, just couldn't compete in the glamour stakes.

As she sees me, her face widens into a bright smile.

'Isabel! Goodness me!' She gives me a kiss on each cheek. 'How long has it been?'

'Three years.' I make room for her on the banquette beside me. 'You took us out to dinner to celebrate Lara getting her Ph.D.'

'Oh, yes, at Le Caprice! I remember.'

Actually, the dinner was at Quaglino's, not Le Caprice. But I'm not going to correct her. Catherine, one of the very top heart surgeons in the country, is not the kind of woman you correct lightly.

'And now here we are at The Wolseley!' she declares, glancing around and signalling a waiter over. 'Lovely food, but I just can't bear all the ghastly celebrity-spotting, can you?'

'Oh God, no. Ghastly.'

'Two glasses of champagne, please,' she says to the waiter, before calling him back again. 'Actually, we'll get a bottle, shall we?'

'Brilliant!' I love Catherine. 'After all, we're here to celebrate! Lara's engagement,' I add, when she looks a little bit blank.

'Oh, well, of course. But before she gets here, you and I must catch up properly! I was dashing to the hospital when you called the other day, and there just wasn't time for a chat. Now, Larissa tells me you have a marvellous boyfriend these days.'

I'm having to think, for a moment, exactly who Larissa is, until I remember that it's Lara's full name. 'Yes, Will. We just moved in together.'

'And you're working as a wedding planner now? Amazing!'

It's kind, the way she says that, just glossing over all the other unsuccessful bits and bobs I've done throughout my chequered career, as though wedding planning was always exactly where I was trying to end up. 'That's right.'

She grins at me. 'You know, it's just the kind of glamorous job I always imagined you'd do! And, of course, you're making my life much easier. I mean, organising a big old frilly wedding is hardly my thing, now, is it?'

I don't want to point out that actually, a *big old frilly* wedding isn't what I'm intending to organise.

'And this dinner you've kindly offered to help me arrange,' she goes on, as the waiter returns with our champagne, an ice bucket, and glasses. 'I just thought it might be a good opportunity for me to get to know your parents a little better. I mean, I've barely seen them since you and Larissa left school!'

'No, it's a lovely idea. In fact, if you'd like, I was going to suggest that I get a friend of mine to cater it for you. He runs his own catering company, in fact, so he could do anything from canapés to an entire three-course dinner.' Or a nine-course symphony of molecular gastronomy, if I don't put the brakes on. 'I'm sure he'd be happy to come down to The Beeches on whatever day you want, and –'

'Actually, I was thinking it might be more convenient for me if we had the dinner in London.' Catherine tastes the champagne the waiter has poured her, and nods. 'I'm based at St Mary's in Paddington for the next couple of weeks, for the duration of some clinical trials I'm heading up, so if your parents are amenable to the idea of coming to town one evening, we could have the dinner at my flat in Maida Vale.'

'Oh, well, I'm sure that would be possible.' Though it does seem slightly counterintuitive to drag my parents all the way up from Shepton Mallet when Catherine's usual residence, after all, is her house in Somerset. Still, I'm not going to say that to Catherine. She doesn't generally brook disagreement all that well, if I recall. 'Um, it might need to be a weekend, though, because Dad doesn't finish at school until six or seven most weekdays.'

'I'm sure they'd love to come up to town for a weekend!' Catherine chinks her glass with mine. 'Take in a show, do the museums . . . oh, here she comes!' she adds, nodding over my shoulder at Lara, who is walking through the revolving doors.

Her face freezes. '*Catherine?*'

'Hello, darling.' Catherine waves Lara over and starts pouring champagne into the spare glass. 'Lovely to see you.'

'It's a surprise to see *you*.' Lara leans down to give her mum a swift kiss on the cheek, not meeting my eye at all. She's wearing a simple outfit of black trousers and a fitted grey shirt, which is unsurprising, given that she sees patients on Saturday mornings, but her hair, unusually for a work day, is left down. 'I wouldn't have thought this was your sort of thing.'

'Oh, well, it isn't, really. But when Isabel said you were going off to look at dresses, I thought you might like it if I came along. I mean, God knows, I wouldn't have wanted *my* mother fussing and flapping about if I'd married your father in a big, white wedding

260

ceremony. But then, I wasn't the kind of person who wanted a big, white wedding ceremony. Obviously, that's not true of you.' She raises her glass and chinks it against Lara's. 'So, I'm here if you want me. No big deal if you don't.'

OK. There are about ten thousand brides-to-be, all around the country at this very moment, wishing to God they had a mother like Catherine instead of the one they've actually got. The one who's spent the last six months holding them to emotional ransom over everything from the guest list to the seating plan, via the matron of honour's hemline.

But Lara doesn't seem all that impressed herself. She just gives a little shrug and takes a sip of her champagne. 'Well. It's nice to have you here.'

'Great!' I go to chink my glass to hers too, and I'm relieved when she reciprocates, albeit in a rather lukewarm fashion. 'So, I don't know if you had a chance to look at any of those magazines I left for you the other day, Lars? Because if you're already narrowing down the kind of dress styles you like, we'll know what to concentrate on when we go to our appointments.'

'Actually, I didn't really have much of a chance to look, Iz, sorry.'

I can see this month's copy of *You and Your Wedding* peeking out of the top of her tote bag. 'We can have a little look now!'

'Iz, really, I'd just like to order something to eat.'

'But there's loads of time!' I reach over and get the

magazine out of her bag before she can stop me. Right away, I can see that she's filled the pages with lots of those little tab-sized Post-its, in yellow, pink and green. 'Lars, this is brilliant! I thought you said you didn't have much chance to look.'

'Ah, but that's Larissa all over!' Catherine is perusing her menu. 'Do you remember her A level revision notes? Colour-coded, cross-referenced, neat little bullet points and summaries all over the place – and you were still convinced you hadn't done enough work, weren't you, darling?'

Lara pulls her lips backwards into something not quite resembling a smile. 'I just spent five minutes flicking through the magazine on my way into the clinic this morning. Pink tabs are for styles I'd definitely rather avoid, yellow are ones I'd try if you twisted my arm, and green are definite possibles.'

God. If Summer Shelley showed as much initiative as this, I'd be laughing.

'Oooh, well, this one's really nice,' I say, opening the magazine to one of the green-tabbed pages where a pretty brunette is pictured wearing a crepe halter-neck gown with delicate beading around the neckline, and a sassy little crystal headpiece that would suit Lara far better than a veil. 'We should definitely be able to find you something like this at Jenny Packham. What do you think, Catherine?'

Catherine peers over at the open page. 'Yes, very pretty.'

'Though you really shouldn't rule out trying on

something a bit more like this.' I've flicked to one of the pink-tabbed pages, featuring a classically romantic dress with a very full skirt, strapless bodice, and wide pale-green sash around the waist. 'You never know until you've tried, and it will make your waist look teeny-tiny.'

'Nope.' Lara shakes her head. 'No meringues.'

'Yes, but it's a very *tasteful* meringue.'

Catherine snorts with laughter, even though I wasn't exactly sure I'd made a joke. 'That's brilliant, Isabel! Though I have to admit,' she goes on, taking the magazine and flicking over a few pages herself, 'they all look a little bit meringuey to me. Honestly, I wouldn't have been caught dead wearing anything like these when I got married!'

'Which time?' Lara asks, coolly.

Catherine doesn't rise to the bait. 'You know very well, Larissa, that when I married your father, I wore a champagne-coloured jumpsuit.' She turns to me. 'Almost drove my mother to suicide, but there was no way I was letting myself be shoe-horned into a fancy frock.'

'Yes, well, it sounds . . . er . . . lovely.'

'Oh God, the thing was hideous! I can hardly look at the photographs. Cheap and nasty and saggy around the crotch . . . and that was just my ex-husband!'

I suppress my instinctive nervous giggle. Lara shoots her mother a Look.

'Come on, Larissa, it's important to keep a sense of humour about all this!'

'That doesn't mean I can't also take it seriously,' Lara says, in the careful, even tone of voice I'm sure she's been using all morning with her patients. 'It's not a crime to want to look nice on my wedding day.'

'Well, obviously, darling. I just don't necessarily agree that you have to hoick yourself into a floaty white dress to achieve that. I mean, it's not as if marriage isn't already enough of a patriarchal institution as it is, without you feeling the need to put on a pretty dress and play the Vestal Virgin for the day.'

I make a mental note to ensure that Catherine and Dad are seated as far away from each other at the wedding reception as humanly possible.

Like, in separate rooms, perhaps.

Because honestly, all Lara needs on the happiest day of her life is her mother and my father going at it hammer and tongs about patriarchal institutions. Much safer to sit Dad next to Lara's current stepmother, Melinda, where the only risk of a nasty scene spoiling the day is if either of them is sufficiently bored to death to make a death-plunge from an upstairs window.

'It's nothing to do with playing a Vestal Virgin, Catherine, it's just about enjoying some tried-and-tested rites of passage –' Lara is cut off by the ringing of Catherine's phone. 'I'm sure you'll need to get that.'

Catherine picks up. 'Dominic, hi . . . well, is he stable? . . . Yes, I told you I was still in town for the weekend . . . I'll jump in a cab . . . All right, bye. I'm so sorry,' she says, draining her champagne glass and reaching across the table to smooth Lara's cheek. 'That was the hospital. Honestly, I've only been there a couple of weeks and they've already decided they can't possibly manage the simplest of surgeries without me.'

'I'm sure you're indispensable,' says Lara.

'Darling, I think a forty-six-year-old father-of-three's arteries are just a little bit more important than a couple of wedding gowns!' Catherine slips her bag on to her shoulder then turns to me for a kiss on both cheeks and a tight, affectionate hug. 'Oh, it was so good to catch up, Isabel! And you'll be in touch to find a date for my dinner?'

'Absolutely. Great to see you, too!'

She leans down and drops a kiss on the top of Lara's head as she slides out from behind the table, then reaches into her wallet for a credit card, which she puts next to her. 'Pop the lunch on this, darling. And if you *do* happen to find a nice dress today, put it on there as well. I'd like that.'

We both watch her as she heads out of the restaurant, through the revolving doors. I open my mouth to speak, but Lara gets there first.

'What in God's name were you *thinking*?'

'I'm so sorry, Lars. I didn't invite her on purpose. I accidentally mentioned our shopping expedition, and I never thought she'd want to come.'

'But did I not specifically say, Iz, that if there was *one* thing you could do for me it was to keep my mother at arm's length?'

'I know.'

'And why didn't you at least warn me, Iz? I'd rather have been prepared!' She slaps the bridal magazine down on to the table, narrowly missing my champagne glass. 'I'd never have turned up with this magazine all marked out if I'd known she was going to be here, all superior about her bloody jumpsuit and her patriarchal institutions! *God*, she winds me up!'

'You stayed very calm.'

'I screwed up,' she mutters, looking a bit upset. 'What the hell was I doing, talking about tried-and-tested rites of passage? Why didn't I just say, "*Oh, bugger off, you snotty cow, and if I want to wear a pouffy white dress, I'll bloody well wear one*"? I'll say it next time I see her,' she adds, savagely, topping up her champagne glass. 'I swear.'

'Look, I really am sorry, Lars. And I know she can be a bit insensitive, but she's far from the worst mother to have in the run-up to a wedding. Look at Susannah Britten-Jones, for Christ's sake, piling all that pressure on poor Licky to marry Vile Marcus. And *my* mum, while we're at it! Don't you remember what she was like when Marley and Daria first announced they were getting married? She dragged poor Daria around every bridal boutique in Bath and then had hysterics in Monsoon when Daria picked out that little suit to wear instead.'

'Oh, come on, Iz, do you really think your mum is in the same category as Catherine, where Bad Mothers are concerned?'

I shrug. 'Let's wait and see. Weddings bring out the worst in her.'

'Well, she's been extremely considerate so far,' Lara retorts. 'She's not been pushy, or interfering, not even when she called to ask what we'd like for our engagement present . . .'

'She *asked* you what you'd like?' I blink at her. 'She didn't just assume you were urgently in need of an electric carving knife or a fish kettle?'

'No! I told her actually that what we'd really appreciate most right now is some John Lewis vouchers to put towards furnishings for whenever we eventually buy the new place, and that's what she's getting us.'

'You asked for *vouchers*? And she's *giving* them to you?'

Because Mum has this . . . well, you could probably almost, without exaggerating, call it a *phobia* of vouchers. I've lost track of the number of times I've asked her – pleaded with her, even – for my birthday present to take the form of a Gap voucher, or an HMV voucher, or even a Boots voucher, all of which she point-blank refuses to do because 'it isn't particularly personal, is it, Iz? I mean, *anyone* could buy you a voucher.'

Whereas only my mother could buy me a dozen soufflé ramekins, or a box set of *Spice Girls in Concert* DVDs, or a chunky blue Aran knit with an image of a giant daisy on the back.

And now she's buying Lara and Matthew *vouchers*?

But I don't want to give Lara the third degree about this, particularly when I know I'm not exactly in her good books at the moment on the whole mother front. And particularly not when she's staring over my shoulder in a slightly glazed manner, like she's doing at the moment . . .

'Lars? Are you OK?'

'Yes, sorry . . . Iz, who *is* that woman? The one with the big nose, in the wrap dress. I recognise her from somewhere.'

I turn round to see who it is she's staring at.

Oh God. It's Sophie Britten-Jones.

She's just sat down at a table the other side of my banquette, ushered into her seat by a toffy-looking guy in a pink shirt and chinos, when her eyes meet mine.

Confusion flashes across her face for a moment before she remembers why she recognises me. 'Oh! Isabel, isn't it?'

'That's right.' I wave across the banquette. 'Hi, Sophie.'

I'm taken aback when she suddenly stands up from her own table and hurries around towards ours. She looks a little bit flustered, her cheeks turning a similar shade to the tight mauve wrap dress she's wearing and I wonder, fleetingly, if she's keen to keep the pink-shirted toff out of this for a particular reason.

'How funny that I should run into you, Isabel,' she says, ignoring Lara, who ignores her right back, flicking through the *You and Your Wedding* and making more inroads into our champagne.

'Funny?'

'Well, I'm actually just up in town to return that pretty Vera Wang frock you arranged for me! And grabbing a quick bite of lunch with an old friend,' she adds, emphasising the word *friend* just a fraction too strongly.

'You're . . . um . . . returning it?'

'Of course! I mean, the thing was hardly worn!' She fixes me with her pale blue eyes and swishes her chestnut hair over one shoulder in the manner I remember from Licky's non-wedding. 'I'm sure the Wedding Shop will take it back. I never usually have trouble with that sort of thing.'

I'm quite sure she doesn't.

'And have you heard from Licky, by the way?' I ask hesitantly. 'Do you know if she's OK?'

'Oh, I think David mentioned that she'd called Dan a couple of days ago. Still in Italy, apparently, though God only knows why. I mean, holidaying alone in the place you were meant to be honeymooning?' She pulls a face. 'Tragic.'

I think of how keen Licky was to go to Rome, and how much nicer it must be for her visiting all her churches and Dan's recommended galleries without Vile Marcus leering at the nudes and trying to chat up the prettiest tour guides. 'Mmm. Well, I must let you get back to your lunch. With your friend.'

'You, too . . .' She glances over my shoulder at Lara and her wedding magazine. 'Oh! It's a *client* lunch? But you were fired, weren't you?'

Did she have to say that *quite* so loudly, for all the other lunchers to hear? 'Actually, I've set up on my own,' I say with dignity. 'It's much better, quite honestly – being my own boss, nobody to answer to . . .'

'Apart from the brides whose weddings you ruin! Oh, I'm *joking*, Isabel.' She lets out several snorts of laughter that makes her seem more horsy than ever, and then stops, quite suddenly. 'You know, you and I should probably swap details, Isabel. I mean, we're as much a new business as you are. Maybe you might like to think about using Broughton Hall for one of your weddings.'

Wait a moment.

I could be on to something here.

I mean, isn't Broughton Hall pretty much the perfect place for Summer Shelley to host her dream wedding? It's an idyllic English location, it's big enough for the number of guests, it's set in its own grounds so there's no need to worry about sneaky paparazzi . . . though actually, that might not be a selling point as far as Summer is concerned.

Sophie, who has obviously mistaken my silence for reluctance, tosses her head irritably. 'Well, forgive me for mentioning it –'

'No, Sophie, you've misunderstood! Actually, I'd be very keen to use Broughton Hall!'

'Really?'

'Absolutely! In fact, I do have one particular bride who's working to an extremely tight time-scale . . . I don't suppose you'd happen to have a slot free for October the seventeenth? That's *this* year,' I add, hastily, before Sophie can ask the inevitable question. 'I know it's hideously short notice, but Summer has a couple of pressing issues . . . that's my bride,' I explain, when Sophie looks confused. 'Summer Shelley – I don't know if you've heard of her? She used to be a pop star, and she models a bit . . .'

'A *celebrity* wedding?' Sophie frowns. 'Oh God, no, Isabel. The date would be fine, but my husband isn't exactly keen on Broughton being hired out for weddings as it is, so I certainly don't think a trashy celeb –'

'But it's going to be terribly tasteful, honestly!' This is not the time to mention the Hollywood theme or the reality TV show. We can cross those bridges when we come to them. 'She's marrying Tim Holland, you know, Sir Peter and Lady Holland's son.'

'*Ohhh.*'

Yes! That's done it. Mention of a multimillionaire, and all of a sudden, her eyes have lit up.

'Well, that sounds like quite a different matter. I mean,' she adds, keen to disguise the fact she's practically hearing cash registers ringing in her head, 'a high-profile wedding like that would be nice publicity for Broughton.'

'Wouldn't it? And didn't you say the date would be possible?'

'We're a brand-new venue, Isabel, nobody else knows about us yet. Of course it's possible.'

I want to punch the air. This is just completely brilliant news!

Oh God – though now I wish I'd not so blithely told her I was working for myself these days. Can I trust her not to mention it to Wendy and Summer? I'd hardly say Sophie was the kind of person I could trust over pretty much anything. Though if she wants Broughton to win this piece of business then it's in her best interests not to send the bride running to another planner who might take them off elsewhere.

'That's fantastic, Sophie . . . just one *small* thing I should probably be clear about before we go ahead.' I clear my throat. 'I haven't actually mentioned anything about my, um, new set-up to my client yet. And I'd appreciate it if we could keep it between us, just for the time being.'

Her eyebrows shoot upwards. 'You haven't *mentioned* that you just got fired for wrecking a client's wedding?'

'Nothing was wrecked. And obviously it's very important for my new client to have total faith in me. Important *for Broughton*, too,' I add pointedly. I feel a bit like someone in a political thriller, a senior civil servant giving the nod and wink to some major arms contractor in exchange for a good deal on oil, perhaps. 'I'm sure you understand, Sophie?'

Obviously Sophie has seen the same political thrillers as I have, because she gets my meaning right away, even though she doesn't actually bother getting into character herself. She simply shrugs, already bored by me and my machinations. 'Whatever you like. I won't breathe a word.' She fishes in her Longchamp bag for a business-card holder, and produces a little cream card. 'All my details are down here. We should speak first thing Monday morning, if your client decides she'd like to go ahead with the Hall. I mean, I am going to need as much time as possible to get all my casual staff organised. Not to mention liaising with my caterers, and the marquee hire . . .'

I'm trying not to get too excited about the fact she's actually *got* staff and caterers and marquee hire. 'Great! So, I'll call you on Monday morning, Sophie, and get the ball rolling.'

'Perfect, Isabel.' She holds a hand out to shake, then nods at Lara, who is looking resigned, bored, and tipsy in equal measure. 'You get back to your client, Isabel. I'll expect your call on Monday.'

Germaine Greer
London

Isabel Bookbinder
~~Individual Weddings~~
Non-Patriarchal Commitment Ceremonies
for Independent Career ~~Women~~ Wimmin
London

Dear Ms Greer

I do not know if you will remember me, but I have written to you ~~many~~ several times in the past to seek your advice on matters of a feminist nature.

Since I last wrote, I have set up my own business (~~Yay for me! Go, girl~~ Sisters doing it for themselves, etc. etc.) offering a planning service to people who are looking to enter into a contract of marriage together, and I was hoping to get some guidance on a few of the basics. Though I personally can see no harm whatsoever in the act of swanning about in a long white dress for one day of your life, it has recently come to my attention that some traditional feminists regard this as a political statement up there with ironing their husband's shirts and giving up work to stay home and perfect their Victoria sponges. Perhaps you could give me the benefit of the current thinking on this?

In addition, while I do not wish to cause any offence to those who have ~~fought on the barricades~~ struggled so hard for women's equality, I am afraid that I simply cannot countenance the ~~hideous~~ possibility that the only acceptable attire for the pro-feminist bride is a

274

champagne-coloured jumpsuit. Surely you can see, ~~Germaine~~ Ms Greer, that it is a Basic Human Right to look reasonably attractive on one's wedding day, and that it is well-nigh impossible to look even remotely presentable, let alone reasonably attractive, when clad in such an item? ~~Let's face it, it's a look that even Kate Moss would struggle to pull off~~ I am not sure I feel comfortable advising such attire given the high stakes involved. What good will it do my fledgeling business if the marriages I am overseeing crumble at the first hurdle, when appalled husbands-to-be turn their heads at the altar to witness their future life partner marching down the aisle with a saggy crotch? While it would be ideal if the relationship was based on mutual respect and affection, and not the dreaded Patriarchal notion that the bride must be a bit of a looker, I fear that we are not living in such a utopia. A bit of careful corsetry, a universally flattering strapless neckline, and a carefully selected shade of ivory, and I think everyone involved would be significantly more content! And perhaps if the bride were to give a speech herself at the reception, and not just allow her husband to speak on her behalf, this would redress the balance and gain the feminist stamp of approval?

I eagerly await your thoughts, but in the meantime, I will go ahead with arranging for my brides to stick with some variant on the Big White Frock, if that is all right with you.

Yours in ~~admiration~~ solidarity

Isabel Bookbinder (Ms)

Chapter Fifteen

By the time Monday morning came around, I'd already had plenty of chance to speak to Summer about Broughton Hall. And I have to say, I think I did a pretty terrific PR job. I waxed so lyrical about the rolling parkland, the golden Cotswold stone and the beauty of the Saloon that Summer had already started calling her mother in Canada to tell them to expect a *Four Weddings and a Funeral*-style event, and that she'd better start looking for a ballgown and diamonds to rent right now.

Though I do think there's just the smallest chance Summer thinks Broughton Hall is an *actual* location from *Four Weddings and a Funeral*. But I'm happy to let the inaccuracy slide. After all, the more enthusiastic Summer is about what is, let's face it, our only option, the better.

Anyway, Sophie Britten-Jones was thrilled when I called her yesterday morning to confirm that we'd like to go ahead. She's already faxed me her hire agreement, which I've signed on Summer's behalf and faxed back to Sophie, and now all she needs is a photocopy of my own contract with Summer for her records. In the meantime, she's sending me one of her brand-new glossy Broughton Hall brochures, so I'll have something concrete to show Wendy and Summer about the venue myself when I meet them later on today at Wendy's offices.

Though I've got quite a lot of other concrete stuff to show them as well. I mean, now that the venue is sorted, I'm really getting things into line. I spent most of yesterday on the phone to the Broughton Hall caterers, who are emailing me their menus and can arrange a tasting any time we want in the next couple of weeks, and I spoke several times to Anita-the-sexy-florist from Licky's wedding, who's coming up to town next week to talk through our flower options.

On the downside, finding a cake-maker is still proving problematic, but the catering manager told me they'd be able to put together a hugely tall, scrummy, sticky croquembouche if all else fails. Oh, and none of the photographers I've left messages for are returning my calls. But at least the basics are coming together.

And thanks to the fact that, unlike wedding paraphernalia, Hollywood accoutrements aren't exactly seasonal, I'm going great guns on all that stuff! In just a few hours of calls yesterday, I've already managed to line up the following:

1) from a hire company in (of all places) Taunton, a red carpet and two rows of red velvet ropes, to be delivered the morning of the wedding along with four giant Oscar statuettes and some huge sweeping

searchlights if we decide it would look fun-tacky rather than tacky-tacky;

2) from a company in Chiswick, a giant inflatable outdoor screen, where we can show black-and-white movies when guests are getting tired of dancing;

3) from an *extremely reliable-sounding* specialist car-hire firm in Cardiff, a stretch limo to ferry Summer between her hotel and Broughton Hall, and a pink Cadillac for the happy couple to make their final departure late in the evening;

4) from the drama departments of Bristol University, more student actors than I can possibly count to play screaming fans, paparazzi, and red-carpet inter-viewers. Less than an hour after I spoke to one of the course administrators, my email account was practically combusting with traffic as dozens and dozens of desperate wannabes got in touch to tell me all the ways in which they think they're perfect for the roles. I think maybe they're all allowed an Equity card after a certain amount of paid work; either that or they all think they're about to be in *Four Weddings and a Funeral*, too.

I mean, is this going to be the most fabulously OTT Hollywood-themed wedding ever, or what?

Honestly, I'm kind of tempted to suggest a similar theme to Lara. Though the thought of what Mum would do given the free rein of a themed wedding doesn't even bear thinking about.

And despite the fact I'm swamped with Summer's

stuff right now, I haven't forgotten about Lara's wedding. I mean, I really am in Top Wedding Planner mode right now! Which is why I've taken the opportunity this morning, before Sophie's glossy brochure gets here, to pop round to Barney's flat in Pimlico to give him a heads-up on his first proper Simple Suppers commission.

As he pulls open his front door to welcome me in, I'm instantly reminded of those pictures in every family photo album of the grinning, moon-faced toddler who's just eaten their first ice-cream cone and is covered from forehead to chin in the stuff. He's lightly coated in a sticky-looking mixture of icing sugar, cocoa powder and melted chocolate. He looks absolutely exhausted, but triumphant.

'Sorry,' he says, waving away my reluctant attempt to give him a kiss on the cheek. 'You didn't give me much notice you were coming, or I'd have made an effort to clean myself up.'

He wouldn't, probably, but it doesn't matter. 'You look shattered.'

'I've been up all night. When you get in the zone, Iz, it's better not to stop.' He shakes his head, leading me through to his kitchen. 'Great creations have been lost that way.'

I glance about the kitchen, which looks a lot like it's been taken over by terrorists intent on creating some kind of cocoa-based weapon of mass destruction. 'And you're in the zone right now?'

'Yup.' He perches on one of the bar stools next to

his tiny kitchen counter and shoves a large ramekin – I think it's one of the dozen Mum gave me, and that I subsequently off-loaded to Barney – in my direction. 'Been perfecting my chocolate soufflé recipe. Have a taste of that and tell me what you think.'

I dip a spoon greedily into the chocolatey mixture and taste. 'Mmm, it's incredible, Barn.'

'I know. That's fifty per cent seventy per cent chocolate, forty per cent eighty-five per cent chocolate, and ten per cent hundred per cent chocolate.'

I know he's been up all night, but this kind of raving can't be normal. 'Barn? Are you all right?'

'Cocoa percentages!' He waves several Lindt wrappers at me. 'The really crucial thing, Iz, with a chocolate soufflé, is to get the bitterness right. My attempts with all hundred per cent cocoa-solid chocolate were far too overpowering, making it with all seventy per cent cocoa-solid chocolate was far too sweet . . . now it's *just right*.' He frowns. 'Though I'm not sure exactly what the overall cocoa percentage of the final product is right now. Do you think we could call your brother in his maths department and see if he can work it out?'

'I promise, Barn, I'll ask him next time I see him.' I take another spoonful of the soufflé as Barney staggers over to start up his coffee machine, which is a souped-up, turbo-action version of the one he persuaded Will to buy. 'Anyway, Barney, how do you think you'd feel about recreating this in a paying customer's home?'

'Oh, I'm not sure that would be entirely fair, Iz. I mean, *I* don't mind coping with the mess, but I don't know if people will be too happy if they see their own beloved kitchens descending into chaos like this.'

'I mean,' I explain, patiently, 'the final version. Your Holy Grail Soufflé. How would you like to make one for paying customers at your first proper dinner party?'

Barney turns to stare at me. 'Are you saying . . . you've got me a job?'

'That's right! Lara's mother! She wants you to cater an engagement dinner for Lara and Matthew. Oh, and her and my parents, of course.'

'Oh, *Iz*.' Barney blows out through his mouth, sending up a cloud of icing sugar. 'Oh, you *star*.'

'It's my pleasure, Barn. And I know you'll do a terrific job. Now, she does just want to keep it pretty simple, and I imagine the kitchen in her flat is pretty basic . . .'

'Basic is fine! Basic is *good*. You don't always need top-of-the-range equipment, Iz, to create culinary fireworks. Oooh, that reminds me, did you manage to track down my old soda siphon the other day? I could have done with it to make a bitter almond foam to go with my chocolate soufflés, and I'm certainly going to need it for a couple of spumas for Lara's mum's dinner.'

Oh, God, that bloody soda siphon. I never did locate it in Will's kitchen cupboards, what with stumbling across Nana Hamilton's sapphire and all the subsequent panic. 'Yes, yes, I did track it down,' I fib, to keep him off my back, 'and I'll bring it the next time I see you. But, Barney, honestly, I don't think this occasion is going to call for any spumas – delicious though they are! Just some homey, cosy food, so that Catherine and my parents can sit around a table, breaking bread together and getting to know each other a little better.' And trying not to stab each other in the arm with their forks, I could add, but don't, because Barney's barely even listening, already wandering to his bookshelf and starting to take down several tomes.

'Cosy, homey . . .' he's muttering. 'Not too many spumas . . .'

I'm just wondering how to refocus him long enough to actually get a cup of coffee out of him when my phone starts to ring.

'Hello, Isabel speaking.'

'Hello, Isabel speaking. It's Dan. Dan Britten-Jones.'

I feel my stomach tip over. 'But how are you . . . how did you get my number?'

'Ah. Well, it's a bit awkward, actually. I probably shouldn't admit this, not after what happened with the last girl . . .' He sighs, long and hard. 'I'm stalking you, Isabel. I know where you live. I know where you work. I know which branch of Starbucks you go to for your morning coffee.'

I might be monumentally freaked out here, but that doesn't stop me glancing at Barney, to make sure he

282

hasn't heard the Starbucks thing. Thankfully, his head is still buried in *Chez Panisse Café Cookbook*.

'I know where you shop,' Dan is carrying on. 'I know where you take your morning jog . . .'

'Ha!' I didn't actually mean to say that quite so loudly. 'You're making it up. I never go for a morning jog! I mean, obviously I do take some form of daily exercise,' I carry on, not wanting him to think I'm a wobble-arsed slob. 'But I don't jog. Old marathon injury, unfortunately.'

'Isabel, I was making it up. It was, believe it or not, a joke.' There's an audibly self-satisfied grin in his voice. 'I got your number from my very favourite sister-in-law.'

'Sophie?'

'That's the one. I believe she had a package for you?'

'Well, yes, but . . . I thought she was going to post it.'

'She was. But I was down at Broughton yesterday and when I realised she was addressing a package to you, I couldn't prevent myself from jumping in and offering to hand-deliver it for her. Ironically, in the light of my previous joke, that means I *do* know where you live.' He pauses. 'I wondered if you'd like me to drop round with it some time later.'

'What?' I realise that I'm coming across as a bit of a monosyllabic half-wit here; I must be, because I've actually stirred Barney from his cookbook to stare at me. 'I mean, I really need to have it for a meeting in town this afternoon. Maybe I could come by your work? Pick it up?'

'Well, if that's more convenient for you . . .'

'It is. Much.' I don't know what it is, but the idea of Dan dropping round to Will's flat – Will's and *my* flat, sorry – freaks me out a bit. 'Just give me the address and I'll be there . . . um . . . before noon?'

'All right. Maybe we can have lunch.'

I gurgle a non-response, and then scribble down the Soho address he gives me on a chocolate-spattered sheet of kitchen paper. 'OK, Dan, thanks. I'll see you in a couple of hours. Bye.'

'*Dan?*' Barney demands, the moment I put my phone down. 'Who's *Dan?*'

'No one. I mean, obviously he's someone. Just no one important.' I cave, under the intensity of Barney's gaze. 'Look, he's just Licky's cousin, OK?'

'Gone-to-the-wrong-church Licky?'

I glare at him. 'How many Lickys do you think I know? Yes, that Licky.'

'So why is her cousin calling you?' Barney gets up to switch on his coffee machine. 'More importantly, why is her cousin calling you and making you go all pink and flustered?'

'I'm not pink and flustered! And he's just calling because he has a package for me.'

'Sounds like he does.'

'A package from Broughton, where I'm arranging my new client's wedding. Summer Shelley, remember? I told you on the phone.'

'Oh, yes, Summer . . .' Barney is momentarily distracted by the thought of a busty blonde with a penchant for posing in her pants. But only momentarily. She's not a chocolate soufflé, after all. 'So you're off to collect this package from this Dan, then, are you?'

'Mm-hm. In fact, I should really get going now, if I'm going to make it to Soho before twelve.'

'It's barely ten o'clock!' Barney stares at me, accusingly. 'Iz? Are you planning to dash back to your flat and get yourself all tarted up for this bloke?'

'No!' Now I know I'm pink and flustered. 'Of course not! For God's sake, Barney, I'm living with Will, aren't I? What the hell would I be doing running about town tarting myself up for some random guy?'

'Not that random,' Barney points out. 'He has your phone number.'

'Yes, well, I didn't give it to him. And you really don't need to worry, Barney.' I hop off my bar stool and pick up my bag. 'You know I love Will. We've only just moved in together. I'm not about to up and leave him!'

'I never said you were.'

'Exactly! Now, look, I've left a message with Lara's mum asking her to give me some dates, so I'll call you as soon as I know anything.'

Barney follows me to the front door. 'I'll wait to hear from you. And give my regards to Will,' he adds pointedly. 'OK?'

'OK, Barney. I will.'

I have popped back to the flat before heading to Soho, actually, because as soon as I'd left Barney's I realised I'd managed to sit on some runny chocolate that must have been on my bar stool. And for heaven's sake, it's not *tarting yourself up* to go home and get changed so that virtual strangers don't think you've had a nasty and embarrassing accident. Obviously I've got to change out of my mucky trousers and into something that doesn't make my bottom look like a national disaster zone. My best Citizens of Humanity jeans, in fact, which just happen to have an extremely miraculous effect on my bottom in all kinds of other ways. Oh, and because I've changed into dark blue jeans I can't very well stay in the dark blue top I've been wearing, so I think I'll slip on this floaty peasant-blousey thing I picked up in COS a few weeks ago, but haven't felt quite thin enough to wear yet. And one of the major advantages of dashing about like a maniac these last few weeks is that I seem accidentally (always a thrill!) to have lost a few pounds off my tummy and hips. A quick emergency de-frizz of the hair, a touch of NARS Multiple, and fifteen minutes attempting to do that thing with the chunky white pencil that makes your eyes look brighter and your Cupid's bow look perkier, and I'm practically a new person!

Not tarted up. Absolutely not tarted up.

Anyway, just because I want to try and make the best of myself before going along to meet Dan Britten-

Jones, it doesn't *mean* anything. For some reason only known to himself (drink? drugs? some kind of undiagnosed mental illness?) he seems to find me reasonably attractive, and I don't want to shatter the illusion he's built up of me by turning up to meet him looking a bit dodgy. Not to mention the fact that men that look like Dan Britten-Jones don't usually give me a second glance. Let's face it, I need to cram in as many valuable self-esteem calories as I possibly can before the inevitable famine sets in again, and I have to make do with the crumbs of an occasional wolf-whistle from a paunchy builder or passing white van man.

I mean, Lara's told me a billion times, having good self-esteem and a positive self-image is extremely important in maintaining a solid relationship with your partner. So even if I *have* tarted myself up, just a very little bit, it's only because of Will.

As I'm heading out of the flat, nice Emma-from-downstairs is letting herself in. She's wrestling with one of those buggies, approximately the size (and cost) of a small car, in which her angelic son is sleeping, and I help her through the outside door with it so she doesn't have to try lifting it herself.

'God, thank you, Isabel,' she says, rather breath-lessly, once the buggy is safely in the hallway, angelic toddler still sound asleep. He's wearing exactly the kind of funky toddler clothes that I wish I could convince Daria to let Hypatia wear – little jeans and a cute hoody, with amazing light-up trainers. 'You know, I always think I want a day off a week, and then by lunchtime I'm always having to restrain myself from ringing the office and begging them to let me move from four days to five. Ooooh, you look nice,' she adds enviously, running a hand through her frazzled hair. 'Off somewhere special?'

'What? No. God, no! Not at all. Just a meeting. Nothing special. Nothing remotely special. I always like to dress up a bit, present a polished face to clients . . .' I realise that Emma is staring at me. 'Anyway! I should be dashing. But we really should get together for that bite to eat some time.'

'Exactly what I was about to say to you! Thursdays are good for us, if it'd suit you. How's the fifteenth?'

The fifteenth is barely forty-eight hours before Summer's wedding, so I probably ought to say no. But I'll have to eat, won't I? And it's not like I'll have miles to travel to Emma and Mark's flat, obviously.

'That sounds great, I'll let Will know.'

'Fab! Oh, and I hope you don't mind, Isabel, but I'll probably do the cooking myself. I had a lovely chat on the phone with your friend from Simple Suppers, but I think he's more the kind of thing I'd use if I had a really *big* dinner to do, you know? Something rather more elaborate . . .' Her cheeks are tinged with pink, and I leap in to rescue her.

'Absolutely. Much better to save the expense for something special, not just me and Will!' I glance at my watch. 'Sorry, Emma, but I really should go now . . .'

She waves me cheerily away, and I set off out to catch the bus towards Soho.

As always happens when I come to this part of town, I'm totally lost within minutes of arriving, wandering the length of Berwick Street at least three times before realising that I'm actually after *Broadwick* Street. Even then it takes me another ten minutes to find the place, tucked down a side street between Broadwick Street and Brewer Street.

I double-check the address I scribbled down, because there's nothing about it from the outside to suggest that it's a gallery at all. It's a small townhouse with a big, black-painted front door and tall, narrow Georgian-style windows that appear to have been blacked out from the inside. I'm just about to get out my phone and try the number Dan called me from earlier when the front door suddenly opens and Dan appears in the doorway.

I'd love to be able to say he looks ridiculous, in baggy khakis, a granddad-collar shirt covered in black stains, bare feet, and horn-rimmed glasses of the Buddy Holly variety. But in fact, he doesn't look ridiculous at all. It doesn't hurt that the shirt is open to reveal rather a lot of his chest or that the frames of the glasses brings out the onyx colour of his eyes. He looks gorgeous. Breathtakingly gorgeous.

'Isabel. You found me.'

Why does he have to make everything sound like the last line of a big-screen epic? 'Yes, well, it was a bit tricky, I always get Broadwick confused with

Berwick, and this doesn't look much like a gallery from the outside.'

He grins and pushes the door open behind him. 'Come on through.'

I make very sure I don't accidentally brush him as I go past, and head into a narrow hallway. There are stairs straight ahead and an open doorway to the right, which Dan leads me through.

OK, *now* it looks like an art gallery. We're in the room with the blacked-out windows, which has bright white-painted walls and beautiful original wooden floorboards. There are a couple of beefy workmen on stepladders doing something complicated with the spot-lighting in the ceiling, and there are empty white plinths dotted around the room, looking as though they're waiting for something to be displayed on them.

'You've caught us in a bit of a mess here, I'm afraid.' Dan folds his arms and surveys the scene. 'We're just preparing for a new exhibition.'

'Oh, anyone good?'

Which is a stupid question, and one that I'm expecting Sarky-Chops to reply to with a dry *No, Isabel, someone utterly shit.* So I'm surprised when he just nods.

'Yeah, actually. Pete Schanschieff.'

He says it like I'm supposed to know the name, so obviously I'm not going to let him know that I don't. 'Oh, I love his stuff.'

'Pete's stuff?' Dan's eyebrows shoot up. 'I'm

impressed. I mean, a lot of people find it very inaccessible. So you liked his exhibition at the Tate Modern last spring?'

Is Dan's surprise because he just thinks, not unreasonably, that I'm a bit of an ignoramus about modern art, or because this Schanschieff bloke is in fact one of those nutters who pickles placentas or performs live autopsies on endangered mountain gorillas, and only someone truly insane could say they actually *liked* it?

Oh God, he isn't the one who did those giant polystyrene cups Licky told me about, is he?

'Well, obviously it wasn't the *most* accessible exhibition.' I'm hedging my bets here. 'But certainly interesting stuff. Very, very interesting.'

He smiles. 'Then you're in luck. He's re-exhibiting most of it here, alongside some of his other works, of course.'

'Ah. A major retrospective,' I say, feeling rather pleased with myself for coming up with this phrase.

Dan fixes me with those intense eyes. 'Yes, I suppose you could call it a major retrospective. You know, you really should come and take a look. You could bring your solicitor. Though Pete's work might not be up his street.'

'I wish you'd stop calling him *my solicitor*,' I snap. 'You make me sound like I've just been arrested or something. And actually, Will is even more a fan of modern art than I am.' I feel a sudden need to defend Will against Dan's unspoken accusation that he's nothing more than a conventional suit. 'I'm sure he'd love to come and see Pete's work.'

'Great. You can both come along to the opening night party in a couple of weeks.' Dan shoots me a look that's almost a challenge. 'Come on back to the office and I'll give you an invitation. Oh, and Sophie's envelope, of course,' he adds, suddenly putting a hand in the small of my back and ushering me down the length of the gallery towards a desk area right at the back. 'Though I don't think I actually did find out from Sophie what it is she's in touch with you about.'

'A wedding at Broughton.' My mind is far more focused on the sensation of his hand through the thin cotton of my peasanty top. 'Got a new client . . . She wants to get married there, only a few weeks . . .'

'A wedding client? So you're still in that game?'

I nod. 'And I've guaranteed my new client I'll only send her to the wrong church if she really, really begs me to!'

Dan doesn't laugh. 'You know, that really wasn't completely your fault, Isabel.'

'Mmm. I wish other people saw it that way.'

'Who cares what other people think?' he shrugs. 'You know what a favour you did Licky. Anyway, it wasn't a total disaster for you, either. You're still working.'

'Only for myself,' I confess, though I've absolutely no idea why I feel the need to.

'Even better. You're obviously a free spirit, Isabel.' He moves closer, which makes me panic slightly until I realise he's just trying to get to the filing cabinet.

'You'll do much better working on your own. Even if it does mean you have to deal with people like Sophie on a one-to-one basis.'

'Actually, Sophie's being very good about the whole thing.'

'Ah. Well. She would be. You're giving her an enormous dollop of cash, I presume.'

'Well, yes, but she's being very helpful, giving me all the contact details of her temp staff, and she's volunteered Maurice to help out with any local errands . . .'

'I bet she has. There's nothing my sister-in-law likes more than a good bit of *help* from Maurice. Preferably when my brother's away, of course.'

Bloody hell. So she's not *only* at it with that pink-shirted toff she was with at The Wolseley.

'You look shocked,' Dan carries on. 'What, you didn't expect her to be carrying on with the lower orders? Well, don't worry, he's not her usual type. Men usually need more than a few quid in the bank to satisfy dear Sophie! Sorry,' he adds, almost without pausing. 'You don't need to hear all this.'

'No, it's OK. It must be difficult. He's your brother.'

'Half-brother, actually. Different mums.'

'*Ohhhh.*'

'Yeah. That's what most people do when they hear that. Explains a lot, doesn't it?' Dan grins, but affectionately. 'He's a funny old stick, David. I know people think he's just this nutter pottering about the

293

place going on about the family antiques, but he's a decent man. And he's changed a lot. When I was little, he was like this complete action man. I worshipped him.'

'We all want to be like our older brothers,' I say, even though I can't honestly recall a time when I wanted to be like Marley. Oh, apart from the times when he'd take my maths homework off me and do, for fun, in five minutes flat what would have taken me an hour of blood, sweat and tears. 'Um, Licky mentioned that David had . . . a bit of trouble not long ago,' I venture, hoping this doesn't make me sound too nosy. 'I hope things are getting better for him now?'

'Mmm. Well, if you call a total nervous breakdown "a bit of trouble".'

'Oh God. I'm really sorry.'

'It's OK. And he is getting better, as a matter of fact. Not having to work at that hellish investment bank has helped a lot. Of course, Sophie doesn't see it that way,' he adds, not even bothering to disguise the savagery of his tone. 'As far as she's concerned, she married him when he was a hotshot banker and she doesn't see why she shouldn't live in the style to which she very happily became accustomed.'

'But she's living at Broughton Hall!'

'Yeah, but according to her, it's just a crumbling old wreck. It doesn't provide her with liquid capital, which is what she really wants. Hence the fact she's started hiring the place out. Anything to cash in.'

I feel a pang of guilt. 'God, Dan, I'm sorry I'm hiring it from her. If I'd known –'

'Not your fault,' he says, matter-of-factly, as he shuts the top drawer of his filing cabinet in a manner that suggests the matter is closed, and goes behind the desk with the card he's taken out, reaching for a pen. 'It's good to hear things are working out for you, Isabel. And that you'll be working at the old ancestral pad for the foreseeable future.'

'Well, not for that much of it. My client is getting married in less than three weeks' time. It's all a bit of a rush.'

He raises an eyebrow as he scribbles on the card. 'Shotgun wedding? Well, let me know if there's anything I can help you with at all. I'm quite sure Sophie's got everything sewn up, but I do still have quite a lot of mates in the area if you need extra muscle . . . I presume you're all right for marquee hire? Barmen? Photographer?'

'You know a local photographer?' I stare at him. 'Actually, that's one of the things I'm having some trouble with.'

'Yeah, I know someone. I could give you his details if you like.'

'Oh, Dan, that would be absolutely brilliant.' I scrabble in my bag for a scrap of paper and a pen. 'What's his name?'

'Dan Britten-Jones.'

I stop writing. 'You do *wedding* photography?'

'There's no need to sound so sceptical, Isabel. I'm a

man of many talents. And yes, as it happens, one of those is wedding photography. How else do you think struggling photographers put themselves through art school?'

'But surely your father could afford . . .' I stop myself. After all, the Britten-Jones family finances are really none of my business. 'But you're a *proper* photographer, aren't you? Licky said you did all kinds of arty things with your ex-girlfriend . . . I mean, that you took arty photographs of her,' I correct myself hastily, seeing Dan's amused look. 'Are you sure you want to be wasting your time bossing tipsy guests around and putting up with Bridezilla tantrums?'

'Doesn't bother me. And besides, if it meant I'd be working with you, it'd bother me even less.'

I don't say anything.

'Look, why don't I send you some snaps from the weddings I shot a few years ago? You can show them to your bride, see if she likes the look of them. No obligation. And in the meantime . . .' He hands me the padded A5 envelope and the card he's just written on, '. . . these are yours.'

'Great. Thank you, Dan.'

'My pleasure. Anyway, it got me what I wanted.' He walks round to my side of the desk. 'I got to see you.'

There's a huge red warning light flashing so vividly in my brain that I'm almost surprised not to see it right there on the white wall in front of me. 'So! Better be dashing!' I stumble backwards. 'Got to get this to my client's manager . . . I call her the Dragon Lady . . . well, not to her face, of course.'

'Of course. Let me see you out.' Dan takes his loping, sloping stride to the front of the gallery, and out into the hallway, where he opens the door for me. 'I really hope you can make it to the party,' he says. 'I'm sure you'd enjoy seeing Pete's stuff.'

'Oh, I'm sure.'

He leans down to give me a kiss – not on both cheeks, as I expect, but just on the one side, halfway between my cheekbone and my mouth. Now that we're all so used to doing that continental mwah-mwah thing on both sides, just the one kiss feels oddly old-fashioned and . . . I don't know . . . intimate.

'You know, I meant what I said the first time I met you, Isabel. You really do have the most fascinating face.'

I don't want to do or say anything that might make my face look anything less good than fascinating – gurning, perhaps, or contorting in embarrassment – so I just step backwards and pull the front door to behind me.

It's only as I set off, briskly, in the direction of Paddington, and Wendy's office, that I glance down at the little invitation card Dan gave me.

'*You Are Invited*,' it says, '*to a Celebration of the Work of Pete Schanschieff, at the Marlow Gallery, Thursday 15 October, 8.30p.m.*

Damn. It's the same night I've just agreed to go to

dinner at Emma and Mark's downstairs. Well, maybe I can put them off for another occasion.

Underneath the printed details, Dan has written, in a surprisingly neat and tidy hand, 'Do join us, Isabel! Bring the solicitor!'

I have to turn it over to read the rest of what he's written, in much smaller letters.

'Or come alone. Entirely up to you.'

Chapter Sixteen

I've almost reached Wendy's office when my phone trills. I'm half-expecting it to be Summer – I know I'm meeting her in five minutes, but isn't it about time for her first call of the day by now? – but actually it's Lara's mother.

'Isabel?' Her voice is brisk and businesslike. 'Catherine Greene here. How are you, my darling?'

'I'm very well, thanks.'

'So, I've had a trawl through the diary, and I think the very best date I can find for this dinner party is this coming Thursday. How would that suit?'

'This *Thursday*?'

'Yes, we agreed a weekend would be better for your parents, didn't we?'

I'm not sure if you're allowed to point out to a professor of cardiology that Thursday isn't, by anyone's standards, the weekend. 'Well, yes, but Dad's school commitments might be a little bit tricky to juggle at short notice, and actually Thursday is one of the days Mum works.'

'Oh, that's not an issue! I'm happy to start late if that would suit them better. Shall we say nine p.m.?'

'Um, I suppose that would be OK . . .'

'And your caterer? He'll be able to make that?'

'God, yes, he'll do *anything*,' I begin, before realising that this might not be the best way to introduce someone whose job it is to come into your home and cook you dinner. 'You know, I'd better check with him, Catherine. But I'm sure he'll be able to juggle things about if necessary.'

'Excellent! Now, my flat's in a portered block, so I'll leave the keys downstairs that morning and you can come along and get yourselves all set up. I'm going to be in surgery all that day, I'm afraid, so I really won't be able to do a thing to get the place looking presentable.'

'Oh, don't worry about that, Catherine. That's for me to deal with.' I buzz Wendy's door, and the receptionist lets me in. 'Can I just double-check that this date is all right with my parents and then get back to you?'

'Of course. Though if they can't do this Thursday, Isabel, then it's really not looking good for any time in the next ten to twelve weeks.'

'Ah. Then I'm sure they'll be fine with it.'

'Do apologise to them on my behalf, won't you, darling?' Catherine sounds regretful. 'I'm used to having to squeeze my social life into my calendar like this but your poor parents may not be.'

'Oh, they won't mind. I'm sure.'

'Fabulous, Isabel, thank you, bye!'

I announce myself to the receptionist and only have to wait for a couple of minutes before I'm waved through.

Zenith TV are here, already starting to set themselves up in Wendy's office. Well, by Zenith TV, I basically just mean Weirdy-Beardy – looking even more intense than the last time I saw him, juggling a clipboard and one of those huge shaggy microphones that look like dead gerbils – and a tiny girl with violently tangerine-coloured hair, who's almost entirely obscured behind approximately three million wires, a film camera, and several rolls of gaffer tape. I suppose I didn't exactly expect an entire outside broadcast team, but seeing just the two of them is a little bit depressing. Mind you, Weirdy-Beardy, for one, certainly seems to be throwing his heart and soul into it, however much I'm sure he'd rather be making a documentary about oil spills, or war crimes, or those endangered mountain gorillas that Dan's gallery artists like to autopsy.

Dragon Lady herself is at her desk jabbering into her phone, but Summer, who's sitting in one of the chairs opposite, sipping a Starbucks coffee, jumps up to greet me.

She's looking prettier and perkier than ever in an outfit she's obviously consciously picked for a 'business meeting': pin-stripe trousers that hug her hips and bottom, an eye-poppingly tight white shirt unbuttoned to reveal spectacular cleavage, and sky-scraper black platforms. Her hair has been swept into a librarian bun, the seriousness of which is somewhat undermined by her favoured shade of baby-pink lip gloss.

'Izzie!' She gives me a kiss and hug, then gestures

around at the Zenith 'crew'. 'What do you think of all this, huh? Isn't it crazy?'

'Yes, crazy . . . I didn't realise they'd be filming here today.'

'Oh, they're filming me *everywhere*.' Summer tries – and fails – to look bored and blasé about the whole thing. 'They already filmed me at my session with Kieron this morning, would you believe? *So* embarrassing. Wasn't it, Sven?'

Weirdy-Beardy mumbles his assent, then turns a very bright shade of pink and faffs self-consciously with his gerbil microphone.

'Oooh, and how do you think I'm looking, by the way? Do you think I've lost weight? Is my bum looking smaller?' She grabs, with difficulty, a chunk of her bottom. 'Kieron says I could still probably shrink it by about half a centimetre, which I think would make all the difference if I want to change into the backless Roberto Cavalli after the sit-down dinner.'

I have a mental image of the roguish, lairy Kieron producing a tape measure and calculator, handily kept about his person for the all-important measurement of Summer's gluteus maximus. His roving eye is one of the reasons I stopped going to my gym, quite honestly, because I didn't like the way he used to ogle my own gluteus (extremely) maximus while I puffed and panted on the step machine. (Obviously the step machine itself – not to mention the treadmill, stationary bike and cross-trainer – were the other reasons I stopped going.)

'Summer, honestly, you're looking absolutely terrific, you don't need to worry about an extra half-centimetre.'

'You're sweet. And you're a total star, Izzie, for finding me a trainer like Kieron. Honestly, he's *amazing*.' She rolls her eyes with an expression that I can't quite make out. Is it appreciation of Kieron's excellent personal-training techniques, or of his rock-hard six-pack and cheeky grin? 'It makes me so excited about the other people you've got lined up for me.'

I stare at her, a bit blankly.

'*You* know, Izzie! My hairdresser, and my on-call beautician, and my therapist . . .'

'Shit, yes. I mean, yes, absolutely, Summer!' Never mind red carpets and giant Oscar statuettes – I *must* remember to make a couple of calls later today on matters of Bride Management. I'll put in a special plea to my hairdresser, Saint Luc; another to lovely Janelle who does my leg-waxes and the occasional spray-tan, and who is Australian and ludicrously laid-back, so almost certainly won't mind about the whole on-call thing; and of course, I must speak to Lara and get her to agree to a couple of sessions. 'It'll all be lined up for you by the end of this week, I promise.'

'I hope so. Because we need a bit more variety for Sven to film. Plus I really think I'd benefit from having a therapist to talk to right now. I'm *so* stressed about everything, Izzie. I mean, seriously, this morning, I actually *hollered* at the poor Starbucks guy because I thought he'd put full-fat milk in my coffee by mistake.' Her eyes are wide, as if in shock. 'Can you believe it? I've *never* done anything like that before.'

'Well, I'm sure that's something the therapist will be able to help you with,' I say, soothingly, shoving to the back of my mind what Lara is going to say when I ask her to book in a couple of sessions for someone with Starbucks Rage. Could I call it 'SR', and hope she doesn't ask me too many questions? 'Anyway, Summer, I've brought along some terrific photos of Broughton Hall –'

'Where?'

'Um. Your wedding venue?'

'Ooooh, yes, please, Izzie, let me see!' Summer scrabbles eagerly for the brochure as I pull it out of the envelope. There's a succession of *Oooohs* and *Aaaaahs* as she studies the photographs of Broughton in all its glory. 'Oh, *gorgeous*,' she suddenly declares, flicking to a picture of the grounds.

'Isn't it? Now, this is where we'd probably be able to host the drinks reception if the weather was decent . . .'

'Not the garden. *Him*.' She points to a spot in the picture where two men are featured strolling underneath a shady chestnut tree. It's David and Dan Britten-Jones.

It's pretty obvious David's not the one Summer is talking about.

'Is he the lord of the manor?' she asks, peering more

closely at Dan, and licking her lips in a lascivious way that suddenly reminds me of the reason we're having this wedding in such a hurry.

'No. He's the lord of the manor's younger brother, actually.'

'Mmm, even *better*. He's, like, the feckless, caddish one, unburdened by the responsibilities of tending the estate.' I think Summer might spend far too long watching dodgy old Elizabeth Hurley bodice-rippers on obscure TV channels. 'Have you met him yet, Izzie?'

'Yes, yes, I've met him a couple of times.'

'You're going *all pink*!' Summer suddenly squeals. 'Is he even better in real life? Is he?'

'He's nothing remotely special,' I say, primly as – thank God – Wendy suddenly slams her phone back into its cradle and hops up out of her seat.

'God, you guys,' she snaps, turning to the Zenith crew, 'could you *not* try to keep it down a bit while I'm in the middle of an important phone call?'

Tangerine Hair, who has been virtually silent with her gaffer tape, and Weirdy-Beardy, who has made all the racket than you'd expect from somebody doing nothing more than staring fixedly at something that looks like a dead gerbil, wisely keep their lips buttoned and say nothing.

'And I see you're finally here,' Wendy adds, to me, even though I'm not remotely late. 'So you've brought the pictures of this venue, then?'

'I absolutely love it, Wendy!' Summer thrusts the brochure at Wendy. 'Isn't it perfect?'

Wendy flicks, rather ungraciously, through the pictures for a moment. 'Well, it certainly *looks* perfect,' she says suspiciously. 'But is it suitable? I mean, are we going to have exclusive use? Are we going to be swarmed by local photographers? Tell me where it is again.'

'It's in the village of Broughton, not far from . . .' I'm about to say Shepton Mallet, but think better of it, '. . . Bath. Deep in the glorious Somerset countryside.' I'm starting to sound a bit like the brochure myself, and I'm suddenly aware that Weirdy-Beardy is motioning Tangerine Hair to put the camera on.

Oooh, here's my first opportunity to promote Isabel Bookbinder: Individual Weddings!

I run a hand through my hair as casually as possible, lick my lips to moisten them, and concentrate on sounding natural as I start talking through the exciting arrangements I've made so far. Summer seems thrilled with all my suggestions – oh, and it's a great big yes to the giant Oscar statuettes, by the way – and even Wendy seems moderately satisfied for a change. I mean, she takes loads of detailed notes, and almost – *almost* – cracks a smile when I mention the screaming fans I've hired from Bristol University. Her smile fades pretty quickly, though, when we get on to the whole matter of her bridesmaid's dress – yes, Summer wants Wendy to be her bridesmaid, apparently; I can't help finding this a little bit depressing – which Summer absolutely insists has to be prom-style and in hot pink, to match her 'colours'.

And then, because I'm aware the time is ticking and we're almost at the end of the meeting, I get us on to the nitty-gritty organisational stuff. We sort out the wording of the e-vite, which we've agreed is the fastest, if not the most glamorous way to get the invitations out in time, before moving on to discussion of the entertainment.

'Now, I suggest we try to think of music that will be in keeping with the overall tenor of the wedding,' I begin, but Summer wrinkles her nose.

'You mean, like, that Jose Carreras or someone? Wouldn't he be incredibly expensive?'

'Um, that's not exactly what I meant . . . I thought, as it's a Hollywood theme, you might like to go for some Rat Pack-style singers, or a Big Band.'

'Well, obviously we want a *big* band, Izzie! I'm not paying a million pounds for this wedding to have a couple of blokes with a keyboard and some drums! Oooh, do you think we could get somebody famous? I really love Take That . . . and Tim's always been this *huge* fan of Prince . . .'

It takes me – and Wendy, actually, who's on my side for once – the best part of twenty minutes to convince Summer that we have neither the time nor the budget to get Take That or Prince, and then I manage to steer her on to the subject of the menu tasting, which I advise Summer she and Tim might like to do by way of a first visit to their venue.

'Oooh, no, I don't want to be eating too much between now and the wedding.' Summer looks horrified. 'And Tim's not that big on eating at all. You can go and do it for us, can't you, Izzie? Hey, maybe if you're lucky, Hot Younger Brother will be there, too!'

'Hot Younger Brother?' Wendy demands.

'God, yes, he's the insanely good-looking guy in that picture.' Summer performs a mock swoon. 'A special friend of Isabel's too, apparently.'

'He's not a special friend in the slightest.' I'm keen to get us off the topic of Dan Britten-Jones. In fact, I'd be quite happy never to have to think about Dan Britten-Jones again in my life. Which is why I just don't understand why my next words come out of my mouth. 'Actually, he's a photographer. And he's volunteered to help us out with photography for the wedding, so if you'd like to see some of his work, Summer, I can ask him for –'

'No need.' Wendy shakes her head. 'The magazine will be covering all that.'

'Magazine?'

'Well, obviously now we've got our venue sorted, I'm going to speak to the magazines about an exclusive deal for Summer and Tim.' Wendy sits back in her chair, hands clasped. '*OK!* have already expressed some interest, and I've scheduled a meeting with *Sure!*, who I'm sure will be extremely keen to talk.'

'*Sure!* magazine?' I blurt, before I can stop myself.

'Yes, Isabel, *Sure!* magazine.' Wendy is staring at me. 'Do you have some kind of a problem with that?'

Well, considering the fact that their features editor

knows that a) I don't work for Pippa Everitt any more because b) I hideously botched the last celebrity wedding I was involved with, then yes, I do have a problem with it.

I mean, if Sunetra D'Souza got wind that I was working on this wedding, I don't think Wendy could persuade Summer to ditch me fast enough. It's all very well Summer thinking that she and I have some special bond, but I'm not sure that bond could survive me being outed as Celebrity Wedding Kryptonite.

'Let me clarify,' I carry on, as coolly as possible given that Wendy is looking at me like she's the Assistant District Attorney and I'm Suspect Number Four in a police line-up. 'What I really mean is that in your position, Summer, I wouldn't touch a magazine deal with a bargepole. And not *Sure!* Especially not *Sure!*'

'Oh, but I really like *Sure!*' says Summer. 'Are they the ones who do Sex Position of the Week?'

Weirdy-Beardy drops his dead-gerbil microphone.

'No, that's *More*,' Wendy says. But she isn't taking her eyes off me. '*Sure!* do all the celeb wedding exclusives, things like that. Which is why I'm surprised that Isabel isn't keen on them.'

'But that's exactly why I'm not keen on them. From my point of view, as a *Top Wedding Planner*, if you want your clients to have a stressful day where their time isn't their own, and their nearest and dearest can't even bring their cameras into the reception without being slapped with a bloody great law-suit, then fine, go ahead and get a magazine deal.'

'I'm not sure I'm that bothered about my nearest and dearest, to be honest,' Summer muses. 'I only really have my mom and Auntie Sue and a couple of others to come over from Canada, and they'll do anything I tell them.'

If I weren't too stressed, I'd feel rather sad about Summer's limited guest list. 'Maybe, but you don't strike me as the kind of girl who wants to lose control over every aspect of her wedding day. I mean, the last wedding I did where *Sure!* were involved, they wouldn't even let the bride have her own choice of car!' I say, truthfully. 'That pink Cadillac I was just telling you about would probably end up replaced by a boring old Rolls. And as for your Hollywood theme – forget it!'

'Oh.' Summer's face falls. 'That would be bad. I do really like my Hollywood theme.'

'Exactly! And it's not like, if you'll forgive me, you and Tim are in need of the money from a magazine deal.'

'It isn't necessarily about the money!' Wendy, aware of the cameras, gives a little laugh, but her teeth are gritted. 'It's the security, for one thing! She was the one –' she jerks a thumb in my direction – 'bleating on about providing Paparazzi flipping Neutrality. Do you have any idea what a headache it's going to be to organise our own security team so that you don't have a bunch of snappers invading the grounds and trying to sneak unauthorised shots of you?'

She realises, just too late, that Summer would

probably like nothing more than stray paparazzi invading her wedding.

'And most of all, think about your *career*, Summer,' she continues, slightly desperately. 'We always said we needed to get you a magazine deal first, and then you'd probably get offers from *I'm a Celebrity* and *Dancing on Ice* . . .'

'Oooooh.' Summer breathes out. 'I'd forgotten about *Dancing on Ice.*'

I can see that I'm in danger of losing her. I lean forward. 'Summer, at the very least, if you *are* going to get a magazine deal, the one and only thing I'd beg of you is that you don't choose *Sure!*'

'So, you mean, it'd be OK if I went with *OK!*?'

'Yes, Summer, I think that would be . . . er . . . OK. Or *Hello!* magazine, even. But honestly, I couldn't just stand by and let you get a deal with *Sure!*. I mean, it's not just your big day at stake. It could be your whole marriage. Haven't you heard of the . . . the Hex of *Sure!*?'

'No!'

'Well, it's like the Curse of *Hello!*, but much, much worse.' I'm just wondering if I'm going to have to start spinning some tale about a bride who sold her wedding to *Sure!* only to wake up on her honeymoon to find that she'd contracted overnight leprosy and her husband was already at it with the chambermaid, when suddenly Summer shakes her head.

'Then that's it. Wendy, I don't want to sell my wedding.'

311

'Summer!' Wendy, seeing her fat twenty per cent commission disappear before her very eyes, is looking alternately desperate and murderous. 'Think of your career.'

'I *am* thinking of my career. I'm thinking of *A Summer Wedding*. And I want the show's viewers to get to know the *real me*, not some cut-out-and-keep bride that some magazine editor is forcing me to be.' Summer dimples, prettily, in the direction of the camera.

I have to admit, she's got a knack for a soundbite.

'Call up and cancel that meeting, Wendy,' Summer orders. 'And I don't want to speak to any other magazines. Just book that hot photographer, Izzie!' She winks at me. 'It'll be nice for the guests to have something pretty to look at on the day apart from just me.'

'Are you sure?' Wendy demands. 'Without even bothering to meet him and see his work?'

'Oh, I don't have time for anything like that! Not with all the appointments Izzie's arranging for me over the next couple weeks. Isn't that right, Izzie?'

'Absolutely!' I get to my feet. 'Anyway, I really ought to be going, if you don't mind. There's a lot to do! Oh, and if you wouldn't mind faxing over a copy of my – I mean, *Pippa's* – contract to the venue, just so that their paperwork is all in order . . .?'

'Oooh, thanks a million,' Wendy snaps. 'It's so nice of you to give me *one* job to do.'

I make sure she's got Broughton Hall's fax number

before gathering my things. 'Well, great to touch base, everyone,' I say, which sounds suitably wedding-planner-ish.

'Thanks, Izzie!' Summer stands up too and gives me a farewell kiss on each cheek. 'God, I'm just *so* excited about it all, you know?'

I'm relieved to hear that Wendy is already on the phone, cancelling her meeting with *Sure!* magazine, as I head back out towards reception.

ISABEL BOOKBINDER: INDIVIDUAL WEDDINGS

SHELLEY/HOLLAND WEDDING, BROUGHTON HALL, 17 OCTOBER

<u>*TO-DO*</u>

- *Call Kevin, catering manager for Broughton Hall, to discuss least possible calorific options for wedding menu*
- *Ask Barney for his opinion on best-tasting lowest-fat/carb/sugar food in advance?*
- *On second thoughts, ask Barney nothing of sort. Will only result in B getting hot under collar about evils of low-fat/carb/sugar food in general; plus maybe better to avoid him until have located bloody soda siphon*
- *Track down Take That management team on remote off-chance they have slot free for private performance at less than three weeks' notice; don't forget to ask for ~~Jason's~~ ~~Mark's~~ ~~Howard's~~ Jason's autograph!!!! Gary Barlow is OK if he's the only one prepared to do it*
- *Track down Prince management team on even more remote off-chance he has slot free for private performance at less than three weeks' notice; don't forget to look up what he calls himself these days and/or find out how you're supposed to pronounce that weird squiggle he used to use instead of proper name*
- *Locate hot-pink prom dress that won't make Wendy look like sunburned penguin.*

Chapter Seventeen

Mum and Dad weren't exactly thrilled about Catherine's this-Thursday-or-never invitation to dinner. Dad, in fact, was actually audibly using the word 'summons' in the background when I called Mum on Tuesday evening, which certainly didn't make me any more relaxed about the chances of this dinner party going well. But they've agreed to come along nevertheless, and are due to get to Catherine's flat in Maida Vale as close to nine tonight as they can possibly make it. Which, if I know Dad and his obsessive time-keeping, will actually be closer to eight-thirty. Eight, even, if he's prepared, for once, to edge above seventy on the motorway.

Catherine's rented pied-à-terre is in one of the huge, imposing mansion blocks that line the Edgware Road, which is where I'm heading now, at five in the afternoon, to meet Barney, who's been there most of the day. He buzzes me in when I arrive, and I take the rather charming original lift up to the sixth floor and head along the corridor to flat number 608, at the back of the building.

I can see Barney before I even reach the door. He's standing with one foot in and one foot out of the flat, looking desperately down the corridor, and there's a phone in his hand.

'I'm just not sure, Professor Greene . . .' he's saying, as he raises his other hand in . . . well, it could be a cutting-edge new greeting, or it could be some sort of threat of implied violence. '. . . Well, it's not really a question of just nipping out to Selfridges and getting the peach purée, Professor Greene, it's a question of whether or not Bellinis will complement my menu . . .'

I try to grab the phone but he blocks me.

'Well, what I'd actually been planning to serve is a delicious akvavit-based cocktail,' he's carrying on. 'Oh, you don't know it? . . . But it's extremely popular all across Scandinavia . . . I appreciate that, Professor Greene. Bye!' He hangs up and practically pulls me into the flat. 'Isabel! I thought you told me Lara's mother was going to be hands-off about all this! Not ringing me on the landline every fifteen minutes to give me some new instruction!' Barney stamps back towards the kitchen, which is tucked away in one corner of the rather bland-looking, anonymous flat, and starts to stir a pan on the stove. 'And why the hell does she want me to serve sweet, sticky Prosecco cocktails instead of my refreshing akvavit and juniper berry punch? What kind of Dane *is* she?'

'Er, not a Dane at all?'

'Ha ha. Very funny.'

'It's not a joke.'

He turns round to stare at me. 'Well, then, who *is* Danish?'

'Will's mother is Danish. But I don't see –'

'*Will's* mother!' Panic passes over his face. 'Oh God, *that's* it. For the love of Christ, why didn't you remind me, Isabel?'

'Because I didn't think it was relevant.' I can feel my heart sinking a little bit. 'It *isn't* relevant, is it, Barney?'

'Only because I've prepared a modern Scandinavian feast for this evening!'

'I see. Well, that's not a problem! I mean, I'm sure modern Scandinavian food is delicious, isn't it?'

Barney doesn't say anything.

'*Isn't it?*'

'Well, *I* like it.' Barney sounds defensive. 'But then I've always been a huge fan of herring. I do understand that not everybody feels the same way.'

'And your menu for this evening is heavy on the herring, is it?'

'Only in a few of the canapés. And in my Herring Three Ways.'

'*Are* there three ways to serve herring?' Apart from liking it, lumping it, or projectile vomiting it all over the walls, that is.

'Of course! We're having one served pickled with a herb mousse – it was supposed to be a herb *spuma*,' he adds accusingly, 'but *somebody* seems to have lost my soda siphon.'

'I haven't lost it!' I fib. 'I know exactly where it is, I just forgot to bring it! But you were saying . . . the other two ways for your herring . . .?'

'One served ceviche-style with citrus fruits,' he

317

continues, mercifully distracted from the damn soda siphon for now, 'and one simply griddled and served with a dill snow.'

'Dill *snow*?'

'Yes, it's this technique I picked up from someone on one of my foodie websites. Or at least, I *will* have picked up once I finally get it right . . .'

'Oh, Barney.'

'Come on, Iz, this is partly your fault! You said you wanted to serve homey food. It's not my fault that Catherine's home isn't Denmark. Anyway, Will's coming tonight, isn't he?'

Will is, in fact, coming tonight. Though I can't shake off this little nagging hope that he's suddenly hit with a big work crisis that means he can't make it after all. It's not that I don't want to spend an evening with him, but more that I'd rather not spend an evening with him where Mum keeps patting him kindly on the shoulder and assuring him that she's sure, if he plays his cards right, he could be enjoying an engagement of his own some time very soon. If there's anything guaranteed to turn Will any more off the idea of marrying me than the (wholly mistaken) idea that I'm becoming obsessed with the idea of marrying him, then that'll be it.

'Yes, Will's coming this evening.'

'There you are, then!' Barney looks relieved. 'I mean, he's *half*-Danish, so I'm sure *he'll* appreciate it.'

'Mmm. Anyway, Barn, I really ought to try and start getting the flat shipshape. It's only three and a half hours till my parents get here.'

'They're not coming any earlier than that, then?' Barney turns to start slicing some kind of oily fish – I can only assume herring – on a chopping board. 'Now that your mum's already up in town?'

'But she isn't already up in town. She's coming up with Dad when he finishes at school.'

Barney shakes his head. 'Nope. I just saw her a couple of hours ago, on my way back from picking up the venison at the Ginger Pig. I was on the bus going past Baker Street tube just as she was coming out of it.'

'Well, it can't have been her. She works on Thursdays. It must have been someone who looks like her.'

'She was wearing a cerise raincoat.'

'Plenty of middle-aged women wear cerise raincoats.'

'With matching shoes. And a matching handbag.'

Oh.

OK, that does make a bit of a difference.

But what on earth would Mum be doing at Baker Street tube? It's not as if that's the kind of area she normally comes to when she visits London – usually she just makes a beeline for John Lewis and then wanders south down Bond Street for a bit of window shopping before her usual pilgrimage (however strenuously she denies it) over to Kensington Gardens to see the Diana Memorial Fountain.

'Look, Barney, I need to make a quick call. You just carry on with the herring. Delicious, I'm sure!'

'Oh, no, I've finished with the herring.' He puts

down his knife and starts marshalling bits of fish on to a plate. 'Next job is smoking my hard-boiled eggs.'

I'm sure I must have misheard that.

I head into the boxy living room – God, it's going to be tough to make this place look romantic and sophisticated for an engagement dinner – and try Mum on her work line.

No answer. Odd.

I try her mobile instead, and she answers after a couple of rings.

'Iz-Wiz? Hang on, it's very noisy here . . . let me move somewhere a bit quieter . . .' It's a couple of moments before the noise level drops, and then she says brightly, 'That's better, isn't it?'

'Mum, where exactly are you?'

'Oh, I'm just out and about in town.'

'In London?'

'No, Isabel, Shepton Mallet. We're not leaving for London for another half-hour.'

'But . . . my friend Barney said he saw you outside Baker Street tube station earlier.'

She gives a giddy laugh. 'I think your friend Barney must have been having a little joke, Isabel.'

'But he was quite sure it was you, Mum. Something about a cerise mac . . .'

'Oh, really, Isabel! I've only met Barney, what, two or three times? How could he possibly be sure that some random lady in a cerise mac was me?'

This is a fair point, I suppose.

'Now, look, I'm just at the newsagent picking up

some chocolates to bring this evening. Should I get those nice mints, you know, the posh ones in the green box that your father likes so much, or do you think Lara's mum would prefer something gooey and Belgian?'

'The Bendicks mints, I think, Mum, but there's no need to go to any trouble.'

'Don't be silly, Isabel! It's been years since I've seen Lara's mum, and she's putting such a lot of effort into throwing this lovely engagement party . . .'

Well, probably lovely. If you discount the herring. the smoked hard-boiled eggs, and the distinct lack of charm in the venue.

'. . . I mean, it's very generous of her, Isabel, especially as I think it's the *usual thing* for the groom's parents to host the engagement celebration . . .'

Great. Dad's insatiable need for everyone to do The Usual Thing has got to Mum, too. At this rate, smoked eggs are going to be the least of my problems.

'. . . I mean, it was your father's family that threw us a party when we were first engaged. And a very nice evening it was, too, even though Granny Jean misread the recipe for the avocado and prawn cocktail and tried to *grill* the skins off the avocados. You know,' she adds, rather mistily, 'I still can't smell singed vegetables without thinking of your father . . .'

'Well, hopefully we'll have an equally terrific evening tonight! And of course, we mustn't forget that we're all here for Matthew and Lara this evening, yes?'

'That's exactly what we're here for! I mean, *there* for,' she adds hastily. 'When your father and I get to London, of course.'

'Good. I'll see you in a few hours, Mum. Bye.'

Four hours later and I'm starting to think that contrary to all my expectations, we might just be in for a decent night.

Catherine's flat, for one thing, looks terrific. I spent a good hour turning it from a soulless greige box into something that wouldn't look out of place in *Elle Deco*, complete with tea-lights on almost every horizontal surface, and little fairylights wound around practically every vertical one. I've also filled every vase I can find with huge sprays of Lara's favourite lilies, remembering to cut out the stamens so that Mum doesn't ruin the evening by proclaiming, every so often, that it smells like a funeral parlour, and I've dug out the least screechy of Catherine's opera CDs to play on the stereo.

I have to say that Isabel Bookbinder: Individual Weddings has really come up trumps for its – for *my* – first full-blown event. It's completely brilliant!

And I needn't even have worried so much about the herring, because Barney's food actually looks rather wonderful. In addition to the chilled pitchers of Scandinavian punch, which we've set up on a table outside on the tiny balcony, he's done a pretty selection of canapés, including soft goat's cheese on home-made crispbread, marinated salmon with juniper berries, and slices of raw herring that don't actually look too bad (especially not if you think of them, as I will encourage the guests to do, as *sashimi* of herring). To follow the canapés will be the mysterious Herring Three Ways, and if that's a total disaster, there's a quite marvellous-smelling main course of venison with a redcurrant jus and mixed-root vegetable rösti, and chocolate soufflé with akvavit-infused cream for pud.

But the best part by far is that everyone seems to be getting on. Despite my worst fears about Dad and Catherine going together like fish and bicycles, they seem to be having an extremely enjoyable discussion out on the balcony with Will – bonding over, of all things, affordable housing for Somerset's key workers. Indeed, Dad looks positively enlivened by the subject, something I never imagined he'd give two hoots about, eagerly leaning forward to tell the sad tale of one of his newest junior staff members who's having to live on her parents' longboat on the Kennet and Avon canal, while Catherine herself regales them both with a similar tale of woe regarding nurses at her Bristol hospital. Will – bless him – is making all the right kind of polite faces and interested noises, and even if he's bored senseless, at least he's not been buttonholed by Mum on engagement talk. Mum herself is at present sitting amongst the fairylights with Lara chatting about the marvels of John Lewis and all the endless possibilities for her vouchers, and Matthew is happily bothering Barney in the kitchen by taking over the mixing of fresh Scandinavian punch. Which means that, by some distance, the least content and relaxed person in the flat tonight is Barney.

In fact, I think I should head in there now and give poor Barn a bit of a morale-boosting pep talk. I've got a pretty good pretext: Will has just told me to tell Barney that the canapés all taste authentically Danish but very delicious too. Which I think I'll just tweak, when I tell Barney, to authentically Danish *and* very delicious too. As a soon-to-be Top Wedding Planner, I know it's important to keep my staff's confidence levels as sky-high as possible. Plus a nice compliment ought to distract him from the gung-ho way that Matthew is slinging about the ingredients for the cocktail.

'Barney!' I trill, as I go into the kitchen. 'You've got some pretty satisfied customers out there. Will says it's the best Danish food he's ever eaten!'

'Really?'

'Yes, really!' Well, it's the *gist* of what Will said, isn't it?

'Then he's going to get a nasty shock when it comes to the main meal.' Barney mops his sweaty brow with a long trail of kitchen roll. 'I almost put white pepper in the rösti when I meant to add salt, and I've made a total mess of my dill snow – *again*. I'm sorry, but I think my Herring Three Ways is going to have to be Herring Two Ways.' He shoots an uncharacteristically violent glare in the direction of Catherine, out on the balcony. 'You know, I *would* have been doing all right if she hadn't got back and started nosing around, distracting me. Good luck with your future mother-in-law, mate,' he adds, over his shoulder, to Matthew.

'Shocking, isn't she?' Matthew grins. 'Not that it matters to me. I wouldn't even care if Lara's mother was Cruella de Vil herself . . .'

'Yes, yes, well, we'll all warn you if she starts wearing a particularly luscious-looking fur coat,' I say briskly, because he's got that starry-eyed look he often gets when he talks about Lara, and I'm not sure Barney is in any mood to be nauseated at the moment. 'I think people are really going to want their drinks freshened right now, Matthew, if you wouldn't mind?'

He rolls his eyes at me as I flap him back to the living room. 'I thought *you* were meant to be in charge of this party, Wizbit.'

'We all know who's *really* in charge of this party,' Barney mutters, slamming a saucepan down on the worktop as though he's auditioning for a part in that musical where the cast rampage around the stage drumming tunelessly on dustbin lids. He really is in just about the worst mood I've ever seen him in. 'I mean, what was the point of her hiring me to cater if she's going to keep butting in with her own suggestions?'

I'm a little bit tired of all this negativity around Catherine, I must say. 'She's a doctor. Bossing people around is part of her daily job description. And she's basically very chilled out, you know.'

Barney snorts.

'Honestly, Barn, she was the most popular mother of anyone at my school! If Dad knew half the things she was happy to let us get up to under her roof, he'd never be happily sitting out there chatting to her today.'

'Yes, well, I'd choose your parents over Catherine any day. Your mum's offered to help with the cooking about five times already this evening.'

I stare at him. 'But Barney, that's incredibly interfering!'

'No it wasn't. Because when I said no, she just backed right off. She didn't come in and start peering into my mixing bowls and sticking her nose in the fridge, and asking me to use half-fat crème fraîche in my herb mousse. I mean, *half-fat crème fraîche*, Iz . . .'

I don't point out to Barney that this doesn't change the fact that Mum came back four more times with offers of the same help he'd just rejected. Or that I'm not entirely certain that this in-home catering lark is the thing for him.

'Bit weird that she lied to you earlier, though,' Barney adds.

'What do you mean?'

'Well, about being in London.'

'Barn, we've been through this. You must have been wrong. She said she wasn't here.'

He shrugs. 'Have it your own way. I was right about the shoes, though, wasn't I?'

'Sorry?'

'The cerise shoes.' He nods in the direction of the living room. 'She's wearing them right now.'

I turn round and have a look at Mum, happily chatting away on the sofa with Lara, accepting a top-up from Matthew with the punch pitcher.

And Barney's right. I must have been in more of a flap when everyone arrived than I realised, because I haven't noticed until now. But Mum is indeed wearing bright cherry-pink peep-toe shoes.

'Of course, I'm sure you'd have noticed if she was wearing the cerise mac, too,' Barney adds, pulling a tray of crispbread out of the oven.

'No . . . I mean, she wasn't wearing a coat . . .'

Which is a bit odd in itself, now I come to think of it. I mean, it's barely twelve degrees outside today, with the looming possibility of rain. Did Mum *really* come all the way up to town with just that chunky cardigan she's wearing?

'Well, I'd ask her again where she was today, if I were you. I mean, those shoes are just too much of a coincidence. And it's not as if she was necessarily doing anything *dodgy*, is it, Iz? I mean, Lara works right near Baker Street, doesn't she?'

'Yes. Yes, she does.'

'There you are, then! Probably she was just meeting up with Lara!' He starts to turn each piece of crispbread, to bake the other side. 'Bit mean of them not to tell you about it, though, Iz, I have to say!'

You know, he's right. Probably Mum *was* meeting up with Lara.

And he's also right that it's a bit mean of them not to tell me about it.

'Oh, by the way, your phone has beeped a couple of times,' Barney adds, nodding in the direction of my handbag, which I slung on the kitchen table earlier. Except that now, to make way for the Scandinavian punch ingredients, Barney's prized Japanese knives, and a pile of herring innards, it's been re-slung into the corner by the fridge. 'I think it's a couple of text messages.'

'Barn, you should have told me right away!' I dart to my bag and rifle in the side pocket for my mobile. 'It might be my client, Summer.'

It isn't, though. It's Dan Britten-Jones.

At least, I assume it's Dan Britten-Jones. I don't recognise the mobile number, but the first text message speaks for itself, really.

Humble (part-time) wedding photographer seeks gorgeous self-employed wedding planner . . . Did you get the pics I sent you of my old wedding work? Do I meet with your bride's approval?

And he's already sent a second message.

Humble wedding photographer wondering why gorgeous wedding planner is ignoring him.

I hate myself for the fact that my heart has started racing, and for the fact that my hands are shaking a little bit as I start replying.

Gorgeous wedding planner isn't ignoring humble wedding photographer, she's just . . .

No, Isabel. No, no, no. For one thing, I can't call

myself gorgeous. It's manifestly not true (decent-to-distinctly-pleasing on a good day, but never properly *gorgeous*). And for another thing, I can't reply to these blatantly flirty texts in a blatantly flirty manner! Not with my boyfriend right in the next room! Not – let's face it – with my boyfriend *anywhere*!

I delete the text and start to recompose.

Hi, Dan, thanks for your messages, not received pics yet but will let you know when they arrive . . .

'Everything going OK in here?' It's Will, popping his head round the kitchen door.

Shit. I drop the phone like it's one of Barney's hot bits of crispbread. It lands on the floor right next to Will's feet, and before I can dart to grab it, he's bent down to pick it up himself.

'What? Oh, yes, yes, everything's fine!' I hold out my hand to get the phone back but Will's wandered past to clap a hand on Barney's shoulder.

'Brilliant food, mate,' he says, to Barney's evident delight. 'Anything I can do to help?'

'No, you're fine, aren't you, Barn? In fact, we both are! No need for you to do anything but relax and enjoy!'

'Right.' Will shoots me a funny look. 'I just thought maybe you might need a hand fixing some drinks, or help getting the table ready? I mean, you looked like you were pretty busy with your phone just now.'

'God, no, not at all. Just some work stuff. It can wait.' I hold out my hand for the phone again, but he doesn't pass it over. What am I supposed to do?

Wrestle it off him? 'Will . . . um . . . I do need my phone back. I was just texting someone.'

'Oh, sure, sorry.' But he doesn't hand the phone over immediately. What he does – and I've no idea why he does this; I mean, am I looking *that* jumpy? – is glance down at the screen for a second. Then he clears his throat. 'Who's Dan?'

'Dan? Well, he's the person I was just texting.'

'Yes. I can tell that.' Will hasn't taken his eyes off me. I'm not sure he's even blinked in the last ten seconds. 'Is it the bloke with the Fiat? The one from Licky's wedding?'

Behind both of us, Barney has suddenly started making a lot of extremely unnecessary noise with pans and baking sheets.

'Mm-hmm, mm-hmm.' I don't know why I'm trying so hard not to sound guilty. It's not like I've done anything with Dan, for heaven's sake. 'That's the one.'

'So it isn't work stuff.'

'What?'

'Well, you don't work with him, do you?'

'Actually, I do. Kind of, I mean. He's probably going to be taking the photos for Summer's wedding.'

'Oh.'

'Yes, so I really should text him back. He's sending me some sample photos, and I need to know when he put them in the post, so I can pin Summer down for a meeting to look at them.' I reach for the phone again, and this time Will hands it to me. Well, he kind of drops it in my hand. Thank God, I'm safe. And I must remember to delete those flirty texts before Will has a chance to get his hands on my phone again. 'So! We should probably leave Barney to finish up in here. All on course for the starter, Barn?'

Unlike Will, who's still eyeballing me like I'm in an identity parade, Barney isn't turning around to look at me. Wordlessly, he sticks up a thumb.

'Great! Let's go and start getting everyone round the table,' I say, herding Will towards the kitchen door. He hesitates for a moment in the narrow hallway, as if he's about to stop and say something, but then he just keeps on walking ahead of me back to the little living room, and straight back out to the balcony.

The moment I see Mum and Lara huddled up gossiping on the sofa, I remember that I'm not the only one who's been making clandestine contact with people they shouldn't. All right, so obviously Mum meeting up with her future daughter-in-law to discuss wedding plans isn't quite the same thing as me conducting flirty text conversations with another man – if, in fact, I *had* been, which I haven't – but I can't help feeling seriously offended about the fact that they've so deliberately excluded me. I mean, *I'm* the wedding planner! *I'm* Lara's best friend!

And I know I moan about Mum a bit too much. But she is *my* mother.

Look, it's not like there's any kind of a *problem* with the two of them getting along so well – gossiping away on the sofa like they are right now, about Kenwood food processors and cotton percale duvet covers. But why the need for all the secrecy? If they did meet for some kind of cosy lunch today, then surely they could have told me about it and invited me along to join them. Just for some dessert, perhaps. A cup of coffee, even . . .

As I head over to them, Mum turns to look up at me, an expression of hurt and disappointment on her face. For a moment, I wonder if she's just mirroring my expression, but then she says, 'Lara's just mentioned, Isabel, that you had a little trip to look for wedding dresses the other day.'

Wait a minute. How did they get from percale duvet covers to this?

Lara is flapping her hands behind Mum and mouthing at me, frantically, '*I'm sorry!!!*'

'We were just doing a preliminary search,' I say. 'I didn't know you'd want to come . . .'

'Not want to come *wedding-dress-shopping*?' Mum stares at me as though I've just suggested that she might like to try going without oxygen for a couple of days. And there's something a bit glassy about the stare, too – something that suggests she really shouldn't be drinking too much more of that Scandinavian punch she's holding. 'When you *know*, Isabel, how devastated I was when Daria wouldn't even try on anything resembling a proper frock?'

'Mum, I think "devastated" is a bit over the top –,' I begin, only to be interrupted by Lara.

'Moira, look, you've misunderstood. It was just a casual visit, we didn't look at any of the really important places.'

'They were *bridal shops*, Lara! They're *all* important places!' Mum raises her voice slightly for a moment before clearly remembering that Lara is her big ally, and that I'm the one who's let her down here. 'I know that, as the groom's mother, I'm not entitled to have an opinion on anything . . .'

'Mum, come on.'

'. . . but seeing as I'm not likely to be the mother of the bride any time soon –'

'Moira, listen, it's all my fault,' Lara interrupts, putting a soothing hand on Mum's arm. 'My schedule is just so packed these days, especially now that Matthew and I are setting aside so much time for house-hunting, and I just wanted to get in a very early look at dresses in case I don't have as much time over the next couple of months as I'd like. And actually, that might be something you can help me with, Moira.'

Mum sniffs. 'Help with what, dear?'

'Well, Isabel kindly gave me loads of bridal magazines the other day, and she said – didn't you, Isabel? – that it might be a good idea for you, Moira, to have a little look through them and give your thoughts on the dresses you like.'

I stare right into Lara's wide, slightly insistent eyes.

The thing is, I know I should be grateful to her for trying to smooth things over. But something inside me is making it impossible for me just to nod, and smile, and go along with it. I mean, *I'm* the one who's actually been lied to here.

I take a deep breath. 'Actually, Lars –'

'So! Are we about to eat, at all?' It's Catherine, stepping through the French windows. She shoots me a conspiratorial grin, and I can't help wondering if she was simultaneously managing to discuss key workers with Dad and Will *and* eavesdrop on what was going on indoors. 'I don't know about anyone else, but I'm getting ravenous! Shall we sit down at the table, and I'll go and check on the chef's progress?'

This is just what I needed, actually, to whisk me out from under the gathering storm clouds. All right, nobody really seems to have commented on it so far, but this is an Isabel Bookbinder: Individual Weddings event, and I can't just sit back having a mood when my caterer needs a bit of protection. I mean, he's got sashimi-grade Japanese knives in that kitchen, and I don't think any of us wants this evening to end in a half-fat-crème-fraîche-induced bloodbath.

I leave Lara and Mum to it on the sofa and follow Catherine at haste into the kitchen.

Chapter Eighteen

OK, so Catherine was a *tiny* bit bossy with Barney in the kitchen, pressuring him to plate up the starters with the result that the Herring Two Ways has become Herring One Way. Which I suppose, really, is just Herring.

But at least now we're all gathered around the tiny table, the atmosphere is just the way I wanted it to be again. The tea- and fairylights are casting the place in a cosy glow, and everyone is elbow to elbow, passing each other the crispbread and pouring each other wine in a way that reminds me of those Mediterranean family gatherings at long, trestle tables under trailing vines. And even if we're nibbling our way slightly nervously through the herring rather than chowing down on huge plates of steaming pasta, at least everybody seems to be having a good time. Even Mum, still a little bit red-eyed and sniffly, is putting a brave face on things and happily knocking back the wine Will has poured her.

Though come to think of it, that might not be the wisest course of action. I mean, it's possible that some of the red eye and sniffliness is as much down to an excess of Scandinavian punch as anything else, in which case she really ought to be on nothing but fizzy water for the rest of the night.

I lean round behind her to get Will's attention on her other side. 'Go a bit steadier with that,' I whisper, jerking my head at the bottle of white in his hand.

'Sorry?'

'The wine. Not so much!'

'Isabel, I've had one glass of punch and half a glass of wine since I got here an hour and a half ago,' he says. Evidently whatever anger – jealousy? – he felt about my text to Dan earlier has been replaced, again, by the same old careful politeness we seem to use with each other most of the time these days. 'I thought I might have one glass with dinner.'

'Not you! Mum!'

'Yes, darling?' Mum thinks I'm talking to her, and pushes her seat backwards a little way so that she can join in the conversation Will and I have been holding behind her shoulders. 'Everything all right with you two?'

'Fine, Mum.'

'Really? I did worry, you know, that it might be rather difficult for you both, sitting down at Lara and Matthew's engagement dinner, when they've not even been going out as long as the two of you. But you seem to be coping with it very well, Iz-Wiz, and as for you, Will, you look quite relaxed! Not too relaxed, though, I hope, because you probably shouldn't leave it too long before –'

'Mum!' I push her chair in closer to the table and

flap at Will to pour some Perrier into her water glass. 'You should have a sip of this.'

'What? Oh, don't be silly, Isabel. Your father's driving home.'

'Even so . . .'

'Well, I need a little bit more wine, anyway, because Matthew's going to make a toast. Aren't you, darling?' Mum reaches round me to pat Matthew's hand, but misses and accidentally pats his Herring instead. 'Didn't you say you were going to make a toast?' she repeats, and then suddenly giggles. 'Or maybe a crispbread would be more appropriate!'

'That's right, Mum.' Matthew raises his glass. 'I *would* just like to propose a toast.' He turns to Lara, who is already gazing at him in rapture. 'Now, I don't want to give too much of a preview of my wedding speech in a few months' time, so let me just say that Lara, you're the best thing that has ever happened to me – even better than England winning the Rugby World Cup!' He grins around the table at his own joke for a moment, and then turns back to face Lara. 'You're the light of my life, Lars, and I can't tell you how happy you made me when you agreed to be my wife.' He chinks his glass to hers and they exchange a smile that, just for a moment, makes my heart ache. 'To my beautiful bride-to-be!'

'Hear, *hear*,' says Dad, approvingly, because toasts are his kind of thing, even if he usually does prefer to be the one making them.

'Hear, hear,' echoes Will, with such heartiness – albeit

rather forced-sounding to my expert ear – that I get this sharp pang of guilt that I was even thinking about text-flirting with Dan Britten-Jones. I mean, would Dan come to one of my stressful family events and join in with such gusto? Or, more likely, would he loiter about the sidelines making sharp witticisms and trying to flirt with Lara? But when I glance at Will to mouth a quick *thank you*, he slides his own eyes away from mine and busies himself with the Perrier bottle again.

'Hear, hear,' Mum adds, rather tearfully, into her wine glass.

All eyes fall on Catherine, who's obviously supposed to add a *hear, hear* of her own. But she doesn't. She simply gives a dazzling, though insincere smile in Matthew's direction. 'Well, nobody's denying she's beautiful, of course! But one doesn't get a Ph.D. just by being pretty!'

Matthew grins back at her. He's either not detected the slight edge in her voice or he's decided to ignore it. 'You're not wrong about that, Catherine! Let's face it, if our kids are geniuses, it'll be thanks to Lara's genes rather than mine!'

I hear a noise that I think is the dishwasher breaking down before realising that it's just Mum, letting out a noisy gasp.

'Oh, *Matthew*, darling, are we going to be grand-parents again already? Is Hypatia going to have a little cousin? Oh, though would she be a cousin if you were, well, unmarried before the baby was born? Not that *I* mind, of course, but John –'

Lara holds up a hand. 'I'm not pregnant, Moira!' she says, with a rather tight smile.

I don't like myself for this, but I can't help thinking rather smugly of Lara's words at The Wolseley: *she's been extremely considerate so far.*

Yes, OK. I *said* I didn't like myself.

'Oh, well, that's all the better, then, isn't it?' Dad says, casting a rather peculiar look in Mum's direction. I'd assume he was trying to shut her up as usual if he didn't look so . . . edgy. 'I mean, not that we'd *really* mind, just like Moira said. But let's just get the wedding out of the way first, shall we?'

'I think there's rather more to "get out of the way" than that.' Catherine has a rather pinched expression around the sides of her mouth that I don't think is just to do with the Herring she's eating. 'What about that paper you were talking about doing with Professor Stevens from UCL, Larissa? I don't think that's the kind of thing you ought to be putting on the back-burner just so you can start a family.'

'I'm not putting anything on any back-burners, Catherine.' Lara takes a sip from her water glass; I think it's one of her delaying tactics, to make sure she thinks before she speaks. 'Margaret Stevens hasn't even started applying for the funding, and she's away on sabbatical at Harvard almost all of next year.'

'Harvard?' Catherine's eyebrows shoot up. 'What a wonderful opportunity. Have you asked if she's looking for a good junior researcher to take with her?'

'It's Harvard, Catherine.' Lara puts down her fork.

'Do you not think the place is already bursting at the seams with good junior researchers?'

There's a slightly awkward silence.

Then Dad clears his throat. 'Is this that paper you were discussing with me the other weekend, Lara? Because it sounded quite fascinating.'

'Oh, it absolutely *is* fascinating, John,' says Catherine, beaming at him brightly. 'And Professor Stevens is one of the most highly respected clinical psychologists in her field. There are plenty of people who'd be pushing as hard as they possibly could to work with her, and not letting anything distract them!'

'A wedding isn't a distraction!' Mum says, staring around at us all as though Catherine's just said something horribly racist and she's the only one who's noticed. 'My friend Barbara's niece actually took *three whole months* off work to sort out her wedding.'

'How extraordinary,' says Catherine. 'And what *was* her work? Some kind of basic office job?'

'No, she was a beauty therapist. And she's a stay-at-home mum now, actually.'

'Ah. Of course she is.'

'Actually, a cousin of mine took a whole month off work before her wedding,' Will suddenly says, in a light tone of voice that suggests he's trying to dissipate the palpable tension. 'And she's a professor of economics.'

'Well! I find that even more extraordinary.' Catherine leans across the table in search of another

340

front to wage her war on. 'A successful, educated woman, *wasting her time* with something as frivolous as that.'

It's time for me to force a serious change of subject. I mean, Will did try, but he's a mere amateur at these things. This evening is in danger of heading as rapidly southwards as Licky's wedding. 'Actually, while we're on the subject of weddings, this might be a great time to discuss Lara and Matthew's plans!' I say hastily. 'Wouldn't you say, Lara?'

Lara shoots me a grateful look, and for a moment, I get that Diana-and-Fergie feeling I was so much looking forward to, before she started sneaking off for clandestine lunches with Mum.

'So, Lars, Matthew, have you thought any more about when you'd like the wedding to take place?'

'Well, we've been thinking of late spring, haven't we, Matt?'

Matthew nods, reaching for the wine bottle to ill-advisedly top Mum's glass up. 'Obviously we'd hope for good weather at that time of year, but if we put up a nice sturdy marquee in the paddock, that should cover all eventualities.'

'Paddock?' Mum is looking confused.

'The paddock at The Beeches, Mum,' says Matthew. 'You remember Catherine's house, in Chilcompton?'

'*That's* where you're having the reception?'

'Ah, well, there's nothing nicer than a good old-fashioned reception in the garden!' says Dad, approvingly. 'Can't tell you what a terrible waste of money it is to go to all the trouble of hiring out a whole hotel when there's a perfectly decent garden going to waste!'

What the hell's happened to *him*? I'd assume it was the Scandinavian punch having as dramatic an effect on his personality as it has on Mum's, if it weren't for the fact that Dad's barely touched a drop of the stuff because of the drive home.

'Well, if they want a nice garden to have the reception in, John, then why not ours?' Mum turns to Lara. Her face is flushed more than ever, and her nose is getting shiny. 'You know, if it's late spring you're thinking of, some of my roses will already be out, and there's probably just enough room for a small marquee at the bottom of the garden next to my rhododo . . . doden . . . rhoden . . .'

'Oh, Moira, that really is so kind.' Lara can't help her eyes sliding towards Mum's empty glass, in some alarm. 'But we couldn't impose all of that on you.'

'It's no imposition! And much more convenient for you, too! I mean, I presume you're planning on having the service at St Peter's in Shepton Mallet, so it'll save your guests from a long trek out to Chilcompton afterwards.'

'They're having a *church* wedding?' It's Catherine's turn to stare round the table as though Mum's just made a racist slur. 'Larissa? What the hell?'

'Actually, we haven't had time to think about that yet.' Lara glances up at Matthew for a helping hand, but he's too busy helping himself to more crispbread. 'I mean, obviously it's something we're considering . . .'

'Considering?' Mum bleats. 'You're only *considering* it? But where would you get married if you *didn't* get married in a church?'

'Now, Moira, there's no need to overreact,' Dad says. 'Marley and Daria didn't get married in a church, after all.'

'Well, of course Marley and Daria didn't get married in a church!' Mum snaps. Actually *snaps*. The first time I've heard her snap at Dad in . . . actually, I don't think I've ever heard her snap at Dad before. 'They're mathematicians! They're not *allowed* to believe in God!'

'Actually, Mum, I don't think there's a specific rule about that,' I say, starting to reach for people's empty dishes. 'Oooh, clean plates! I'll pass all your compliments to Barney in the kitchen, of course, and –'

'But don't you think it would be hypocritical for *you* to marry in church, Larissa?' Catherine is leaning towards her. 'Just like . . . sorry, who is this Marley chap?'

'He's Matthew's brother, Catherine,' Lara says, icily. 'I have mentioned him once or twice.'

Catherine is unembarrassed. 'I mean, you've barely set foot inside a church since you were a child.'

'I went to church when Dad's triplets were christened six years ago.'

'Oh, well! If it's your *father's* hypocrisy we're talking about –'

'We're not talking about anyone's hypocrisy.' Lara's voice rises. 'We're talking about *my wedding*.'

'And Matthew's wedding too,' Catherine says, meaningfully.

'What's that supposed to mean?'

'Well, maybe *Matthew's* the one who wants to get married in a church.'

'Actually, I'm not all that bothered either way,' Matthew muses, chewing on a bit of crispbread. 'Whatever you want, really, babe.'

'*Babe*?' Catherine's eyebrows shoot upwards. 'Goodness me, Matthew. All that time you spend with sports-mad teenage boys is clearly having a rather detrimental effect on your vocabulary!'

There's another brief silence, more awkward even than the last. I think, now, that even Matthew might have noticed that there's tension at the table.

'Catherine, there's certainly nothing wrong with being a teacher,' says Dad, lightly, 'if that's what you're implying.'

'A *games* teacher,' Catherine says, not quite so lightly.

This is too much for Lara, who shoves back her chair. 'Oh, and *doctors* make such ideal husbands, don't they, Mother? Why else would you have married three of them?'

'Well, at least I found them mentally challenging,' Catherine retorts.

Mum gasps. 'My son is not mentally challenged!'

'So, venison for everyone?' I trill, clattering the

plates in an attempt to stop anyone else from speaking.

Will has got to his feet, too, and is already making a move for the kitchen. 'I'll tell Barney to start bringing it through.'

'Great! I hope we're all still hungry!'

'Actually, I'm not.' Lara gets up too, reaching for her handbag. 'I'm sorry, Moira, John, but Matthew and I really must be leaving now.'

'Larissa, for God's sake, you're overreacting . . .'

Lara simply ignores Catherine, jabbing a bewildered Matthew in the ribs until he, too, gets up. 'Would you tell Barney how lovely the food was, please, Iz?'

'Lars, come on, don't go.'

'No, Iz. I'm sorry. And thank you, for organising such a . . . a special evening. Come on, Matthew.'

My brother follows her out of the room, and a moment later, we hear the front door closing.

I'm actually pretty grateful, for once, for Dad's obsession with finding a nearby parking space, as me and Will help him manoeuvre a quietly weeping Mum along the pavement and into the passenger seat of the Volvo. Once we've settled her in, I hop into the back, because they're going to drop us off in Battersea on the way south-west out of London.

I'm all geared up for some kind of diatribe about how I've ruined yet another family occasion by allowing Mum to be served lethal akvavit-based cocktails, but actually Dad stays silent all the way through the park, until, just as we pass the looming bulk of the Albert Hall, he clears his throat.

'It's going to be a rather long journey home. I wonder if we might be better off finding a simple hotel for the night.'

'I think that's a very good idea, John,' Will says. 'There's a Holiday Inn in Putney that I know is quite reasonable. If you like, I'll look them up as soon as we get back to the flat and I can call ahead and book you a room.'

'That's a brilliant idea, Will!' I say, desperate to let him know how much I appreciate his help. 'And Putney isn't too far for you to make it tonight at all, Dad. I mean, it could be difficult for you to pull over on the motorway if Mum needs to be sick or something.'

'Well, I doubt that would be an issue. In thirty-five years of marriage, I've never known your mother to be sick from drinking too much.'

I accidentally catch his eye in the rear-view mirror. 'But *has* she ever actually drunk this much before?'

'Well, that's a fair point you make, actually, Isabel.' Dad sounds mildly surprised, as though he's just witnessed a chimpanzee making a cup of tea. 'She does like her occasional Baileys, of course. But I've not seen her inebriated for many years. Probably not since our own engagement party, now I come to think of it. Though that was probably just to wash down my mother's avocado prawns.'

I think this is his attempt at lightening the situation,

but you never can tell with Dad. And jokes about Grandma Jean are so few and far between that I daren't assume it's anything of the sort.

We lapse back into silence until we cross Albert Bridge, when Will has to start giving Dad precise directions.

'Seems like a nice area,' he says, as we slide into a parking space just over the road from the flat.

'Yes, it's great.'

'Though I hope you don't let Isabel walk back beside the park late at night, Will. You know, it isn't sensible to take a path alongside a big open space like that. You never know who might be lurking in there.'

'Well, as long as it wasn't someone who could squeeze through the six-inch gap between the railings to grab me, Dad, I think I'd be fine.'

'There's no need to be cheeky.' He sounds offended. 'I'm only trying to look out for your safety.'

'Don't worry, John,' Will says, already unbuckling his seat belt. 'I wouldn't want Isabel doing anything of the sort. Her safety is of paramount importance to me. Now, shall I just nip inside and make that call to the Holiday Inn? Might be easier if I just go and do it quickly now, save you having to – er – disturb Moira. Though you're obviously very welcome to come in for a coffee . . .?'

'No, better not, I think,' Dad says. 'But I'd appreciate you phoning ahead.'

'No problem.' Will slips out of the car and makes his way towards the front door. It's only a couple of minutes before he's heading back out towards us again, giving a thumbs up. He leans down at Dad's open window. 'All fine, John, they're expecting you.'

God, he's so *capable*. It's one of the things I always fancied about him, and even these peculiar barriers that have come up between us these last couple of weeks can't prevent me from wanting to leap out of the car and throw myself into his arms. Obviously I can't, though, not with him and Dad shaking each other's hands and exchanging see-you-soons, and then Will saying he'll leave us to it and go inside and put the kettle on. Which is a bit odd, as neither he nor I are big late-night tea drinkers. But there's no time to dispute this, as he's already walking towards the flat, leaving just us Bookbinders behind to say our good nights to each other.

I unbuckle my seat belt. 'OK, Dad, will you phone me when you've checked in to the Holiday Inn? Just so I know you've got there OK?'

He frowns. 'I wouldn't want to wake you.'

'I'll still be awake. Or can you text?'

'Can I do that with this?' He reaches back into the glove compartment and pulls out an extremely new, unused-looking BlackBerry. 'The senior staff have been badgering me to get one of these for ages,' he add, stabbing ineffectually at a couple of keys. 'I mean, I've no idea how the thing works. Totally overrated as a form of communication, if you ask me. Not to mention the fatal impact they're having on language, and spelling, and –'

'Actually, Dad, you can just get Mum to call me first thing tomorrow,' I say, before he can work himself up with anger about all the other reasons a BlackBerry is the work of the devil, aside from the obvious one that it's just that he doesn't know how to use it.

'Yes, well. It's probably better.'

I climb out of the car and go round to the passenger side. Mum's window is open – I think Dad was hoping the chill blast of air on her face might mitigate the effects of the akvavit – so I lean through and give her a quick kiss on the cheek. ''Night, Mum.'

There's not even a grunt in reply. She's out for the count, her head lolling sideways and her feet propped up on a plastic carrier that's been stuffed with . . .

With what looks a lot like a pink trenchcoat.

I can see one row of buttons, and the buckled belt trailing out of the carrier, as though it's been hastily bunged in there to prevent anyone – to prevent *me* – from seeing it.

'Dad?' I ask suddenly, seeing my opportunity before I've actually got time to think about whether I want to take it. 'This might sound like a weird question, but was Mum up in town this afternoon? Before the party, I mean?'

'What?'

'Well, I'm not saying anyone's making stuff up or anything, but Barney . . .'

'The herring obsessive?'

'. . . the *chef* – He thought he saw Mum near Baker Street this afternoon. And Mum said she wasn't, but then I saw her shoes . . . and now her mac –'

I'm not making any sense – it has been a long day, after all – so it's not surprising when Dad suddenly cuts me off. 'Baker Street, you say?'

Oh, now that *is* surprising. I was assuming he'd just scoff and tell me not to be so silly, and that the shoes and mac are just a coincidence and Barney must have imagined it. 'Er . . . yes, that's right.'

His mouth purses, just for a moment. 'I don't think that can possibly have been the case, Isabel.'

'Oh. So she did come up in the car with you?'

'Yes, Isabel! I think I'd have noticed if she didn't!' Dad turns the engine back on, irritably. 'We really should be making tracks now.'

'Of course. And thanks for coming all this way. I'm sorry . . . well, I'm sorry it didn't exactly go according to plan.'

'Don't be silly, Isabel,' he says, though some of his irritation seems to have diminished. 'It wasn't your fault. In actual fact, you managed to organise a very pleasant party.'

I blink at him, wordless with astonishment.

'Matthew was rather silly, giving your mother all that lethal punch. And as for Catherine . . .' Dad sucks in some air, and then blows it out again. 'She may be an extremely bright and interesting woman, but she has all the basic human decency of a swamp dweller. Really, it's astounding that Lara's turned out such a sweet and charming girl, with a mother like that!'

The thing I'm really astounded about is that I appear to be getting off scot-free, for once. But I've been the object of Dad's ire often enough to feel the need to defend the current targets. 'I think Matthew just wanted Mum to relax and have a good time. And Catherine really isn't as bad as everyone thinks, honestly, Dad. She's just got very strong opinions on certain things.'

'Yes. Having my son as her future son-in-law, for one,' Dad says drily.

'Really, Dad, I don't think she meant –'

'Oh, I think she did, Isabel. And she's entitled to her opinion, of course. But from what I gather, she's not exactly been the most hands-on parent for most of Lara's life, so the thing I find really unforgivable is that she seems to think she has some kind of divine right to start interfering now.'

I don't say anything. Because actually, I can't argue with much of that.

'Well, you'd better be getting inside. It's cold.' Dad hovers for a moment as if he's unsure what to do. And then, quite suddenly, he reaches across Mum, out of the open window, and gives my hand a very quick squeeze. 'Good night, Isabel. It was – well, it *should* have been – a nice evening.'

He waits until I've opened the front door and have crossed, safely, over the threshold before he pulls away, indicating carefully as he turns the corner.

Chapter Nineteen

Well, that's a bit weird.

It's barely eight fifteen in the morning and there are voices in the corridor, outside my bedroom.

Have we taken in a lodger? Did Will invite a friend for a sleepover last night?

Do thirty-five-year-old solicitors have sleepovers?

I pull my head out from under the pillow just as the door opens, and Will sticks his head around it.

'Iz? Are you awake?'

'Mnhn-hnnh.' *I* may be awake, but obviously that information hasn't yet transmitted itself to my lips, tongue or vocal cords.

'Your mother's here.'

'*What?*'

He closes the door behind him. 'I've just sent her along to make tea in the kitchen,' he whispers. Actually, it's less loud, even, than a whisper; I think he has the measure of Mum, and realises it's perfectly possible for her to have produced a Holiday Inn toothbrush glass from inside her handbag and have it pressed up against our bedroom door for a good old snoop. 'Didn't you hear her ringing the bell five minutes ago?'

'No . . . I was fast asleep.' I would add something flirty about the reason for our respective late starts this morning, which is that Will practically pounced on me when I got in last night. Or I practically pounced on him. What with all the panting and grabbing and clothes-shedding, it wasn't really clear who was pouncing on whom. Certainly it was clear that Will's ruse about leaving me in the car to say good night to Mum and Dad while he 'put the kettle on' was just that – a ruse. Because what he was actually doing was giving our bedroom a hasty spruce-up – making the bed, all the better to fall passionately into; lighting a couple of my Diptyque candles, all the better for romantic candle-lit romping. But what exactly prompted his sudden amorousness, I've no idea. I mean, I know why *I* suddenly came over all frisky, after that sexy display of alpha-male capability (all right, it was only booking a Holiday Inn in Putney, not heading up a hostile merger on Wall Street, but I'm easily impressed), but I don't know what it was that I did that got him all fired up.

Unless it was something to do with Dan Britten-Jones, and that text message.

Well, whatever it was, I have to say, it made a very refreshing change from the chilly politeness of the past few weeks. Last night, for the first time since I moved in, we were a lot less Jane Austen and a lot more Jilly Cooper.

'Well, did she say what she was *doing* here?' I hiss.

Will shakes his head, reaching for the blue-and-white Paul Smith tie that – ooh, *yes*, I remember – is still loosely knotted around one of our bed-posts, and slipping it round his neck. 'No. I assumed you were expecting her.'

'No! I thought they were heading back to Shepton Mallet first thing this morning!' I jump out of bed and dart to the mirror, checking my face for any outward signs of last night's fun and games. But no, my blissful glow has been replaced by a wild-eyed look of confusion. 'Frankly, after last night, I'm amazed she's even upright.'

'Isabel? Are you in there?' The bedroom door is edging open, and Mum's voice is floating round it.

'Mum!' The last thing I want is her coming into the bedroom, so I leap out of bed with a speed that would impress Usain Bolt. 'Yes, Mum, I am in here,' I say, peering round the door. 'But Will's just getting ready for work. Can you wait a minute?'

'Oh, of course!' Her eyes are wide, and faintly ringed with an overload of Touche Éclat that doesn't quite hide the dark circles beneath them. She's in the same clothes as yesterday – though still minus the cerise mac – and her hair looks flat, and urgently in need of her usual daily shampoo and condition. 'I was just making some tea, and then I thought maybe Will would prefer coffee, but I'm afraid I don't know how to begin using that huge machine.'

'Tea is fine, Mum –'

'And actually, Moira, I really do need to be getting

off to work,' Will interrupts, coming up behind me and opening the bedroom door so he can get past.

'Oh.' Mum looks disappointed. 'What a shame. I was hoping we'd all be able to have a good old gossip about the engagement party.' She lowers her voice conspiratorially, as though Catherine might have bugged our flat. 'Wasn't it a dreadful night?'

'Well, of course *certain people* didn't behave themselves all that well,' says Will, which somehow manages to agree to nothing while at the same time making Mum feel he's shoulder to shoulder with her in the matter. 'But it was a terrific party otherwise. I mean, Iz does have a talent for organising these things, doesn't she?'

Yup, I was absolutely right to have extremely hot sex last night with this man. He really is a treasure.

'Oh, well, of course she does!' Mum says. 'But that only made it all the worse – that she'd gone to all that trouble, and your nice friend Barnaby did all that delicious food . . . and as for poor Lara and Matthew, their night was just completely ruined!'

'Well, they do say the path of true love never runs smooth.' Will leans down and gives me a swift kiss, then gives Mum a farewell peck on the cheek as he reaches for the briefcase on the hall table. 'But I think we can all pretty much rely on the fact that a wedding will dig a whopping great pothole in the middle of it! Lovely to see you, Moira. Have a good day, Iz.'

We both stare after him as he pulls the front door shut.

'What was he talking about, Iz-Wiz?' Mum asks, after a moment. 'Potholes . . . paths . . .'

'Never mind, Mum.' The glow of last night has receded, instantly, to a feeble flicker. I feel a bit like the Ready Brek Man with a blown fuse. I swallow, hard. 'It doesn't matter.'

'Well, maybe it *should* matter! I mean, it sounds like he's not all that keen on the idea of weddings full stop!'

'Mum, lots of men aren't that keen on the idea of weddings. It's no big deal.'

'You see, this is the thing that concerned me about you two moving in together,' she's carrying on, following me along the hallway towards the kitchen, where there are absolutely no signs that she ever began making tea, not even a boiling kettle. 'It may be old-fashioned, Iz-Wiz, but there are some people who'd say that no man is going to buy the cow when he can get the milk for free!'

I don't say anything. I need a coffee. And after Will's throwaway comment as he headed out the door, a huge, stodgy, comfort-food-laden breakfast would fit the bill as well.

'Oh *dear*, Isabel.' Mum is actually wringing her hands now. 'I mean, it didn't sound promising at all, the more I think about it. When you moved in together, I thought it might not be too long before the two of you were announcing an engagement just like Lara and Matthew, and now I don't know . . .'

'But you just said you were concerned about us moving in together! Because Will would get his . . . his

356

milk for free! You can't say you expected an engagement as well.'

'Just because I was *concerned*, darling, didn't mean I wasn't *hopeful*.'

I flick on the kettle and reach into the cupboard for my coffee filters, snatching a digestive from the open packet while I'm at it. 'Anyway, Mum, I don't believe you've come here to discuss my situation with Will.'

'Oh! So it *is* a situation . . .'

'Mum. What are you doing here? I mean, not that I'm not pleased to see you,' I add, when I realise I may have sounded a bit harsh. 'But you know I have to work, and you didn't say you were staying in town today.'

'Well, I'm not, really. I mean, I wasn't planning to.' She sits down at the kitchen table and puts her cardigan over the back of another chair, not at all as if she's *not planning* to stick around. 'But, Isabel, your father mentioned this morning, before he left to get to school, that you'd been quizzing him about this supposed sighting of me yesterday . . .'

'I wasn't *quizzing* him.'

'. . . and I suppose I felt I should come and tell you, Iz, that your friend Barnaby was right. I *was* in town yesterday afternoon.'

I turn round and stare at her. 'What?'

'I came up early to have a little look at wedding dresses in the shops on Chiltern Street.'

I lean back against the worktop, struggling to look casual. 'With Lara, yes?'

'No! Not with Lara! By myself.'

'By yourself?' This is unexpected, and not altogether convincing. 'Not . . . I don't know . . . with Barbara or anything?'

'Oh. Oh, yes, that would have been a good idea.' Mum is turning slightly pink. 'But no, Isabel. I came alone.'

'But what on earth for?'

'I just wanted to get an idea of the kind of styles that are fashionable at the moment, so I could offer a worthwhile opinion if I came out dress-hunting with you and Lara.' She stares, fixedly, at the floor. 'That's why I was so upset yesterday when I knew you'd been to look at dresses without me.'

I'd be finding all this quite heartbreaking if it weren't for the fact that it still sounds extremely odd.

'Then why did you tell me you weren't here? And Dad, too – he told me you'd driven up together.'

'Yes, well, your father was only lying because he realised *I* had, and that I must have wanted to keep it a secret from you.'

It's a smooth, plausible answer. Almost *too* smooth and plausible?

I mean, you can't kid a kidder.

'So why were you keeping it a secret? I mean, there's no shame, Mum, in getting a bit overexcited about this wedding. I've got pretty overexcited about it myself!'

'Really?' Mum peers up at me and, to my shock, I can see she's got tears in her eyes. 'So you understand?'

'Well, of course I understand! Mum, please . . .' I hurry to her and put my arms around her shoulders as the tears start to stream down her cheeks. 'Why on earth are you crying?'

'I'm just finding it all rather emotional at the moment . . . It's why that awful woman upset me so much last night, you know.'

'Mum.' I pull back and look at her. 'Come on. *That awful woman* is going to be Matthew's mother-in-law. Can't you try to get along?'

She makes a sound that's halfway between a sniff and a hiccup. 'She doesn't deserve it, you know! All the happiness that comes from having a close, loving family, a family you've actually *strived* to maintain over so many years.'

'I know, Mum.' I pat her shoulder, hoping the tears won't start again. 'She's not exactly the traditional sort.'

'I'll say! And you know what I think, Isabel? I think she's a coyote.'

'A what?'

'Oh, I read all about it, Iz-Wiz, in the *Sunday Times Style* section the other week. Older women, preying on younger men.'

'A *cougar*, Mum.'

'Yes, that might have been it.' Mum sniffles. 'Anyway, all those nasty things she was saying about Matthew were obviously just because she's all eaten up with jealousy inside that she can't get herself a handsome young man like that any more.'

359

I can't deny I'm slightly relieved as my mobile starts to ring. Less so when I grab it from my bag and see that it's Summer.

'Mum, I really have to take this. It's my bride.'

Mum flaps a hand as she fishes in her own bag for a tissue.

'Summer?' I pick up. 'Don't worry, I haven't forgotten, I'm meeting you at Tiffany's at ten sharp to choose your wedding jewellery.'

'Oh, hi, Izzie!' Summer sings down the phone. 'Actually, I've decided my wedding jewellery can wait. I mean, Tim and I are having so many little spats in the run-up to the wedding that he just keeps increasing the amount he says I can spend on the jewellery every time he apologises. I could be up to a hundred thousand in a week's time!'

I silently question, not for the first time, Summer's real motivation for marrying Tim Holland.

'Anyway, I'm here right now with Wendy . . . say hi, Wendy!'

'Hi,' comes an unenthusiastic grunt.

'Hi, Wendy. Nice to hear your voice.'

'And Wendy's just told me she saw an advert on the tube this morning for this big wedding show, in Battersea Park,' Summer continues. 'You didn't mention anything about that, Izzie!'

'The Designer Wedding Show? Well, no, I didn't mention it, because I didn't think it was particularly worth a visit for you, Summer.'

'But Wendy thinks it'll make a *great* segment on the

show! She's been getting worried about us not having enough action – well, apart from when Kieron picks me up and pretends to chuck me around!' she giggles. 'Honestly, Izzie, he was *so* funny yesterday, mucking about with his Swiss balls . . .'

I don't want to hear about Kieron's balls, Swiss or otherwise. I'm far more taken up with the fact that Summer is obviously about to summon me to meet her and Wendy (and the Zenith TV crew) at the Designer Wedding Show in the park.

Because what the hell do I do if Pippa Everitt is there?

I mean, admittedly, it's unlikely. I heard Pippa bitch about wedding fairs on more than one occasion, and I know for a fact that she turned down a VIP invite to the National Wedding Show before ranting at length about what a waste of her valuable time it would be, and not even a couple of free glasses of cheap champagne could induce her to spend half a day being badgered by suppliers she wouldn't cross the room to spit on if they were on fire. OK, I paraphrase, but that was about the gist of it.

But I'm not sure it's a risk I really want to take, nevertheless.

'Well, it sounds great, Summer, but probably it doesn't make any sense for me to come along with you.'

'Don't be silly, Izzie! *Obviously* you have to be there! How are we going to film any of the really good people showing at the fair if we don't have you there to introduce us? And Wendy thought it would be fun for you to catch up with all your friends and colleagues in the business.'

Oh, Wendy did, did she?

'Well, actually, Summer, I think you'd be surprised how few suppliers I could really call my friends,' I say, trying to keep my tone very light in case Wendy's listening in. 'I mean, wedding planning is a terribly *solitary* profession, at the end of the day. We hunt alone. Like . . . like wolves.' I hope to God that wolves *do* hunt alone; it's not something I'd suspect Summer to know, but I wouldn't put it past Wendy to haul out her iPhone and check it out on Wikipedia.

'Whatever, Izzie, but this show is all about my wedding, and I want my wedding planner to be filmed with me at the wedding show.' Summer isn't about to take no for an answer. 'I'm not taking no for an answer,' she continues, confirming my suspicions. 'We'll meet you inside at ten thirty. OK?'

'But, Summer . . .'

'No arguments, Izzie! See you then.'

I put down the phone.

'Is there a problem, Iz-Wiz?' Mum asks, blowing her nose.

'Yes. No. Maybe. I just have another quick call to make,' I say, heading for the privacy of the bedroom. 'Why don't you get that cup of tea you were talking about?'

As soon as I'm safely behind a closed door, I dial

Pippa Everitt's landline number with slightly trembling fingers. I'm relieved when an unfamiliar voice answers.

'Oh, hello, is that Pippa Everitt the wedding planner?' I ask, putting on the poshest accent I can possibly manage. I mean, forget silver spoons, I sound like I was born with a whole cutlery canteen in my mouth.

'Actually, this is Camille, her assistant.' Unbelievably, she sounds posher still. God, Pippa must be so thrilled she got shot of me. 'Would you like to speak to Pippa?'

'No, no, I'm sure you can help! I'm . . . er . . . Ishbel, calling from the Designer Wedding Show in Battersea Park. Now, we have Pippa down on our VIP list, but I just wanted to check we'd got that right?'

'Oh, no, you must have made a mistake. Pippa isn't going to the fair at all.'

'*Really*? Not at all? And definitely not today? You're quite sure?'

'Yes, absolutely sure.' Camille sounds slightly annoyed at my challenge to her competence. 'She's out of town on a venue visit all day, in fact, so I really don't appreciate you people calling up and badgering her to come along to an event which is a manifest waste of her valuable time!'

Wow. Pippa really has lucked out with her mini-me Camille.

'I do apologise. Didn't mean to badger! Have a lovely day, now!'

Actually, this event could be OK after all.

Not to mention the fact that I could use it to win back a few valuable brownie points with poor old Mum, and cheer her up a bit.

Cheer myself up a bit, too. Will's departing remark about weddings is still niggling at the back of my mind, and I wish I knew why he felt such a need to make a point. Especially after things were so much warmer between us – positively equatorial, in fact – last night.

Which reminds me, talking of hotness. I must get around to replying to Dan Britten-Jones' text, or he really will think I'm ignoring him.

I scroll down to find both his texts, and start replying to one of them.

Hi, Dan, sorry for the delay, no, the pictures haven't arrived yet but I'll keep an eye out . . .

Then – and it's weird, because my fingers almost seem to have taken on a life of their own – I stop writing that one, delete it, and start a fresh one.

Humble Wedding Planner informing Gorgeous Wedding Photographer that she wasn't ignoring him. Humble Wedding Planner busy last night at engagement event. Humble Wedding Planner will let Gorgeous Wedding Photographer know as soon as Mad Bride has seen his pictures.

I press Send. Then, without letting myself dwell on what I've just done a moment longer, I open the bedroom door and head back into the kitchen to ask Mum if she'd like to stay up in town and come and look at some wedding dresses after all. She's so excited that I barely notice the almost-instant bleep from my mobile. And it's another five minutes or so before I even check it to see what Dan has replied.

So you think I'm gorgeous, do you?

Mum is under the strictest possible instructions to keep a low profile at the wedding show, and I've made her even happier than she already is about the visit by assuring her that I'll join her for a good look around, just the two of us, as soon as I've finished with Summer, Wendy and the TV crew.

'Now, you make notes on anything you think Lara might like,' I tell her, as we head across Battersea Park towards the huge semi-permanent marquee near Chelsea Bridge, and I buy us both entrance tickets at the official kiosk. 'Dresses, cakes, stationers, florists . . .'

Mum's eyes are shining, all trace of tears long gone. 'Don't worry, Iz-Wiz, I'll make a note of everything! Now, dresses are the first priority, don't you think?' She wriggles her shoulder in excitement. 'I just can't wait to see what kinds of things are trendy at the moment!'

'You mean, apart from the stuff you saw on Chiltern Street yesterday?'

'Oh, well, of course.' Mum suddenly busies herself studying the little brochure that came with our tickets. 'Now, I think I'll go and settle down with a coffee at one of the bars first, Iz-Wiz, while you get started with your client. Maybe we'll bump into each other on the way round!'

'Yes . . . though if we do, Mum, you *must* remember not to say anything about me working for myself instead of for Pippa Everitt, OK?'

Mum performs that little zipping-up-your-mouth mime. 'You can trust me, Iz-Wiz!'

I leave her queuing for a cappuccino at the coffee bar just outside the main entrance, and then head through the doors into the marquee itself.

Good God.

It's no wonder Pippa avoids these things like the plague.

The huge marquee which, Tardis-like, seems even bigger inside than out, is teeming with women. And not just any women – hawk-eyed, lean, *hungry*-looking women, circling in packs like wild animals on the Serengeti. Honestly, it's making me come over a bit David Attenborough inside my head . . . *Observe the Great British Bride in her natural habitat . . . though at first it may be hard to distinguish her from the others in her pride, if you look closer you can spot the leanest and hungriest-looking of the group, generally also clutching a fat ring-binder and deliberately displaying her left hand as a signal to the other Brides that she, too, is the proud owner of a one-carat diamond . . .*

And it isn't just the brides and their entourages that are filling the place with noise and movement. There are also dozens and dozens of stalls and stands, each one fronted by what looks like a spare cast member from *Village of the Damned* – wild-eyed, brightly smiling salespeople, attempting to stop passers-by with tastes of wedding cake, or a look at one of their beautiful portfolios of photographs, or a peek at their selection of exquisite lace veils . . .

In fact, talking of exquisite lace veils, I can see Summer at that stand right now. Let's face it, she's pretty eye-catching – even if it weren't for the bright blonde hair or the candy-coloured hoodie and matching mini-skirt, you can hardly miss the TV crew milling around her. There's Weirdy-Beardy, looking . . . well, weird and beardy. And just a little bit pervy, if I'm honest, because he can't seem to take his eyes off Summer's smooth, tanned legs in her mini-skirt. Plus, of course, there's Tangerine Hair, who has, since I last saw her, become Egg-Yolk Yellow Hair. It's actually a bit of an improvement.

I catch Summer's eye and wave as I head over.

'Oh, Izzie!' She greets me with a little hug. 'Thank God you're here. Now listen, will you tell this lady that we're doing her, like, a *huge* favour here? I mean, footage of me trying on her stuff might end up on the opening credits of the show! But she's still being difficult about it.' She nods at the stall-holder, a stocky, wide woman in flowing palazzo pants and a silk jacket who looks more like an oblong than any woman – any *person* – I've ever seen before in my life.

'Look, madam, if you're not going to be buying anything, then I'm afraid I really don't want you messing around with my collection,' she's saying irritably to Wendy. 'I don't care if you *are* from the BBC . . .'

'We told her we're from the BBC?' I whisper to Weirdy-Beardy, who blinks rather guiltily back at me.

'Well, I *did* work for the BBC, even if it was just an internship,' he mutters. 'And it usually gets you in everywhere.'

'Oh, you're here now!' Wendy's voice is directed at me. 'Isabel, come and tell this woman you're a top wedding planner, and that you'll never let any of your clients wear so much as a wisp of lace from her precious bloody collection if she doesn't let us film Summer trying on some of these big flouncy old things.'

I give a nervous laugh. 'Oh, Wendy, I don't think there's any need for threats!'

'And she can be Elizabeth Taylor's personal wedding planner, for all I care,' the Human Oblong says, folding her arms belligerently. 'If you're not interested in buying any of my "big flouncy old things", then I'm not interested in you filming them.'

'Look,' I say, putting a hand on Wendy's arm and drawing her away, 'we're obviously not getting anywhere here. Why don't we go around and get some nice footage of Summer at some of the other stalls? I mean, there's this amazing-looking chocolate fountain stall right here.' I nod at the stall opposite, which has the words 'Chocs Away' emblazoned across its awning. 'Wouldn't it make good TV to have Summer trying it out?

Weirdy-Beardy stares in Summer's direction. 'I suppose. Eating melted chocolate –'

'Great!' I cut him off before he can say anything more explicit. 'Well, let's start there, then, shall we, Summer?'

Summer wrinkles her nose. 'I don't know . . . aren't chocolate fountains a little bit nineties?'

'And more to the point, what the hell does a chocolate fountain have to do with Hollywood?' Wendy demands.

'Oh, well, Hollywood is *all* about the chocolate fountain right now,' I say. 'Elton John had them at his latest Oscars after-party . . . Angelina Jolie has donated several of them to her favoured orphanages . . .'

I stop as my phone suddenly rings, but glancing down at it, I can see that it's just Mum, so I let it go to voicemail.

Summer's baby-blue eyes have widened at this link to the A list. 'Then I *have* to have one at my wedding.' She links arms with me and hauls me across to the other side of the central aisle to the Chocs Away stand.

There are several fountains on the go – a tall cascade of luscious dark chocolate, surrounded by piled-high strawberries; an even taller fountain right beside it with milk chocolate and some mini beignets; and a white chocolate one that's instantly caught Summer's eye, probably because it comes with pleasingly retro pink-and-white marshmallows for dipping.

'Ooooh, *Izzie*! That would go brilliantly with my colour scheme!'

'Yes, wouldn't it? We could put one in the chill-out zone, if you'd like, or we might be able to have three or four set up in between the tables after the main course, if people would prefer chocolate fountain to pudding.'

A beaming young salesman is coming over, proffering plates of chopped fruit. 'Please, ladies, feel free to dig in!' he says. 'And perhaps I can run you through our full range of high-end chocolate fountains? Now, what I think has taken your fancy here is our premium White Chocolate Cascade, for the true White Chocolate lover.'

Bloody hell, Mum has started ringing me *again*. I reach into my bag and press the Decline button.

'I know a lot of people think white chocolate is just for kids,' the salesman is continuing, 'but we think most of us are just big kids at heart!'

'Ooooooh, so is *this* the kind Angelina Jolie gives to the orphans?' Summer asks, reverentially.

'Um . . . I'm not sure we've ever had the pleasure of working with Miss Jolie.' Quick on his feet, the salesman is keen not to let an order slip away. 'But I can say quite categorically that yes, this is very much the model that she *would* choose.'

He stops and glares at me as, for the third time in the last minute and a half, my phone rings.

'Isabel, can you please just get that, and tell whoever it is to fuck off?' Wendy snaps, mopping the perspiration from her upper lip. 'How is Sven supposed to get any decent footage with that bloody awful ring going every five seconds?'

'Sorry. Just give me one sec . . .' I step a few feet away and answer my phone. 'Mum? Please, you have to leave me alone while I'm working!'

'I'm sorry, Iz-Wiz, but I thought I really should call!' Mum is whispering extremely hoarsely. 'To warn you!'

'Warn me? About what?'

'I've just seen her arriving, Iz! She and her friends just stopped off for a cappuccino, and now they're heading inside!'

'*Who* are?'

'That WAG, Isabel. The one whose wedding you ruined. Well, all right, darling, not *ruined* exactly –'

'Frankie Miller?' Automatically, my head snaps up and I stare towards the entrance doors. Sure enough, I can see them coming through. It's a veritable posse of glamazons: a steely-looking brunette who I vaguely recognise as another über-WAG, and who is obviously the bride (bulging file, blinding ring), flanked by a shorter, sulky, probably related brunette on one side, and Frankie Miller on the other. 'Oh *shit*.'

'Isabel! There's no need for that kind of language!' Mum drops her voice to a whisper again. 'But I was right to warn you, wasn't I, darling? I mean, doesn't *she* know you don't work for Pippa Everitt any more? You don't want to run into her with your new client, do you?'

'Yes, Mum, you were right to warn me. I have to

go.' I end the call, regretting with every fibre of my being that I've brought us here, to Chocs Away, slap bang on the central aisle. I mean, Frankie and her friends are going to have to go right past us if they want to get anywhere at all. And we're hardly bloody invisible, are we, with an entire camera crew standing right beside us?

Or rather, standing right beside *Summer*.

Yes! This is it. I could just slip away, into the interior of one of these other stalls, hide out until Frankie and her cohorts go past, and then discreetly make my exit from the marquee altogether. I mean, I can just tell Summer, afterwards, that I suddenly had a crippling stomach ache, or . . . or that the overpoweringly sweet smell of this white chocolate suddenly made me feel sick . . .

'What the fuck?' A voice suddenly rises above the noise of the crowd. It's broad Liverpool. It's Frankie. And I think she's just spotted the camera. 'Is that a *TV crew* there?'

As she starts shoving her way through the chocolate-dipping masses, I dart into the stall right behind me, almost knocking over a tulle-covered shop dummy as I go.

Oh *God*. How have I made *this* mistake?

I'm inside the veil stall. The *double-fronted* veil stall, I now realise.

'Oh, for God's sake. Didn't I tell you I had no interest in letting you film in here?' It's the Human Oblong, marching towards me.

'Yes, I know, I'm so sorry . . . I just fancied a bit of a second look . . . your range is simply stunning . . .'

Outside, there are more raised voices.

'We don't wanna get filmed today,' Frankie is saying loudly, and agitatedly. 'We was told there wasn't going to be any press here.'

'We're not press.' This is Wendy, equally loud and not much less agitated. 'We're just here to make a programme . . . for the BBC, as it happens. Nobody's interested in filming you.'

'You mean this'll get shown on TV?' This is the other WAG. Peeking around one of the tulle-shrouded shop dummies, I can see that she's putting her hands on her hips and squaring up to Wendy. 'My fiancé doesn't like me being shown on TV without permission. Even when they show me in the crowd at Stamford Bridge, he goes mental.'

'Well, I'm sorry about that, but we've as much right to be here as you,' says Wendy, staunchly. 'Cameras and all.'

Actually, I don't think they have.

'Actually, I don't think you have,' says Frankie, sharp as a razor. 'Got permission to film, have you? Should I go and ask one of the security people on the door?'

'Excuse me?' The Human Oblong has come up right behind me. She's regarding me with ill-concealed dislike. 'If you're not going to be buying anything, madam, then I really am going to have to ask you to leave. You've been hanging around that blasted chocolate fountain, and I don't want my merchandise unsaleable thanks to you! So if you don't mind . . .' She makes a little motion with her palms, as if to usher me away.

'I'm not going out there! I mean . . . er . . . I *am* going to be buying something!'

She frowns. 'I think your clients made it quite clear they weren't the biggest fans of my designs.'

The voices outside in the aisle are getting louder, Summer's joining them this time.

'Actually, we're here with a top wedding planner,' she's saying, 'so I really think it's OK for us to do a little bit of filming . . . Oh! Where's she gone? Wendy? Can you see Izzie?'

OK. It's no longer just a case of getting out of here. This whole thing really needs to get broken up before Summer starts calling out my name like she's looking for a lost puppy. How long is it going to take Frankie to twig that *Summer's* Izzie-the-Wedding-Planner might just be *her* Isabel-the-Wedding-Destroyer?

I grab one of the full-length veils that's hanging from a peg on the stall's back wall.

'You know, this one really is perfect,' I say, jamming the comb at the front into my hairline, and pulling forward the layers of lace until I'm shrouded in the thing. 'I'll take it!'

'Take it? But . . . are *you* getting married?'

'Well, not exactly. But then I always say, when you find something you really like, it's best just to get it right there and then, so you don't regret missing out later!' I flap at the heavy, beaded lace so I'm able to unzip my handbag and pull out my wallet. 'How much?'

'It's three hundred and sixty-five pounds.'

I swallow hard. 'Can you recommend anything a bit cheaper?'

'Yes, I can recommend something cheaper.' She points over my veiled shoulder. 'Somewhere over there, I believe, is the Berketex stand, where veils are not hand-sewn from finest English lace, beaded with Swarovski crystals . . .'

'OK, fine. It's worth every penny.' I shove my credit card at her, praying it isn't going to get rejected, and listen with bated breath to the furore outside.

'All right, fine, we're *not* from the BBC,' Wendy is saying, angrily 'but that still doesn't mean we've sneaked in to try to get secret footage of a load of footballer's wives . . .'

Thank God, my card's gone through. 'Well, you've really made my dreams come true!' I tell the Human Oblong, gathering the folds of the veil around me and lifting it up at the front so I don't trip.

She's staring at me in astonishment. 'But . . . don't you want me to pack it into a bag for you?'

'Oh God, no. I'm going to wear this right now.' I'm already on my way out. 'I mean, if you can't leave a wedding fair in a lovely big veil, then when *can* you?'

I don't know if it's the slanging match going on in their midst, or if it's because everyone here is so addled with wedding-fever that the sight of someone dashing past them in a cathedral-length veil isn't the slightest remarkable, but I get to the main doors without a hiccup. Then I throw back the tulle and grab the nearest security guard.

'Trouble in Aisle B. Unauthorised filming. Camera crew not meant to be here,' I mutter. And I'm relieved to see him heading across the marquee to break up the spat as I pull nearly four hundred quid's worth of veil out of my hair and go to haul Mum away from her cappuccino, towards the safety of the park.

YOU AND YOUR WEDDING *MAGAZINE*

HELP! I'VE JUST COME DOWN WITH WSS!!

You know the feeling – the church is booked, the guest list is written, but still it seems like you have a million jobs to do, and no time to do them in. You've bent your mum's ear twice a day for months, your bridesmaids are already avoiding your calls, and you fiancé has taken up permanent residence in the pub. Yes, you've fallen victim to WSS – that's Wedding Stress Syndrome to you and me. But don't worry, help is at hand!! Our very own Wedding Guru, top planner Isabel Bookbinder, gives us her tried-and-tested advice on how to stay sane as your Big Day approaches – if there's anyone who understands Wedding Stress Syndrome, it's Isabel!

'First things first: avoid wedding shows like the plague. Nothing – and I mean nothing – is more guaranteed to get your blood pressure rising and your heart pounding (classic signs of full-blown WSS) than a morning spent in a Tardis-like tent with a ~~mob of wild-eyed harpies~~ multitude of fellow brides-to-be, all ~~hellbent~~ determined to snare their perfect dress, florist or chocolate fountain! Far better for your mental health to make these kinds of important decisions from the comfort and privacy of your own home. Forget net-a-porter, eBay and excessive quantities of free porn: this is precisely what the internet was invented for.

'No matter how strong the temptation, do not feel obliged to throw any kind of engagement soiree. Yes, it

could be a terrific trial-run for your party-planning skills before you get stuck into your wedding arrangements; it could be a great first opportunity for both families to meet; it could just seem like a really good excuse to buy a fabulous new outfit and flash your sparkly new engagement ring at all and sundry. But don't forget that it could also be a terrific trial-run for people to practise their falling-out skills; a great first opportunity for your caterer to showcase his inexplicable love of North Atlantic oily fish; and a good excuse for your mum to get embarrassingly drunk on Scandinavian-spirit-based cocktails. If you really must insist on celebrating your engagement, why not consider a quiet evening in with a carefully chosen group of well-behaved friends, your darling fiancé and a nice easy Chinese takeaway? Alternatively, just treat yourself to a congratulatory spa day and admire your engagement ring while a nice silent beauty therapist gives you a luxury paraffin-wax hand treatment and manicure.

'No matter what the circumstances, I couldn't honestly advise hiring a film crew to follow you around in the run-up to your wedding. They will only draw attention to you at the most inconvenient of times, leading to acute attacks of WSS when you least expect them.

'Just in case anyone's looking, I do have an unworn (and never likely to be worn) exquisite handmade lace-and-Swarovski-crystal veil up for grabs. Thanks to a sudden attack of WSS, I paid nearly four hundred quid for the ~~bloody~~ thing, but I'm perfectly prepared to accept a hundred and fifty if it goes to a good home. ~~To be honest,~~

~~I'd even be prepared to give it away so it doesn't just sit about gathering dust and making my boyfriend think I'm obsessed by the idea of getting married~~ *Please email me at isabelb@individualweddings.com if you're interested!'*

Chapter Twenty

Even though I think she's eventually forgiven me for my role in the disastrous visit to the wedding fair the other week, Summer is still adamant that she won't take on board the extra calories that a menu tasting would require. So for this morning's scheduled trip to Broughton to do just that, I took Barney, instead, as an expert proxy. This was in many ways no bad thing – I had more fun than I think I'd have had with Summer and the Dragon Lady herself breathing down my neck – but it does mean that, with only three days to go, the bride and groom still haven't seen their venue.

If I was a suspicious person, I'd almost be starting to wonder if some of the excitement is wearing off before they've even made it down the aisle. And even though I'm not a suspicious person, even the remotest possibility of my second-ever wedding hitting the skids the way the first did is enough to make me ever so slightly anxious.

Which is why, even though I'm feeling rather dozy after my tasting of cappuccino of white bean (embarrassingly dated, according to Barney) and pot-roasted guinea fowl (so tough it might as well have been guinea *pig*, according to Barney), I give Summer a call the moment I've parted ways with Barney at Paddington Station – with about a million assurances that yes, I *will* bring his soda siphon the next time I see him – and jumped into a taxi.

'Just checking in to see how things are!' I sing at her, enthusiastically, as soon as she answers. 'And I wanted to fill you in on the fabulous menu tasting this morning!'

'Oh, yeah, right, that was today, wasn't it?' she puffs. 'How was the food?'

'Well, my foodie friend . . . I mean, our, er, *specialist catering consultant*, had a few suggestions that I think the chef was very happy to take on board.' This is a little bit of verbal Photoshopping. In fact, after Barney had complained not only about the bean soup and the guinea fowl/pig but also that the chef's Asian dipping sauce was too heavy on the soy and too light on the wasabi, that the chef's saffron risotto was insufficiently *al dente* and that his toffee-praline Pavlova was an insult to Pavlovas, the pair of them practically had a blood-feud going. Thankfully I managed to engineer a slight thaw when I convinced Sophie Britten-Jones to tell her chef that poor Barney suffers from something called Gastro-Tourette's, where he can't restrain himself from saying incredibly rude things about other people's cooking. 'Of course, there isn't very much time to make big changes, but they're certainly amenable to making a few tweaks here and there.'

'Oh, OK, well, that sounds good . . .' Summer is puffing even harder now. 'Sorry, Izzie, you've just caught me in the middle of my workout with Kieron.'

I send a little prayer to whichever patron saint is in charge of successful weddings that this is all I've caught her doing with Kieron.

'Hey, that reminds me,' she goes on. 'I need you to arrange for a taxi to collect Kieron at the train station on Friday night and drive him to my hotel, OK?'

'Summer!' I blurt, before I can stop myself. 'Are you sure . . . look, you'll be getting married the next day!'

'So?'

'Well, I'm just not sure it's all that appropriate.'

'*Christ*, Iz, it's only for a last-minute abs workout! So unless you *want* me to have a big roll of flab on my stomach on the big day . . . oh, hey, while I'm on the subject of that, I really need you to speak to that hot photographer and make sure he's *absolutely clear* that he can only shoot me side-on, or three-quarters to the camera. *Not* square to the camera, or I'll look like a heffalump.'

'Fine, Summer, I'll speak to him.' The mere thought of picking up the phone to speak to Dan sets my heart racing a little bit. We've not had any contact since those flirty texts the week before last, apart from the brief call I made a few days ago to tell him his sample photos had arrived and met with Summer's approval, but he was right in the middle of a meeting with one of his artists and so we didn't have long to chat. Still, he managed to send enough electricity crackling over the airwaves to power a small town. And given that there's not been too much electricity crackling my way from Will ever since the night of Lara's engagement party, I'll take any kind of spark I can get.

Not that I'm blaming Will, by the way. Not entirely. I think he'd have been more than happy to have a rerun of the whole tearing-each-other's-clothes off thing the very next night, but I just couldn't get myself in the mood. I mean, it's not all that easy to tear somebody's clothes off when you'd much rather just sit down with that person and hammer out the reasoning behind their little 'throwaway' comments about the general hideousness of weddings. Anyway, I've been incredibly busy with work ever since. Which Will, of all people, ought to understand. And I think he does understand, because he's given up attempting to tear anything off me. Mostly he just sticks his head round the door of my study and offers to make me hot drinks.

'And you'll book that taxi for Kieron too, yeah?' Summer is asking, reminding me that she's still puffing away on the other end of the phone.

Oh, let her have her so-called last-minute abs workout. I mean, I'm not exactly the moral police right now, am I?

'All right, Summer, I'll get that done. But really, I was just calling about the tasting, and to remind you that you've got your session with the psychologist tomorrow afternoon.'

The psychologist, by the way, being Lara. I think

she's still feeling a bit guilty about walking out of Catherine's dinner party, because she's agreed that she'll make time for a one-off last-minute therapy appointment with Summer.

'So, everything still OK on that front?' I double-check. 'We're still on?'

'Well, of course I'm still on!' Now Summer sounds as though she's put me on to speaker-phone, and I think I can hear a rowing-machine noise in the background. 'I can't wait to meet my celebrity psychologist!'

'Yes . . . but you know that Lara – I mean, Dr Alliston – isn't exactly a *celebrity* psychologist.'

'*Oh*! So, she hasn't, like, been on TV or anything?'

'Well, not to my knowledge –'

'But *all* the best shrinks are on TV,' she interrupts me, sounding dangerously close to Little Miss Grouchy again. 'I thought you were getting me some-body amazing!'

'Oh, well, all I mean is that I haven't actually *seen* any of the TV she's done,' I say, hastily. 'And I do know she's done quite a lot on the radio as well.' This, at least, isn't a total lie. Lara has been on the radio – on Woman's Hour, once, when the well-known TV psychologist they'd booked to talk about rising stress levels in the workplace had to cancel at the last minute because she had too much to do.

'*Kieron*!' Summer suddenly shrieks, not listening to me any more. 'You *know* that tickles!'

This is my cue to let her get on with her workout –

or whatever the hell it is that she and Kieron are actually up to – and give Lara a quick call to reconfirm tomorrow's five o'clock appointment.

'Lara, hi!' I say, as soon as she picks up. 'Are you at work yet?'

'No, I'm just on my way in.'

I glance at my watch. 'At twelve o'clock?'

'Yeah, well, I slept badly. I only had paperwork to do this morning anyway, so I'll catch up.'

Instantly, I feel bad that I'm neglecting her in favour of Summer. 'All this wedding stuff must really be getting to you!'

'What? Oh. Um, yeah. It is, a bit.'

'A bit? You're having sleepless nights! Look, I promise you, as soon as Summer's wedding is all out of the way, I'm really going to hit the ground running with plans for you and Matthew, OK?'

'Mmm. About that.' I hear her take a deep breath. 'Look, I've been having a bit of a rethink, and I'm just not sure Matthew and I are all that fussed about a big, formal wedding.'

'Of course you're not sure,' I say soothingly. 'It's a big deal. And I know the planning can all seem a bit daunting, especially when we haven't even got the basics in place yet.'

'It's not the planning that seems daunting, Iz. It's *it*. The wedding itself. Actually, I'm wondering about suggesting to Matthew that we bring the date forward a bit, and just do something incredibly simple – a registry office, and a meal at a nice restaurant.'

'Are you kidding me?'

'Look, you know I've never exactly been one for the whole dream wedding thing, and after your mum . . .' She stops.

'After my mum started piling on the pressure? After your mum started banging on about the frilly white dress? Come on, Lara!' I say, sounding more like an overexcitable life coach than I'd intended. 'You can't let them get to you, not when the stakes are so high!'

Lara doesn't say anything for a moment. Then she says, 'Iz, all I really want to do is marry Matthew as soon as possible. Time really is of the essence.'

'Look, soon as we've got some of the early decisions set in stone, the weeks and months will fly by.'

'That's not my point . . .'

'I tell you what, why don't we grab a bite to eat after your session with Summer tomorrow, and we can have a bit more of a chat about the arrangements? I'm heading in to the clinic anyway, to keep an eye on things with Summer.'

'Do you think you *need* to keep an eye on her?' Lara sounds rather alarmed.

'Oh, not at all!' I say, hastily. 'Just being professional! So, dinner tomorrow night? It'll be on me.'

'Iz, I don't know . . . I told you I have a lot of paperwork to catch up on.'

I'm getting an uncomfortable, unfamiliar feeling. Is she trying to fob me off?

'It's only a quick dinner,' I say, hearing a pathetic

note in my voice that transports me back over twenty years in time, to the day I first spotted Lara show-casing her perfect skipping technique in the play-ground, and knew I'd do anything – anything – to get her to be friends with me. 'I promise, just an hour or so.'

Lara doesn't say anything for a moment. Then, suddenly, she says, 'OK, a quick bite, then. But Iz, seriously – you have to start accepting that I might not want this big wedding. I don't want you to turn up and bombard me with wedding stuff.'

'I wouldn't dream of it. Anyway, I'm too swamped with Summer's wedding this weekend to think about any details for you and Matthew yet. We'll just chat about it over a nice glass of wine, OK?' I'm actually pretty keen to get her off the phone now. Because I've just had this completely brilliant idea.

As my taxi carries on rumbling through the park, I dial the number for Nancy Tavistock's boutique. When somebody answers, I get them to put me through to my old friend Dannii, who runs things while Nancy is globe-trotting. Only a couple of minutes later, and I've got Lara a special after-closing-time appointment at six o'clock tomorrow evening, which we can easily make after her session with Summer. It'll be perfect! I mean, I know she said she didn't want me bombarding her with wedding stuff just yet, but this isn't *bombarding*. This is the really fun part. Honestly, if there's anything that'll make her feel a bit special, and get her in the mind-set for the kind of wedding I know she really wants, it'll be a trying-on sesh at Nancy's. The dresses are out of this world, and if I can use my contacts there to negotiate a hefty discount on the four grand plus, which Nancy's wedding gowns usually cost, I'll be the best wedding planner *and* the best friend she could possibly think of.

I'm a tiny bit alarmed, as I walk down Marylebone High Street at half-past five the following evening, to see that there appears to be an impromptu rugby scrum outside the doors of Lara's clinic.

There are about a dozen leather-jacketed men with big weaponised cameras, jostling each other as they snap away, calling out, 'Over here!' and 'Show us yer knockers, love!' I'm just hoping – OK, *praying* – that this has nothing to do with Summer when I spot Weirdy-Beardy and (in an interesting development) Aquamarine Hair, standing a little way back from the mêlée with their own camera. And then there's a break in the rugby scrum for a moment and I see Summer herself, peering out of the glass door that leads into Lara's clinic. I have to say, she's doing a terrifically awful job of looking like she doesn't want to be recognised, in white drain-pipe jeans, a navel-baring cropped top, gigantic Dior shades and a Yankees baseball cap pulled low over cutesy, girlie pigtails.

'Just go *away*,' she's pleading through the six-inch gap in the door. 'This is *private business*. It's *nothing to do with you.* Tim and I have a right to visit our sex therapist in peace . . .'

At this, as she quite obviously intended, the paparazzi practically self-combust. Even if I have my doubts that they know exactly who Summer is, they certainly know who Tim Holland is, and a picture of a playboy heir heading into an apparent sex therapy clinic with a buxom blonde is probably worth a few quid. And as I fight my way through them and get to the door myself, I can see that there's a scruffy bloke who I vaguely recognise as Tim Holland standing next to Summer. He's got the same soft, puffy, albeit good-looking features I recognise from his photos in the gossip magazines, and he's an odd mismatch with Summer's glamorous bling in baggy trousers, a granddad shirt and a tweedy flat cap that (I assume) he's wearing ironically. I only just have time to register that this is, in fact, the first wedding-related event he's bothered to show up to when Summer sees me and opens the door a fraction wider to let me in.

'Izzie! God, I'm so glad to see you!' Her eyes are sparkling. 'Can you *believe* all this?'

Now that I'm indoors, I can see Wendy, who is hovering by the clinic's reception desk with an expression of triumph, and Lara, who is standing beside her wearing an expression of righteous anger.

'Lara, I'm so sorry about this,' I begin. 'I had no idea –'

'I should bloody well hope not!' she hisses at me.

389

'God, Iz, do you have any idea of the kind of trouble I could get into for all this?'

'I know. I'm sorry.' I glare at Wendy. 'Nobody should have been contacting the paparazzi.'

'It's not just the paparazzi!' Lara folds her arms. 'Did you know about this film crew they were planning on bringing into the session with them?'

'I assumed, Isabel, that you'd cleared this with Dr Lara beforehand,' Wendy comes over to us. 'Obviously we want footage of the session for the show. I can't see what she's making such a fuss about.'

'It is Dr *Alliston*,' Lara says, adopting the careful, controlled tone she's often advised me to use when dealing with a particularly difficult member of my family. 'And the reason I am making *such a fuss*, as you call it, is because I have to take into account all kinds of ethical issues to do with privacy.'

'Honestly, Dr Lara, I don't mind people knowing all about my private business!' Summer dimples at her. 'Do you need me to sign, like, some kind of a waiver, saying I won't sue you?'

'It's not about you!' Lara is turning pink. 'It's about my other clients! And my colleagues' clients! We can't have photographers besieging the building when people are coming and going for extremely private therapy. Oh, and as for the implication that this is a sex therapy clinic –'

'OK.' Wendy holds up her hands. 'I apologise for that. I shouldn't have advised Summer to say it.'

'But Dr Lara,' Summer says, 'allowing the cameras

to film my session could be so, like, *inspiring* for the viewers. Think of how many people we could be reaching out to – girls who have eating disorders, or, like, women trapped in abusive relationships . . .'

'Have you suffered an eating disorder?' Lara demands. 'Or been trapped in an abusive relationship?'

'Well, no, but I was thinking I might *say* I had.'

'It's exactly the kind of drama that we think the show needs,' Wendy adds, briskly, 'and some of our research suggests that it could make Summer a lot more popular with female consumers in their teens to mid-twenties, who are the target audience for the shows we want Summer to be asked on to. You know – *Celebrity Big Brother* and *I'm a Celebrity, Get Me Out of Here*.'

Judging from the look on Lara's face, I think it's time to wrap this up.

'Well! Obviously this hasn't quite worked out the way I think we all wanted. But some very important lessons have been learned!'

'Yes, Isabel.' Wendy glares at me. 'I hope you *have* learned your lesson.'

'Now, Summer, Wendy, I think it's probably best if we try and get you a taxi or something, don't you? I'm sure Dr Lara – I mean, Dr Alliston – would very much like to have her clinic return to normal.'

'There is a back exit you can use, if you prefer,' Lara says frostily.

'Oh, no, we can cope with the paps, can't we, babe?' Summer slings an arm around Tim.

'Well, I don't know, Summ.' His voice is throaty –

a smoker's voice – and there's a certain dozy look in his eyes that makes me wonder exactly what kind of cigarettes he favours. 'If there *is* a back exit . . .'

'Don't be absurd, Tim,' snaps Wendy. 'Just put your head down and say "no comment".'

'Oooh, and Wendy, you'd better give Sven a call on his mobile.' Summer is looking across the scrum of paparazzi to where Weirdy-Beardy and Aquamarine Hair are still standing, rather forlornly, with their camera. 'Tell him he'll probably want to film us coming out.'

After the call is made, it's a couple of minutes before Summer and Wendy judge the moment right for the big exit, and I pull Lara out of the view of the flashing cameras as they head out on to New Cavendish Street.

'Well, you and me might as well use the back exit,' she says wearily. 'Follow me.'

I do as she says, following her through a couple of doors out into the mercifully quiet mews behind the clinic.

'Lara, again, I'm so sorry about all this.'

'All right, all right.' She slumps against the wall for a moment, looking shattered. 'It's not your fault.'

'Honestly, I didn't know Wendy was going to make the whole thing a press call. And as for the film crew –'

'I *said*, all right!'

OK. So she's really fed up. And I can't exactly blame her.

On the other hand, now I'm even more pleased that I've arranged the surprise visit to Nancy Tavistock's boutique. A fun hour trying on gorgeous dresses might put this screw-up behind us.

'Look, let's just go and grab a glass of wine at Providores.' Lara straightens back up and smoothes down her crumpled pencil skirt. 'We can get some tapas there, too. I'm not sure I'm in the mood for a full-on dinner.'

'Well, if it's wine you're after, how does a nice glass of champagne sound?' I beam at her.

She doesn't beam back. 'Why?' she asks warily.

'I've got us an appointment with my friend Dannii at Nancy Tavistock's! To try on some of the most gorgeous wedding dresses you've ever seen!' I attempt to link arms with her, but she pulls away.

'Isabel, I told you. I didn't want a load of wedding stuff tonight.'

'But this is Nancy Tavistock's! It's not just any old load of wedding stuff.'

'Exactly. I'm not sure how you think I'm magically going to be able to afford one of Nancy's dresses.'

'Oh, well, I'm pretty certain I should be able to get you a tasty discount. And even if I can't, it'll be fun to try them on, won't it?'

'Not really, no.' There's a slightly despairing note in Lara's voice. 'Look, I told you I wanted to talk about scaling down the whole wedding. And doing it as quickly as possible.'

For God's sake, what is her sudden obsession with

time? Anyone would think . . . Wait a minute. I know I asked her before, and I already got this wrong with Summer, but . . .

'Lara, you're not pregnant, are you?'

'Christ, Isabel, why on earth do you keep asking me that?'

'Because you want to have the wedding really fast . . . you're knackered . . . irritable . . .'

'No, Iz. I am not pregnant. Not remotely. There can be other reasons for wanting to have a wedding quickly, you know.'

Well, yes, but I find it very hard to believe that Lara has a sex tape she's trying to hide from her future in-laws.

'OK, fine, but even if you do want a small, quick wedding, you'll still need a dress, won't you? I mean, unless you want to get married in a pair of jeans and a T-shirt!' I give a little laugh, but it sounds so forced that I immediately regret it. I take a deep breath. 'Lara, is there some reason you don't want to go dress-shopping with me? I mean, I know Catherine's dinner party didn't exactly go to plan, and I know you're unimpressed with how I just handled things with Summer, but if it's that you think I'm a bad wedding planner . . .'

'I don't think that.' She reaches out suddenly and squeezes my hand. 'Honestly, Iz, I think you're doing an amazing job. And if it means that much to you, let's go.'

'If it means that much to *me*?'

'No, I didn't mean . . . let's just do it, OK? I'm sure Dannii is waiting.'

I'm more glad than ever that Lara's clinic is only a short walk away from Nancy's boutique, because I'm not sure how much longer I could stand the rather awkward silence that's sprung up between us. Still, I can tell that Lara is gearing herself up to be enthusiastic in public, at any rate, because she plasters a bright smile over her face the moment Dannii comes to unlock the shop's door. And I can feel myself smiling too, because it's great to see Dannii again. She was always my favourite of Nancy's staff, as sweet as she is stylish, and despite her glossy looks she's a million miles away from being a bitchy fashionista. Ever the professional, she has indeed laid on the customary bottle of champagne (OK, Prosecco, but who's taking notes?) and she pours us a glass each, all the while oooh-ing and aaah-ing at Nana Hamilton's – sorry, at *Lara's* – engagement ring. When she realises that I'm not only the wedding planner but also the best friend *and* the future sister-in-law, she practically erupts with excitement, and tops up our glasses with a generous amount of fizz before locking the shop door, tilting the blinds, and starting to pull a selection of dresses from the racks dotted sparsely around the boutique.

'Now, you're so gorgeously petite that we don't want anything that will overwhelm you,' she explains to Lara, while I make myself comfortable on the chaise longue and start trying to work out how to use the camera function on my iPhone. 'Something like this might be a good place to start . . .' She holds up a stunning ivory column dress with spaghetti straps and some simple beading around the bodice. 'And I certainly wouldn't advise you to go with a full-length veil, unless you're already thinking about a very traditional church ceremony?'

'No,' says Lara. She's twisting a lock of hair rather edgily around her finger, and looking uncomfortable, even though I can tell she doesn't want to be rude. Let's face it, despite her odd mood, she's pretty much congenitally *incapable* of rudeness. 'Actually, Dannii, that's one of the many decisions we haven't even come close to making yet. And I certainly don't want anything too OTT on the dress front, because we're really hoping to keep things very simple.'

'Oh, well, then this dress would be perfect!' I say. 'Go on, Lars, try it! I'm dying to see you in it.'

Lara shoots me a look before slipping behind the screen. It's just a few moments before she emerges.

I'm all poised with my iPhone, ready to document the moment so that maybe I could use it as part of my best woman's speech, possibly with some kind of slide projector . . . But to my disappointment, it's not the tears-in-the-eyes moment I was hoping for. She looks lovely – of course she looks lovely – but the dress is too big in the front, making her look a bit like Gwyneth Paltrow in that hideous pink thing at the Oscars, and she's pulling awkwardly at the shoulder straps and frowning.

'It's nice,' she says, in response to Dannii's automatic squeal, 'but far too revealing for me, I'm afraid.'

Dannii primps the loose fabric a bit so that Lara can see what it might look like if it actually fitted properly. 'Well, it is quite a plunging neckline, which some brides can feel a little bit uncomfortable with, even when it's a perfect fit. Usually it's the ones with the overprotective fathers who tend to be worried about what Dad will have to say about it before he walks them up the aisle!'

'Well, that's not a problem for me. My dad's not the overprotective sort. Anyway, he's not going to be walking me up the aisle.'

'Lara!' I can't believe I'm hearing this. 'When did you make that decision?'

'It's not a *decision*. It's just a . . . thing.'

'But he'll be devastated!'

Lara folds her arms across the drooping bust and shoots me a sceptical look. 'You know my dad. Do you *honestly* think he'll be devastated?'

'Well, upset, then. Put out. Cheesed off.'

'Isabel, he walked out on us for his new girlfriend when I was twelve years old.' She's not bitter, just matter-of-fact. But I can't help thinking that, if the church-or-no-church debate was deemed unacceptable to have in front of Dannii, this kind of private family detail should probably be off-limits too. 'I don't think he'd have much right to be cheesed off, and I don't think he *will* be cheesed off.'

'So, who *do* you want to walk you up the aisle, then?'

'God, Isabel, I don't know. Maybe Stefan. Maybe nobody. It's not a big deal. And like I tried to tell you earlier, I'm not even sure there's going to *be* an aisle.'

'Well, of course there's going to be an aisle. Even if you do decide to get married in a registry office, there'll be an aisle.'

'Not if there are only a dozen people there, there won't be.'

'Oooh, a small wedding can be so lovely!' Dannii sings out, before I can say anything. 'So chic, and none of that nonsense about inviting Great-Auntie So-and-so . . .'

'What the hell's the matter with you?' I stare at Lara. 'A dozen people? Even with just our immediate families, we're already practically a dozen!'

'Like I've been trying to tell you –,' Lara's using that controlled tone she tried on Wendy earlier – 'I want to keep this thing very low-key.'

'But it's your *wedding day*. Remember – the joyful, celebratory wedding day with my annoying brother that you've been dreaming of for the last fifteen years?'

'I know that! I just think there's no point stressing out about having The Most Perfect Day, when –' She stops, and stares at the floor.

'When *what*, Lara?'

'When things can go wrong that you have absolutely no control over,' she suddenly blurts. 'When you never know what kind of things can happen to mess it all up.'

I stare at her. 'So you *do* think I'm going to make a mess of it?'

'No! Not you, Isabel. That isn't what I meant –'

Dannii suddenly interrupts, playing the peace-maker. 'Well! Perhaps you'd like to try on something else?' She holds out a strapless dress with an A-line skirt in layers of pale ivory chiffon. 'It's a very classic look, of course. The mothers of the bride always seem to love this one!'

'Oh, my mother's not a big one for wedding dresses, full stop.' Lara grabs the dress from Dannii, not seeming to notice that she's scrunching the delicate layers of chiffon in her hands. 'If she even clears her diary for the day itself, it'll be a bloody miracle.'

'She's not that bad,' I tell a rather shocked-looking Dannii. 'She's just a very busy doctor.'

'No, she's not "just" a very busy doctor, actually, Isabel. If that was the only problem with Catherine, she wouldn't have started picking on Matthew the other night, or upsetting your poor parents.'

'Matthew can look after himself,' I say, attempting my own version of Lara's controlled tone. I could probably do with a bit more practice. 'And I'm not sure why you always feel the need to jump to my parents' defence these days. Let's face it, it's not as if they were brilliantly behaved either. Mum getting drunk –'

'She was just nervous, for crying out loud!' Lara is turning pink. 'Give her a break, for once in your life!'

'For God's sake, Lara, she's not here right now! And as far as I know, she hasn't bugged the place. You don't have to keep up the Model Daughter-in-Law act every single minute of the day!'

Dannii is shooting confused glances between us, as her happy vision of two best friends/sisters-in-law/wedding planner and bride shopping for a dress together gradually disintegrates before her very eyes.

'It isn't an act, Isabel.' Lara's chin juts out, the way it does when she's upset about something. 'I care very much about your family.'

There's something about the way she says this, something about the tone of her voice and the way she's looking at me that means she might just as well have added two unspoken words.

Unlike you.

I get to my feet. 'Right, well, I'll leave you to it, then shall I? I mean, it's quite obvious that I'm not the person you want here to help you pick out your dress.'

'What do you mean?'

'Well, it just seems that all this wedding stuff you're so unenthusiastic about with me is a lot more fun for you when my mum's around.'

'That's ridiculous, Isabel. What on earth are you talking about?'

'I'm talking about the John Lewis bloody wedding list. I'm talking about your mother-and-daughter bonding trips to look at dresses on Chiltern Street. I'm talking about the cosy phone conversations you're always having behind my back . . .'

'Iz, you're misunderstanding that. Look, you and me can do more wedding stuff together . . .'

'But I don't want your charity! This was supposed to be fun! Something we were doing together, you and me, like Di and Fergie, remember?'

Lara doesn't say anything. And I'm not sure I have very much left to say either. I sling my bag over my shoulder, mutter a thank-you-I'm-sorry in Dannii's direction and head for the door. Then I wait outside the boutique for a good few minutes, wondering if – hoping that – Lara might follow me outside.

When she still hasn't, after ten minutes, I start walking to the tube, alone.

Chapter Twenty-One

My row with Lara has really put the tin lid on it, then.

I'm a joke. A total fucking joke.

My tube journey to Sloane Square is just long enough for me to make a mental list of all the ways I've screwed up over the last few weeks, and by the time I'm exiting the barriers to begin my walk over the bridge to Battersea, I think I've come up with a pretty comprehensive set of reasons why I may, just possibly, be the biggest loser on the entire planet.

I mean, really. Let's examine the evidence here. So far, in my illustrious new career as a wedding planner, I've sent two brides to the wrong churches and ensured that one of them didn't even manage to make it up the aisle at all. Summer's Hollywood-themed wedding, which was always going to be walking a fine line between adorably kitsch and hideously tacky, is almost certainly going to be the latter – that is, if *she* even makes it up the aisle at all, thanks to the fact she appears to be cheating on her husband-to-be with the personal trainer that *I* arranged for her. My first-ever professional engagement party descended into chaos at least partly because I didn't keep a weather eye on the guests' booze intake. And now, worst of all, even my own best friend doesn't trust me to plan her wedding to my own brother.

The only thing that's kept me from bursting into noisy tears on the tube and annoying my fellow rush-hour passengers is the possibility that Lara might have left me a message on my phone. Not apologising – I'm not the kind of person who likes to hold out for big apologies – but explaining. I mean, maybe there really is another reason why she seems to prefer discussing wedding stuff with Mum rather than with me, or another reason why she's frantically down-scaling the size of her wedding, other than the fact she's decided I couldn't possibly cope with organising it.

But there isn't a message. Nothing on my voicemail. No texts.

Oh, I tell a lie. There are two messages, both from Summer, the first one asking me if I think it's OK for her to drink sparkling water in the run-up to Saturday, or if I think switching to still water would be less bloating; and the second one asking me if I could bring her a silk pillowcase on Friday so that she doesn't wake up on Saturday morning with big creases down the side of her face.

Honestly, it's all I can do not to hurl my phone over the side of Albert Bridge deep into the dark, swirling waters of the Thames below, then turn round and start walking to Victoria, jump on a train to Gatwick and fly anywhere, *anywhere* in the world for a few weeks. Sit on a beach, stare at the sea, get my head into shape and work out where it's all going wrong.

But I can't, of course. All I can do – all I *do* do – is turn the ringer off on my phone so that, at the very least, I won't be plagued by Summer calling me at half-hourly intervals throughout the evening and into the night. And so that I don't spend the next few hours waiting, miserably, for the 'Lara's Theme' ringtone I've assigned to Lara that might mean she was calling me after all.

As I open the outside front door to Will's flat – sorry, to *our* flat – and head on up the stairs, there's a sudden click from the door to Flat A, and a voice calls up the stairs after me.

'Oh, hey! Isabel!'

It's Emma-from-downstairs, waving at me.

'Oh, sorry, you obviously want to drop your bag and jacket off inside your flat before,' she carries on.

'Before?'

'Before you come inside for a drink and dinner? Remember?'

Shit. What with everything that's happened today, I've completely forgotten.

'I hadn't forgotten . . .' I fib, just as Emma's grin widens.

'OK, I have a confession. I'd kind of forgotten about it too, until Will knocked on the door about half an hour ago. Anyway, why don't you just come on in and have a hard-earned glass of Pinot Grigio? I can sneak a sip!'

Well, I can hardly say no, can I? Let's face it, all I was really planning on doing this evening was drinking myself into a miserable stupor on Pinot Grigio anyway.

'The boys are already out the back,' Emma continues, pushing the door wider open with her hip, 'doing manly things with Jake and a football, I'm sure. Honestly, the patio's only about six feet square, but I sometimes think Mark imagines it's actually Wembley Stadium.'

I follow her into a huge double reception room that I recognise is the same layout as Will's flat upstairs, but with the sitting room and the kitchen knocked into one. The living area is a cosy mix of squashy chocolate-coloured leather sofas, quirky Murano glass lamps and garish plastic toys, and the big open-plan kitchen has freestanding units in my favourite duck-egg blue, and an island unit cluttered with open wine bottles, bowls of Kettle chips and nearly bare sprigs of rosemary. The pale cream walls are variously decorated with framed pictures of angelic blond Jake, a gorgeous black-and-white photo of Emma and Mark on their wedding day, beaming at each other with total adoration, and bits of rice pudding that I assume are Jake's tea, and not a deliberate design decision. French doors lead out from the kitchen to the little patio garden, where Will and Mark, both still in their work suits, are gently tapping a half-sized football back and forth to an overexcited blond toddler.

I stare about the place, not moving.

Because this is weird. Seeing Will's flat – *our* flat – in

this totally different incarnation. Not that there's anything wrong with Will's flat, obviously. It's just that standing in this one, with its family-friendly layout, and the neatly piled toys, with the homey, comforting scent of roasting lamb wafting from the kitchen, is making me feel like I've slipped, Alice-through-the-Looking-Glass-style, into a parallel universe.

A parallel universe, incidentally, where even a heavily pregnant working woman with a toddler can make her home more welcoming than I ever could. Just the kind of morale boost I need this evening.

'I know, I know . . .' Emma is apologising frantically. 'It's a mess with Jake's toys out, I'm really sorry! And I bunged the roast in the oven only half an hour ago so it'll still be a while before we eat . . .'

'Don't be ridiculous.' That came out far sharper than I was intending, so I hastily soften it with a smile and a pat on her arm. 'Honestly, Emma, I can't even rustle up more than beans on toast without getting my friend Barney to cook for me! Oooh, is that the wine you were talking about?' I go on, my eye lighting on the chilled bottle that's sitting on the work-surface. I think Emma might be shooting me a slightly odd look as I make a beeline for it and glance around for a glass, but she's nice enough not to comment.

'Why don't you take it outside and get comfortable?' she suggests, reaching up to a shelf to take down a large wine glass, pouring in a generous amount, and then, after a moment, just handing me the rest of the bottle. 'You can take a couple of beers outside for the boys too. I've just got to baste the lamb and then I'll be out in a minute.'

I take a large gulp from my wine glass before following her instructions and heading outside to the patio.

'Isabel!' Mark puts down Jake, who's wriggling and giggling under his arm, and comes towards me to give me a kiss on each cheek. 'How brilliant to see you. And even better that you've brought us a fresh round. Say hello to Isabel, Jakey – isn't she a nice lady for never complaining when you make a racket down here?'

'Honestly, I never even notice,' I say, waving at Jake. He waves back, which is an improvement on Hypatia, and I'm just about to try out that whole patented Princess Di thing (I seem to have her on the brain these days) of squatting down to talk to him on his level when suddenly he starts giggling, his plump little body almost doubling up in delight as he points to something to the left of me.

It's Will. He's puffed out both his cheeks, crossed his eyes and stuck his thumbs in his ears so his fingers can waggle at the side of his head.

He looks ridiculous.

He looks amazing.

'He's a natural,' says Mark, ushering me towards the bistro table as Will shoots a grin and a wave in my direction, then picks up Jake and turns him upside down as though he's about to throw him in the sandpit.

'Yes, he does seem to be . . .' The icky, miserable, hopeless feeling I carried back from Lara's dress appointment is lifting, ever so slightly. I've never been one of those women who go all funny over big men with small babies, but I can't say I'm unmoved by the sight of Will mucking about like this. I mean, probably I shouldn't let it get my hopes up or anything, but it's better than watching him sitting in the corner checking his BlackBerry and wincing every time Jake makes a sound. In fact, maybe my astonished stare is getting to him, because once Jake is happily settled at the sandpit with a new-looking truck (did Will buy a *present*? God, he thinks of everything, doesn't he?) he comes over and joins me and Mark at the table.

'Hi,' he says, leaning down to give me a quick kiss. 'Everything OK?'

'Yes, yes, fine.' I reach for my wine glass and take another large gulp. 'Bit of a tough day, that's all!'

'Oh, yes, Will tells me you're a wedding planner.' Mark hands a beer to Will before topping up my glass again. 'I imagine tough days are par for the course!'

'Well, some more than others.'

'God, Em and I could have done with you when we were getting married. Total nightmare, the whole thing! Her mother, my mother, both our sisters . . . a whole lot of fuss about the length of the bridesmaids' dresses . . .' He shudders. 'Nothing but drama from start to finish.'

'I'm sure you had a fabulous day in the end,

though,' I tell him. 'That photo in the kitchen certainly looks like it.'

'Ah, that was because the day was nearly over and we'd drunk our body weight in champagne,' says Emma, stepping out on to the patio to join us. 'The perfect recipe for blissed-out wedding pictures!'

But I can tell, by the little glance that she and Mark have just shared, that she's being falsely modest. It's all too obvious just how much they adore each other.

There's a sudden shriek from Jake, who appears to have discovered a new way to manoeuvre his truck through the sandpit but might as well have just struck oil in there for all his excitement.

'God, sorry!' Emma rolls her eyes apologetically. 'You two must hate us on a Sunday morning when you're trying to have a lie-in up there.'

'Isabel's already said she's not at all bothered by it!' Mark grins at me. 'She had her chance and now she must for ever hold her peace.'

'Well, she's a better woman than I am,' Emma retorts. 'Honestly, Isabel, before I had Jakey, I'd have cheerfully murdered anyone who dared wake me up with a two-year-old at the weekend. And once you have one of these little monsters yourselves –,' she reaches out to tickle Jake's tummy – 'you'll be cursing us as the people who took away your last chance of a weekend lie-in while you still had the chance.'

I give a nervous laugh, because I'm not entirely sure what to say to this, not with Will sitting right next to me. I take yet another long drink from my wine glass, and I'm just about to say something vague and non-committal about that kind of thing being a little way off when Will suddenly speaks up.

'Actually, Emma, Isabel and I are quite emphatically *not* planning babies, thank you very much!'

What? I mean, where the hell did that come from?

First he slags off weddings, and now babies too?

I can feel my face turning pink, and I try to catch his eye, but he seems to be studiously avoiding mine.

'Oh, you think that now,' Mark is saying, 'but just you wait, mate, until everyone you know has them! That's what did for me and Em, wasn't it, love? We started feeling like we were the last people on the planet who hadn't got around to propagating yet!'

'But that's hardly the point, is it?' Will is speaking very fast. 'I mean, peer pressure is one thing when it's about drinking a bottle of cider round the back of the athletics shed, but it's not exactly a good reason to go around having babies left, right and centre!' He gives an awkward laugh of his own. 'And let's face it, this city isn't exactly in the grip of a falling population . . .'

I can't believe I'm hearing this. More to the point, I can't believe I'm hearing this *in public*. And only a few minutes after I've just watched him messing around with Jake.

I'm suddenly reminded, out of the blue, of this feeling I used to get every year at Christmas. Dad had this strict policy, even when we were really tiny, of sitting us down on Christmas morning and

410

making us choose one of our biggest presents to donate to the children's ward at the Bristol Royal Infirmary. And while this might be a terrific idea when you're old enough to understand it, when you're four years old all you really understand is that you're not going to get to keep the Tiny Tears doll you've been dreaming of since early September. And it's pretty miserable.

Roughly as miserable as the feeling you get twenty-five years later when the sight of what a proper grown-up future could look like is laid out before you like an enticing Christmas gift, only to be snatched away before you've even had the chance to touch it.

OK, so Will doesn't want marriage. He's made that plain enough these last few weeks. And now, apparently, he doesn't want babies either. And if sitting here in this garden with this happy couple and their cute-as-a-button kid isn't enough to make Will think that he *might* want to marry me, or have babies with me, then I'm not sure what kind of a future we have together.

And if I thought my day couldn't have got any worse after my row with Lara, then obviously I was wrong.

'God, Isabel, sorry, we shouldn't have even said anything . . .' Emma's face has turned beetroot-red as she cottons on to the frosty, silent atmosphere around the bistro table.

'It's OK.' I'm feeling pretty beetroot-red myself right now. I stand up. I just want to get out of here, as fast as I possibly can, before I start crying. 'Actually, I'm not sure I have time to stay, Emma,' I mumble, already heading for the door. 'So sorry, but lots of work . . .'

'Oh, Isabel, please don't go!' Emma wails, as Will gets to his feet and heads into the living room after me.

'Iz, stop! What's going on?' He catches up with me as I reach the front door. 'Is everything all right?'

'No, everything's not all right.' I can't even look at him. I yank the door open. 'Everything's shit.'

'But, Iz, you can't just run off like this!' His voice is appalled, though whether by the awkwardness of what's just occurred or the embarrassment of my hasty departure, I'm not sure. 'Emma and Mark have invited us for dinner . . .'

'Well, *you* stay then.' I shrug his hand off my shoulder with more violence than I thought I was capable of, and just keep moving. 'I'm getting out of here.'

'Isabel, for God's sake!'

'Just leave me alone, Will. Just . . . leave me alone.'

Chapter Twenty-Two

It was only as I stumbled into the back of a taxi near the flat, when the driver asked me where I wanted to go, that I remembered something else that's going on this evening.

Dan's gallery party.

Well, look, I might as well go there as anywhere. I mean, fuck it. If Will's not in it for the long haul then I'm going to have to get used to being single again. Footloose and fancy-free and all that. Why shouldn't I head off to a party hosted by a gorgeous bloke who's got a bit of a thing for me? Some harmless flirting might make this hideous day just a little bit more bearable.

I'm sure that's not just my large and hastily drunk glass of Pinot Grigio talking.

By the time I get to Soho, the party at the Marlow Gallery is in full swing. There are people spilling out of the front door on to the pavement outside, and I can hear the bass line of some extremely loud music that's far too cutting-edge for me to be able to identify resonating from the inside of the townhouse.

I have to say, I think it was probably a good thing, now, that I drank that large glass of wine at Emma and Mark's. It's never the easiest thing in the world to arrive at a party on your own, and especially not a party like this, where all the other guests look as if they should have their own late-night alternative comedy show on E4, or like they're just one change of drummer away from a double-platinum album and a world stadium tour. There are a lot of slogan T-shirts, a lot of vintagey accessories, and a lot of trendy facial hair (and that's just the women, ha ha).

I whip off the cotton cardigan I've been wearing over a black camisole, so at least I look like I've made a bit of an effort, not to mention a little bit sexier, in case Dan *does* happen to be in the mood for flirting with me in person, and shove it into my handbag. Then I take a deep breath and make my way inside, only to be immediately backed into the nearest corner by an extremely zealous couple with unnervingly fixed pupils and indeterminate European accents (Dutch? Croatian? It's so noisy and I'm so rubbish at identifying accents, that it's impossible to tell) who start haranguing me about their passion for the artist's work. I agree with them heartily that it's very *powerful*, and terribly *majestic*, but I'm getting a little alarmed when the bloke leans in far too close, breathes cigarette-scented air in my face, and tells me that actually, they're both finding the entire exhibition profoundly *erotic*, when thank God, I see a familiar face heading along the narrow hallway towards me.

It's Licky.

'Wizkins! I didn't expect to see you here!' she squeals, flinging her arms around me.

'Me neither!' I extricate myself from the von Creepingtons, who watch me go like a pair of children might watch an ice-cream van vanish, without stopping, over the horizon. 'You look *incredible*.'

This isn't just the Pinot Grigio talking, by the way. If anything, it's an understatement. Licky is transformed from the lumpy, unhappy bride-to-be she was the last time I saw her. Her frizzy, sandy hair is cascading over her shoulders, crackling with life, her eyes are gorgeously made up with smouldering, smoky eyeliner, and she's showing off sun-kissed shoulders in a billowing, multicoloured maxidress, with fabulous gold hoop earrings brushing her collarbones.

'You look like . . . like an ancient Goddess of Plenty,' I blurt at her, as she pulls me through the side door into the main body of the gallery. It's packed with chattering, drinking people, none of them showing all that much interest in what I thought was meant to be the main event, which is the pictures on the walls – which, naturally, look as though they've been scrawled by a colour-blind toddler – and the sculptures on the plinths – which, of course, look to me like nothing more than twisty lumps of metal.

'Oh, that's probably because of these earrings.' She grabs a couple of iced vodka shots from a passing waiter and hands me one. We chink glasses and down them in unison. 'They're based on ancient Roman jewellery that was found in Pompeii. Gennaro bought them for me, from this sweet little jeweller's in Salerno. There's a necklace too, but I thought it might be a bit much worn all at once . . .'

'Hang on.' I stare at her. 'Who's Gennaro?'

Despite the dim lighting in the gallery, I can see Licky's face flush. 'We met at his family's *agriturismo* in Campania.'

'Campania? I thought you were in Rome.'

'Well, I was, but I met this nice American family at a café in Piazza Navona, and they told me all about this amazing place they'd stayed further south, and I'd seen everything I wanted to see in Rome, so I just . . . headed off!' Her voice betrays the fact that, even after the event, she's surprised she did it. 'Honestly, Isabel, his family's place is so beautiful, only twenty miles from Naples, and they make their own olive oil, and they have four beautiful horses, and if I go back to work there, which obviously would just be the most fabulous opportunity, Gennaro says they'll buy more horses and I could start up my own little riding school for the guests.'

'Licks, this sounds wonderful!' The vodka – I think it might have been lime flavoured, but I drank it too fast to tell – is spreading a nice, warm feeling throughout my chest, and I'm already starting to feel glad I came to this party, instead of just sitting around miserably at home. I flag down another waiter and pick a couple more shots off his tray. 'Especially after Vile Marcus . . . I mean, Marcus.'

'I know!' Licky waves away her second vodka shot, so I finish my own and then polish hers off, for a little bit more of that nice, warm feeling. Oooh, and it is lime-flavoured, definitely. I am glad I worked that one out. 'And the best part is,' she carries on, 'I'm completely sure Daddy would have loved Gennaro, whereas I always had my doubts how he'd feel about Marcus.' Her eyes are getting a bit moist, so I give her hand a squeeze.

'I'm sure. Gennaro sounds wonderful.'

'Well, it's early days yet . . . Oooh, I should show you a photo!' She delves into her dress pocket for her mobile. 'Now, here he is with Vittorio and Francesco, his little nephews – you'd die if you saw them, Iz, they're *so* beautiful . . .' She shows me a photo of an olive-skinned man with smiling eyes, his arms loosely around the shoulders of two small, equally smiley boys. 'And here Gennaro is again at his favourite bar in the village . . .'

In the absence of any more lime vodka shots appearing on the horizon, I accept a glass of champagne from the waiter who's proffering them and take a few sedate sips as I watch her scroll through her photos of various photogenic Neapolitan locations, until it all suddenly reminds me of the rustic Italian wedding I wanted to have with Will, so I polish off the rest of my champagne and start looking around for another couple of glasses.

'Oh God, I'm so sorry, Wiz,' Licky says, realising I've switched off. 'Here's me going on and on about

Gennaro and I haven't even asked how things are with you. How's the wedding-planning career going? Ooooh, I remember now, Dan-Dan told me you're doing a big celebrity wedding at Broughton this weekend! And he's doing the photos.'

'That's right.' Thank God, a waiter is headed our way with fresh supplies, not only of champagne but also of some yummy-looking mini jacket potatoes that I could probably do with, to line my stomach. I am starting to feel just a little bit unsteady on my feet, to be perfectly honest. 'Will you be around?'

'Um, not sure about that, actually.' Licky is turning rather pink again. 'I'm kind of avoiding Mummy at the moment, you see. I mean, I know Daddy would have loved Gennaro, but Mummy . . . well, she's a different kettle of fish. Thinking it might be better to tell her about him over the phone.'

'Yes,' I agree wholeheartedly, as a vision of Susannah Britten-Jones's reaction to Licky's big news flits through my mind. I swipe two champagne flutes from the waiter, plus a couple of the jacket potatoes. 'So, where are you staying at the moment? Oooooh – if you need a flatmate, maybe we could find a place together!'

Licky frowns. 'Together? But I thought you were living with your boyfriend?'

'How do you know that?'

'Dan-Dan told me. I'm staying with him at the moment, actually – he's been such a star since I got back, Iz.'

418

'And he mentioned that I was living with Will? So does he . . . um . . . mention me a lot, then?'

'Now and then!' Licky suddenly giggles, nudging me in the ribs. 'Ooooh, *Izzie*, you don't fancy him too, do you?'

'Well, obviously he's very attractive and everything, but . . .'

'Is that why you're here?' She stops giggling, and her eyebrows shoot upwards into near-perfect upside-down Vs. '*Wizzie*! You've come to his party to get off with him?'

'Of course not!' I bluster ineffectually. 'I mean, I have a boyfriend.'

'Oh, yes.' She thinks for a moment, and then frowns. 'Then why are you looking for a flatmate? Aren't things going well? I mean, it's supposed to be the honeymoon phase, isn't it, immediately after you've started living together? Oooh, Dan-Dan!' she suddenly squeals, flinging her arms around Dan, who's just walked up beside me.

He hugs her back. 'I hardly think you can lecture people on honeymoon phases, Licks. You're the one who went away on yours alone and came back with a brand-new bloke!'

Licky giggles and shoves him a couple of times, which is a good distraction from the fact that his arrival has made me go all hot and sweaty.

I mean, now that he's actually standing here next to me in all his mop-haired, molten-eyed, muscular glory, I'm suddenly not feeling quite so sure about this whole seduction thing after all. Not because he isn't looking gorgeous, but because he absolutely, seriously *is*. And because I'm just a wobbly-kneed, booze-fortified wreck of a human being who's come all the way to Soho for a fling with someone who isn't my boyfriend.

Oh God – is that why I'm here? A *fling*? I've been telling myself I'm just here to flirt with him, but has my subconscious been playing a trick on me? It could be the utter misery I've been feeling, or it could be the large quantity of alcohol I've recently consumed, but is the nasty truth of my real intentions coming out?

'Ooooh, mini fish and chips!' Licky is saying, as she suddenly spots another waiter go by with a fresh tray of canapés. 'Anyone else want any?'

'No, thanks. I'm not hungry.'

'Thirsty, though, I see,' says Dan, as Licky makes a beeline for the waiter. He nods at my half-empty champagne glass.

'It's been a hard day.'

'Oh?' Without taking his eyes off me, he stops one of the waiters and mutters something to him about coming back with a bottle. 'Nothing to do with the fact you're here on your own, I hope?'

I polish off my – second? third? – glass. 'How do you even know I'm here on my own?'

He sketches a hand in the direction of my camisole top and pencil skirt. 'Well, I'm not any kind of an expert, but that doesn't look to me like the kind of outfit somebody would wear out to a party with their solicitor boyfriend.'

For all that I'm feeling deeply wounded by Will, I can't help a spark of irritation that Dan is having a dig at Will again. 'For God's sake, do you really think all solicitors are straight out of the pages of a Charles Dickens novel? For all you know, Will does nothing but . . . but smoke crack cocaine and dance on a podium at all-night raves.'

'And is that what he's doing this evening?'

'No.' I stare at the floor, over his shoulder, anywhere but into Dan's teasing molten-chocolate eyes. 'He's eating roast lamb with our downstairs neighbours. But that's not the point.'

'No, well, as far as I'm concerned, the only point is that you're here. Looking terrific.'

'Well, I came to see the exhibition, of course.'

'Of course. I completely forgot, you told me what a big fan you were of the artist.'

'Paul.'

'Pete.'

Shit. 'Precisely.' I take a couple of wobbly steps closer to the nearest plinth, and peer at the twisty lump of metal it in a manner that I hope looks both knowledgeable and discerning. 'Oh, well, this is ever so witty,' I say, because this is just the kind of thing people are always saying on Dad's pretentious BBC2 artsy programmes.

'Oh, you think?' Dan steps closer too, so that he's still right beside me.

Was this the wrong thing to say? 'Well, I mean, very *challenging* too, obviously.'

'Ah. Challenging.'

'Yes.' I peer more closely at the little label on the side of the plinth. '*Mia, Resting*', it says, '£25,000.' 'Bloody hell! That's a lot to pay for . . .' I'm about to say 'a twisty lump of metal', but stop myself just in time. '. . . for a sculpture of Mia resting. I mean, you'd think if people wanted to pay that much for a sculpture of this Mia, they'd prefer one of her actually doing something – ski-jumping, perhaps, or abseiling . . .'

'Well, that's certainly a good point, Isabel. Though I used to go out with Mia, and I have to say I don't ever remember her doing anything quite so physically exerting.'

I remember now that Licky has mentioned this Mia ex of Dan's before. Instantly, I get a flash of jealousy. 'Well, she looks great in this sculpture!'

A slightly wicked grin passes over his face. 'I'm surprised you can tell, Isabel, from that particular view of her.'

What?

Ohhh . . . now that I turn my head to one side, and look a lot more closely at it . . . You know, I wouldn't have called it *Mia, Resting* quite so much as *Mia, Spreadeagled*.

I can feel my cheeks practically bursting into flame. The von Creepingtons' assessment of the artwork now seems creepier than ever. 'Well, what a brave girl Mia must be,' I blurt. 'Is she here tonight? It would be great to meet her face to face, instead of . . . um . . .'

Dan is watching my discomfort with a slow smile

spreading over his face. 'She's not here,' he says. 'I'm all yours tonight. And in person,' he adds deliberately. 'Not just on the other end of a text message.'

I don't say anything. I mean, if my nerve was faltering before, it's all but obliterated now. I mean, how is boring old me supposed to compete with uninhibited, bohemian Mia?

'Hey, how do you fancy grabbing some air?' Dan suddenly asks, reaching for my hand. 'I've a nice little roof terrace at the top of this building. We can go up there and have a nice quiet chat.'

Oh. So maybe Dan thinks I can compete with uninhibited, bohemian Mia.

'That sounds . . .' *Stupid, Isabel. Hideously ill-advised. An awful, awful idea, devised by a drunken lunatic.* '. . . great.'

'Excellent. Why don't you follow me?'

So here I am. This is it. All geared up for my fling.

I must say, though, Dan's description of this as a 'roof terrace' is being a bit generous. I'd been imagining a kind of Mediterranean idyll, complete with terracotta pots of lavender and climbing plants winding around a romantic pergola. What we're on now is more what I'd call a 'bit of flat roof surrounded by a dangerously crumbling brick wall'. Still, I don't want to be churlish. The lights are twinkling prettily below us in Soho, there are a couple of little cast-iron chairs, and I'm up here with a chilled bottle of champagne and sexy, charming Dan. It may not be

Mediterranean, but it's pretty idyllic by most people's standards. The stuff dreams are made of, right?

I shiver, suddenly, as a sharp breeze hits us.

'Chilly?' Dan has popped the bottle and is pouring me a glass. 'Would you like my jacket?'

'No, thank you.' I'm not, actually, chilly. In fact, after the heat and noise of the party, it's nice to feel the breeze against my skin.

'Well, maybe some more champagne will warm you up a bit, then.' He hands me a glass, and chinks his own against it. 'Here's to you.'

'Here's to *you*.'

'All right, then. Here's to us.' He holds my gaze as we both take a long drink, and then he steps closer to me. 'So . . . Isabel.'

'So . . . Dan.' I can feel my heart beating faster, and hope he's not close enough to hear it himself. 'It's very nice to be here,' I say, in the sultriest, throatiest tone I can muster.

'Are you all right?' A little frown dents his forehead. 'You sound kind of hoarse.'

'No, I'm fine.' Better stick to my normal voice, then. 'Absolutely fine.'

'OK, good. Because you really should take my jacket if you're worried about catching cold, you know.' He puts both hands on my shoulders. 'I know you've got a big weekend coming up.'

No. No, I do not want him to be nice to me. I want him to push me up against this crumbling wall (well, maybe from a health and safety perspective, it'd be

424

better if he pushed me up against the door that leads back inside) and ravish me. Being nice to me just reminds me of Will. And Will is the very last person I want to be thinking about right now.

'I'm really fine. And I told you, I don't need your jacket.'

'Well, I'm not going to argue with that. I mean, you look pretty great in what you're wearing at the moment.' Now Dan's voice has gone a bit low and sultry. Of course, it doesn't make him sound like he's getting a cold. It makes him sexier than ever. 'You're very beautiful, Isabel, I hope you realise . . . hey, are you *sure* you're OK?' he suddenly says, stepping backwards and taking his hands off my shoulders. 'You just went a bit . . . cross-eyed.'

'Oh, don't worry about that!' I'm feeling more light-headed than ever. 'It's just the alcohol.'

'Right . . . Look, perhaps you shouldn't have any more to drink, Isabel.' He tries to take my champagne glass out of my hands, but gives up when I think he realises a struggle would be unseemly. 'I don't want to take advantage of you if you don't really know what you're doing.'

'Dan, Dan, Dan . . .' I attempt a low, knowing chuckle, and then knock back most of the contents of my champagne glass just to prove I'm not as drunk as he thinks I am. Oh – if that *does* prove that I'm not as drunk as he thinks I am. I'm getting a little bit confused by stuff like . . . details. 'I can assure you, I know *exactly* what I'm doing. I mean, I've never had any complaints.'

He takes a deep breath. 'OK. I really didn't realise you were in this state. I mean, I just thought, after that text message you sent me, and everything . . . but I'd never have brought you up here if I'd known you were that out of it.'

'Don't worry about that! I mean, I'd never have *come* up here if I wasn't a bit out of it! God, I mean, I've barely got the nerve to cheat on my boyfriend drunk. I'd hardly be able to do it sober!'

Dan actually grimaces. 'Just what I wanted to hear.'

'Oh, no, you mustn't feel bad, or anything! I'm not *really* cheating on him.' I polish off the rest of my champagne before Dan manages to pull the glass away from me. 'I mean, things are pretty much over between us, is the point.'

'You've split up?'

'Well, not yet. But it's just a matter of time, Dan, I assure you. I mean, if he refuses to even think about marrying me, and the idea of having babies with me repulses him, then we're hardly in it for the long haul!' I'm dimly aware that I'm rambling, but I can't seem to stop myself. 'Oh God – not that I want to freak you out, or anything! I'm not scheming to get *you* to marry me and father my children, in case that's what you're looking so worried about . . .'

'That's not what I'm looking so worried about.'

'. . . because all I really want to do with you right now is get flung.'

'Flung?'

'Do I mean flinged?'

'Isabel . . .' He reaches out and tucks a strand of hair behind my ear. It's a gesture that reminds me so much of Will that I actually feel a physical spasm in my stomach. On the other hand, maybe it's just the mini jacket potatoes making a bid for freedom. 'You're not making very much sense. I think it's probably best if I just get you in a cab and . . . oh, shit.' He stares at me. 'Are you *crying*?'

I open my mouth to say 'Nope, absolutely not,' but that isn't exactly what comes out. What does come out, if I'm perfectly honest, is more of a wail.

'Oh, for the love of God,' Dan mutters, but not unkindly, as he pats my shoulder and fumbles around in his pocket for what turns out to be a non-existent handkerchief.

'I'm sorry,' I blub, as soon as I can string words together. 'I should never have come up here with you.'

'Well, no, you probably shouldn't, but we all make mistakes. Now, let's get you downstairs, sweetheart, and –'

'I'm serious! I've screwed everything up. And you know what's the biggest screw-up of all?'

'Not getting a taxi home and getting safely into bed – that'd be a pretty big screw-up!' Dan is half-guiding, half-pulling me towards the door.

'No, the biggest screw-up of all was moving in with Will.' There's a nasty feeling of nausea creeping up my gullet, which I'm hoping to God is just a symptom of extreme embarrassment. 'I was perfectly OK before that, you know? I never even *thought* about the wedding thing, let alone the baby thing! But right now it's all I can think about!'

'Isabel.' He stops, for a moment, and looks right at me. 'Go a bit easy on yourself. It's not exactly surprising that you're thinking about weddings all the time, is it? I mean, it's your job. And didn't you tell me your best friend and your brother were getting married too?'

This just brings a fresh hot-spring of tears to my eyes. 'Yes, but they don't even want me to plan it for them, that's how much of a joke I am –'

'Oh, I'm sure you're mistaken about that,' Dan goes on, quite rightly cutting me off before I actually start howling again. 'Anyway, my point is that it's no wonder you've gone a bit wedding-mad. It's a bit like letting somebody go mad in a sweet shop when they're meant to be on a diet.'

OK – now I'm seriously confused. And the fact that the roof terrace seems actually to be shifting under my feet isn't helping make any sense of Will's words . . . sorry, I mean *Dan's* words . . . 'Are you saying I need to go on a diet?'

'No! I'm saying nothing of the sort.'

'Oh, I think I get it. It's a whatsit . . . a mephator . . . so is Will the diet? Or is he the sweet shop?'

'He's neither.' Dan has almost got me to the door. 'He's just the guy you're in love with.'

'You're right. That's who he is. Sorry, Dan – can you just wait a minute?'

428

I pull away from him just in time. And I'm praying there's nobody standing in the street four floors below as I lean over the crumbling wall, and throw up a stream of Pinot Grigio, lime vodka, champagne, and half-digested mini jacket potato into the night air.

Chapter Twenty-Three

The moment I woke up, I realised I'd spent the night somewhere I shouldn't.

The bed sheets were the wrong texture. My pyjamas were the wrong size. And Dan Britten-Jones was sleeping beside me.

Sleeping like a log, I should say, because he didn't even stir when I slid out of bed and gathered up my things – shoes, bag, clothes (cringe), underwear (double-cringe) – before shutting myself in the bathroom and putting them all back on. Nor did he move a muscle as I crept back out of the bathroom right past him and let myself out of the front door, only a few metres from his bedroom.

God, what *happened* in that bedroom last night?

My last clear memory is the roof terrace. And throwing up off the side of it. Everything after that is hazy, at best. There was definitely a taxi, at some point, and by logical conclusions, I must have been in it with Dan. There might have been tea offered, or possibly coffee, because I can definitely remember sipping some kind of hot liquid from a mug and enjoying the way the steam rose up and soothed my sore eyes and throat. Beyond those details, my mind is a blank, and everything else is just assumption.

Though the obvious assumption, based on the fact that I woke up six inches away from Dan, my feet intertwined with his at the bottom of the bed, really isn't one I want to think about right now. According to my watch, it's almost seven o'clock in the morning, and I have to get home.

I stand on the kerb, blinking at the passing traffic for a couple of moments and wondering where the hell in this huge capital city I actually am. Dan never mentioned where he lived, did he? I squint for a street sign and see one further down the road, then as I start walking towards it I reach into my bag for my iPhone. If I enter the street name in on Google Maps, that'll tell me where I am . . .

Oh, I've just lucked out, because I can see a black taxi heading along the road towards me. I hail it, mumble Will's address at the driver, and get in.

'Christ's sake,' the driver says, staring at me in the rear-view mirror. 'Can't you just walk it?'

'Walk what?'

'The ten minutes it'll take to get there.'

I stare back at him. 'We're in Battersea?'

'Well, where did you think you were?'

I can't believe Dan did this to me. He knew full well where Will's flat was because he had the address from that envelope Sophie sent me, and he still couldn't see fit to drop me off there on his way back home last night. God, so much for all that crap I can dimly remember him coming out with on the terrace last night. All that bollocks about not wanting to take advantage of me when I was drunk . . . not wanting to take advantage of me when I was still not quite so drunk that I'd agree to anything, I think he meant.

'Look, would you just drive me, please?' I say, in a shaky voice. 'I'll pay you double . . . whatever you want . . .'

'Oh, forget about it,' the driver sighs, obviously taking pity on me and pulling away from the kerb.

It's then that I glance down at my iPhone screen.

Jesus.

Fifty-six missed calls.

How the hell did that happen? Was I so out of it all night that I didn't even hear my phone ring, not once?

Was it, perhaps, the fact that – like an idiot – I switched my ringer off to avoid late-night harassment from Summer?

'Looks like somebody's in trouble,' the taxi driver is suddenly saying.

How can he possibly have seen my phone screen from where he's sitting? I think for a moment, until I realise that he isn't looking at my phone screen, he's looking at Will's flat, which is where we've just pulled up. There's a police car parked on the double yellow lines right outside the block. A policewoman, all fur- rowed brow and Juliet Bravo hair, is getting out of the passenger side, and the front door to Will's block is opening. Will himself is coming out.

He looks . . . actually, words can't describe how he looks. His skin is kind of grey, his eyes are panda-ringed and he's aged about twenty years over the course of one night. He's still in the same suit trousers and shirt he was wearing yesterday but with a hooded sweatshirt over the top. Something about this combination of the formal and informal clothing makes him look like a schoolboy on the team coach, coming back from an away football match.

I don't know how someone can look so old and so young all at once, but the effect is heartbreaking.

Just as I'm wondering whether it mightn't be better all round for me to slump down in the back of the taxi, tell the driver to floor it, and send Will a hasty text message with some line about how I was round at Lara's last night and I forgot the time, Juliet Bravo glances over her shoulder and meets my eyes. I'm not exactly a champion lip-reader, but it wouldn't take one to work out that she's saying 'Is that her?' She gestures in the direction of my taxi, and Will's bleary eyes follow where she's pointing.

It's too late. Now I have to get out and face the music.

I reach through the partition and shove a tenner in the driver's direction, then clamber out without waiting for the change.

'Yes, that's her,' I hear Will saying to the police-woman, before the rest of what he's saying is drowned out by the noise of the double-decker bus rumbling between us. By the time it's gone, and I'm crossing over, I can hear that he's offering all kinds of thank-yous and apologies, and that Juliet Bravo is patting him on the arm and saying she quite understands. Mind you, I'm not sure she understands as much as she's claiming, because as I approach, she shoots me a look of total disgust and says, 'Next time you fancy going AWOL all night, love, you might like to try answering your phone.'

'I'm so sorry,' I mumble. 'I'd switched the ringer off to avoid my client calling me at all hours . . .'

Juliet Bravo's expression tells me that she doesn't accept this as an explanation for wasting valuable police time. Which, I can't help feeling, despite being totally on the back foot here, is just a tiny bit unfair. I mean, I'm not the one who called the police out, am I? But it seems that Will is still Mr Popular around here, because she pats him on the arm again a couple of times before clambering back into the car and driving away.

I stare at Will. He stares at me.

'I'm sorry,' I begin. 'I totally lost track of the time.'

Will opens his mouth as if he's about to speak, but appears to change his mind. He just gestures, wearily, towards the front door.

'Will, seriously, you didn't need to go calling the police,' I carry on, starting up the stairs, Will following me with a leaden tread. 'It was just a silly mistake! I was over at Lara's, and –'

'Isabel?' I hear Lara's voice before I see her, but a moment later, she's at the open flat door. 'Fucking hell!' she practically shrieks, in a voice that matches her own drained face and wild hair. 'Where *were* you?'

'With you, allegedly,' mutters Will. 'All night.'

Before I can say anything, Lara grabs me and pulls me into a fierce, angry hug. 'For God's sake, don't try telling him you were with Barney, either,' she hisses into my left ear. 'He's been here making soup since three-thirty this morning.'

'Soup?' This is all a bit much, although it certainly explains the aroma of onions and chicken stock that is emanating from the kitchen down the hallway. 'I don't believe all this,' I go on, looking from Lara to Will and back again. 'You called the police? Barney came and made soup? But he doesn't even *like* soup.'

'Well, what did you expect us to do?' Lara's face is turning pink. 'You just disappeared, Isabel! Will said you just ran out of the neighbours' dinner, and then you stayed out all night without even saying if you were OK. Of *course* we called the police!'

'Right . . . I suppose so . . .'

'Anyway, we only called the police once you hadn't answered the *fiftieth call*! And Matthew was starting to talk about calling your parents . . .'

'Which we don't have to do now, thank God.' Matthew is stalking out of the kitchen, slinging his own hooded top on as he comes. He glowers at me, reaches over to ruffle my hair, and then glowers at me again. 'Nice one, Iz-Wiz. But next time you decide to go a bit mad and then go missing, maybe you could not do it the day before Lars and I both have nightmare days at work coming up?'

'I'm really sorry –'

'Let's get home and grab an hour's sleep,' Matthew interrupts me, putting an arm around Lara's shoulder and moving her towards the front door. 'You should do the same, mate,' he adds, to Will, who is just standing propped up by the wall. 'You look like you need it.'

There's a bit of a team-bonding feeling that I'm totally left out of. Will starts thanking them for coming, and nobody even really seems to notice as I slip towards the kitchen. Barney is standing at the stove-top stirring a huge silver pan that I didn't even know we owned. It's weird, but even amongst all the stress and drama of the last five minutes, the very first thing that pops into my head is that I still haven't managed to find that damn soda siphon.

'*Iz*!' He reaches out to give me a brief hug, his face breaking into a smile. 'I'm so relieved to see you!'

Relief washes over me too; it's so nice to be faced with at least one person who's not stony-faced and judgemental. 'So you're not furious with me, like the others?'

'I'm *mostly* relieved. But as it happens, I'm pretty cross with you too.'

'Because you've ended up having to make soup?' I quip. But Barney isn't having any of it.

'No, Isabel, not because I've ended up having to make soup! Poor Will, the state he was in, I thought a bowl of chicken soup might be the thing to settle his stomach.'

Those pangs of guilt are kicking in again. 'He . . . was in a state?'

'Well, what do you expect? He thought something terrible might have happened to you! And I've had to stand here for hours wrestling with whether or not to tell him that I didn't think anything terrible had happened to you . . .' he lowers his voice. '. . . but that you might be *doing* something terrible.'

'What do you mean?'

'Is this all about that Dan bloke?' he hisses at me. 'Because that's where I thought you were. Now, I was waiting to say anything to Will until I absolutely had to, because I know he was already a bit funny about you texting him, but –' He breaks off hastily as Will comes into the room. 'Well, it's probably best if I leave you two to it,' he says, slipping his apron over his head and turning the gas low on the pan. 'This should be kept simmering for another hour or so, just until it's nicely reduced – and that means *simmering*, Iz, not on a rolling boil . . . but probably you're not too bothered about that right now!' he adds hastily, as I shoot him a look. 'Just enjoy it with some nice crusty bread whenever it's ready, and don't forget to season!'

He hoicks on his newly branded Simple Suppers! rucksack, pats Will on the shoulder, then turns and mouths, 'Good luck' at me before he leaves the kitchen. The front door clicks shut behind him a moment later.

Will is the first one to break the silence.

'I should go and have a shower. I need to be in by eight-thirty this morning.'

'Will, look, I'm really sorry,' I suddenly blurt. 'I was

stupid, about turning off the ringer. I know you must have been really worried . . .'

'Well, of course I was, Isabel.' He's still not looking directly at me. 'I'm not exactly the sort to have an overactive imagination, but obviously I was worried something dreadful had happened. After all, when your girlfriend runs out of dinner in a total state, and doesn't say where she's going, and then as the clock ticks by you still haven't heard from her, and she isn't answering her phone, and her friends don't know where she's gone, or her clients, for that matter –'

'Oh God, you didn't call Summer, did you?'

'I called everyone I could think of, Isabel. Which is when I started to get really worried. Though now, of course . . .' He gives one of those shrugs again, his shoulders slumping further this time. 'Now that I know you're actually alive and well, I'm starting to feel pretty fucking stupid for being so worried.'

I'm shocked. Will doesn't swear. He has to be really, really angry for him to actually swear.

'OK, I can tell you're really, really angry –' I begin, but he interrupts me again.

'So where were you?'

'Well, like I said, I went to this party . . .'

'All *night*?'

'Look, I got a bit drunk – actually, I was sick . . .'

'Spare me the sob story!'

I can't help bristling. And as soon as I do bristle, I realise that it's a much less unpleasant feeling than dreadful, crushing guilt. 'Look, I know you've been awake all night, but you don't have to snap at me like that.'

'Fine, OK, I tell you what, why don't *I* stay out all night, without any warning and without answering my phone? Then we'll see if you're so blasé about, as you call it, being *awake all night.*'

'I'm not blasé! And I've apologised for leaving my phone off! And you don't have to keep staring at me like you're trying to work out if . . . I don't know, if I've gone out and *murdered* someone or something!'

'Isabel. I'm not trying to work out if you've gone and murdered someone. Believe it or not, that scenario didn't actually cross my mind.'

'Well, what scenario did, then?'

Will doesn't say anything for a moment. Then he says, in the lowest, quietest voice I think I've ever heard him speak in, 'I don't want to talk about this any more.'

I feel a rush of blood to my head. I mean, all right, I've (probably) done something unforgivable and (possibly) lost any right whatsoever to take the moral high ground. But for him to be so certain of his own position on the moral high ground that he doesn't even feel the need to descend from it for a single moment to start flinging the unspoken accusation . . . Well, it's just a little too much to bear.

'OK, fine,' I snap. 'Don't talk about it! Let's leave all the important discussions until we're in the neighbours' garden, shall we?'

'Isabel, are *you* having a go at *me* about something?

After the night I just had, trying not to convince myself you were dead in a ditch somewhere?'

God, I hate ditches. The moment you accidentally mislead people into thinking you might have been dead in one, you seem instantly to lose any hope of making valid criticisms of your own.

'I'm not having a go,' I say, trying to keep my own voice level. 'I'm just saying that maybe there was more reason for me to go out to Dan's party last night than you're acknowledging . . .'

Oh shit.

That's done it.

'Dan?' Will is rocketing, instantly, from the moral high ground right up to moral Everest. 'Dan in the Fiat? Dan your text-message buddy? *That's* where you were last night?'

'Will, look, it was only his party in the sense of it being at his art gallery . . . and he's working at Summer's wedding tomorrow so I had to go and speak to him.'

'Ah, yes, of course. Lest we forget. You're *working* together. And it shouldn't bother me at all that he texts you to call you gorgeous. That's obviously the sign of a professional relationship.'

I forgot to delete the text messages, didn't I? And even though summoning up outrage that Will has read my text messages doesn't seem entirely appropriate right now, it's about the only chance of outrage that I've got. 'You read my texts? How dare –' I break off as Will turns, grabbing his jacket, and heads for the door. 'You can't just leave! I thought you said you were going to have a shower!'

'I can have one in the gym at work.'

'But I want to talk! Not about last night, but about *us*! And I have to go to Somerset for the wedding, so if we don't talk now –'

'There's nothing to talk about.' He slips off his hooded top, pulls on his jacket, and opens the door, all without turning around. 'Maybe I'll see you on Sunday. Good luck with the wedding.'

From: izbo@googlemail.com
To: danbj@marlowgallery.co.uk
Subject: Thanks a fucking lot

Dan

~~What in God's name~~

~~Do you have any idea~~

OK, look. I'm prepared to accept my fair share of the blame. Obviously it doesn't look very good for me that I a) sent you flirty text messages, b) came all the way to your party with the express purpose of ~~being flung~~ having a fling, and c) then got extremely drunk and went up to a romantic (if a bit ropey) roof terrace with you. So I'm happy to take a large portion of the responsibility here.

That said, I cannot possibly condone your actions vis-à-vis taking me back to your flat last night. You knew full fucking well that your flat is only minutes away from my boyfriend's!! And yet you still could not be bothered to think about dropping me back there, thereby saving me the terrible task of having to explain where I had been all night. ~~If you could have seen Will's face~~

~~I don't think he's ever going to forgive me~~

~~I just wish I hadn't screwed things up so badly~~

442

Chapter Twenty-Four

Despite the fact I spent Thursday night behaving like a stupid teenager – or, in some ways, precisely *because* of the fact I spent Thursday night behaving like a stupid teenager – I know I've got to pull myself together and try and be professional, at least for the duration of this weekend. After all, it's not Summer's fault I got so drunk that I ended up doing God-knows-what with Dan Britten-Jones; she still deserves the wedding of her dreams, no matter how miserable I happen to be feeling.

Anyway, there's been almost no time to feel miserable, because there's been far too much to do. From the moment I left London yesterday afternoon, I've been working my way through a seemingly endless succession of To-Do Lists: one for food and drink (have we got enough mineral water available? has the chef remembered to do the starters for the vegetarians and the nut allergy sufferers?); one for entertainment (who do I speak to if there's a problem with the inflatable movie screen? what time will the string quartet want their meal break?); one for décor (can Anita the florist get white rose petals to scatter along the aisle like we decided, or are we limited to pink ones? where can we find a ten-foot long pink table-cloth to replace the one that's mysteriously vanished from the top table?); and one for imponderables (should I arrange for a St John Ambulance crew in case any of Tim's ex-Priory friends go on a drink-and-coke binge? should I replace the posh Roger & Gallet toiletries in the Portaloos with posher Molton Brown ones?).

This doesn't take into account the entirely separate To-Do Lists I have for Summer herself, by the way, co-ordinating such matters as the spa treatments she's booked at her hotel, transport down from London for her hairdresser, makeup artist, and (of course) Kieron, delivery of her wedding dress, shoes, and custom-made Swarovski crystal tiara and (as a kind of last-minute afterthought, I do wish she'd mentioned this earlier) taxis to pick up her visiting Canadian relatives from Heathrow on Saturday morning and drive them all the way to Somerset.

Still, somehow I seem to have kept on top of it all, and now we're T minus two hours seventeen minutes, as we'd say if this were an episode of *24*, and I'm heading over from Broughton to Summer's hotel for a last-minute visit, just to see how things are going. I'm assuming that if anything disastrous was happening (bride locked in bathroom refusing to come out, for example, but even I couldn't be unlucky enough to be faced with that scenario again) Wendy would have been on the phone to me complaining by now, but I still can't help the fluttery feeling in my stomach as I pull into the car park in Mum's Micra that I've borrowed for the day. I mean, I can't say that Summer was exactly in the *best* mood yesterday, when she and Tim showed up to see Broughton for the first time. Though I suspect that might have been more to do with the shamefully over-the-top cow eyes Sophie Britten-Jones kept making in Tim's direction as she took them on the tour, and not so much to do with the venue itself, which she rather grudgingly admitted was beautiful.

But I don't need a bride in a good mood. I just need a bride who's going to turn up. My ambitions for Summer's marriage, I hate to say it, stretch no further than that.

I'm not even out of the car before I realise that a very familiar Fiat is pulling up in the space opposite.

It's Dan.

I get out of the car, trying to compose my face into a expression of total calm and composure, when what I'd dearly love to do right now is hurl myself across the car park and howl at him that he's a selfish, narcissistic turd-bag who ought to come with his own health warning.

'Hey!' He folds himself out of the Fiat, shielding his eyes from the bright sunlight and smiling at me. 'Perfect timing.'

'Yes. Perfect timing.' I shut my car door. 'Though, of course, we've both got work to do, so I don't have time to chat.'

Leaving his camera equipment in his car, he jogs

across the car park and catches up with me as I head for the hotel. 'Somebody's feeling a bit hostile today.'

'Yes, well, I wonder why that might be.'

He grins. 'Well, when you find out, do you think you could tell me? Because I'm not sure I'm going to like stroppy, angry Isabel as much as I like funny, friendly Isabel.'

I stop walking. His casual tone has incensed me, and I want to wipe the smile off his face. 'Then I really don't think you're going to like reporting-you-to-the-police Isabel!'

'Sorry?'

No matter that this is only bluster – at least this has shaken him. 'Look, I know I might have been stupidly drunk, and obviously I did come to your party with the express intention of having a fling with you, but I still think you should have been certain I was giving you my consent before you had sex with me.'

Slowly – very slowly – but surely, that grin is spreading across his face again. 'Ahhh. That's what I like to see. Funny Isabel back again!'

I stare at him, outraged. 'You think I'm joking?'

'You think I had sex with you?'

'*Didn't* you?'

'No, Isabel, I didn't.'

I'm about to say 'a likely story,' but he carries on.

'I mean, I've always thought you were gorgeous and everything – you already know that – but you're not gorgeous enough for me to be able to overlook the vomit and the tears. Oh, and the semi-consciousness.

I mean, call me boring and vanilla, but that's never really done it for me.'

'Oh.' My face has started burning. 'Right . . .'

'And anyway, even if I had been possessed by some kind of masochistic desire to have sex with you that night, Licky was hardly going to let me get away with it, was she?'

'Licky?'

'Don't you remember her coming back with us in the taxi? Getting you in the bath and hosing you down to try to sober you up?'

Now he's said this, I am getting this blurry memory . . . Licky flapping her hands at a taxi driver to get him to pull over so I could be sick out of the open cab door . . . Licky propping me up on the edge of a bath so she could get my shoes undone and pull a clean pyjama top over my head . . .

'Well, take it from me, she was there. Call her yourself and ask her if you don't believe me.' Now Dan is looking slightly offended.

'No, no, I believe you . . . I just thought . . . well, when I woke up and you were in bed next to me . . .'

'I only came in halfway through the night, because poor Licks was having a nightmare of a time trying to sleep through your snoring. I thought under the circumstances that it was more gentlemanly to let her take the sofa in the sitting room.'

Now my cheeks have gone somewhere beyond flaming and are rapidly heading towards thermo-nuclear. Bad enough that I've just falsely accused Dan

447

of something roughly akin to date rape – but to find out that I was *snoring* . . . I don't think I'll ever live the embarrassment down.

'Aw, don't worry about it, Isabel!' Dan reaches out a hand and lays it on my shoulder. 'You were having a bad night. If it helps at all, I still think you're gorgeous.'

'No! It doesn't help! I'm the biggest idiot on the planet! And I've messed everything up with Will because of you . . . well, because of *me* . . .'

'Really? Because the way you were babbling on on Thursday night, it sounds like your Will is just as much to blame for things going wrong as you are. Something about him refusing to marry you, and telling the neighbours he didn't want kids . . .?'

'Yes, maybe, but at least he didn't just go out and get hammered and spend the night with some devastatingly attractive girl to get back at me.'

'Interesting. I just thought you thought I was *gorgeous*. But apparently it's *devastatingly attractive*.'

'Yes, all right, you're Daniel Craig, Brad Pitt and Johnny Depp all rolled into one, OK?' I swat his hand away. 'But that's not the point. You're not . . . Will.'

Dan says nothing for a long moment. 'Well, I can't argue with that, can I?'

'No. I'm sorry, Dan. And I'm sorry about Thursday night.'

'That's all right. I've had my heart broken before. I'm sure I'll get over it.' He smiles at me. 'Anyway, we can't stand about chewing the fat all day, can we? I'd better go and get my cameras. And don't you have a wedding to run?'

'God, yes, I need to go and see if Summer's OK.'

He stops me just before I turn back in the direction of the hotel. 'For what it's worth, Iz, I'm sure your solicitor will end up forgiving you. So you might as well save yourself some of the agony and forgive yourself.'

Well, so much for my hopes of getting a bride in a good mood. Summer may not have locked herself in the bathroom, but after just five minutes of her company in her hotel suite, I'm kind of wishing she would just lock herself away somewhere and save us all the agony of putting up with her foul temper. Dan is struggling to get any decent pictures and even Saint Luc the hairdresser, who's quite used to diva displays from his clients, is looking weary as he attempts to talk Summer out of the particular up-do she's set her sights on.

'But we agreed on a classic chignon,' he keeps saying. 'Elegant. Timeless. These spiral curls you are asking for, they are neither elegant nor timeless.'

'But they're what I want,' Summer declares, her chin jutting out. Were it not for this and the scowl lining her face, she'd look incredible – her Kieron-honed curves poured into pure white lace underwear and barely covered by the tiniest of silk kimonos. Honestly, I'm amazed that Weirdy-Beardy can even hold his camera steady. And from the look on his face, he's pretty amazed at his self-control too. 'And you have to do what I want, Luc. I'm the bride.'

Luc casts me a look of despair, so I decide to speak up. 'Honestly, Summer, I think it's better if we stick to what we decided with your hair. It'll go so much better with the dress, and you might regret it otherwise when you see the photos . . . isn't that true, Dan?'

'My hairstyle is the last thing I'm going to regret about today,' Summer snaps at me, before Dan can answer. It's at least the tenth time she's snapped at me since I got here. 'Believe me, Izzie.'

'Well, of course you're having a last-minute attack of nerves. That's quite usual!'

'Don't tell me what's usual! Is it *usual* that the groom doesn't even text the bride the night before the wedding to wish her good night?'

Ugh. I really don't want to think about text messages right now. 'I'm sure he was busy . . . family arriving . . .'

'Five grams of coke arriving, more like,' she snorts – rather appropriately. 'Tim was on the phone to his stupid dealer most of the way along the motorway yesterday.'

'Um, right.' I make a mental note to see if I can get that St John Ambulance booked at late notice after all. 'But seriously, Summer, as soon as he sees you walking down that aisle, he'll forget everything else! And that beautiful chignon Luc had planned for you will just make you look so stunning.'

'I want *ringlets*.'

'But I do not even have curling tongs with me,' Luc says despairingly.

'That's OK. I do. Wendy!' Summer yells, to where Wendy is sitting rather grumpily, still in her pyjamas, having her base applied by Edie the makeup artist. 'Can you go to my room and get my tongs? The big barrel ones, not the mini handbag ones.'

'It's all right,' I say, seeing Wendy's eye-roll. 'I'll get them.'

'No, you won't, Izzie. You'll go downstairs and get another bottle of champagne.' She waggles the empty bottle that's sitting on the dressing table. 'And tell them I want the vintage Laurent Perrier one this time, not, like, the crappy regular stuff. If I'm going to marry a millionaire, I might as well see *some* benefits.'

I'm perfectly happy to duck out for a few moments, so I leave the suite and its bad atmosphere behind and head on down to reception to ask for the fresh delivery of champagne. And I ask them for a separate glass, while I'm at it, because I'd quite like a couple of minutes to sit, calmly, with a nerve-settling drink, and focus on everything there is to do over the next eight hours. Usually I'd be using the time to put in a quick call to Lara or Will for a bit of moral support, but obviously those avenues are closed to me . . .

'She still being a bit of a cow up there?'

The voice behind me makes me jump. It's Aquamarine Hair – or rather, as she is today, Hot-

Pink Hair – coming in from what must have been a rather long cigarette break in the grounds.

'Oh, hi . . .' This is terrible; I have no idea what her real name is. And after all those big ideas I had about treating junior people well when I was working as a wedding planner on my own. Still, she doesn't actually work *for* me, so it's not quite as bad, is it? 'I think she's just having an attack of last-minute nerves,' I say. 'That's all.'

'Mmm. Of course, you know *why* she's having a rethink? I think she's cottoned on to what me and Sven saw last night.'

Wait. This is all too much information. And I'm stuck on the word *rethink*. 'She's not rethinking . . . is she? I mean, she can't! There's been a million quid spent on this wedding!' I realise, rather too late, that this isn't quite the appropriate response. 'I mean, what did you and Weir . . . I mean, *Sven*, see last night?'

She lowers her voice. 'Well, I told Sven I thought we should get some footage of the marquee, right, while it was all empty late at night and half-finished. I thought it would be all atmospheric, you know, and kind of calm-before-the-storm . . .'

'Yes, yes.' I don't want Hot-Pink Hair's Emmy-winning pitch. 'Very atmospheric, I'm sure.'

'Yeah, well, it *would've* been, if it had been empty. But she was there, wasn't she? That stuck-up cow who owns the house?'

'Sophie?'

'Mm-hm. And *not* alone.'

For God's sake, does she imagine we've accidentally stepped out of the pages of an Agatha Christie novel, where we've all got acres of time to stand around while she reveals the mystery? 'Well, who was she with?'

'Tim, of course. At it like rabbits, the pair of them. And I'd avoid getting too close to the top table this evening if I were you.'

Oh Christ.

Well, if nothing else, this might explain the disappearance of the ten-foot-long pink tablecloth.

'Sven's not said anything to her yet,' Hot-Pink Hair continues, 'but –'

'To who?'

'To Summer.'

'To *Summer*? On her *wedding day*? Is he completely mad?'

She blinks at me as though I'm completely mad. 'So . . . you *wouldn't* tell her?'

'No!' I realise I've raised my voice. 'Of course I wouldn't tell her!'

'Well, I get that you've got a vested interest –'

'It's nothing to do with that! I mean, I don't have a vested interest.' I push away the guilty feeling that's jabbing me in the stomach. 'Look, Summer has been looking forward to her dream wedding for . . . well, for weeks. Who am I to take that away from her?'

'Yeah, but now that you know about this . . .'

'Yes, well, I wish you hadn't told me!'

'Sorry. I just thought you might like to know why she's being such a bitch today.'

'So does she actually *know*?' I can feel panic rising. 'You said Sven hadn't said anything yet.'

'No, but she's not a total idiot,' Hot-Pink Hair says, with some feeling. 'Even if we don't say anything, or show her the footage –'

There's *footage*? Despite the fact the bottle of champagne – and my glass – have now appeared in the hands of the cheery receptionist, I'm not about to take it back up to Summer's suite until I'm sure everything is completely under control right here.

'OK, look, I'm begging you, don't let Summer see any footage. And don't say anything about it. Not you or Sven.'

'But I feel kind of bad, knowing about it.' Hot-Pink Hair runs a hand through her locks, and I wonder if she's (rather sweetly) toned her shade in with Summer's wedding colours for the day. 'She's a nice girl, in her own way.'

'I know she is. And a year from now, if Tim Holland is still playing away, with Sophie Britten-Jones or anyone else, I'll make it my own personal duty to inform Summer about it.'

She shoots me a sceptical look.

'I will! In fact, it's all part of an Isabel Bookbinder wedding package. It's called a . . . a *marriage audit*.'

'I thought you worked for someone called Pippa something,' she replies, more astutely than I'd given her credit for.

'All part of a *Pippa Everitt* wedding package. But we do feel very strongly, in these kinds of circumstances, that the very best course of action is simply to let the wedding go ahead. We're just like priests, in a confession booth! We may hear terrible things, but it's not our responsibility to actually do anything about them.'

Hot-Pink Hair wrinkles her nose. 'I'm not *entirely* sure that's right, actually . . .'

'Listen. Honestly.' I look right at her, hoping she'll see how serious this is. 'You mustn't say anything. It's not any business of yours or mine.'

'What about Sven?'

'Or Sven's!' For God's sake. 'Promise me you'll keep it to yourselves?'

She thinks for a moment, then shrugs. 'You're the wedding planner. You know what's best.'

'Exactly!'

I'd rather not think too much about whether those two sentences actually go together, to be honest. I'll be much better off just taking this champagne up to the suite, and making sure Summer looks perfectly pretty for her walk down the aisle.

Chapter Twenty-Five

All right, then. We are now T minus fifteen minutes, and everything at Broughton Hall is ready for the arrival of the bride. And not just all the things I've arranged and anticipated, but some I haven't, too – like the small but growing scrum of photographers down at the bottom of the driveway. All right, they're not actually trespassing on to private property, but nevertheless they're making a bit of a mockery of any concept I might have had of paparazzi neutrality. Not that I think Summer and Wendy are going to mind; far from it, although I'm not sure they'd be quite so happy if they realised that the bulk of the snappers seem to be from the local press rather than the national tabloids. I can't help a sneaking suspicion that Mum has been blabbing her mouth off around the offices of the *Central Somerset Gazette*.

Still, everything else is in place and raring to go. Freshly arrived on their coach from Bristol, my three-dozen student actors are doing sterling work screaming and hollering at the guests as they walk up the red carpet. Inside the entrance hall, Sophie's staff are circulating with chilled flutes of champagne while the string quartet lustily scrape their way through Great

Movie Themes – *Lawrence of Arabia* and *Murder on the Orient-Express* have dominated for most of the last half-hour, but thankfully they've just moved on to a medley of James Bond tunes and now the far more romantic strains of 'Nobody Does It Better' are echoing around the hallway. Dan is charming people left, right and centre as he moves amongst the guests with requests for photos, blending effortlessly in both with the older toffs who must be Sir Peter and Lady Holland's invitees, and the younger crowd, who are obviously Tim's friends. And Tim himself has at least made it on time, greeting his parents' friends at the entrance to the Saloon as though butter wouldn't melt in his mouth, with no outward sign of last night's extra-curricular shenanigans.

Sophie Britten-Jones, though, is a different matter. As I head into the Saloon with a glass of cold water for the newly arrived registrar, she stops me halfway up the petal-strewn aisle. She's looking rather flushed with excitement and dressed to the nines in a rather tight navy dress, not unlike the Vera Wang brides-maid's dress she wore to Licky's non-wedding, a little cream crocheted jacket and a cream-coloured pillbox hat on her head.

'Isabel. Time for a quick word?'

'Sophie, you look just like a guest.'

'Oh, well, I am a guest! Tim wondered if I'd like to join in all the fun.'

'What?'

'Well, we were talking yesterday, Isabel, and it

turns out we have a lot of friends in common – from the old days, up in London, you know? And so many of them are going to be here today that it would almost be weird if I wasn't part of the wedding party!'

I take a deep breath. 'Sophie. I'm not sure what you're trying to do here . . .'

'Well, I'm just trying to get you to pop an extra seat at one of the tables for dinner, of course!' She shakes back her chestnut mane. 'Obviously I'm not *too* fussy about where I end up, but I am an old acquaintance of Tim's brother-in-law, and I know Angus, the best man, from the old days at Chinawhite . . . anyway, I know you'll do your best to put me somewhere good!'

I take a deep breath. 'No, Sophie. I'm not going to do anything of the sort.'

'What do you mean?'

'Well, it may have escaped your notice, but I have a bride due here in less than ten minutes, so I don't have the time to start mucking about with a seating plan. And more to the point, I don't have the inclination.'

'Oh, really?'

'Yes, really! For God's sake, Sophie . . .' I lower my voice. 'I'm not going to facilitate you moving in on Tim Holland at his own wedding! I don't care how rich he is, or how desperate you are.'

Her eyes narrow instantly. 'What did you call me?'

I don't want to call her desperate again, because she's pretty scary. But I'm not about to back down. 'I know what went on last night, Sophie, and I just can't condone it.'

'Oh, can't you, Miss Prissy Knickers?'

'No! He's getting married today!'

'Big fucking deal.' Sophie adjusts her pillbox hat by a couple of millimetres. 'He's not married *yet*.'

I can't believe what I'm hearing. 'That really isn't the point! And aren't you conveniently forgetting that you *are* married?'

'To *David*.'

'What's wrong with David?' I feel rather protective of him all of a sudden, knowing Dan's concerns for his older brother. 'Anyway, just because you don't like the person you married, doesn't mean you have any right to go around wrecking Summer's relationship.'

'He shouldn't even be marrying her, you know?' she hisses. 'His friends loathe her. His family are mortiied by the entire thing. They'll be divorced before the year is out. And she's only after him for his money.'

'Yes, well, it takes one to know one,' I flash back, before I can stop myself. 'Now, please, Sophie, I need to give this drink to the registrar. And then I have to start getting the guests seated. If you want a seat at the reception, then I'm afraid you're going to have to sort it out yourself.'

If I was truly feisty, and not a bit of a wimp, my legs wouldn't be shaking as I walk away from her. But thank God, by the time I've turned back from the registrar's table, and busied myself primping Anita's display of lilies for a good few moments, Sophie has gone.

Right. Well, I wasn't just bluffing when I said I had to start getting the guests seated. Several rows towards the back have already started filling up (I think with Tim's ex-Priory chums; they look as though they're planning to get up to all kinds of nefarious doings at the back) and I need to make sure the bride and groom's families are seated comfortably in the front rows well before the bride's arrival. I don't imagine Tim's family will need too much help shoving their way to the front, but I do want to make sure that Summer's family, having been forgotten about at the airport, at least feel that they're being given some special treatment. I can see a couple of nervous-looking blonde ladies, with more than a hint of Summer about their low-cut dresses and teetering heels, hovering around the middle of the aisle, so I sweep up to them to introduce myself.

As I suspected, they are in fact Summer's relatives – 'Mom and Auntie Sue,' they inform me – so I lead them towards the front row on the left-hand side, where the bride's family traditionally sit.

Oh. Some people have already put their handbags down here. Three of them, laid out on every other seat.

'I'm so sorry,' I say, swooping on the bags and gathering them up carefully in my arms. 'Someone else obviously wanted the best seats in the house! Please, take a seat and you can have a little look through the Order of Service. It'll give you a taste of what to expect from a traditional English wedding. "With this ring, I thee wed," and all that! You make yourselves comfortable and I'll just go and find out who these handbags belong to.'

I'm stopped, about five feet down the aisle, by an

imperious-looking woman in charcoal-grey tweed and a large black hat.

'Excuse me,' she demands, 'but what do you think you're doing with my handbag?'

'Oh, these are yours?'

'Mine, my niece's, and my sister-in-law's.' She reaches out and snatches all three handbags from me. 'We *had* actually reserved some seats in the front row.'

'Right, well, I'm so sorry, but actually that row is reserved for family.'

'And who do you think *I* am?'

'Um . . . who *are* you?'

'The groom's mother, of course!' Her eyes, shadowed beneath the brim of her huge hat – a hat that, combined with the grey tweed suit, is far more appropriate for a funeral than a wedding; though I'm sure that's the point – are fixed on me with dislike. 'I had quite expressly put those bags down there to keep that row for my brother and his family. You had no right to remove them!'

I'm filled with a new-found respect for Summer. I mean, all right, she might only be marrying Tim for the money, but if she's prepared to take on board this battle-axe of a mother-in-law then she deserves every single brass farthing. 'Yes, but I'm so sorry, Lady Holland – that left-hand row is actually meant for the bride's *immediate* family. You know, her mother, and her auntie . . .'

Those shadowed eyes slice sideways, over my

shoulder, so that Lady Holland is looking directly at the Nice Lady Relatives. 'Good God,' she says, in none-too-soft a voice. '*Those* are my son's impending in-laws?'

'Lady Holland!'

'Well, it's just too much!' she snaps, actually stamping one court-shoe-clad foot like an irritable pony. 'This whole grisly affair, the press outside, that ghastly, common red carpet –'

'Lady Holland, I'm the wedding planner,' I interrupt, before she can say anything else she might regret. Actually, who am I kidding? She's not going to regret a single ill-tempered word. *I'm* the one who's going to regret it if I have to stand here and listen to her slag off all the hard work I've put in over the last three and a half weeks. 'I'm responsible for that ghastly, common red carpet, not your future daughter-in-law.'

'No, you're not!'

'Sorry?'

'You're not the wedding planner! Pippa Norton is the wedding planner. Tim mentioned it to me only a couple of days ago.'

'Pippa Norton?' I blink at her.

'Oh, well, I'm sure she works under her maiden name. Everton? Everard?'

'Everitt.'

'That's the one. But to me she's just Pippa Norton.'

I can feel my heart racing unpleasantly fast. 'You . . . *know* Pippa Everitt?'

'Of course I know her! She's married to my godson, Henry! Both on their way inside now, I'm sure, though I haven't actually seen them yet. Still, if she's in charge, she could be busy in the marquee or something.'

No. *No*. I clutch the back of one of the chairs. Pippa Everitt cannot be a guest at this wedding. This cannot be happening to me.

'In fact,' Lady Holland is going on, 'I'm surprised Henry's mother didn't mention that Pippa was working on Timothy's wedding when I ran into her at Le Caprice last week. Embarrassment, probably, if she'd known what a hideous job Pippa was going to make of it!'

OK. The important thing to do is to stay calm. After all, it's not as if there's anything that can actually be done, now, about the fact that I've told Wendy and Summer I've been working for Pippa Everitt. By everyone's reckoning I've done a decent job getting this whole day up and running. The worst Wendy can do now is subject me to a torrent of verbal abuse and swear never to let me work with one of her clients again, which is hardly going to come as a terrible hardship . . .

'Oh, speak of the devil. I knew she'd be here any minute!' Lady Holland is gesturing over my shoulder, back down the aisle. 'Henry! Pippa!'

I'm trapped. Completely and utterly trapped. There's no four-hundred-quid veil I can throw over myself. No sneaky exit. Pippa Everitt is waving at

Lady Holland, she's spotted me, and she's heading right for us.

I am, quite literally, frozen.

'*Isabel*?' She's staring at me, distracted by my presence even as she air-kisses Lady Holland on each cheek. 'What are you doing here?'

'Claiming she's doing your job,' Lady Holland snorts, moving past Pippa to kiss Henry, Pippa's blond, bland husband, who is standing a few feet away looking . . . well, looking tall. It's about his only distinguishing characteristic. 'I must say, Pipps, I hardly thought this wedding was your usual style! I do hope all this Hollywood nonsense is tongue-in-cheek.'

Pippa's eyes dart from Lady Holland to me and back again. 'I don't understand. Has Isabel said that I planned this wedding?'

'*No*, Pippa, I told you, dear!' Lady Holland tosses her head. 'She's been saying *she's* planned the wedding. Oh, Lord, is that Daphne Simpson-Burnett?' she suddenly mutters, gazing towards the doors. 'I have to stop her before she gets anywhere near those Canadian creatures, or I'll never hear the end of it . . .'

She barrels away down the aisle, and Pippa takes a step closer towards me.

'What's going on?'

'Well, it's just great to see you, Pippa, first of all –'

'Have you planned this wedding? And why does Lady Holland think *I've* planned it?'

'. . . you're looking wonderful,' I go on, feeling

sweat pooling in my lower back. 'Is this dress by Alice Temperley? It's perfect on you.'

'Will you shut the fuck up about my bloody dress and tell me what's going on?' Pippa is looking me up and down. 'You're in a work suit. You *have* planned this wedding, haven't you?'

'Look, Pippa, I just want to say that I hope this indicates how much I learned from you . . .'

'It doesn't indicate anything. I simply don't understand.' Pippa turns to her husband for support or answers, but quickly turns back when she realises she's more likely to get support or answers out of one of the linen-covered chairs. 'You got the *Holland* wedding? After that bloody fiasco at that hideous WAG wedding.'

I take a deep breath. 'You have a lot of excellent points to make, Pippa, and I'm really looking forward to discussing them with you, perhaps over a glass of champagne at the reception. But at the moment, I have a wedding ceremony to get through, I'm sure you understand, so –'

'No, I do not want to discuss it with you over a glass of champagne!' Her bony hands are on her even bonier hips. 'I want an explanation, Isabel. If you've told people I was responsible for this, then I absolutely have a right to know about it.'

'Is everything all right here?' Attracted, like a vulture, by the raised voices and air of tension, Sophie has appeared at Pippa's elbow. 'Is there a problem with seating? Can I help at all?'

I shoot her a look. 'It's fine, Sophie, I'm completely in control of it –'

'No, it is not fine!' Pippa glowers at me before switching her attention to Sophie. 'Who are you, exactly?'

'I'm Sophie Britten-Jones. I own this place. So if there's any kind of a problem . . .?'

'You're the owner?' Pippa's eyebrows shoot upwards. 'So you've been liaising with the wedding planner?'

'With Isabel, yes.' Sophie glances at me. 'What have you done to upset this lady, Isabel?'

'I've not done anything. Honestly, Sophie, Pippa, I think it's best if we all just head to our starting positions . . .'

'Has she told you she's working for me?' Pippa demands, ignoring me completely as she turns towards Sophie. 'Has she said Pippa Everitt Weddings is behind this event?'

I can see Sophie's eyes widen, and I can tell that, like me, she's remembering our conversation at The Wolseley, where we agreed – *clearly* agreed – that it was in both our best interests if she didn't let on what she knew about me being fired from Pippa's company.

And a split second later, I can tell that she's also remembering the conversation we had right here, only minutes ago, where I refused to rearrange the seating plan to suit her twisted agenda.

Her eyes flash, briefly, in triumph. 'So *you're* Pippa

Everitt?' she gushes. 'Isabel's talked so much about working for you.'

'She doesn't work for me,' Pippa snaps. 'I fired her a month ago!'

'But I've seen your name on the contract. I'm quite sure of it.' Sophie flashes a little glance in my direction. 'The bride's manager sent me a copy, I'm sure it's easily to hand in my office just downstairs. That would clear everything up, wouldn't it?'

I could kill Sophie. I could absolutely kill her.

Pippa is staring at me, her face white with fury. 'Did you *steal* one of my contracts, Isabel?'

'No! Pippa, please let me explain . . . yes?' I can't help snapping, as somebody taps my shoulder behind me. 'Oh, Wendy!' It's she who's tried to attract my attention. And to be honest, she didn't need to tap my shoulder to do it. She could have just wandered past and my eye would instantly have been drawn to her. Because she's the most peculiar-looking bridesmaid I think I've ever seen. In her hot-pink satin bridesmaid's dress, her hair bouffed up in a style I can't believe Saint Luc would ever have agreed to without the threat of extreme violence, and shifting uncomfortably from side to side in unfamiliar spindly heels, she looks, just as I suspected, like a sunburned penguin.

'Can you come with me, please, Isabel?' she asks, in a voice that's a million miles from her usual gruff tone. 'I know you're busy.'

'No, no, it's OK.' Anything to get away from the

surrounding harridans. 'Ladies, please, you'll have to excuse me for just one moment . . .'

'It'll be a bit longer than that,' Wendy mutters, as I start following her.

'Why? Is there a problem?'

'Yes, Isabel. There is a problem.'

I'm just about to ask if it's something insurmountable, or if it's something – a broken nail, a scuffed shoe – that we can solve with a bit of DIY and a lot of ingenuity, when Wendy continues.

'It's Summer. She's not coming.'

'Not coming?' I actually laugh. 'What, to her own wedding?'

'Exactly. To her own wedding.'

The white limousine is stopped almost halfway down the driveway, just about where Dan's Fiat and Will's Golf almost ran headlong into each other a few weeks ago. Back up on the drive behind us, the student actors have already started to disperse now that all the guests have gone indoors, heading round to the catering vans near the marquee for their promised cups of tea and hot bacon rolls. We're too far from the gates to see clearly the photographers at the bottom of the driveway, but I can see flashing bulbs and hear shouting, and I'm praying that Summer isn't about to do anything stupid, like climb out and start posing. But as Wendy and I approach, both of us shivering in the chill breeze, one of the rear windows winds down, and Summer's face peers out.

I have to say – I *hate* to say, under the circumstances – she looks ravishing. The pure white silk of her wedding dress is beautiful against her lightly tanned skin, and a combination of Edie's makeup skills and sheer, unbridled happiness have left her face glowing.

She may not be getting married today, but she's the most radiant bride I think I've ever seen.

'Izzie,' she says, grinning nervously at me. 'Do you really, really hate me right now?'

Right beside her, his hand resting lovingly around her bare shoulders, is Weirdy-Beardy. He grins at me too and shoots a thumbs up in my direction that, still in shock from Wendy's debrief as she hurried me out of the Hall and down the drive, I return.

I mean, *Weirdy-Beardy*? Not, as I'd been assuming, fit, sexy Kieron. I know there's no accounting for taste, but I'm just totally astounded that Weirdy-Beardy is the one Summer's been carrying on with these last few weeks.

And to be fair, they actually look pretty good together, cuddled up in the back of the limo. Now that he's smiling and happy, he's much nicer-looking than I'd noticed before – a lot less weird and, despite the fact he hasn't noticeably shaved since I saw him last, slightly less beardy. And most important of all, he couldn't be looking more adoringly at Summer if she was all dressed up in a babydoll nightie and clutching an entire litter of squishy Labrador puppies.

'I know you won't be too cross with me,' Summer

carries on. 'I mean, even Wendy isn't that cross with me, and I thought she'd be the one to totally explode. I knew you'd be nice about it. And you are going to be nice, aren't you?'

'Well, of course I'm going to be nice, Summer,' I say, faintly. 'I mean, whatever makes you happy . . .'

'Sven makes me happy!' Summer turns her face towards Weirdy-Beardy's, and the pair of them beam, starry-eyed, at each other. 'Ever since practically the first day we met!'

'That's lovely . . . but couldn't you, maybe, have mentioned this a bit sooner?' I grip the top of the car window-frame. 'Any time sooner than three minutes before the ceremony was due to start? I mean, just a thought . . .'

'I know, I know. I guess I should have. But this whole wedding thing has been like an express train that I didn't know how to get off. And then when Sven showed me what he'd filmed of Tim and that woman last night . . . well, it kind of made me rethink everything a little.'

Evidently my talk with Hot-Pink Hair earlier was either too little or too late. Either way, she didn't – or couldn't – stop Weirdy-Beardy from spilling the beans. 'Of course. And I totally understand that. But Summer, there are guests waiting. This wedding has cost a million quid . . .' I take a deep breath, trying not to let myself slip into panic as yet another wedding for which I am responsible hits the skids. 'OK, look, why don't you just come on in, have the ceremony, enjoy the party, and then a few months down the line, you can probably file for a quickie divorce?'

Summer blinks at me. 'Are you *serious*?'

'Absolutely I am.' Even as I'm saying this, I can hardly believe that the words are coming out of my mouth. 'It'll be less humiliating for poor Tim,' I add, which is absolutely true – although I have my suspicions that Tim is so sky-high right now that he might not even notice Summer's no-show. 'And then there's *A Summer Wedding* to think about . . .'

'I've tried that.' Wendy pipes up, behind me. 'Didn't get me very far!'

Summer pulls a regretful face. 'Guys, I really am sorry. But honestly, I can't marry Tim. Not when it's Sven I really want.'

I don't know what to say to this. The fact that they've chosen the eleventh hour to declare their love is pretty inconvenient, it's true, but it's not as if they're doing anything worse than Tim and Sophie were doing last night. To be fair to Summer, at least she's got the guts to stand up and be counted.

'So if you could go in there and tell Tim I won't be showing up after all,' Summer is carrying on, 'I'd really appreciate it, Izzie.'

Wait a minute. What about her guts? Standing up and being counted? 'Summer, don't you think you ought to be the one to tell him? He'll be heartbroken.'

'Oh, jeez, Izzie, I know he's going to be a little embarrassed, but do you actually think he's going to be heartbroken? I mean, his folks will be so pleased, they'll shove another couple of million in his trust fund just to celebrate! He'll be OK. And maybe him and that Sophie girl can get together, and then he really won't notice I'm gone!'

'I'll tell him for you, Summer,' says Wendy, wearily. 'And I don't mind telling the rest of the guests you won't be showing up. Then maybe we can all get out of these ridiculous outfits and go to the pub.'

'Oh, you're a star, Wend. You too, Izzie! Hey, when me and Sven get married, we'll make absolutely sure you're the one to plan our wedding! Even if you have to come all the way to Canada to do it! Sven's thinking of coming back there with me, actually, and seeing if he can get funding for this amazing film about Native North American Indians he's been thinking of making. I'm even thinking we could have a traditional Native American wedding ceremony, to promote it! How does that sound, Izzie? Something you could do for us?'

'I suppose . . .'

'Fabulous.' Summer blows me a little kiss. 'Oh, and tell my mom I'll call her, OK?'

What else can I say? I can't force her to attend her own wedding. And she looks so totally, completely happy that I can't stop myself from leaning through the open limo window and giving her a quick, tight hug. 'It's been nice working with you, Summer. Good luck with everything.'

She hugs me back, and Weirdy-Beardy gives me another of his silent thumbs ups before murmuring something in her ear. 'Yeah, we should really get going now. Sven wants to take me back to London to see his flat in Clapham.' She pronounces it Clap-Ham, and I can't help wonder if any of her adoration is going to fade, just ever so slightly, when she comes to terms with the reality of a relationship with a non-millionaire. I really hope not. 'See you at my next wedding, Izzie! I'll call you Monday, Wendy!'

We watch together as the limo uses the surrounding parkland for a tricky three-point turn and then heads back down the driveway to an explosion of flashbulbs and even louder shouting.

'Well, it's made the paparazzi's day. At least someone's happy,' Wendy murmurs, as she reaches under the waistband of her puffball skirt and pulls a packet of cigarettes out from the waistband of her tights. A moment later she pulls her lighter from the depths of her hot-pink bouquet and lights up, puffing out a stream of smoke. 'Fucking hell. I could do with a drink.'

'There's plenty in there.' I jerk my head back towards the Hall. 'About a hundred bottles of champagne and a hundred and fifty bottles of wine, to be precise.'

'Two hundred and fifty bottles,' Wendy says, almost in wonderment. 'Sale or return?'

I shake my head. 'Nope. It's all still got to be paid for. Even if there's not an actual wedding . . .'

'*Isabel Bookbinder*!' It's almost an unholy shriek that comes from behind us, and we both turn round to see Pippa Everitt tottering out of the Hall towards us, Sophie Britten-Jones at her shoulder. Pippa is waving a thin sheet of paper, rather like whatshis-name the Prime Minister in that black-and-white footage where he tells everyone we're not going to go to war with the Nazis, and Sophie is wearing an expression of glee. 'How *dare* you?'

Wendy drops her cigarette to the gravel. 'What do Patsy and Edina want with you?'

I swallow hard. 'Look, Wendy, I haven't been entirely honest with you up till now –'

It's too late. Pippa is brandishing the faxed contract right at me. 'I could have you prosecuted, you know!' she spits. 'I could sue you for every penny you've got.'

'Pippa, I really can explain . . .'

'*Pippa*?' Wendy stares between us. 'Your boss, Pippa?'

'No, OK, she isn't my boss. And I'm really sorry that I lied to you, Wendy, but I wanted this job more than anything . . .'

'You do know what this means, don't you?' Pippa is saying on. 'The fact that it's *my name* on here? It means that this is *my wedding*. So unless you want me to take you to court over this, I suggest you make me a very rapid transfer of funds.'

'Funds?'

'Yes, Isabel, funds! The commission you've earned on this wedding. Sophie tells me it must be a hundred grand. Well, it's mine. And I want it in my bank account first thing Monday morning.'

I stare at her. 'But, Pippa, I haven't even got all the money yet!' And now that Summer has bailed, maybe

I'll never get it. After all, are Tim's parents going to be happy to shell out my final fifty grand payment when there wasn't even a wedding? Will their pleasure at seeing the back of Summer extend that far?

'Tough,' she snarls. 'The full whack, in my account, or I'll be phoning my solicitors quicker than you can say "total fucking charlatan".'

'Hey!' Wendy points a finger at her. 'Don't call Isabel a charlatan. She did a bloody good job on this wedding, at the end of the day!'

I can feel tears pricking my eyes at Wendy's unexpected defence of me, and I'm just about to thank her when my phone starts ringing in my handbag. It stops a moment later, then starts up again.

It's Lara. It's our emergency distress code, the one we've used for twenty years, long before we each had our own mobiles and we wanted to alert each other that the ringing family telephone was for us, and that it required urgent privacy.

'Don't tell me – that's today's bride,' Pippa sneers, 'ringing to say she's being helicoptered to the wrong location in the wrong dress.'

'I have to take this,' I mumble.

'Oh, yeah, that's right, run away from the trouble,' I hear Pippa say. 'Well, don't you worry, Isabel, I'm not going anywhere!'

I answer my phone. 'Hello?'

'Iz? That you?'

'Yes, Lars, it's me,' I gulp. 'Having a little bit of a nightmare here, actually.'

'At Summer's wedding? At Broughton?' Her tone is taut and urgent. 'That's where you are right now?'

'Well, it was supposed to be Summer's wedding –'

She interrupts. 'Right, Iz, we're going to find a cab number and send someone there to pick you up, OK? Matthew and I are on our way down the motorway right now, but you'll want to get there as fast as you can.'

'Want to get where?'

She takes a deep breath. 'The hospital.'

It's weird, but the moment she says it, everything makes sense.

Mum's funny moods recently. Her tears and odd behaviour at Catherine's dinner party. Her terrible, pale, drawn look when she picked me up at the station, and all that strange stuff about wanting more grandchildren before it's too late.

I can feel my heart racing, even though it seems to be right up inside my head instead of in my chest where it's supposed to be. 'It's Mum,' I say, 'isn't it?'

'No, Isabel.' Lara sounds surprised, and more concerned about me than ever. 'It's your dad.'

Chapter Twenty-Six

You know, I've never been one of those people who profess, whenever hospitals are mentioned, 'God, I *hate* hospitals.' It's always seemed like such a pointlessly obvious thing to say, right up there with, 'God, I *love* breathing oxygen' or 'God, I'd *love* to meet Daniel Craig, have him fall wildly in lust with me and make passionate, frantic love to me on the deck of a private yacht.' I mean, for crying out loud, who *likes* hospitals? What kind of twisted sicko would you have to be to actually enjoy going to a place that looks like a giant multistorey car park, and that is filled with scary signs directing you to the Oncology department, and the Casualty department, and the Cardiology department, and that has that icky, slightly sweet smell of disinfectant that reminds me of all the times in infant school when people were sick and the cleaning lady would come in to mop up the vomit with a steel bucket and mop?

Maybe this deep-repressed sensory memory is what's making me feel sick again right now.

A man at an information desk behind a glass screen stares at me as I stumble through the entrance doors of the Bristol Royal Infirmary towards him.

'Did you just get out of a *limousine*?' he asks, before I can get a word out.

'Yes . . . I was at a wedding . . .'

It's Wendy I have to thank for the limousine, by the way, and therefore for me getting here so fast after Lara's phone call. It turns out that, on top of being a bit of a dragon, she's completely brilliant in a crisis. Within the space of five minutes, she saw off Pippa and Sophie (both scornfully claiming that I was obviously making up the whole thing), requisitioned a cup of tea and a bacon roll ('for the shock') from one of the acting students, and commandeered one of the waiting limousine drivers to take me to Bristol. As she closed the car door on me, she squeezed my shoulder and said, 'Don't worry about a thing, Isabel, I'll handle the Hollands. You just go and be with your family.' It's actually making my eyes prickle just thinking about it.

But this is no time for sentimentality. I clear my throat. 'Accident and Emergency, please. My father's been brought in. His name is John Alastair Bookbinder, he's sixty-three . . .'

Evidently the man behind the glass – is that *bulletproof*? And if so, should I be scared of my fellow hospital visitors? – has nothing to do with actual admissions, because he just points me in the direction of Accident and Emergency without looking Dad up on his computer screen. It's on the ground floor, off to the left of the entrance I've just come in, past the gift shop, so I start to hurry there at a half-walk, half-trot.

478

Maybe I've got this wrong, but isn't there some kind of rule about running in hospitals? Or is that just swimming pools? Certainly I can't see anybody else running, even the ones who look as white-faced and panicky as I suspect I do.

I'm passing the gift shop when I realise that one of the white-faced, panicky people I've just walked by is Mum.

She's staring blankly at a display of rather dismal-looking carnations near the shop's entrance, wearing clothes that I know in a million years she would never have actually chosen to go out in – her gardening outfit of saggy-bottomed Capri pants, a loose Breton T-shirt and muddy white Keds – and she looks about a hundred years old.

'Mum.'

'Isabel?' She turns, her entire face seeming to dissolve. 'Oh, *Isabel* . . .'

'What happened, Mum? Is he all right? Have you seen him?'

'I came in from the garden to put on some crumpets and a nice pot of tea, and he was just *lying there*, Iz-Wiz!'

'But do you know why? Was it a stroke? A heart attack?' I swallow hard. 'Was he conscious?'

'He came round a few minutes before the ambulance got there. Oh, Iz-Wiz, if only he'd agreed to go and see the doctors! I've spent weeks trying to persuade him to see this nice neurologist up in London . . .'

'On Harley Street.' A lot of things are making sense to me now. 'That's why you were in town that afternoon.'

'That's right.' Mum is too distraught to bother justifying her strange claims of visits to Chiltern Street to look at wedding dresses. 'I even went and met him myself, to tell him all about the terrible headaches your father's been having, because he just wouldn't go himself.'

I can't help the flash of anger that runs through me. No wonder Mum's looked so dreadful and behaved so oddly recently. Just because Dad is too stubborn to admit there might be something seriously wrong with him, poor Mum has endured all these weeks of worrying about it alone. Honestly, even when he's lying in a hospital bed, he still has the potential to get right up my nose.

'You should have seen him, Isabel, lying there on the kitchen floor like that. If only I'd thought about the crumpets earlier, I might have got to him sooner! Or maybe if he'd *had* a crumpet, it might have fortified him a bit and he wouldn't have collapsed.'

'It's not your fault, Mum. Honestly, I don't think a crumpet would have helped.' I put my arm around her shoulders while she weeps gently for a good couple of minutes. 'It's OK.'

'Anyway, I thought you were at Broughton Hall,' she says, when she can speak. 'I told Lara and Matthew not to bother you until you'd finished.'

'Don't be ridiculous!'

'But the wedding –'

'Doesn't matter.' This isn't the time to go into the whys and wherefores, to explain that the wedding was off long before Dad collapsed, crumpet-less. 'So, do we know anything? Can we go and see him?'

'They won't let me see him yet. I think he's been taken for an MRI scan. And nobody's saying very much.'

'Look, Mum, why don't we get you a coffee and something to eat, and then I'll go and see if I can find a doctor, OK? See if there's anything else they can tell us.'

Halfway between the gift shop and Casualty I locate a coffee stand, the quality of which would have Barney carted off to the Cardiology ward faster than you could say 'Mint-Choc Cappuccino', where I get Mum a strong tea and, because I've switched into Britain-in-the-Blitz mode and I'm aware that sugar is good for shock, a slightly stale croissant for her to nibble. Then I take her to the A&E waiting room and find her a seat in the quietest possible corner. Given that it's still only six-ish on a Saturday evening, at least the place isn't overrun with drunks and pub-fighters just yet, and thankfully nobody around is displaying the kind of open wounds that might upset Mum, apart from a ten-year-old boy with no front teeth, who looks as if he might have just come from playing rugby on concrete. But even he's looking pretty stoical, man enough in fact to be comforting his own, weeping mother, so I feel OK about leaving

Mum for a few minutes while I go and see if there's anyone who can tell me what's going on with Dad.

I'm just trying to convince the cynical-looking reception staff to tell me if they have any idea how long an MRI might take when all of a sudden I hear a familiar voice on the other side of the open double doors that separate the waiting room from the actual ward.

'No, I don't know exactly what he's in for, for heaven's sake! You're meant to be able to tell *me* that! All I know is that his name is James Bookbinder, and he was brought in from Shepton Mallet about an hour ago.'

It's Lara's mother. She's truly resplendent in white coat, Katharine Hepburn trousers and platform boots, her hair upswept in a chignon that would have even Saint Luc murmuring his admiration. Her hands are on her hips as she berates the poor nurse whom she's obviously decided to hold responsible for the Infirmary's slipping standards.

'Are you saying my daughter has her information *wrong*?' she demands, waggling her mobile at the nurse, who has just mumbled something that clearly irks her even more. 'Because I think if you listen to her message, it will be very clear that she knows precisely what she is talking about, and –'

'Catherine!' Forget about no-running rules; I practically break into a sprint to get to her. 'I didn't know if you were still in London for your clinical trials.'

'No, no, that's all over now.' She gives me a brisk hug. 'Are you all right, Isabel?'

'I'm just so glad you're here to help!'

'Well, I could do a lot *more* to help if the idiots who do what passes for work around here would just take five seconds to check their records.'

'Actually, it's John Bookbinder, not James,' I blurt, apologetically, at the put-upon nurse. 'His date of birth is the fourth of May. I don't know his blood type but if he needs any kind of transfusion, there's me and two brothers on their way whose blood you could use. Or if he needs an organ of any kind, like a . . . a kidney or anything, I'd be more than happy to let him have one of mine!' This is probably a pointless offer, as the problem is obviously his brain, and even if it *was* possible to give a brain transplant, Dad would be far better off with Marley's than mine. But I think it might help to let the medical staff know there's a wealth of genetic resources at their disposal if they want them. 'Stem cells, even . . .'

'Isabel, it's OK.' Catherine puts a hand on my arm. 'I'm sure none of that will be necessary.'

'Or relevant,' mutters the nurse, who's been checking the computer at the station behind us. 'He's up in Imaging at the moment. Dr Mitchell is going to see him when the scan's been done.'

'Mitchell? Oh, for God's sake, I've never even heard of him.'

'Her,' retorts the nurse, pointedly.

Catherine shakes off this (somewhat counterfeminist, surely?) mistaken assumption with a toss of her hair. 'Isabel, look, why don't you go back out there and try to relax, and I'll go and see if I can't find someone who's actually been out of medical school for more than five minutes to take over your father's case. All right, my darling?'

I gulp a bit, and manage to say that yes, that is all right, and then just as I'm about to say thank you, she turns and whisks her way through the double doors, along the pale beige corridor.

So we sit, and we wait. About twenty minutes after Catherine disappears, Marley shows up. Don't get me wrong, I'm glad he's come, and obviously Mum is thrilled to see him, but he's actually more of a trial than a support. Ever since he's arrived, all he's done is sit in a tense and nerve-grating silence, clutching Mum's hand so hard that both their sets of knuckles turn white. And I wouldn't mind, but I thought mathematicians were supposed to be terribly empirical and logical. I'd quite appreciate a discussion about the odds of everything being all right – let's face it, *odds* are what Marley's entire Ph.D. thesis was based on – and in the absence of that I'd appreciate it if he didn't just sit there looking utterly stricken, occasionally letting out a tortured, 'Oh, *Mum*,' every time she starts crying again.

Honestly, when Lara and Matthew finally come round the corner of the waiting room, I could kiss both of them. Actually, I *do* kiss both of them. Matthew responds with a distracted peck on the cheek and a swift hug before nipping past me to Marley and Mum, but Lara opens her arms, throws them around me and says, 'Iz, it's all going to be OK. I'm absolutely sure of it.'

Instantly, I believe her. I mean, she's a doctor too, isn't she? All right, maybe not a *medical* doctor, but she's absolutely the smartest person I know, and if she tells me with such conviction that it's going to be all right, then who am I to doubt it?

'Now, what do you need?' she continues briskly, standing back and regarding me at arm's length. 'Coffee? Tea? Oooh, I know, emergency KitKats!'

'No, no, I'm all right, thank you, Lars.'

'And Catherine? Did she get my message? Have you seen her?'

'Yes, she's been brilliant. She's chasing down some doctor who she wants to take over Dad's treatment.'

'Ah. Presumably whoever was already assigned wasn't up to her standards.' Lara rolls her eyes, though not unkindly. 'Well, I'm glad she's on the case. We can trust her.'

There's something about the word 'we' that makes my throat clench up again. It's just such a relief, after dealing with Mum and Marley, to know that Lara's going to be with me through all this.

'Thank you,' I croak, 'for coming here so fast. And for calling me at the wedding.'

'For God's sake, Iz, where else would I be? And of

course I called you! I knew you'd be pretty pissed off if I was here and you weren't!' She grins, though rather anxiously. 'We can make jokes about our row now, can't we? I mean, we are friends again?'

'Of course we are.' I squeeze her hand. 'It was the stupidest row. I'm the stupidest person. And I'm sorry. I shouldn't have been jealous.' I take a deep breath, because I want to ask her something that's been on my mind ever since her call earlier. Something that I think explains her weird mood at Nancy Tavistock's boutique the day of our row, not to mention her sudden obsession with keeping the wedding low key. 'You knew, didn't you? About Dad, and his headaches, and this Harley Street neurologist? Mum told you. And that's why you wanted to keep the wedding small, and not have your dad walk you down the aisle, and all that stuff. Because you were worried about how me and Matthew would feel if our own dad wasn't there.'

Her cheeks flush pink. 'Yes. But, Iz, you know, your mum only told me because she was getting herself all worked up about Matthew and you, and how you'd take it if anything happened to your dad. It wasn't as if she singled me out instead of you, or anything . . .'

'Lars, it's OK!'

'. . . and I felt awful for not being able to tell you, Iz, but your mum went on and on about . . . I mean, she made it quite clear,' she corrects herself carefully, 'that she didn't want to worry you. I think she was just using me as a bit of a professional sounding board.'

'Honestly, you don't have to justify anything. I'm glad she had you to talk to. I'm sure you were terrific. It's exactly why this family needs you.'

Lara makes a funny gulping noise, and her lower lip wobbles for a moment, before she does an almost-visible motion of pulling herself together. 'Well, you may not need an emergency KitKat,' she begins, 'but I could certainly do with – Mother!'

This isn't an out-of-the-blue Freudian slip or anything. Catherine has comes out of the A&E department doors, and she's heading towards us.

Instantly, I do that thing I always do when there's turbulence on planes, which is to stare at the cabin crew to see if they're a) carrying on as normal; b) *pretending* to carry on as normal while actually starting to freak out; or c) actually freaking out. But Catherine is even better trained than cabin crew. She has a poker face the like of which I've never seen before.

'Larissa, darling,' she says, as she reaches us, before turning towards Mum and my brothers. 'And hello, Matthew . . . Maureen . . .' She doesn't even bother to try having an inaccurate stab at Marley's name at all. 'Well, I've tracked John down, and I've asked a very senior neurosurgeon friend of mine if he'll take over this case.'

'He needs surgery?' Mum gasps, as Marley looks even more stricken and Matthew does that manly

I-won't-cry-not-here thing of slumping forwards in his chair, elbows on his knees, staring at the floor tiles.

'Nobody knows that yet, Maureen, but I wanted to be sure he was getting the absolute best advice available. And Mr Jansari is the absolute best.'

'*Rishi* Jansari?' Lara suddenly demands. 'March to November 1996 Rishi Jansari? The one who took us to his holiday cottage in Penrith? Oh, Catherine, you're not trying to get back with him again, are you?'

Catherine's cheeks flush ever so slightly. 'Never mind my romantic life, Larissa. Rishi is one of the best neurosurgeons in the country, and Isabel's father will be in excellent hands with him.'

It's just struck me as odd that she said 'Isabel's father' rather than 'Matthew's father' or 'John' or even 'Jimmy', 'Jack' or 'Jason', when she turns to me and puts a hand on my arm.

'Isabel, he's told me to tell you he'd like to see you.'

I blink at her, stupidly. 'Mr Jansari wants to see me?'

'No, Isabel, your dad.'

'*Me*?'

'Yes.'

'But . . . what on earth for?' That came out wrong. 'I mean, are you sure he said me? Not . . . Mum? Or Marley?' Or Matthew, or Lara, or the ten-year-old boy with the concrete rugby injuries? Because aren't I one of the very last people Dad would be calling to come and see him? Not the very first?

'Well, I know he wants to see all of you. Especially

488

you, Maureen,' Catherine nods rather regally at Mum. 'But you're the one he's asked for right away, Isabel. Do you want to follow me through?'

The thing is, nobody else seems to realise just what a surprise this is. Apart from Lara, that is, who shoots me a look.

'You OK, Iz?'

'I'm fine,' I fib, as I go after Catherine towards the double doors. 'I'll be back in a few minutes.'

It's a little bit scary, following Catherine at a brisk pace along the beige corridor, then past lots of little cubicles with their curtains drawn, from behind which electronic humming and the occasional beep emanates. I think I need to steel myself for how Dad's going to look. He'll have a lot of those humming, bleeping machine hooked up to him, probably, and there'll be a lot of wires, maybe even . . . oh God, will there be a feeding tube? Intravenous drips . . .? But as Catherine pulls back the curtain at the cubicle we've just reached, all I see is Dad.

He's sitting up in bed.

And he looks . . . fine.

Well. All things being considered, he looks fine. He's wearing a horrible pale green hospital-issue gown that would make anyone look sick even if they were fit as a fiddle, and there's a large piece of putty-coloured plaster on the side of his head where he must have bashed himself as he fell earlier. His eyes are closed, and he does look tired. But other than that, he really does look OK. There are no wires. There are no

489

bleeping machines. There is a chart at the end of this bed, and there are more pieces of plaster in the crook of his arm where I assume they've taken blood. But that's all. Nothing worse than that.

'John?' says Catherine, in a much less gentle voice than I was planning to use. 'How are you feeling?'

Dad's eyes fly open. For a moment, he looks disoriented, but then his eyes light on Catherine and me, hovering by the curtain.

'Catherine,' he says, and then, 'Isabel.'

'Well, I'll just leave you two to have a quick chat, shall I?' says Catherine, briskly. 'John, you're in excellent hands with Mr Jansari, so I'm going to head back up to my ward rounds and then I'll pop back down in an hour or so. The nurses have been told to keep me informed when you're moved to a different ward.'

'Right. Well, thank you, Catherine,' says Dad. He's looking rather stiff and uncomfortable, the way he always does when he's slightly beholden to somebody and he doesn't quite know how to display his gratitude. 'You've really been a marvellous help. I'm very grateful, and I'm sure Moira is, too.'

She looks confused, briefly, about who Moira could be, but she's not a woman to be unsettled for long. 'You're very welcome, John. I'll have a word with Mr Jansari on my way out, see if there's anything I can tell your family for you.'

And then she's gone, whisking the curtains closed again behind her.

'Dad . . .' I can hear the wobble in my own voice, so I busy myself pulling up the grey plastic chair to the left of the bed, and arranging myself on it, until I can be sure I'll be able to speak properly. 'Dad, how are you feeling?'

'Well.' He clears his throat. 'The doctors have been excellent, and the nurses have been extremely helpful and obliging.'

That's all well and good, but I don't want to sit here listening to a report on the quality of the staff at Bristol Royal Infirmary. Not after the terrible shock we've all had. I lean forward. 'That's nice, Dad, but I asked you how you were feeling.'

'I know.' He sighs, briefly. 'Well, I feel fine.' He taps his injured forehead, ruefully. 'I do have rather a headache, of course, but then that's largely been the case for the last couple of months.'

'Dad, why the hell didn't you go to see the doctor?' I suddenly blurt. 'You've obviously not been feeling well for a while, and Mum was going spare trying to persuade you to see this neurologist . . . maybe if you'd gone to see him weeks ago it could have prevented things getting worse. The . . . the tumour, I mean, or whatever it is that's –'

'Well, of course it isn't a tumour, Isabel.'

'They've told you that?' I feel a flood of relief. 'From the scan?'

'Yes. This Jansari chap came by with the results a few minutes ago.' Dad isn't meeting my eye; he seems abnormally fascinated by a loose thread on the hem of his bed sheet. 'And as for why I didn't go to see the neurologist, it's simply the case that I've been far too busy with work. I wasn't trying to avoid it, nor was I refusing to face up to the reality that . . . that I might be seriously ill . . .' His voice trails off. He starts to pick at the loose thread, worrying at it between the tips of his fingers. Then, after a few moments, he says, in a quiet voice, 'But I acknowledge that I should have gone to see the doctor. It would have saved your mother a lot of what now looks like totally unnecessary worry. Obviously I regret that. I regret that very much indeed.'

He looks so small – crushed, almost – that I have this overwhelming urge to fling my arms around him, burst into tears, and tell him he's not allowed to die, not ever. But I don't know how he'd react to that. Tell me not to cause a scene, probably, and give me a mini-lecture on how we all have to die someday, and that his mother got so old and ill that, actually, everyone who cared about her was relieved rather than sad when she eventually passed away. So I don't.

'So, have they told you anything more about what might be wrong?' I ask. 'I mean, obviously the scan has ruled out anything *malignant*, which is good?'

'Yes, it is good. Though unfortunately, I'm not out of the woods yet. This Jansari – he seems a good chap, very well regarded, and it turns out I've taught both of his nephews – bright boys, one went to Oxford . . .'

'Dad.'

'. . . yes, well, anyway. Mr Jansari says there's absolutely no cause for undue alarm, but he does want to run some further tests, just to rule out the possibility of anything, er, degenerative.'

'*Degenerative*?'

'Yes, yes, no cause for alarm.' He clears his throat. 'I mean, obviously he wants to be a hundred per cent sure that we're not looking at Parkinson's or Alzheimer's – but then he did say that the headaches were rather more likely to be caused by simple tension, and that maybe . . . well, maybe a few good massages might alleviate some nasty muscle knots in my neck and shoulders . . .'

'But you collapsed!'

'Ah, yes, well, according to Mr Jansari, that was probably caused by a combination of the sharp pain in my head and acutely low blood sugar.'

I don't believe it: Mum's bloody crumpets could have prevented this after all. On the other hand, if he hadn't collapsed, he'd never have ended up in hospital getting the MRI scan. And I'm too relieved, for the moment, to be annoyed about all the stress he's put Mum through. 'So let me get this straight. You could have Alzheimer's. Or, most likely, you could just have a pain in the neck.'

'That's correct.' For a moment, the ghost of a smile hovers around his mouth. 'Of course, if it *does* turn out to be Alzheimer's, then I'll end up *being* rather a pain in the neck!'

'Don't joke, Dad.' Without meaning to, I reach out and take his hand, just to stop him worrying away at that bloody loose thread. 'You wouldn't be a pain in the neck.'

'Well, that is what I wanted to talk to you about, Isabel, while I had the chance.' He gestures around his cubicle. 'It's not often you and I get an opportunity like this, is it?'

'An opportunity to sit in a hospital ward and discuss degenerative diseases? No, that's true.'

'What I wanted to say to you is this.' He looks up from the sheets, right at me. '*If* it turned out to be Alzheimer's, then I want you to know, Isabel, that I'd be relying on you.'

'What do you mean?'

'Well, Marley could handle the family finances, of course, and I'm sure he and Matthew would be able to help your mother make decisions for me if I lost the ability . . .'

'Dad . . .'

'. . . but most of all, I'd want you to keep everybody positive, and not let anyone give up, go down in the dumps. That's the most important thing. And nobody else could do it for me, Isabel. Only you.'

I can't help it. I burst into tears.

Dad pats my arms, and murmurs a couple of kindly things like, 'Oh, you silly-billy,' and 'Now, come along, Wizbit, stiff upper lip, probably just a bit of nasty neck strain,' and then the curtain gets whisked back and the put-upon nurse appears to say they're moving

494

Dad up to a bed in a proper ward, and that if he wants to have a quick word with any other family members, it's probably easier to do it now. All this, by the way, while she shoots me a succession of deeply unimpressed looks that seem to tell me she's never seen such an overreaction to a little bit of a tension headache, and that if I really want something to cry about I should spend a day in her shoes.

Then Dad tells me he'd like a quick word with Mum because she'll need to bring his pyjamas and a toothbrush, and asks me if I could go back to the waiting room and send her through. So I hiccup a bit, give him kiss on the cheek, and then I head back out past all the cubicles, down the long beige corridor towards the waiting room.

And that's when I see Will.

I don't know how he knew to come here – I suspect Lara's hand in this – but he's peering anxiously through the glass in the double doors. His face lights up when he sees me coming.

I speed up and press the button to open the doors, already speaking as he pulls them open from the other side. 'Dad's OK! Well, chances are he's OK. Chances are that all this drama could have been prevented if he'd just gone for a shoulder massage and had a hot bath . . .'

Will pulls me, almost roughly, into a giant bear-hug. 'I'm so glad,' he mutters, into my hair. 'You should have called me. Not Lara. *You* should have called me.'

'I know. But I thought . . . look, nothing happened with Dan,' I blurt. 'I was a total idiot. I only even went to his stupid party because I was upset about those things you said at Emma and Mark's.'

He stands back. 'What things I said at Emma and Mark's?'

'Oh, you know.' It seems unimportant now, now that he's here with me, his T-shirt and jeans all rumpled from the seat belt and in the glasses he wears when he hasn't had time to put his contact lenses in, and that I wish he'd wear more often because they make him look so gorgeous. 'All that stuff about you not wanting children.'

'You mean all that stuff about *you* not wanting children.'

'Um, no. I didn't say anything. You were the one talking about the size of the population, and saying peer pressure wouldn't induce us to have kids.'

'Because I was trying to help you out!' He sounds bewildered. 'When Emma was going on about how we'd be having our own little monsters soon. You looked so horrified, Iz, I was just trying to take the pressure off you. I know all those things like marriage and babies terrify you.'

'But I was only looking horrified because *you're* terrified by marriage and babies.'

'When did I ever say that?'

'You didn't have to say it, Will. You've made it pretty obvious, ever since I moved in, that the very last thing on your mind is asking me to marry you. And it's OK, honestly, I don't mind, not any more! I'd rather be with you than have the ring, and the wet-room, and the kids . . .'

'But I thought I was doing everything the way you wanted! I mean, you seemed pretty freaked out by Lara's engagement, and the last thing I wanted was to do anything to frighten you off when you'd only just agreed to move back in with me again. Not to mention the fact that you didn't exactly seem to be jumping for joy at the thought of us getting a joint mortgage.'

'It's a mortgage,' I point out. 'Does anyone jump for joy at the thought of a mortgage? And couldn't you have told me what you were thinking?'

'Couldn't you have told me what *you* were thinking?'

It's a reasonable point. I can't argue with it. More to the point, I don't want to argue with it. I just want to put my arms around him again, and have him put his arms around me, and know that we're going to be OK together. As if he's read my mind – well, it wouldn't hurt for him to start now – he pulls me towards him again.

'I should go and tell Mum and the others what's going on,' I say, rather muffled, into his chest. 'Come with me?'

'You only have to ask.' He leans down and kisses me, his lips soft against mine. 'That's what I'm here for. That's the whole point of me. You know that, don't you?'

I breathe him in; he smells of petrol, and shower gel, and his flat. Of our flat.

'Yes, Will.' I smile up at him. 'I do.'

Seven Months Later

It's a warm day for early May, and the sun is beaming down brightly from a clear blue sky. Let's face it, there's no better omen for the start of a perfect marriage than perfectly beautiful weather for your wedding day. There were a few unsettling drops of rain lurking about while we were getting ready this morning, but ever since the cars arrived to take us to the church, there hasn't even been the slightest hint of a cloud. And it's stayed that way throughout the service, throughout the photo session in the church-yard, throughout the drinks reception and now for the buffet supper – which, quite incredibly, we managed to shift outside at the very last minute, to take advantage of the golden sunset. Lara was a little bit unsure at first, because she wanted me to relax and enjoy the day rather than spend my time directing people to move trestle tables, chairs, and platters of food, but as I told her, it's not every day you get to be the planner *and* the chief bridesmaid at a wedding. It's a big responsibility, and I'll only relax when I know I've made the day as perfect for her as it possibly can be.

Mind you, I'm starting to feel pretty chilled out now, as the sun sinks into the horizon. The speeches are successfully over, the cake is successfully cut, and Lara and Matthew have just performed their first dance, back in the marquee, to the three-piece jazz band's version of 'When I Fall in Love'. Honestly, I don't think there was a dry eye in the house.

In fact, that's why I'm heading out of the marquee right now, to pop up into Catherine's house and see if I can find a fresh box of tissues for Mum. The dance practically finished her off, but the truth is she's barely stopped sobbing since Lara appeared at the church door in her beautiful Nancy Tavistock dress earlier this afternoon. There was a bit of a lull during the photos and the champagne-drinking on Catherine's back lawn, but she started up again with a vengeance the moment the speeches started. Obviously Matthew's speech was a bit of a tear-jerker – God, my brother can be soppy at times, and I've had at least half a dozen of the single female guests come up to me since to tell me, fervently, that I must tell Lara how lucky she is to have a husband like him – but Dad's speech really got Mum's waterworks flowing, too. Well, *speech* is probably overdoing it a bit. All he really did was stand up after Lara's dad and say a few words about how happy he was to be welcoming Lara formally into the family after all these years, and how if she made even half as good a wife as she'd been a best friend to me, then Matthew really is the luckiest man on the planet.

OK. Maybe Mum wasn't the only one who's been needing tissues. But even if I did get a little bit choked up at Dad's speech, Catherine's speech immediately after it redressed some of the balance. Bless her, I think she was actually trying to be nice, but it all sort of turned into a bit of a lecture about how getting married shouldn't mean you suddenly feel the need to iron your husband's shirts and wash his smelly rugby socks, and how she'd have managed much longer and happier marriages if her husbands had realised this. She did wind it all up, though, with a nice toast to Matthew who, in her words, 'never takes my daughter for granted, and seems like the kind of man who knows where the ironing board is'.

Well, Lara was happy enough about it, anyway, and that's the main thing.

I hurry across the field towards Catherine's garden, and then into the house through the back doors. I've left the tissues, along with all the other wedding-planner bits and bobs I thought I might need today, in the kitchen, so I head there right away. Barney is darting between the counter and the stove, simultaneously slicing bread and heating up butter in three huge frying pans, while his new assistant Amy stands helplessly on the sidelines and watches.

'Barney,' I say, 'I've told you already! There's no point in hiring Amy if you won't actually let her do anything.'

'I am going to let her do something, Iz! I'm going to let her *plate up* as soon as I've got these mini Welsh rarebits ready!'

'Well, I'm not sure she's been all the way through catering college for plating up. Anyway, Barn, are you sure we need Welsh rarebits? I think people are still pretty full from all the amazing food earlier.'

Barney lets out a snort of derision. 'You're being nice, Iz, but there were some serious screw-ups in that buffet. I over-did the rare roast beef, and I should never have tried curing my own ham, and my rosemary focaccia was woefully under-seasoned, even Amy thought so . . .'

'It was all brilliant, Barney, I promise you. I heard nothing but praise from everyone. Even Catherine said how much she liked it, and you know how hard she is to please.'

'Really?'

'Yes, really.'

'And what about those friends of Lara's from university – you know, the one whose wedding you're doing in September? Did they like it?'

Barney is talking about Eloise and Rob, who have recently hired me to plan their wedding in Suffolk four months from now. They're not my only Suffolk wedding coming up, in fact – I'm doing another near Ipswich in June, and I've just had a call this week from a couple wanting to fix a date for a wedding by the sea in Aldeburgh this time next year – but they're probably the only ones who are going to require outside caterers, and so it's a good excuse to hook up with Barney.

'They seemed to be loving it,' I tell Barney. 'The ham in particular.'

'Oh God, well, I wouldn't do the same thing for

502

their wedding! I swear, the stress of curing that ham nearly killed us, didn't it, Amy?'

Amy murmurs something approaching assent, and starts to tidy up the scattered breadcrumbs.

'Anyway, I'm already thinking they look like the kind of people who'd appreciate some really good modern Italian,' Barney carries on, wiping his hands down the front of his Simple Suppers! apron and starting to rummage through one of his equipment boxes. 'My squid tartare, my deconstructed carbonara . . .'

'Um, yes, terrific, but there's really plenty of time to think about the details,' I begin, just as Barney pulls the piece of equipment he's been rummaging for out of the plastic box. It's his soda siphon.

I don't believe this. I've searched high and low for that bloody thing these last few months. And now here it is, bold as brass – well, bold as brushed aluminium – in Barney's hot little hands.

'What?' He's noticed me staring.

'Your soda siphon! You never said you'd found it!'

'But I've had it back for ages.' Barney looks genuinely puzzled. 'Will gave it back to me a few months ago. Remember, that time you stayed out all night, and the police came round?'

'And you couldn't have mentioned it before? I've scoured the kitchen for it!'

'Well, you never said. Anyway, how did you think I was going to make my mini rarebits without my mustard-and-Tabasco spuma?'

I give up. The main thing is, he's got the wretched

thing back, and he can foam up unlikely ingredients to his heart's content. 'Barn, look, why don't you just leave some stuff to Amy and come and enjoy the last couple of hours of the wedding? You are meant to be one of the guests, you know!'

Obviously, it's fruitless, though he does agree that he'll come and have a dance with me when he brings the mini rarebits over, so I can head back to the marquee with Mum's tissues, happy in the knowledge that I've tried my very best.

I take a few moments on the way back over to the marquee to admire it for a moment. It's nothing like as huge and fabulous as the one we hired for Summer's wedding, but I've done a good job of making it look pretty special, draped with the twinkling fairylights that I'm thinking might become my wedding-planning signature, and decorated inside with the gorgeous red roses that Anita let us have at cost, now that she's working with me on pretty much all my weddings. God, listen to me – that sounds like I'm on practically a wedding a week! Well, I'm not – but I'm not far off a wedding a month. Honestly, things have been going a lot better for me since I actually set the business up properly, after Summer's wedding. The Hollands paid up my full fee, thank heavens – as it turned out, Summer's no-show really did put smiles on their faces – and even though I had to pay it all straight back out again to Pippa (the hardest cheque I've ever had to write) at least she's leaving me alone to get on with my own business in peace.

Anyway, even though Summer's wedding itself didn't earn me a penny, *A Summer Wedding* is a different matter, bringing the clients rolling in since it aired on the Zone Reality channel (not the Living channel, as poor Summer wanted) just after Christmas. And it was a little bit of a hit in the end, believe it or not. I think the fact that there never actually *was* a wedding gave the producers a bit of a USP, and the yards of free publicity splashed all over the trashy weekly mags and the Sunday tabloids didn't exactly hurt either. Still, I'm a bit amazed that anybody actually watched it, and even more amazed that I didn't, in the event of it, come across as totally useless. In fact, once I'd got over the sheer horror of seeing myself on screen (it's true what they say, the camera really *does* add ten pounds; *fifteen*, actually, if you want Will's considered opinion) I could appreciate that I was coming across pretty well. There wasn't too much of me, thank God, especially as the lion's share of the screen time belonged, of course, to Summer and to Wendy, who's become a bit of a cult heroine, and is apparently in talks to appear on *I'm a Celebrity, Get Me Out of Here,* and front her own reality show about her life as a celeb PR agent. But thanks to whoever edited *A Summer Wedding*, whenever I did pop up on screen I looked and sounded industrious, creative and, most important of all, distinctly approachable. And it's not just Mum who told me this – though she *did* tell me, of course, several times a day, basking as she was in the barrage of compliments. I also heard it from the brides-to-be who contacted me after they saw the show. The first call I got, just a few days after the second episode aired, led to my first (successful) professional wedding back in March: a nice, traditional church-and-marquee do, rather like this, in Suffolk. After that, I did another small do in early April at a restaurant in London, and then, of course, the one I've been waiting for – Lara and Matthew's.

We've kept the day pretty simple, just like Lara wanted, with a happy compromise between the church service (for Mum) and the reception here (for Catherine), and as soon as Lara stopped worrying that we were all going to be mourning Dad's death at her wedding, she stopped all her resistance to her own dad walking her down the aisle. And I've really eased off on the whole Bride Management thing, too, because it was freaking Lara out a bit, and obviously the most important job I have is to make the bride feel happy and at ease.

I mean, I haven't dropped it entirely. I did insist on booking Lara a good few weekly manicures to get her hands into decent condition for the wedding ring, and obviously I took her shopping for some great new bikinis and kaftans for the honeymoon in Greece, and I could hardly let her show up in that stunning strapless Nancy Tavistock without a pre-wedding exfoliation and spray tan, but those are probably all things I'd have done as her chief bridesmaid anyway . . .

Oh, I can see Will. He's coming out of the marquee at a snail's pace, almost bent double, because Hypatia has clearly decided she fancies a bit of a toddle, and he's holding her hand. They both look up as they see me coming, and Will smiles.

Mum was right, by the way. Will *does* look good in a morning suit. Especially now, at the end of a long day, when he's loosened his tie ever so slightly, and his hair has gone a bit sticky-up and messy.

'Somebody was just asking after you,' Will says, as I head straight for them.

I blink down at Hypatia, who's looking both serious and seriously cute in the dove-grey flower girl's dress that – shock! horror! – Daria has actually permitted her to wear. '*Really?*'

'Well, no.' Will grins at me, lowering his voice. 'She was actually saying "bowl, bowl," because she wanted some more dessert, but your dad overheard her and thought she was saying "bell, bell". For Isabel, see?'

'Yes . . .' It's nice of Dad to try. And to be fair, Hypatia's been lovely with me all day, sticking to my side like glue for most of the photographs, and even letting me look after her most precious toy, Derek the Digger (Lord only knows what happened to the new-generation Tiny Tears doll I bought her for her first birthday, though I suspect it's been banished to the attic for fear of gender-stereotyping). 'Well, we've been twins today, haven't we, Hypatia? You and me?' I squat down and tickle her tummy. 'Both of us in our bridesmaids' dresses, like two peas in a pod!'

'Yeah, but Hypatia's the really cute one,' Will says. He lets go of Hypatia's hand as she spots Dad, and makes a rather waddling beeline for him. 'I had to say that while she was still here,' he adds, in a theatrical whisper, as we both straighten up to full height and he puts his arms round my shoulders. 'You really do look terrific, Iz. Have done all day.'

'Thank you.'

'And you've done a brilliant job here, you know.'

'You think?' God, Barney's insecurity must be catching. 'Have you heard people talking about it? Mum? Dad's family? Dad?'

'All of them, Iz, and saying nothing but good things. Oh, apart from your Auntie Clem. She didn't realise I was your boyfriend – I think she may think you're a lesbian?'

'It's a long story.'

'Right, well, she obviously doesn't realise I was with you, because she came up to me during the buffet and said it was all very well everyone saying how marvellous you were on the TV, but that as far as she was concerned, Lara's bridesmaids' dresses were drab, the hymns were inappropriate, and the ham was too salty. In no particular order.'

'Well, it wouldn't be a Bookbinder wedding without one moaning minnie,' I say, rolling my eyes.

'Exactly. Nothing like keeping up a grand old tradition.'

Neither of us says anything for a moment. I'm kind of wishing I hadn't said anything about Bookbinder weddings, in case Will thought I was dropping a hint – which I absolutely wasn't, by the way. I mean, everything is so much better between us now that we've stopped stressing out about which of us wants what, and when. So good, in fact, that we've even started making a few home improvements to the flat. Nothing totally insane like a wet-room, thank heavens – just some new bookshelves in the living room, and a fresh paint job in the bedroom, and we've been talking about updating the kitchen so that we can have an island unit just like Emma and Mark's below. It feels a bit like putting down a few roots, but without having to move to Twickenham.

Mind you, Lara and Matthew's new house is gorgeous, so I suppose you could do worse than move to Twickenham. It's very nice, after all.

Will is looking at me as though he's trying to guess what I'm thinking. 'Isabel . . .'

'*Isabel*!' It's my name, in stereo, as Mum hollers it from out of the marquee towards us. 'Lara and Matthew are leaving in a few minutes! You have to come for the throwing of the bouquet!'

Oh God. Could she make it any more obvious?

'Could you make it any more obvious?' I hiss at her, as Will and I head back to the marquee.

'What, darling? It's just a nice tradition!' Mum is resplendent in sapphire blue, the colour of Nana Hamilton's engagement ring, from her strappy sandals to her jaunty straw beret. And she's gone even further down the matching route by insisting that Dad's tie and waistcoat be made from the same shade. He's standing beside her now, holding Hypatia, and he shoots me a look that's half-smile, half-exasperation.

'Catherine has banned all the girls from her side of the family from joining in,' he says, 'so I'm afraid we need you to keep up the numbers.'

I fix him with a look of my own. Dad and I are doing more of this these days: it's not exactly a flood of communication, but it's certainly what you might call a 'shared understanding'. 'That's the reason, is it?'

'Well, of course it is, Iz-Wiz.' Mum looks offended that I've even asked, a sure sign that she's feeling sheepish. 'Honestly, there's no need to be so touchy. We all know you've no intention of getting married, that you're a big career girl now.'

'Moira!' Dad glances at her, shifting Hypatia's weight to his other side. It's something he's very careful of now, since his physio confirmed that his terrible headaches were, indeed, all down to back and neck strain.

'Well, John, all I mean is that now she's a famous wedding planner she isn't going to have the *time* to get married herself!'

'Mum, I'm not a famous wedding planner.'

'You were on TV! And you saw that review clipping I posted you from the *Radio Times*, Isabel, where they called you the voice of calm!'

Even though this makes it sound a much bigger deal than it really was – it wasn't a *review*, as such, just a couple of lines of caption on the listings page so they could justify using a picture of Summer busting out of her wedding dress – I still can't help my little glow of pride. *In the final episode of guilty reality TV pleasure* A Summer Wedding, *put-upon but unfailingly perky planner Isabel remains a still, small voice of calm when unexpected events threaten to derail D-lister Summer's big day…*

Yes, OK, I know it by heart. But it was a big moment for me, reading that. Almost as much of a big moment as it was for Mum, who regards the *Radio Times* as a bastion of taste and discernment only a notch or two below *Delia's Complete Cookery Course.*

'I'm just trying to tell her that she's done a wonderful job on this wedding!' Mum is carrying on. 'And that we're very proud of her.'

I can't work out whether I'm thrilled that they're proud of me, or just a tiny bit put out that everyone's decided I'm never going to get married, but I can see the waterworks threatening again, so I take Mum's arm and we go towards the dance floor, where Lara is waiting.

OK: it's total rubbish that they needed me to make up the numbers. There are about twenty girls all lining up – my female cousins, my male cousins' girlfriends, colleagues of Lara's from the clinic and Matthew's from school. In the midst of them all is Lara, clutching her bouquet. Even with smudged makeup from a day of damp eyes, and slightly frizzed hair from an hour of dancing, she looks absolutely incredible. The dress we picked out, with Mum's help (and with that hefty discount, yay me!) hangs perfectly on her small, slim frame, and the simple crystal hairband that she wanted to wear instead of a fussy veil seems to bring out the sparkle in her eyes. She catches my eye now, and gives me a quick thumbs up.

'Thank you,' she mouths at me, her face glowing with pleasure. 'For everything.'

I smile back at her, feeling pretty glowy myself. 'You're welcome,' I mouth back, 'Mrs Bookbinder.'

Her lip wobbles a bit then, but before she can get teary, Matthew starts waving at her from behind the group of girls, jabbing at his watch. From the look on his face, he can't wait to get her into the wedding car and away from all the madness for some newlywed time alone.

'OK, OK. Everybody ready?' Lara turns her back to us all, lifts her lily-of-the-valley bouquet high in the air, and chucks it over her shoulders towards us.

There are a few shrieks, a bit of good-natured scrambling, quite a bit more less good-natured scrambling . . . and then I realise something weird. None of the girls has caught the bouquet.

Will has caught it.

He must have been standing right behind me the whole time, and I didn't realise it.

'Will . . .' I blink up at him, bemused. 'What on earth are you going to do with that?'

'Well, obviously you know a lot more about wedding traditions than I do. But I thought the girl who ends up with the bouquet is meant to be the next

512

one in line to be married.' He closes my hand around the bouquet's stem, interlacing his fingers with mine, and then his face breaks into the most incredible smile I've ever seen. 'I think this was meant for you.'

The Glamorous (Double) Life of Isabel Bookbinder

Holly McQueen

'A marvellously funny debut' Jilly Cooper

Isabel Bookbinder might not be leading the most glamorous life ever – measuring column inches at the *Saturday Mercury* isn't exactly the job of her dreams – but luckily she's developed a foolproof plan to change all that.

Reasons to become a bestselling author:
- Plentiful opportunities to swish new Super-hair
- Sophisticated launch parties (with smoked salmon blinis)
- Am bound to captivate the delicious Joe Madison
- Can finally prove to father that Really Am Not a Waster

Potential setbacks:
- Don't yet have 'Yoko' bag, as carried by arch rival Gina D
- Hmm. Am inadvertently at the centre of a major political sex scandal
- Paparazzi are doorstepping my parents and boring boyfriend Russell
- Haven't *actually* got round to putting pen to paper yet

Admittedly some of the setbacks are a little daunting, but Isabel's sure that a woman of her ingenuity – and creativity – can find a way . . .

arrow books

The Fabulously Fashionable Life of Isabel Bookbinder

Holly McQueen

When aspiring designer Isabel Bookbinder bags a job with Nancy 'Fashion Aristocracy' Tavistock, she's sure her career is finally on track. Dazzlingly glamorous, this is a world that she feels truly passionate about – after all, she knows her Geiger from her Louboutin, her Primark from her Prada, and she's *always* poring over fashion magazines. Well, ok, the fashion pages of *heat.*

So, learning from the very best, the future's looking bright for Isabel Bookbinder: Top International Fashion Designer. Within days she's putting the final touches to her debut collection, has dreamt up a perfume line, *Isabelissimo*, and is very nearly a friend of John Galliano. And on top of that she might even have fallen in love.

Yet nothing ever runs smoothly for Isabel and fabulously fashionable as her life is, it soon seems to be spiralling a little out of her control . . .

Praise for Holly McQueen:

'Marvellously funny' Jilly Cooper

'Does exactly what it says on the tin: if you like Sophie Kinsella's Shopaholic books and you miss Bridget Jones, then meet Isabel' Louise Bagshawe, *Mail on Sunday*

arrow books

The Secret Life of a Slummy Mummy

Fiona Neill

For Lucy Sweeney, motherhood isn't all astanga yoga and Cath Kidston prints. It's been years since the dirty laundry pile was less than a metre high, months since Lucy remembered to have sex with her husband, and a week since she last did the school run wearing pyjamas.

Motherhood, it seems, has more pitfalls than she might have expected. Caught between perfectionist Yummy Mummy No 1 and hypercompetitive Alpha Mum, Lucy is in danger of losing the parenting plot. And worst of all, she's alarmingly distracted by Sexy Domesticated Dad. It's only a matter of time before the dirty laundry quite literally blows up in her face . . .

'This slice of angst and affluenza is several cuts above the rest . . . witty, observant and supremely intelligent.' *The Times*

'There is something of Bridget Jones's hopeless-but-adorable quality about Lucy . . . Neill's hilarious depiction of the manifold daily perils of stay-at-home motherhood is so convincing that it soon looks like the most challenging job in the world – and Lucy is all the more sympathetic simply for staying afloat.' *Daily Telegraph*

arrow books

ALSO AVAILABLE IN ARROW

Friends, Lovers and Other Indiscretions

Fiona Neill

From the author of *The Secret Life of a Slummy Mummy*

It's 2008 and the credit crunch is starting to bite. Sam and Laura Diamond and their friends are approaching forty and feeling a lot less certain about life. Laura dreams of having a third child, while Sam longs to give up his job and have a vasectomy. Wild child turned corporate lawyer Janey Dart finds herself unexpectedly pregnant and married to a wealthy hedge fund manager who loathes her friends. While Sam's oldest friend, restaurant-owner Jonathan Sleet, can't control his roving eye, so it's no surprise that back on his organic farm in Suffolk his wife Hannah is finding distractions of her own.

When they all come together for a holiday, things get really interesting, because six friends, two decades of tangled fortunes and a complicated secret from the past make for an explosive combination . . .

'Funny, and packed with observations of wince-making accuracy . . . Superb entertainment' *The Times*

'Neill's characters are so cleverly depicted, you feel as if you've met at least one of them before' *Vogue*

arrow books

The Truth About Melody Browne

Lisa Jewell

The wonderful new novel from the *Sunday Times* bestselling author of *Ralph's Party*.

When she was nine years old, Melody Browne's house burned down, taking every toy, every photograph, every item of clothing and old Christmas card with it. But more than that – Melody Browne can remember nothing before her ninth birthday. Now in her early thirties, Melody lives in London with her seventeen-year-old son. She's made a good life for herself and her son and she likes it that way.

Until one night whilst attending a hypnotist show with her first date in years she faints – and when she comes round she starts to remember. Slowly, day by day, Melody begins to piece together the real story of her childhood. But with every mystery she solves another one materialises, with every question she answers another appears. And Melody begins to wonder if she'll ever know the truth about her past . . .

Praise for *The Truth About Melody Browne*

A touching, insightful and gripping story which I simply couldn't put down.' Sophie Kinsella

'Stunning.' *heat* 5 stars

'Classic storytelling' Elle

arrow books

Heiresses

Lulu Taylor

They were born to the scent of success. Now they stand to lose it all . . .

Fame, fashion and scandal, the Trevellyan heiresses are the height of success, glamour and style.

But when it comes to . . .

. . . WEALTH: Jemima's indulgent lifestyle knows no limits; Tara's one purpose in life, no matter the sacrifice, is to be financially independent of her family and husband; and Poppy wants to escape its trappings without losing the comfort their family money brings.

. . . LUST: Jemima's obsession relieves the boredom of her marriage; while Tara's seemingly 'perfect' life doesn't allow for such indulgences; and Poppy, spoiled by attention and love throughout her life, has yet to expose herself to the thrill of really living and loving dangerously.

. . . FAMILY: it's all they've ever known, and now the legacy of their parents, a vast and ailing perfume empire, has been left in their trust. But will they be able to turn their passion into profit? And in making a fresh start, can they face their family's past?

arrow books

We think *Confetti Confidential* is as good as Sophie Kinsella's bestselling novels!

If you don't agree, we'll give you your money back!

Simply send this book with your name, address and your original receipt to the below address and we will send you a cheque for the full purchase price.

Arrow Marketing Department
Random House
20 Vauxhall Bridge Road
London SW1V 2SA